SOMETIMES WE TELL THE TRUTH

SOMETIMES WE TELL THE TRUTH

A NOVEL BY

KIM ZARINS

SIMON PULSE
New York   London   Toronto   Sydney   New Delhi

SIMON PULSE

An imprint of Simon & Schuster Children's Publishing Division

1230 Avenue of the Americas, New York, New York 10020

First Simon Pulse hardcover edition September 2016

Text copyright © 2016 by Kim Zarins

Illustrations copyright © 2016 by Adam J. Turnbull/colagene.com

All rights reserved, including the right of reproduction in whole or in part in any form.

SIMON PULSE and colophon are registered trademarks of Simon & Schuster, Inc.

For information about special discounts for bulk purchases, please contact Simon & Schuster Special Sales at 1-866-506-1949 or business@simonandschuster.com.

The Simon & Schuster Speakers Bureau can bring authors to your live event. For more information or to book an event contact the Simon & Schuster Speakers Bureau at 1-866-248-3049 or visit our website at www.simonspeakers.com.

Jacket designed by Karina Granda

Interior designed by Steve Scott

The illustrations for this book were rendered digitally.

The text of this book was set in Adobe Jensen Pro and Avenir.

Manufactured in the United States of America

2 4 6 8 10 9 7 5 3 1

This book has been cataloged with the Library of Congress.

ISBN 978-1-4814-6499-4 (hc)

ISBN 978-1-4814-6501-4 (eBook)

To everyone who craves stories on this road trip called life;
to Rachel, Michael, and Emma, who helped me tell this one;
and to Mark and Arthur, for sharing this road trip with me

DRAMATIS PERSONAE

ALISON: Venus with a gap-toothed smile; her favorite color is red

MR. BAILEY: our civics teacher; the guy taking us on this field trip; came up with this whole storytelling competition

BRIONY: captain of the cheerleading squad; prom queen; Kai's girlfriend

BRYCE: Rooster's buddy; general goof-off; loves his forked beard; Saga's boyfriend

CANNON: my friend since sophomore year; entrepreneurial spirit; hacker; suspended but meeting me in D.C. anyhow

CECE: total feminist

COOKIE: pothead philosopher

FRANKLIN: obscenely rich son of chronic Alp-skiing parents; throws legendary parties and has a maid clean it all up after; drives a Boxster; good-looking, though in that artificially tanned, whitened-teeth way; Mouse's boyfriend

FRYE: lanky dude; total player; mooch

JEFF: me . . . not much to say here

KAI: star quarterback; good-looking and perfect, but so much more likeable than Franklin; Briony's boyfriend

LUPE: smart; prelaw; Reiko's best friend; recently Marcus's girlfriend

MACE: has the worst acne ever, combined with weird facial flaking and eyebrow dandruff; big and mean enough to beat the crap out of you if you care to point this out; used to be friends with Pard but is now a loner

MARCUS: quotes Aristotle at the start of every damn paper he writes; the kind of person who sophomore year tells you a tomato is a fruit, and when you argue over it he wants to use the Socratic method to determine *fruitness* when you'd rather just say tomatoes don't belong in fruit salad and thus can't be called fruits; inexplicably Lupe's boyfriend; I might be jealous he's going to Harvard

MARI: really good writer, but kind of a rival; editor for our lit journal, *The Southwarks*; hangs out with Sophie

MOUSE: very cute cheerleader; a completely cheerful person who is only too happy to play a supporting role to her boyfriend, Franklin, and her cheer captain, Briony

PARD: pale, thin haired, high voiced, tiny guy with extreme fashion sense; we used to be best friends; it's complicated

PARSON: hard-core Christian who actually practices what he preaches; handsome, perfect, and moral, yet it's impossible to hate him

REEVE: friendless little tattletale; bundle of nerves; so skinny he doesn't have calves

REIKO: smart; premed; really pretty; alarmingly ready to throw herself at Frye; my ex

ROOSTER: redheaded linebacker; skull like a battering ram, body like a mountain, language like a gutter; a slapstick, emphatic sort of person

SAGA: lusts for clothes and would possibly kill for them; likes beards; Bryce's girlfriend

SOPHIE: smart; prelaw; very shy; Mari's friend

THE BUS DRIVER: drives the bus

JUST A GENERAL PROLOGUE

My mother drives me to school like I'm little again, and I stir awake when she turns off the engine. It's still nowhere close to sunrise, and my classmates huddle under the streetlamps in the parking lot, some staying warm by smoking. I pray to God my mom doesn't notice them.

No such luck. She peers through the windshield, and a familiar look of pain flashes in her eyes. She doesn't get super upset, though, just gets dead serious and whispers, "Do you have your meds?"

I tug the zipper on my backpack's pocket, show her I know how to pack and triple-check the important stuff, and, by implication, have everything else under control.

"If anything happens, no matter what time, no matter where you are, call me, and I'll come right away."

"Everything's fine, Mom."

"Take your pillow," she says for the millionth time.

"Love you," I say, which means both *good-bye* and *no way in hell*. And she lets me go.

I shuffle toward the group. We're well into April, but at this hour it's cold, so I tuck my hands in my sleeves.

My breath mists, but I have nothing on the chain-smokers exhaling those vast clouds. A part of me would love to try it, but the whole (now) *only child with asthma* situation makes a boy promise certain things to his mother.

1

I catch Pard watching me. He exhales sideways, like a parent just caught him in the act. Something in his face, some trace of a question left over from last week, makes me turn my back on him.

I focus on my pack and duffel, make sure I've got my shit together. No one has said hi to me yet.

They would have if Cannon were here, but Cannon isn't coming. Not today.

I nod to myself like I've confirmed packing what I meant to pack, and then edge closer to Reiko and that circle of girls. Her friends are recapping prom, which is just another reminder of how popular she's become.

"Hey," I manage.

She takes in my groggy face and gives me a little squeeze. "Aww, Jeff."

I grit my teeth and smile. We dated our freshman year, but now she treats me like I'm a kid—like she has matured and I haven't.

The girls go on talking, cheerful despite the hour, and start chatting up their latest admissions offers. Reiko's going to Penn, or maybe Georgetown. She says she's going to check out the campus again while we're in D.C. this weekend. I nod and wonder if she'd let me tag along, since I got into Georgetown too. Maybe now is my chance to ask her.

"You look so sleepy," Reiko says, and pats my cheek. If she likes touching me so much, then why did she break up with

2

me? Except I know the answer to that already.

I just nod, because sleepiness excuses social ineptitude.

The girls go back to discussing their college plans while clutching pillows and putting on lip gloss, which is hot to watch and generally looking like my dream slumber party come true. Being invisible is sometimes a pretty sweet deal. I wonder how I can sit next to any of these girls for the six-hour ride. Maybe share a pillow . . .

But then Frye strolls up. I'm hoping he'll decide to mooch a cigarette, like he mooches a ride every day to get to school, and leave us nonsmokers alone. Instead, he parks himself right in Reiko's physical space and says, "Whoa, how can you look this good this early in the morning?"

He's probably not hitting on her. I mean, Frye gets in *every-one's* space. There have been a couple times when I even wondered if Frye were coming on to me, but then realized he gets *thatsuperclose* to everyone. Still, I smell his mouthwash from here.

I sneak my hand over my mouth and quietly check on my own breath.

Reiko ruffles Frye's hair. She has to bend backward to do it, because he's that close to her, leaning over, palm-tree style. She laughs, and he laughs, and then she laughs some more. When did this thing start? He's saying something about these YouTube videos teaching him how to give massages, and the girls are like, *Show us!* So he slides his hands over Reiko's shoulders, and I pretend to check my phone, because I can't watch.

3

The yellow bus pulls up the same time Mr. Bailey does. He's toting a huge thermos of coffee. No wonder he's smiling.

"Hey, kids! Let's do this!"

Everyone reaches for their packs, and I wonder for the hundredth time who will sit with me now that Cannon isn't coming.

On cue, my phone vibrates, for real. At 5:15 a.m.

U on the way?

I text him back. *Lining up. Sucks you aren't coming.*

Screw them!

Yeah, I text. *Unfair. Of all the days to be suspended, it had to be today.*

Don't worry. I have a plan. Revenge!

My breath catches. Cannon always has a plan, and while I miss having him here, his plans sometimes scare me. Especially after the senior prank. How do you tell your only real friend that he went too far? He'd only say what he's said countless times before: that I need to get out of my shell. Can't argue with that.

What plan? I ask.

His reply's as cheerfully cryptic as a fortune cookie. *I'm going to kidnap you. :)*

I think of all the things Cannon has pulled off—high stakes poker matches, parties with insane amounts of alcohol, and then, yes, hacking—and I'm nervous. He means well, but still.

What?? I text back.

Pick you up when u get here. Meet some G friends. Party.

4

G *friends* could mean girlfriends, or not. He's still on this mission to make me go to Georgetown. He's been talking up this guy who will get me connected to the scene there. But I don't buy his plan to meet me in D.C. *You're going to drive six hours just to show me around Georgetown?*

Not going to. I'm HERE. Gonna help you make connections for next year. Introduce u, have fun. I'm gonna pass out. Later.

Suddenly my chest feels tight, and it has nothing to do with the smoke. I don't know what Cannon has planned. Yes, I got into Georgetown, and he'd said he knew someone there I should meet. Was he really going to introduce me to that guy? It's kind of nice he wants to help, except I'm not sure who this guy is, or what he'd expect from me. I never fully know what to expect from Cannon. It's never just fun with him. He'll get you into a party, the kind you see in movies, and then at some point he has a signature he wants you to copy, and you don't know whose it is or what it's for, but you sign a check, a really small amount, just a prank, but you feel like maybe you shouldn't. You just do your little part, and then he does what he does with it.

Quintessential Cannon. I know somehow that he'll have Mr. Bailey's itinerary, and he'll be there, but running off to meet his friends is risky. He knows I can't have any trouble this semester, that I actually want to get into the schools where I'm wait-listed, so why would he do this to me?

I look up and see that I'm alone outside the bus.

I climb the iconic rubber-tread steps that seemed so huge in

5

second grade. Come to think of it, the steps still feel huge. Buses are just weird that way.

I hesitate just inside, front and center, and it's like being onstage without a script as I scan for a seat that will not lower an already shaky social standing.

Front left, Reeve faces the back of the bus with his knees on his seat, so I get an unwanted view of his scrawny ass. He whips around to stare me down with his unibrow power. He's a pretty weird sight, and I wouldn't mind telling him so, but he's poised with his clipboard to record every offense against him and every breach in school regulations. He's been class treasurer for two years and founded the school's Discipline Committee (a committee of one), which basically makes him a modernized hall monitor.

I can't sit at the front of the bus.

I try to look confident, like I'm actually going to be a famous author, and one day the popular guys in the back will say to their kids and grandkids around the Thanksgiving table, "Jeff Chaucer, you say? Yeah, back in high school, he wrote my paper on Virginia Woolf—I still have it."

Reeve returns to his spying position as I pass him. Luckily, there are a couple free seats farther back . . . except when I get there, it turns out these spaces aren't free after all.

Plugged into his headphones, Mace is slumped alone where I couldn't see him before.

And, like fate, Pard has the seat across the aisle. His shoes

6

are propped on the seat, and he's curled around his sketchbook so I can't see it, but it's there, and he's drawing, like always. The little Band-Aid he's been wearing on his finger is gone. I'm still not used to him without his hat—he looks just like he did freshman year, like we're in a time warp, but of course, everything has changed. He doesn't acknowledge I'm right here staring.

Now I have a dilemma. When a person walks this far into a bus, you can't turn back. It's social death. Sitting near Reeve would suck, but sitting near these two guys from my past would also suck. Mace cracks his knuckles like he wants to crack my head. Even if I wanted to risk that, I won't risk Mace's epic acne, facial flakes, and eyebrow dandruff.

That leaves Pard, who alternates between nibbling his pencil and sketching with his head down in an *I don't see you standing right there* pose. I don't ask for favors, not from him, not standing in the aisle, where people are watching. But I'm Cannon's friend. I can do this.

"Move over," I tell his scalp. Pard's hair is still wet from the shower and combed, but so thin I can see his head underneath, even paler than his hair. Kind of weird-looking, yet vulnerable—just like his face, which has never seen a shave. I'm not exaggerating either. Not one shave, and he's almost eighteen. No wonder I'm thinking of freshman year when I see his face frozen in time like that.

His head snaps up, and his brown eyes are proof that he's not albino (though let's not rule out the possibility that he's wearing

7

contacts). They also reveal the soul of a Balrog. Right now those furious eyes say how much he hates me, even as he puts his feet down and signals for me to climb over. I try to creep past without touching him, but the backs of my calves awkwardly brush his knees. The unwanted contact makes me scoot so far over that I'd fall out if it weren't for the window, permanently shut.

Pard rolls his eyes and then goes back to his sketchbook, always angled so I can't see, like he does when we're both in the library with our doctor's notes excusing us from PE. I don't know why Pard never has PE, but I'm out whenever it's too strenuous. (Yes, my mother made this happen.)

"Okay, everyone," Mr. Bailey says. "It's a six-hour drive, plus breaks. Let's just relax and enjoy the ride, okay?" He delivers the rules: no getting out of your seat, no eating, no drinking, no this, no that. "Any questions?"

Of course, this is an open invitation.

"Are we there yet?"

"Can I go to the bathroom?"

"Can we get a commemorative tattoo when we get there?"

This from Alison, sitting like a queen bee, back center with her two football stars on either side. With one leg propped over Rooster's huge knee, she's leaning back into Kai's shoulder. From his right, Kai's girlfriend, Briony, casts spitfire looks, but Alison doesn't notice. Briony must lie awake at night wondering what guys see in Alison Chavez. Unlike Briony, with the blond hair, the bikini body, the baby blue eyes, Alison isn't that kind of

8

pretty. But she's got your attention like no one else. I don't just mean clothes, though today's outfit is cowboy boots, red stockings, and a lacy baby-doll dress, all on a five-foot-eleven-inch body. I mean *her*. When Alison flashes that gap-toothed smile like she's up to something, you want to be up on it with her. You want to be the one who says the funny line that makes her tip her chin and laugh with nothing held back. And maybe I love her with something like tenderness, because in this large, lonely world, she's the only girl who has ever grabbed my ass.

As the bus starts moving and pulls away from campus, the back row breaks into stupid songs and starts churning like a mosh pit. A suspiciously shaped balloon bounces over our heads, and Bryce shouts, "Whale condom launched!"

Male voices chant, *Keep it up, keep it up!*

Poor Mr. Bailey. He's a young teacher, and I think young teachers get hopeful that we'll like them, and we do. But that doesn't mean we won't give them crap. Nothing personal.

But Mr. Bailey hasn't looked at us in the same way since the senior prank, like any kid he sees might be one of the hoodlums who trashed his house in a night of pizza and revelry, while he was at the all-weekend civics teacher conference. We didn't trash it *that* badly and thought he'd take it in stride, maybe even see it as a sign that we think he's cool, but he was furious. He doesn't have enough to convict us, only suspect. Pard's done detention but seems to have told nothing. Yes, there was evidence, but it pointed only to Pard, not to Cannon. Or to me. And the guys on the bus think the only secret to keep is trashing his house, so we're safe there, too.

Cannon's right. Everything is fine.

"Keep it down!" Mr. Bailey shouts, and the guys give a deflated *aww* when he snatches the balloon away.

Once the bus hits the freeway, Rooster whips out his ukulele, and it's hilarious to see this gigantic redhead with this ittybitty uke, but for a linebacker, Rooster's playing well. Alison sings some inappropriate lyrics, bodies sway into each other, and people have more fun than they should be having on a bus. Bryce passes me a plastic cup without explaining, and one sip burns all the way down. I ignore Pard's jealous glances.

The noise picks up, and there's a crash in the back row. An empty beer bottle rolls down the aisle.

So it begins, even before we've left quaint Canterbury, Connecticut.

"Pipe down!" Mr. Bailey holds his hands like a victim in a stickup, and then, prompting the driver to pull over but not waiting for the bus to park, he grips the seats as he makes his way down the aisle. He traps the bottle under his foot and emits the mighty sigh of a severely put-upon adult. "I am *this close* to turning around."

Cookie, curled in the back corner as if he's one of the popular kids (but really just because he's thoroughly baked), says all dreamy-like, "It wasn't ours, man. It was on the bus when we got here."

Mr. Bailey raises an eyebrow. "The driver told me his normal rounds are with kindergartners."

Cookie's mouth hangs open before he manages to reply, "I love Goldfish."

Mr. Bailey gives us all this constipated look, as if he's straining to connect the trashing of his house with the bottle in his hand. He grips the back of Mace's seat and points his nose toward the rowdy back row like he means business. "All right. We are going to behave ourselves and not give me any more trouble. I have this." He brandishes the bottle as evidence of our collective sin. "And between this and your little prank"—he glares at Rooster's faintly purple-yellow forehead, like it might be the reason for the dent in his bedroom door (it is)—"I can get some of you suspended. I mean it. You've pushed me way too far."

Suspended. That can't happen. Not while I'm wait-listed at Cornell and the other low-level Ivies. Yes, I have Georgetown in the bag, unless a suspension could ruin that, but I'm not sure I want to be a lawyer or a civil servant or whatever politics-happy Georgetown alums tend to do. I want a couple options before my whole life is paved in front of me. It's already a problem that I'm not doing so well in Mr. Bailey's class. Suspension would blow my chances.

Mr. Bailey lifts his chin with grim satisfaction. He has our attention and pauses, apparently considering what to do with us. He looks badass somehow, crossing his arms while holding the bottle. "I have an idea," he finally says. "I need all of you to be quiet and respectful on this ride. To keep us busy, we'll play a game. We'll pass the time telling stories. It will be a competition. One story for each of you. You'll all pay attention to each other— no zoning out on phones. Whoever tells the best story will get a free A in Civics, and all detention and suspension material forgiven . . . even if I find out what happened that night. And I *will* find out. So, play to win a free A. Or act out on this trip and be disqualified, and potentially suspended."

We all soak this in. It's so quiet I hear another bottle rolling around somewhere.

"All right, then. Let's do this. Maybe you'll learn something from each other. Remember, you all have brains—"

"And if we work together, we can solve the world's biggest problems!" the class chants in unison, with a hefty dose of mock cheerfulness.

Mr. Bailey gives me an encouraging, pep-talk look, and then I watch his face sour as he notices the cup beside me that I'm failing to hide. There's iron in his eyes, like he's deciding what to do. He extends his hand for the cup, sniffs, and frowns.

He addresses everyone, while looking right at me. "You all might want to think hard on the story you'll be telling. Jeff, I'll talk to you later."

My heart pounds, and I'm relieved when Mr. Bailey breaks that stare.

I'll probably get suspended on my own, without Cannon's help.

Kai raises a hand. "What kind of story? Our life story?"

12

Kai is the most popular senior there is, all quarterback awesome and sandwiched between Briony and Alison, like, all the time, yet he suddenly looks nervous about telling his life story, even though everyone would totally want his life.

Mr. Bailey does that *let me carefully consider your question* teacher thing with his eyebrows. "Well, you can talk about yourself as a way of introduction, but I'd like each of you to come up with a fictional story. Modern times, ancient times, based on real life or not at all—doesn't matter. Just something really interesting to hold our attention."

Briony sulks. "What's the point? Jeff will win."

Everyone looks at me resentfully. All those eyes.

"I—I'm not as good as everyone thinks," I stammer.

Choruses of *Yeah, right* rise all around. Apparently, I'm supposed to be a genius just because I wrote that Morpheus story about dreams and desire and death. When it came out in *The Southwarks* last spring, it was like the school exploded. Teachers congratulated me. Popular kids started being nice to me, and not just for being Cannon's friend. More like they thought I had some power to put souls onto printed pages. And I kind of thought I could. It was so magical. Writing that story happened by itself. It's like all my years with *Sandman* and old myths just turned on the tap. It was the best thing to ever come out of me. The absolute best. My dad wept. *He wept.*

And now it's gone. The tap's off. I look within me, and there's nothing there.

The bus lurches back onto the freeway.

Seated again in the front now, Mr. Bailey asks Reeve for a spare sheet of paper, so we can have a drawing of our names to see who goes first. Reluctant to lose a sheet from his clipboard, Reeve complains until Mr. Bailey offers a few extra credit points.

"What *have* you been writing lately?" Pard asks me in that cynical, unnerving way he has. His voice, like his smooth face, somehow missed out on puberty.

"Oh, I started something."

The peach-fuzz corner of his mouth quirks. "And?"

"I'm working on it. It got a little away from me."

Pale eyebrows lift in a *fancy that* look of contempt.

"What's the title?"

"'The House of Fame.'"

"Fame," he repeats, all hollow-like. "How autobiographical."

Rooster stops playing his uke when Mr. Bailey draws a name from his hat. I'm watching, glued, while the silence and the word "fame" take a choke hold. I'm praying that Mr. Bailey doesn't call on me, praying my name slips out of the hat and disappears, because I know today I'll lose Mr. Bailey's game, my college prospects, and my reputation. Pard's words sting. I do want fame. I want these guys to think I'm good. But they'll either figure it out right now, or within the next six hours, that I have no story. Those sequels they've asked for? New stuff? I have nothing.

Mr. Bailey draws out a slip of paper.

14

"Kai, you're up!"

Thank you, God, I semi-pray. The back two rows go wild. Kai high-fives Rooster. How can anyone be delighted at being sprung with telling a story? But he's too cool to freak out.

"Awesome. Can I tell any kind of story? Like, can I tell a war story?"

Mr. Bailey waves a permissive hand. "Sure."

Kai nods, like ideas are already starting to form. "Okay, hold on, I just need an angle. You know, like, should these be Navy SEALs or Trojans or what?"

Bryce leans into the aisle, and his forked beard hangs for all to see. Yes, Bryce sports a wicked black forked beard, which makes him look like Satan on Xanax. Or maybe he's on the brownies Cookie had for breakfast. "Dude, do *zombies*! You have to do zombies!"

Kai's eyes lose focus while all the story's pieces lock into place. Finally, he says, "Zombies. That'll work. I like it."

KAI'S TALE

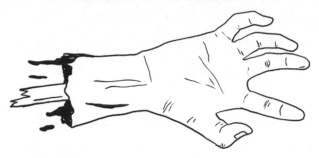

Okay, so there's this war of the zombies. Lots of decapitations and body parts and awesomeness, and since it's two armies of the dead, they're unstoppable. They can get their hand cut off, stick it back on, and keep on fighting. Total Armageddon. And if humans get in the way, they die. So the humans pray to the gods to stop these monsters, and the gods take that whole battlefield and plunge it down into the underworld. Except the gods miss two zombies. One is helping his brother limp off the battlefield, just as the ground under their feet starts to collapse.

"Wait," Bryce calls out. "What do you mean *limp* off the battlefield? I thought they repaired themselves right away. Not getting the zombie physiology recovery system here."

"Well, the more you get your limbs severed, the longer it takes, okay?" Kai explains. "You get into overload and can't keep up. Actually, the way it works is that if you get completely hacked up and scattered, that's it for you. So if you start losing body parts, you either need to get to a calm place to recover, or you need a body brother to share his parts with you."

The guys go nuts over this idea. *Ooo, body brother! Tell us how that works!*

"Like, if you have serious losses and can't regrow your arm, a body brother can cut off his arm and save you. And you'd do the same for him."

"That is *so* cool!" Bryce booms. "Rooster, be my body brother!"

"Dude, totally." Alison gets her foot thrown from its meaty pedestal as Rooster leaps up and chest bumps over Bryce's seat.

Bryce shouts, "Yeah," all pumped. "Man, I'd even give you my beard, if you needed it." They'd make a wild pair of body brothers besides the size difference, with Bryce's forked beard, black eyes and hair, and olive skin, and Rooster's pale blue eyes, freckled Scottish skin, and mass of red hair.

"Would you let him tell his story?" Briony snaps. She smiles encouragement at Kai—not that he needs any. He's laughing and enjoying his rowdy friends. Kai never pushes for the limelight. It just happens naturally.

Okay, okay. Anyhow, part swapping's what these two brothers had done for each other for years and years. Arc and Palam weren't brothers while living, and maybe they even came from countries that used to be at war against each other—who knows? But by now, as zombies, they share the same flesh. The same smell. After countless battles together, they only made it through this last one by luck.

But since there are only two of them, Arc and Palam are no

match for the human army that pours in, now that things are safe for humans. The president imprisons the two zombies for scientific study.

Lupe's new boyfriend, Marcus, cuts in. "Wait, there are gods in this story *and* the president of the United States?" He blinks twice, hard, like on some subconscious level he's shocked he asked such a dumb-ass question. I mean, Marcus is the smart one, all Harvard-bound, but this is *fiction*. I instinctively look at Pard, almost like the old days, but he's facing Kai, sketching for all he's worth.

"Cut me some slack, Marcus. I'm working it out as I go," Kai tells him.

The lab guys run tests on the zombie brothers to figure out how they work, and the zombies remain prisoners, but they bear it the best they can. Everything changes when they see a gorgeous girl helping out in the lab. She works on the other side of the glass, doing something with test tubes. They don't know it yet, but this is Emily, the president's daughter. She wants a career in science rather than politics, so she works at the lab after school. Arc puts his hands on the glass, and Palam touches his heart. They are totally stunned by the beauty of this warm-blooded young woman.

Falling in love is the happiest moment of their unlives. But then things start to go wrong.

"You shouldn't be in love," Palam says. "A true brother would stand aside when his brother is in love. And I love her."

"I saw her first," Arc throws back. "And I'm not going to tell you to stand aside. We both love her, but we can't *both* have her. So we'll just have to let her choose."

This is the first time the brothers have a falling-out. They'd been warriors bonded together for ages, but it just takes one girl to change everything.

"I don't get it," Alison cuts in. "She's on the other side of the glass. So what are they fighting over?"

"Over *her*!" Briony blurts out.

"This is a pure power struggle," Kai adds. "They're fighting over the right just to want her, even if it's hopeless."

Month after month they pine for Emily, who works in the labs all the time but still has nothing to do with them. It's a bitter and long year for the zombies—imprisoned, hopelessly in love, and no longer brothers at heart.

Then, unexpectedly, a zombie delegate arrives and negotiates to release one prisoner—just Arc, not Palam. So Arc is free to go to the underworld. Only he can't leave Emily, so he disguises himself and becomes one of the lab employees. Keeping out of Palam's sights, Arc works near Emily for years, never revealing his love or the secret of his identity.

When a fire destroys the labs, Palam escapes in the commotion. He'd been watching Emily all these years too, and he's dying to marry her. He plans to go to the underworld, raise an army, and freak the hell out of the president until he wins Emily's hand in marriage.

But Palam has a big shock when he smacks into Arc on his way out of D.C.

The brothers stare each other down with their mismatched eyes, because even those body parts were shared . . .

"Cool," Rooster says, kind of hushed.

. . . and they start to fight. I mean, *really* fight. They draw blood, but they aren't stopping there. It's like they want to cut off all the body parts that they've shared all these years. Even if it kills them both—because killing your body brother is pretty much your own death sentence, with no chance to be revived.

All the commotion brings out the army, and the president and Emily too. Emily identifies them as the lab zombies, and this becomes the moment of truth for Arc and Palam. Arc confesses his love for Emily as the reason why he stayed and disguised himself. The president is seriously grossed out. Then Palam tells the president, "Go ahead and kill both of us, but kill Arc first, so I know he'll never have Emily."

The president orders the execution, but Emily breaks into tears. She can't believe her dad would execute them just for being zombies. "They have no choice being that way," she cries.

"But they love you!" her dad says.

"That's not a crime either," she tells him. "I won't let anyone die because of me."

The president, who looks at lot like Mr. Bailey, says, "Okay, we'll have them compete in the American way. On live television, with cool obstacle course features and costume designs. The winner of the duel will get Emily's hand in marriage."

Emily's eyes bug out. "Uh, how about just a date, Dad . . . and then we'll see how it goes?"

The president raises an eyebrow. Clearly, that's not an option. And so the duel is planned.

The television slot is scheduled, and lots of publicity goes into it. All the big Super Bowl Sunday advertisers, and so on.

There are just three people not caught up in all the hype. They're only thinking of their hearts' desires. Arc prays to his favorite god that he'll win the duel. Palam prays to his favorite god that he'll marry Emily. Emily prays to her favorite goddess that no one will get killed and also that she won't end up marrying anyone.

But Emily's prayers are denied.

The players take their places. Arc isn't dressed in street clothes anymore. He's in a blue and silver outfit cut to show his muscular blue-black flesh. Palam wears red and gold to distinguish them, since their bodies are almost identical.

When the gun goes off, they start running all over the set, each zombie looking for a weapon that can snuff out the other.

22

The rules are that they can't kill each other outright, but they have to make the other surrender. And to make a zombie surrender pretty much means cutting him open and taking out all his guts.

Arc scores a lucky break, though. Palam gets his foot stuck in a pipe, and it's pretty easy for Arc to cut him through at the hip with a machete. Palam hops around, trying to fight back, but he's weaponless and missing a leg, and then an arm, and so on. So Palam has to surrender.

Arc rejoices in his big victory and flashes a smile at Emily up in the stands, but his moment of triumph is short. Maybe it was the prayers or maybe it was all the media hype, but one of the underworld gods had learned about the duel. Invisible to all and bearing his poisonous blade, the god slashes at all Arc's organs at once.

Arc turns purple, and black blood comes pouring out of his ears. Even Palam, missing an arm and a leg, isn't nearly as wounded. In fact, with some help from the pit crew bringing him his parts, Palam's arm and leg are already reattaching themselves enough that he can crawl to Arc's side. Even though he's lost Emily, Palam has eyes only for Arc. To see Arc near death brings out all the old memories of saving and being saved.

Palam pleads, "What do you need? Tell me what part, and I'll give it to you."

But Arc shakes his head. He speaks with difficulty. "Emily? Where is she?"

Palam realizes Arc wants to speak only to his beloved, not to him, and it cuts him in a way he's never felt before.

Emily pushes her way through the crowds and throws herself at Arc. She cries, "Arc! No! Please don't die!"

Arc takes Emily's hand into his purple fingers and musters up the strength for speech. "Emily, the gods are calling me to Hell. I'm sorry I'll never get to know you, to love you as I wanted to, but if you are looking for a good man, please consider Palam. He was the truest brother I ever had. It was only our love for you that shook up our love for each other." Then he gasps, as if he can't speak anymore.

Hearing this, Palam rushes back to Arc's side and holds the body he knows like his own. "Tell me what part you need," he begs. "Tell me! I can save you!" But Arc fades fast and dies in Palam's embrace. Palam weeps a long time, and the eye that once was Arc's weeps as much as his own.

Everyone waits to hear what will happen next, but Kai says, "That's all, folks!" and we burst into applause.

The popular crowd gets all fist-bumpy, and everyone else wants to tell Kai he's good but can't, because Rooster and Bryce, and especially Franklin, are hogging Kai up. Franklin's been relatively quiet so far—like it's so demeaning being in an icky bus when he could be lounging in his thirty-five-hundred-square-foot mansion—but now he seems resigned to roughing it for the weekend. He spreads himself out, with Mouse curling

24

into him, all the while chatting alpha-male style with Kai. It's all so popular and cozy a portrait that I want to sneak back to the parking lot with a blowtorch and rip off the catalytic converter from Franklin's black Boxster.

Mari, fellow writer and semi-rival, calls out loudly over everyone's heads, "So, Jeff, what did you think?" She smiles at me, her face framed by that beanie she's worn all winter.

It's like a switch turned off everyone's chatter. I do that flinching *you mean me?* look, as if she meant a different Jeff. Kai moves his head so Franklin isn't in his way, and everyone's waiting to hear what I, the future famous writer, will say.

I am not the best at speaking to a whole bus full of people.

"You should be a writer," I tell him.

His eyebrows crawl up his face, and he still looks impossibly cool. "Really? I was wondering if the brother thing was cheesy. If I should have kept it a love story. I didn't even fill in if Palam marries Emily. The brother thing just took over."

I can see he really wants me to answer. "The brother theme was the best part. It was an unexpected way to resolve the love triangle. And zombies were perfect. I mean, they were made to fight, and once you see them fighting each other—over love—it really captures how hard it is for these guys just to live a normal life after all that war."

He gives a chill little nod, but I catch some hint of pain and sorrow in his eyes and the set of his mouth. "Thanks. I appreciate that."

25

And then Briony flings her arms around him.

I turn and see Pard with his sketchbook. When Pard sketches from life, he pins his object with a lion's stare, and I was surprised Kai didn't notice or get thrown by it. Now he's finishing up, with a few different pencils scattered in his lap, and for an instant I see the portrait.

It's beautiful. Not just because it looks like Kai, though it does. It's shaded right to get his dark skin, has the powerful but streamlined build, the cheekbones and the short black hair, the strong hands hanging loose at his knees. But what takes my breath away is the look on Kai's face. It's that haunted look he gave to Mr. Bailey when he asked if he'd have to tell his life story. Pard captured the story behind the story. And somehow I know it's Kai's soul, put down on a piece of paper.

Pard claps the book shut and glares at me. Not the artist's stare. The glare he gives when he wants to erase you.

"You're good," I mutter, because he deserves to hear it.

"I am," he says back. Then he reopens his book and looks at me sideways, dropping his voice. "You know about his brother, right?" I shake my head, and he draws in a bit of background. "The vet."

I scrunch my eyes. "He helps animals?"

He pins me with a look that makes me feel childish. "The veteran. At eighteen, you're this brave hero going out to help your country. Out there, things happen around you, *to* you. You get hurt inside and outside. For the pain they get you hooked on

26

Vicodin, OxyContin, morphine, whatever. Before you know it, you're dumped back, just nineteen years old and spent, and to feed your addiction you get hooked on heroin. Forget the hero thing. Now everyone wonders what the hell is wrong with you. It doesn't take long."

Alison points out the city rushing by and, beyond it, the waters surrounding Long Island. "Look, we're already passing New Haven!"

Pushing up her chic writer glasses, Mari leans into the aisle to face the back row. "That's where you're going next year, right, Kai? Yale? That's so awesome."

Jealousy all over his face, Reeve mutters something about his scores being twenty points higher than Kai's. It's clear that Reeve thinks Kai got in because he's black and not because he's a straight-A student and star of the football team and a coach for underserved kids in robotics (their team won a national championship). Not because he can tell a brilliant story with zero time to prep. I give Reeve the stink eye because he sucks, but also because I'm still hurting from Yale's rejection too, and Reeve seems like a great target for channeling all my disappointment.

It looks like Kai isn't going to say anything, but Reiko's best friend, Lupe, who takes no shit from anyone on earning her admission to Dartmouth, snaps, "Check your privilege, Reeve."

"Oh right, my privilege to get told off for stating the facts," Reeve grumbles.

"Asshole," Lupe snarls, and Reeve counters with a testy "I heard that" as he scribbles on his clipboard.

"*Anyway*," Briony segues, rolling her eyes. "Yale is lucky to have you, but I'm even luckier. UConn's just an hour away."

She snuggles into Kai, and they look good together, prom

king and queen. But maybe the real love story—for Kai, at least—is brother love. I can see it in his eyes, the way he's processing the story he just told. How he didn't want to tell his life story, but there are pieces of his life there. Body brother parts that make the story live.

For me, brother thoughts become sister thoughts, and it hits a nerve that I don't like to think about. I was so young at the time, and when my parents said she was gone, I was like, "Gone where?" I just didn't get why Bee wasn't coming back.

I told all that to Pard freshman year, right after I stumbled on that photo of the girl in the bikini top who otherwise looked just like him. I asked, "Who is she?" He barely kept it together. He looked at me like he didn't want to say. "She was my twin."

Was his twin. Her name was Ellie. Pard could barely speak. He must have been feeling like hell, remembering her, so I thought it was only fair to tell him about my sister, to share that I knew how bad it was. I think it only made him feel worse. It's not exactly a club you want to join.

I never brought it up again.

"Hey," Rooster booms like he's incapable of normal speech volume. "What I want to know is how this zombie body part sharing works. Like, if your dick gets cut off—"

"That is so inappropriate!" Reeve scribbles something furiously.

"What, you're going to write me a tardy slip for saying 'dick'? My dick is never tardy."

Mr. Bailey cuts in. "That's enough, Rooster. I think we should move on to the next story."

He reaches in the hat to draw the next name, but Rooster booms, "Okay, kiddies! Have I got a story for *you*. It's a love triangle done right. Not that our man Kai here doesn't know how to tell a good story, but I have a better one."

Mr. Bailey holds up a slip. "Now, now, Rooster, I already drew out Cookie's name. You'll have to wait."

"Can't wait for Cookie, Bailey-man. I have to tell it now, or my love triangle will be out of place. Gotta tell it right-o." He hiccups.

"He's *inebriated!*" Reeve pulls at his collar like he can barely breathe. He points an accusing red pen toward the back so we can all see Exhibit A of Alcohol Abuse. "We are on a trip to pay our respects to our nation's forefathers, and this is how you behave. *Disgusting.* Absolutely disgusting."

"You should try it sometime." Rooster roars with laughter, and as Mr. Bailey tries to calm everyone down, Rooster steamrolls ahead with his story.

ROOSTER'S TALE

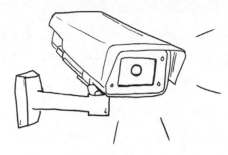

My tale is from . . . the future!

So, years from now, Reeve finally gets laid.

"What?!" Reeve half screams, and Mr. Bailey gives a warning. *"Rooster."*

I mean, *fictionally*, there's this middle-aged skinny guy. He's on the Disciplinary Committee—oops, I mean, he's like a hall monitor for some big power company. He wanders the corporate offices and makes sure employees aren't texting or kissing or stuff like that. Anything fun gets reported, and he's the best employee at turning in people to get them fired. So he makes a fair pot of money to live off of. And when he goes home, he plays hall monitor there, too, because he always has a boarder or two subleasing in his house. He's a real fun landlord, I can tell you.

All he lacks is a woman. Then he gets one. She's originally just his tenant. And, oh man, is she hot. I mean *hot*. Limber, all high energy, you know? And Alison is totally young, probably half his age—

31

"Hey!" Alison elbows Rooster in the ribs. "I'm am *so* not going to get it on with Reeve."

Rooster clasps his huge meaty hands in a gesture of prayer and contrition. "Of course not! Any resemblance to actual persons is entirely unintentional in this work of fiction. And, besides, I'll make sure this fictional young woman gets a much better time than anything said middle-aged, balding, office hall monitor can provide."

She puts both feet up in Rooster's lap. "Carry on. But I *am* listening."

He bows dramatically. "My lady, you are the fairest audience this humble bard can hope for."

As I was saying, this fictitious, beautiful, young Alison has hit upon hard times. She can't pay rent, and the old hall monitor guy wants her so bad, he asks her to marry him. She reluctantly agrees. It's either that or the street. And he puts the ring on her finger, does the courthouse routine making her a Mrs., and tells her she'll never have to worry about being evicted from now on. And then, of course, he monitors her every time she goes out, every time she goes in. *Real* close relationship.

Enter new character. Nick is the new tenant in the house, taking up Alison's old room. Nick moves in with his few things and his guitar strapped around his back. Has some books and scientific equipment, too, because he's putting himself through college. Going to work on global warming. And you can guess that some serious global warming fires up between Alison and Nick. Totally outshines the diamond ring on Alison's finger, and who can blame them?

But they can't do or say anything, because the surveillance cameras are everywhere, plus hidden mics in the kitchen, living room, the bedrooms, you name it. There's even a mic in the bathroom down the hall. That's right, the Reeve-man—I mean, the old guy, let's call him John Hall—listens to everyone piss. Luckily, there aren't any cameras to visually record said pissing. But the hall cameras catch who goes in and who goes out, so Nick and Alison can't even make out in the tub. The only way to communicate is by writing on the foggy mirror after a shower. Nick would take a shower, and then Alison would go in to change the toilet paper roll, and there'd be a message for her, and she'd reply, and he'd then go to the bathroom before the mirror lost its fog. The lovebirds started a little correspondence this way:

Him, Day 1: LUV U. ♥
Her, Day 1: U 2.
Him, Day 2: Sex?
Her, Day 2: Can't.
Him, Day 2: Pleezzzz?
Him, Day 3: Dying for you! PLEASE!
Her, Day 3: OK . . . But how?

Our poor would-be lovers are in a quandary, but Nick got an A in Civics at Southwark High, and he knows he has the brains to solve the world's biggest problems.

Everyone turns to see the look on Mr. Bailey's face.

"Oh, go on," he says, all grouchy, and we know he's totally hooked to find out what happens next.

So, a week later, Alison reads a note from Nick on the bathroom mirror:

Him, Day 10: Got an idea . . .

Just hoping Nick would figure out a plan, she goes about her business, always careful, of course, since she figures that twinkle on her diamond is actually a tracking device. One day she's shopping downtown, and when she passes by the church, she notices that the weird choirmaster is blowing her kisses. Abe—well, everyone calls him Blondie because of his white-blond hair—totally has a crush on Alison. He's also working on a plan to win her love.

Pard has had many, *many* nicknames during his years at Southwark, and his hair has been a running joke for years. Once he told me the problem is that people initially mistake his hair for being beautiful just for its color. They stare. On a closer look, they notice it's not just straight but thin and oily, and there's just not quite enough of it for his head. I feel bad for him when he instinctively tries to tug down the brim of a hat he no longer owns. He misses that hat.

Then Pard picks up his pencil and starts sketching like this means war.

So, a couple days later, Nick takes sick. Really sick.

"I think we should check on him," Alison tells her husband.

Old John Hall rubs his gray stubble. "Hmm, let me check the tapes."

And that's exactly what the old fart does. He overhears Nick groaning and tossing around in bed, and in the daylight hours the camera catches him there, doing nothing but writhing in the sheets.

John gets out his clipboard and knocks on the door.

"Hnnnuuh?" groans Nick.

"Nicholas, are you ill?"

"Very," replies a weak voice. "Come in."

Reeve—I mean, John—finds Nick all pale and trembly in bed.

"Oh, Mr. Hall," Nick moans. "We're doomed. It's all going to end."

John shakes Nick's shoulder. "Doomed? What's the matter, boy? Out with the truth!"

"Sir, no one wants to know the truth." He holds out his arms to show strange bruises. "It's radiation. I've always been

35

sensitive to it. That's why I've been studying global warming. I was hoping to get to the bottom of CRPP . . . you know, Complex Radiation Proximity Poisoning. It's the interference between solar flare activity coming from space with the technology-made radiation trapped by our atmosphere. It's deadly. Look . . ."

Nick pulls out an iPad and shows the old man images that would freak out anybody. Pictures of people with missing hair and covered with boils and scars and those bruises Nick has, all from radiation poisoning. He shows pics of animals with two heads, the whole horror show. Then he gets to the point.

"My skin always reacts before a radiation onslaught, and I can tell this next one is going to wipe out the whole country. Maybe the world."

John's wide eyes go from the tablet to Nick, back and forth. "Good God! What can we do? How do we save ourselves?"

Nick shakes his head. "I don't know if we can. The radiation will pour through the windows, doors, walls. Now, obviously, if we could go underground, like in some sort of a bunker, that would help, but I don't know. . . ."

John grabs Nick's sleeve. "My basement! That's underground."

Nick cocks his head, thinking. "I'd have to take a look. I feel pretty weak, but I'll try to get up. This is a matter of life or death. We might have only hours to get ready."

John helps Nick out of bed and holds carefully on to his

elbow, leading him down the stairs to the surveillance head-quarters. The room is full of monitors, so John can see what's happening at home and at work.

Nick touches the walls. "Solid. No windows—that's good. And this equipment you have here . . . would it be able to produce a strong white noise? The strong wavelength would help break up any radioactive particles."

John nods excitedly. "Yes, I could do that."

"Good," Nick says. "But even with that, the room might not be deep enough to protect our bodies. If the floor were dirt, I'd bury us under there. Dirt is wonderful protection; combined with the protection of this basement, even a couple of feet of dirt would work. Maybe we could get a plastic pool filled with dirt for the radiation to bounce off? Then we could just hunker down here and, after the radiation spill, maybe in two days or so, we could come out again." Nick pauses, rubbing his chin. "Yeah, that should work. It will be sad, though. So many people will die from the poisoning, all because politicians have concealed the truth from the American people and let corporations drive ecological policy."

John springs to action. "Right! I'll go downtown and buy us each a plastic pool. You mean a little kiddie pool, right? Any particular kind of dirt?"

"Any pH-balanced dirt will counteract radiation," Nick tells him. "Oh, and get three pools. We don't want to leave Alison to this grim death."

"Of course not," John says. "Nicholas, wait right here. I will be back in thirty minutes!"

And once the goods are procured, John leads Alison by the hand to the surveillance headquarters. Her mouth quivers a little as she takes in the news of the impending disaster.

Nick and Alison bury John Hall first in his pink plastic tub. He's bedded in organic soil, the high-grade kind that the farmer's market people tell you about. The tip of a straw pokes out the top of the mound, to allow for breathing.

"I'm going to turn on the white noise," Nick says to the mound. "Ready?"

He hears a muffled *Nmph* in response.

Nick cranks up the white noise. He disables the audiovisual recording software . . . or, at least, he thinks he does. Then he puts a sprig of geraniums on John's mound, just for effect.

He pinches Alison's ass. "Let's go," he whispers. And upstairs they go.

And what a romp they have!

Poor Alison was so tired of sex with Hall Monitor John, you know, practically getting fingerprinted while you're doing it, and it's good, so good, to have a hot-blooded body pressed to her. They do it all in John and Alison's bed. Alison's free as a bird, and she sings as she frolics.

And the whole time, though they don't know it, the live feed sends footage straight to the basement. If John could see even one minute of that long, long night, he could have filled his clipboard with all those naughty things they were doing. But even though he's in the dreaded surveillance room, John can't see a thing, and the white noise drowns out the lovemaking. At his feet looms an oversize screen with images of Nick on Alison, Alison on Nick, and every other position they could discover. The flat-screen is like a tombstone inscribed with John Hall's worst nightmare, and he's buried under it, his body shifting as if his restless soul were trying to watch the show.

So Alison and Nick go at it all night long, and pretty much pass out right before dawn . . .

. . . when who should show up but Blondie!

He throws pebbles at the window, one after another, and then starts serenading Alison with that cooey-fluty voice of his.

"Ooo-ooou, Aa-li-son! Suh-WEEEE-tie pie! Ooo-ooou!"

Everyone rolls with laughter. All except for Reeve and Pard. Reeve scribbles furiously on his clipboard, and he mutters loudly how John Hall would have put tracking devices on Nick and Alison to ensure they were in their kiddie pools as well. Pard, on the other hand, doesn't make a move. He knows I'm watching him and doesn't turn around. If I were a friend, I'd say something, do something. But I don't, and so I feel like a traitor as I laugh along with the others.

"Ooooo-oooou! How about a kiss for me, my dovey-dear?"

And Blondie breaks out a number from *The Sound of Music*, like, *do-re-mi* and all that shit.

"What the hell is going on?" Nick asks.

Alison rolls her eyes. "It's Blondie, that choirmaster. I think he's hoping John will be sleeping, and I'll let him come up for a kiss. He wrote me a note a few weeks ago saying he wanted to try that. He's such a freak."

"Swee-tie!" Blondie calls again, his voice as sweet as honey.

Alison groans. Then she gets a sly look on her face.

"It's still dark," she tells Nick. "I'm going to have some fun."

So she tiptoes to the window. "Blondie, *shhh*. My husband is sleeping. If you want that kiss, come up, but let's do it quickly!"

Blondie's little squeal is so loud that both Alison and Nick can hear it all the way upstairs. He's thinking this is his lucky-ducky day!

Nick props up his head on one elbow to see what Alison is up to. As Blondie starts climbing the rickety fire escape stairs, Alison leans her naked ass out the window. She winks at Nick, then calls out to Blondie.

"Quickly, my love!"

And Blondie kisses Alison. Just not where he thought he'd be kissing her.

Alison and Nick hear Blondie gasp. Then they hear the sound of his feet backing up and a yelp as he struggles for balance.

"What? What just happened? Alison? What's going on?"

Alison laughs and claps the window shut. Then she snuggles

back into bed with Nick, and they joke about where they should kiss each other next.

Meanwhile, Blondie may be stupid, but he's got enough sense to hear them laughing inside and to remember the feel of the thing he'd kissed.

He's going to get even. Oh yes.

Blondie runs to the church. The fence was being soldered by a repairman, who was already at the job to avoid the heat of day. Blondie carefully picks up a red-hot poker, and off he goes, hell-bent on revenge. Back to the window.

"Ooo-ooou, Aa-li-son!" he sings. "Sweeee-tie pie!"

The honey in his voice is gone, but he sings as sweetly as a heart cracked and filled with rage possibly can.

"He's back!" whispers Alison. "He can't seriously want more?"

"Maybe he's weird that way," Nick says. "Let me have him this time. I want him to kiss my ass too."

So this time, Nick leans *his* ass out the window. "I'm ready, baby!" he crows in a falsetto, and he lets out a fart to help Blondie find him in the darkness.

And Blondie gooses him. With the poker. Nick never saw it coming, but you can believe it's damn hot.

The scream that erupts from Nick wakes the whole street. It's an apocalyptic sound, piercing every wall, every nook, every cranny—down, down, down into the basement. Down, down, down, through the dirt in the plastic pool. And John hears.

And John knows the end of the world has come.

Still buried under the dirt, he presses a button on his phone that he's saved for this very moment. A small, but monumental act.

His Twitter feed posts: *Farewell, Earthlings. We who survive will find each other here and build a new nation.*

And 3.7 million people retweet.

@HallMonitor is the number one trend that day on Twitter.

You see, when John first learned about the apocalypse, he had set his feed to post audiovisual footage of his basement, living room, and bedroom every ten minutes. It would continue to do so until he deactivated the autofeed. Or until the world would be destroyed. His hope, he had tweeted, was that if he was trapped in his home, he would be found and rescued.

This means his twenty-three original followers read his warning about imminent radiation outpourings and his intention to entomb himself in his basement for safety. Then they watched Nick and Alison screw each other all night long.

He'd gained a lot of followers by morning.

So, while Nick mourns his roasted ass and applies cold compresses, someone pounds on the door. There is nothing for Alison to do but throw on some clothes and answer it.

A man in a suit stands there with a clipboard. "I am here on behalf of Proximus Power Management to see John Hall, our employee . . . for the moment."

Alison doesn't know how to explain this one. "He's . . . uh . . ."

"In his basement in a tub filled with dirt," finishes the man.

Alison's jaw drops. "How did you—"

"Know? Everyone in the world knows what went on here last night."

The suit hurries downstairs, clipboard in hand. Turns out that when you work for a nuclear power company, you shouldn't tell the world that poor radiation handling is causing a world disaster. And that's it. John gets fired and becomes an international icon of stupidity, Blondie does time for ass branding, Alison becomes a reality show star, and Nick sells pics of his ass and does interviews on talk shows, in a standing position.

That's the end, and you're welcome.

The applause is wild. Bryce slaps his pecs like a gorilla, Kai high-fives Rooster, Briony rolls her eyes but giggles madly, and Alison starts a bus-wide body wave.

But not everyone cheers Rooster on.

Reeve splutters and thumps his pen on his clipboard over and over. "That was . . . how shall I say it? That was deeply offensive. *Deeply.* But you got the details all wrong. Why don't I tell the next story, and pay you back for all your lies?"

"Remember, this is fiction," Mr. Bailey interjects.

"Yeah, don't stand in the way of art!" Bryce calls out.

Reeve waves his clipboard and whines about inflammatory storytelling while Mr. Bailey unsuccessfully tries to calm him down.

Meanwhile, I hold still like a frightened animal to see what Pard will do. While I love Rooster's story, it was mean to give that pathetic character Pard's nickname and voice. Even the poker seemed to be added with Pard in mind. Pard is all sugar voiced and platinum haired, but he's made of steel.

"You," he says softly. "It was you, wasn't it?"

Rooster looks confused, and Pard mouths *My hat.*

Besides loads of bottles, pizza boxes, and a bra, Mr. Bailey has one special memento from the senior prank that happened at his house not two weeks ago while he was stuck at that teacher conference: one gray fedora, punched through the middle and hanging as if by a perfect Frisbee toss on a cuckoo clock out of reach. It might still be there, for all I know.

Rooster holds out his hands like he's pushing the thought away. "No way, dude! Like I'd really want Mr. Bailey to start questioning you and risk you telling on us. It thought it was Fr—"

"It wasn't me," Frye practically snarls. "I'm not taking shit for something I didn't do." Frye is legendary at ultimate Frisbee, so we all thought he did it, but the accusation blew over without any proof.

Pard glances at Frye but settles on Rooster. "I'm just trying to figure out who doesn't like me, and you're the type to find pranks funny. You know, wild party, and I take the fall. Wild story, and I take the fall. Is this your way of bragging?"

Rooster holds out his flat palm like a traffic cop. "Dude, we're cool. I only used you because I wanted to do your voice. That's it."

"Oh, fine. All is forgiven, then," Pard says drily. "The ridiculous thought of me being in love and squeaking lyrics just could not be passed up. Very funny, my voice." Pard looks at Alison without the worship she must be used to getting. "Made *you* laugh."

And, with that, he turns in his seat, conversation at an end.

"Aw, come on," Rooster whines. "It was just fun."

"Yeah, but not for him," Alison replies. She sighs.

Pard ignores them and pretends to take an interest in Mr. Bailey and Reeve, still carrying on about slander.

Five seconds later, Alison has a hand on Pard's shoulder.

"I suppose you're here to kiss and make up," he says, voice flat.

She raises an eyebrow. "Not exactly *kiss*."

"Shame, because by reputation we're both great kissers, even if sexual orientation keeps us tragically apart. I could lay all that aside, though, this once."

A collective murmur disapproves of Pard praising his own erotic charm and flirting with the most desirable girl at our school, but he's ballsy, talking to Alison like that, and she rewards him with an amused smile.

"I'm sorry I laughed," she says, "but I would *never* trick you into kissing my ass."

"That's only because me kissing any part of you has never crossed your mind," he says cattily. "Which is a disappointment, frankly, coming from such an open-minded person like you."

"Is that so?" She gives him this hot look I can't describe, like she's accepting a challenge.

45

And then things move really fast. She pushes her way onto the seat and, before I know it, they're kissing. Not a little peck, but a hard, hungry kiss.

People gasp, and a few whisper-shout some variation of *What the hell?* because Alison is known for doing whatever strikes her fancy, but this time she may have gone too far. She surely hears the shocked murmurs all around, but doesn't seem to care.

"Get under," she says into Pard's mouth, and I think she means get low so that Mr. Bailey won't see them—although, at the moment, Mr. Bailey is on the receiving end of a core dump of all the injustices Reeve has ever faced at Southwark High. But maybe she means getting under literally, because she's on top of him suddenly. They need their own room, but there I am, pressed against the window, and it's not enough space for them or for me.

Pard has his head in my lap, but mostly I see the back of Alison's head, her hair falling and exposing the back of her neck. His hands move up and down her back, her hair. All I can hear are those wet, sticky, slurping noises I've known only in dreams. And all I can feel is Pard's head shifting in my lap as he gives and gets in this porn-star kiss.

Mace and I meet eyes, and then I look back to the scene raging in my lap.

"What's going on back there?" thunders Mr. Bailey.

Alison detaches herself, and a string of saliva stretches and then slaps Pard's lower lip. She sits up fast but pinches his thigh as their legs untangle.

"Nothing, Mr. Bailey. Just looking for a contact lens."

"Well, it's my turn," whines Reeve.

Alison laughs a derisive, *oh no it's not* laugh and gets up. Unfortunately, Pard is still in my lap. It's like his muscles have deflated. She mouths *Later*, which might mean he'll get another chance, and with a wink she's gone.

I really don't care if he gets another chance or not. I just hope that, if he does, it's back at her hotel room when we get to D.C. I don't think I can survive another rerun of this scene.

Mr. Bailey's voice sounds distant to my ears, like he's in an echo chamber. "Now, now, Reeve. It's Cookie's turn."

"But I have to go now—otherwise my story won't make sense," Reeve insists.

Pard just lies there, and his voice, all husky, rises from my lap, which voices should never do. "By God, it's possible," he says to no one in particular. I hope all he means is that it's possible for a scrawny guy like him to make out with a hot girl like Alison, but I'm afraid he means something entirely different.

With Alison gone and people busy commenting on what just happened, it's just me with this guy who used to like me, which made me flee, but now we're hanging out with his head in my lap, and he has this soft, dreamy smile on his lips. I'm looking at those lips, and our eyes lock.

"Get up," I tell him. My voice comes out strained.

He tips up his chin, looking me over. I don't know how he can look so relaxed, so in command. His lips are thin and wet

47

and uncharacteristically smiling. I don't know how to process this smile. There's no Balrog anger left in his eyes, but he's still made of fire.

"Enjoyed that, didn't you?" he says.

I'm not about to answer that, because anything I say would be sort of undercut by the fact that his head has been *right there* rubbing against me the whole time, and so I turn without responding and stare out the window, pretending to be mesmerized by the flicker of metal guard rails rushing past. Pard's head, still heavy in my lap, shifts when he laughs at me.

When Pard came out of the closet sophomore year, he came out wearing the fedora. His posture changed, and his walk changed too. More and more often, he let his hips move and let that slinky side of him show. But he kept his fedora defensively angled as if to protect his eyes from the looks he was getting in the hallways. Or looks from me. Half the time when we sat at our anti-PE library table, we didn't make eye contact. It was easy not to.

Pard sits up, and his hair sticks out in the back from all that friction in my lap. He smiles ear to ear without the brim of a hat dimming the unguarded pleasure written all over his face. Alison's fairy-tale kiss has transformed him. He's in bliss. It doesn't seem to bother him that everyone's whispering and rolling their eyes, or even that Frye took pics with his phone. Sitting way too close, he studies me as if *my* face had changed by the kiss.

I kind of wish I were wearing a hat to hide behind.

Meanwhile, Reeve's whiny voice drones on. He whips out notes and reports on who was smoking this morning, who was drinking. I, of course, am on that list.

"You're all headed to mediocrity," he says, grinning over his clipboard. "But especially meatheads like Rooster."

Meatheads. Rooster picks up on it right away. He slaps Alison on the thigh and says with mock hurt, "Ouch. He called me a *meathead.* I have a boo-boo on my heart."

Alison laughs her sexy laugh. "Awww, Roo." And she kisses him—not on his mouth, but on his left pec, where the boo-boo is.

Rooster is not a meathead. I mean, he's a dumb jock, but he knows how to play the moment. He kept his cool when Alison jumped Pard's bones. I could hear him trying to make light of it with Kai and again when she sat back down, even though it must have killed him to see his crush crushing against Pard, of all people.

Briony takes up Rooster's cause and acts like she's defending a child. "Reeve is so mean," she says, and Mouse and Lupe and Reiko chime in.

Reeve stutters, as he does when he's not working with a script from his clipboard. "I am n-not mean! Go ahead and attack me and then claim I'm the mean one. Outrageous. Absolutely insulting."

Meanwhile, Pard's watching me. Staring. I wish he were

drawing as usual, which would keep him too busy to lob all these sticky smiles my way. Something has seriously shifted, and instead of Pard acting pissed at me, he's acting . . . what? I don't know and I don't care. I pretend to be engrossed in my phone.

"Tell me what you're thinking," he says, and I swear to God, his aura touches me. This thick, warm mess of an aura. If he thinks we're going to have a heart-to-heart over my perspective of what just happened, he's seriously delusional. So I slam the door on him in the harshest possible way.

"I just saw two girls kissing."

I'm being offensive, but I need to stomp out whatever it is he's trying to start.

Instead, he tilts his head and asks quietly, almost sexy-like (though obviously not sexy), "So . . . which girl turned you on?"

Maybe I deserve that, but I'm speechless. I mumble Alison's name, of course, while his aura brushes up against me like one of those cats that rub up against your leg because it knows you hate cats.

I need to say something, anything, to beat off that fuzzy warmth snaking through me. "Maybe you should worry what Greg will do when he finds out you practically had sex on the bus." Okay, that came off as something Reeve would say. Like, *I'm telling.* And saying "sex on the bus" out loud completely disturbs me. I don't want to verbalize even remotely what happened in my lap. Pard having this sex life. Being good at it. Being good at it in my lap.

If anything, his predatory smile intensifies, and I brace for a comparison to Reeve, but it's worse than that. "Is this your coded way of finding out if I'm still seeing him?"

I cradle my phone and text Cannon.

Save me. The only seat on the bus was next 2 Pard or Mace. Hell is real.

"I'm free," he says, so close to my ear that I shiver. "Just so you know."

I'm so shocked I can't move. I'm back in late summer after ninth grade, wanting to hide, deleting his phone messages, his texts asking where I am and why I won't write back. I'm lucky I don't crack my phone from squeezing it so hard.

Mr. Bailey unintentionally rescues me. "Pard? Reeve is trying to tell his story, if you'd care to listen."

The moment has passed. I flip Pard off, and he scoots toward the aisle. He looks a little more like himself again. Angry.

"Exactly," says Reeve. "Show some respect."

A groan comes from the back.

"I heard that, Rooster!" Reeve shouts. "Time to pay you back for your story. Here's *your* future."

REEVE'S TALE

Very well. So, currently, Rooster seems like he has it all, but guess what happens before graduation? In his hubris he impregnates a fellow student.

"What's hubris?" Rooster asks, turning to Alison. "Some kind of pubic hair?"

She shrugs. "Makes sense to me."

"*Huuubris,*" Bryce sings.

But Reeve laughs like Bert on *Sesame Street*. An evil Bert with a similar unibrow, but much more of a beaky nose. *Heh-heh-heh.*

"Rooster, your lack of vocabulary speaks volumes about your future, as well as that of your compadres. In fact, hubris signifies pride, and you will lose all your pride and friends when you have the effrontery to impregnate the lovely Briony."

Kai's eyebrows launch up to his hairline, and Briony freaks.

"Ew, gross!" she screams, and Rooster, glancing at Briony's and Kai's reactions, looks like a dog that's pooped on the carpet.

"Calm down, everyone. Reeve, change all the names, or your story ends here."

"Certainly, Mr. Bailey."

So, our protagonist, Cocky—*heh-heh-heh*—flunks out of school and has to work at the mini-market by the gas station. He moves into the basement with his girlfriend, um, Briana. They have a baby named, um, Allie, and later get married.

Alison raises an eyebrow, and I think she's going to interrupt, but then she just laughs and caresses her "daddy." Rooster purrs like a lion. They kind of settle into each other incestuously and listen to the story.

Years later Cocky loses his job and has to get work at a mini-market in the middle of nowhere. Literally just a shop off a forgotten freeway. So, his wife, Briana, and daughter, Allie, who is just starting at some no-name community college, move into the one-bedroom connected to the store. Yes, indeed, they all had to sleep in the same room. To top things off, Briana has a second child, and now they have to fit a crib in the already overstuffed bedroom. The baby yowls every night and will only settle down after a late night feeding and stroll with her mom.

It's a rather dull life, I must say, and the only fun Cocky has is pranking the occasional customer—only no one has been around in a long time.

Now I will introduce two college students, graduates from our own Southwark High. They are on their way to Brown, and all their worldly goods are packed in their Subaru. I'll play the main one, but for the story, we'll call him Mitch.

I smile ear to ear. I mean, *Mitch*. It's as if in his fantasy life, Reeve is one of the popular meatheads he claims to despise. It's like catching him pulling a varsity jacket over his bony shoulders.

And my friend will be our own Jeff Chaucer.

"What?! Leave me *out*." I try to look tough (like a Mitch), but immediately everyone's throwing out fake names, and they decide to name us Bert and Ernie. Alison claims she once dated an older guy named Bert, and Reeve gets way too excited when he hears that.

"Can you do Ernie's laugh?" Pard asks, and there's still a lot of bliss-smacked predator to him, but that edge of mockery is also back, which might be progress.

Reeve, meanwhile, swaggers a bit as he launches back into his tale.

So these guys come in and see this dumpy little store, and they see Cocky, a big bald guy, sitting back watching TV, like his store is his living room, which it is. I should add that Cocky is a corpulent fellow. Over the years, all his muscle has turned to fat, and he has trouble getting out of his chair when the college students arrive. This makes them snicker, and Cocky wants revenge.

Ernie asks to use the bathroom, and Cocky has it all worked out. With a smile on his face, he gives Ernie a key.

That leaves Bert for him to deal with. Cocky looks out the window and sees the Subaru packed with gear.

"Car looks pretty dirty," he says. "A wash is only five bucks."

"Just coffee, thanks," Bert says, and he buys an overpriced cup. Cocky hands it over with a grin, and Bert takes a sip. It tastes like the dirt it was made from.

Then Allie walks into the store, and Bert's jaw drops. "Hi there," he says, and she smiles at him.

Cocky doesn't like that, but he uses it to his advantage. "Allie, want to help Bert get his car washed?"

"Sure," she says.

Bert can't say no to that, even though he has to cough up five dollars.

While Bert is scrounging for change, Cocky tells his daughter the plan to prank the boys. She zips outside with Bert's car keys.

When Bert joins her, she already has the car queued at the machine drive-through.

"Let's go," she says, and Bert climbs in the passenger side, and they ride into the darkness with all the water jets and sponges.

Unbeknownst to Bert, the back windows are all rolled down. He sniffs. "Does it smell soapy in here?"

Allie laughs and then makes him forget everything when she gives Bert a big kiss. With tongue!

The real Alison leans forward. "No way! I am not making out with you, *Bert*."

Reeve's laugh is more nervous than evil. *Heh-heh-heh.* "Let's just move on."

When they get out of the wash, Allie parks the car right where it had been. It's not all that clean, but Bert has no complaints . . . until he notices the soggy mess inside.

"Everything is ruined."

Allie laughs. "Oh, it's just a joke. Lighten up!"

Just then Bert hears shouting.

It's Ernie, who has been locked in the bathroom the whole time.

"Bert, get me out! It reeks in here!"

Bert rushes to Cocky to demand help. Cocky unlocks the door. Out comes Ernie and the stench of an unwashed bathroom so filthy that a guy has to pee standing on the counter top.

Ernie glares murder at Cocky. All three of them head back to the store, when they see another sight:

The Subaru's tires are flat.

And Allie is tiptoeing away, carrying a harpoon.

"That does it!" shouts Bert. "I'm calling the cops."

"No, wait, it was an accident!" blurts Cocky. "I'm sure she just tripped carrying that thing."

The young men stare at him. "Tripped four times? Holding a harpoon?"

Cocky casts his daughter a look like she's gone too far, even though he told her to do it, then turns back to the angry boys. He's worried they might call the cops. "My daughter got carried away there. I'll make it up to you guys. You can crash here tonight. I should be able to put on some temporary tires that will get you through. There's no need to get upset. I'll even throw in dinner, on the house. How's that for a handsome offer?"

The guys agree, or pretend to, at least. When Cocky goes into the garage to find cheap tires, Bert says, "I've had it with this guy."

Ernie agrees. "But there's not much we can do."

"Or is there?" Bert chuckles.

That night, after a dinner of heated up micro meals from the convenience store, they have to figure out the sleeping arrangements. It's tight in the tiny, one-bedroom apartment off the store that the whole family shares, and putting up two other people makes it almost impossible. Cocky and Briana decide that they should sleep in their usual bed, with the crib at the end, and they put up the young men in Allie's double bed. Allie herself will sleep on a rollaway in the storage closet.

Before long, everyone is asleep, except the two friends, because Cocky snores like a walrus.

Bert rolls toward Ernie. "I'll see you later."

"Where are you going?"

He winks. "To Allie's. I thought she might enjoy a visit."

Ernie gasps. "What about Cocky?"

A snore shakes the room. Bert grins, then flicks off the sheets. "Serves him right. See you around."

"Wait, don't!"

But Bert is already sneaking to the storage closet. It swings open without a sound. Allie is asleep, but Bert jumps in the bed and passionately rolls on top of her.

"And then she wakes up and screams that a rapist is attacking her?"

Alison has her arms crossed, and everyone's whispering and weighing in. The image of Reeve climbing on top of a sleeping girl is way too horrible a visual.

"No, she doesn't . . . I mean, no . . . ," Reeve counters. "It's my story, and she woke up wanting it. Knowing Bert is hot and could do it with her."

"No. She doesn't," Alison says, and her voice has a finality to it.

"But she *has* to," Reeve whines. "It's part of the plan. It's the whole point of the story. Cocky screws over the boys all day, and they screw him over all night."

58

Alison raises that eyebrow. "Then why didn't Bert jump on top of Cocky?"

Reeve gets this exasperated look on his face. "Because he'd kill me . . . and I am not a homosexual."

Alison heaves a big sigh. "Look, I'll help you write your story." And she takes over.

So, Bert climbs on top of Allie, but Allie wakes up and tells him she doesn't want him, so Bert stops. Right?

Reeve is devastated. "Right."

There's pity in Alison's smile as she continues her revised version.

Allie points out that it's rude to make love to people without their permission. She takes his arm and leads him back to his bed. She explains to him that you should make sure the person wants it, and she'll show him how. She sees Ernie there, watching them with eyes wide open. Allie asks Ernie, "Want to sleep with me tonight?" And Ernie says . . .

Alison looks at me with those brown eyes snapping with energy. "What does Ernie say?"

"Sure," I squeak. Earlier, I thought Pard had been messing with my head more than I could take, but now my head-mess knows no bounds.

Alison flicks a hand as if to say, *There you have it.* She finishes telling the story her way.

Then Allie puts Bert in his bed and pulls Ernie out, and she leads Ernie to her little rollaway in the closet. And Ernie is sweet and innocent, Allie's favorite flavor. She teaches him first how to kiss, and they play around in various states of undress until they are making love again and again. They play the night away, until Ernie needs to sneak back to his bed in the morning.

"How's that?" she asks.

"Fine," I say, breathless. My heart's beating fast, and my voice betrays me.

Her smile is wicked, like she's mock-scolding my naughty mind. "I was talking to Reeve."

"Oh." I turn to the window and pretend to look for Long Island. I want to die.

"W-well," Reeve stutters, "have it your way. I don't want to offend the fairer sex. Anyhow. Allow me to continue."

Bert lies in the bed, alone, none too happy at being rejected by the lovely young woman. So he dozes off. He wakes up an hour later to a baby crying. He's been warned about the baby's habit of waking up every night. The room is pitch dark, but the other bed creaks, and he knows Briana is taking the baby out for a night walk, and maybe even a breast-feeding.

Bert gets up and moves the crib to the foot of his bed. Then he takes off his clothes and waits under the covers.

Briana comes back and passes his bed, and then retraces her steps. She puts the sleeping baby in the crib and crawls in next to him.

"I almost got in the wrong bed!" she whispers to the man she thinks is her husband.

"Hmm," Bert groans heavily, hiding his voice to keep the game of musical beds a secret. He runs his hand over her breast, and she rolls toward him. Then they start making out, all tongues and grinding and sex. The real deal. *Heh-heh-heh.* Over and over, and she is totally into it. She moans, "Cocky, you're on fire tonight." They fall asleep naked in each other's arms.

Well, when Ernie finally returns to the room, tiptoeing in the dark, he almost gets into bed with Bert and Briana, but the baby crib warns him that this is the wrong bed.

So he gets into bed with Cocky instead.

Then he scoots up real close and tells Cocky every kinky thing he did with Allie that night.

He's totally shocked when Cocky rolls over and grabs him by the throat.

"It's me, you moron," Cocky growls. "How dare you sleep with my daughter?"

Briana calls from the other bed. "Cocky, is that you? But I thought I was having sex with you in *this* bed."

"So. Much. *Ew,*" moans Briony.

Cocky roars, "You guys slept with my daughter *and* my wife!" The only reason Ernie doesn't get strangled is that Cocky lunges for Bert while still holding on to Ernie. Cocky's plan seems to be to grab both of them by the necks at the same time.

Everyone is screaming, all while at least partly naked, and Briana slaps Bert, and the baby starts bawling, and Allie rushes into the dark room with her harpoon in hand in time to hear Cocky roaring loudly as he chases Bert and Ernie around the room.

Clutching the baby, Briana shrieks at her daughter, "Help your father!"

So Allie takes a swing with her harpoon. Everyone hears a *thunk*, and a body falls to the floor.

By now the gray light of dawn breaks over the horizon, and in seconds everyone can see the truth: not Bert or Ernie on the floor, but Cocky.

Allie has clocked her own esteemed progenitor with solid iron.

Bert says, "Well, ladies, we had a terrific time, and now we'll be on our way."

So they get into their musty Subaru and drive to school. The end.

Reeve's story was so mean spirited—not to mention so rape-happy—that everyone and especially the girls rant about what a load of sexism it was.

"And he wonders why he can't get laid," Reiko says to Frye with a snort.

Briony is also beside herself, insisting to everyone that she (1) would never sleep with Rooster and (2) would kill herself before she let Reeve touch her body.

Point #1 is extremely awkward for Rooster. I mean, the first word that came out of Briony's mouth when Reeve claimed she'd slept with Rooster was "gross," and now she adds that she'd never sleep with him. And Rooster can't tell Briony off, because she's Kai's girlfriend. So he just sits there, dumbstruck.

I'm looking at Rooster through Briony's eyes, and I see it. He's a football star, and popular, but not hot. There comes a point when a guy gets so huge that he's like another species. Girls squeal when he picks them up, but not because his body makes their hearts flutter. They save the flutter thing for guys like Kai, with those smooth shoulders and small waist. Even skinny-assed Frye sees far more action than Rooster does. It's weird, because Rooster has had some hot girlfriends, but I'm wondering if any of them ever made *him* feel hot. I'm guessing not. And I wonder if that bites.

I'm grateful Alison isn't giving a huge speech about how mating with me would be the most disgusting experience in a menu of horrific life options. Still, I'm feeling low from being set up in a fictional one-night stand that no girl in real life would ever tolerate.

"What did you think of the story, Jeff?" Mari is asking my professional opinion again, which feels suspicious. Maybe she wants to see if I'm one of those pigheaded, sexist authors.

Obviously, I know which side to take in this war. "It was vindictive. And raping a woman to get back at a man is totally off."

"No one got raped!" Reeve screeches.

"What about Briana?" Cece demands loudly, even though she's sitting near Reeve at the front. She's been grumbling about the sexism in the other stories and seems to have reached her tipping point. "That was not consensual."

"Anyone sleeping with Reeve would hardly do it consensually," Lupe quips.

"Deception is his only hope," Reiko adds.

"Hence his story," Lupe concludes, and the two of them smile somewhat cruelly.

I don't know how Reeve can hear all this without shriveling up and dying.

He raps the clipboard with his pen, *rat-tat-tat*. "So, let me get this straight. You guys can pull pranks, and it's fun, but when I do, it's vindictive and evil and sexually aggressive. What a bunch of BS. The truth is that you're scared of my intelligence, because

64

if I chose to use it against you, you wouldn't stand a chance."

Things are about to take a nasty turn, when Alison speaks up. "There's one good thing about this story."

Her eyes twinkle with mischief that is actually not at Reeve's expense. She might be the only person on the whole bus not ganging up on him.

"Two words: 'musical beds.' *That* is something I need to try."

Most of the girls are skeptical, but the guys can't help but want in on that game, especially if Alison is playing.

Suddenly people are whispering "musical beds" and swapping seats. They pair off quietly while Mr. Bailey gets into this big sexism debate with Cece up front.

Changing seats to ditch Pard sounds terrific, but I don't know who would sit with me. I don't even know how to ask someone. I turn around to find Bryce, but he's already out of his seat, sliding in with Rooster like that's a done deal. I look over at Reiko, but she's already leaning over Frye to get Lupe's attention.

"Over here, goddess," Pard says softly.

Alison grins and squeezes in with him. With us.

He's got this smug smile on his face, meant for me to see. I can't believe Pard has beat me to it . . . with *her*. Now I have to leave or be a complete loser in front of Alison.

I see Cookie slouched in the back corner and pounce.

"Cookie!" I have to raise my voice, because he is that zoned out, and Mr. Bailey turns his head, but he's not really looking. Cece is still ranting in full swing.

Cookie flashes a peace sign. I take that as a yes to the question I didn't ask, then crawl over Pard and Alison and hustle to the back. Alison slaps my ass as I rush down the aisle. Unless it was Pard.

I sandwich myself in the back row between Saga and Cookie. Instantly, I know the smell of pot and cigarette smoke will probably trigger my asthma, but there's no other option. I can last until the first pit stop.

"I'm thirsty," Cookie says, and he looks at me like I might have a tall glass of milk.

"What the heck is going on here?" Mr. Bailey cranes his neck. "You all changed seats?"

"Sir, I did no such thing," Reeve says, clicking his pen. "But I have it all here, exactly what happened while Cece distracted you."

Cece slaps her seat like she's had it. "I wasn't *distracting* him! I was pointing out that these tales are offensive." She faces the whole bus and looks a little lost because Rooster isn't in his spot, Saga is, but she finds him two rows ahead and narrows her eyes. "These stories all objectify women. First they are forced into marriage, and then they are an object for a man to use. It's disgusting."

"Aw, it's just fun," Rooster says.

Cece leans out like she wants to crawl over the seats and smack him. "Using women for your own sexual gratification is not *fun*."

"Yeah, it is," Rooster says, but quietly to Bryce beside him.

66

Knees jutting into the aisle, Mr. Bailey props his chin with his fist, like a perkier version of that statue *The Thinker*. "I expect all of you to be offended at least once today. It's unlikely we could have this many people telling this many stories without finding some of them very problematic."

"Then let's make rules to keep that from happening," Cece says.

Mr. Bailey frowns. "I don't think that's possible. And I don't think it's appropriate."

Cece retorts, "You think it's appropriate to tell inappropriate stories?"

"I think it's appropriate to let everyone tell their own story. That doesn't mean people are universally praised for the tales they tell. We're all listening and reacting to what we're hearing, and we're all talking, all learning. That works for me. Now, let's get on with it. I already drew out Cookie's name."

Cece throws herself down on her seat with a *thump*.

Meanwhile, Cookie blinks like a baby animal new to daylight while everyone waits for his story.

COOKIE'S TALE

"What?" he asks. "What did I do?"

Lupe twists in her seat. "It's your turn, doofus!"

Cookie blinks in sweet, clueless surprise. "A story? My own?"

"Your very own widdle story," Bryce answers.

Cookie nods. He rests his head on my shoulder, and I try to lean away, but the more I lean, the more he falls on me.

"Come on!" Saga swats him on the head, and his hat falls off, waking him up.

"*O-kay*," he says slowly.

I like water.

He pauses, just for a moment.

Water in a Dixie cup is nice, but I mean on a lake. Still water is *still* water. When you're lying on a boat and you hear the slap of water on the hull. *Slap . . . slap . . . slap.* So chill. Usually, when you hear the *slap . . . slap*, you see the sunbeams reflected on the water and your boat and wherever. It's like the sun-slap, you know? But with light, not water.

Rooster angles to see around Bryce. "Yo, is there a point here?"

"It's poetry, man," Cookie says.

"Well, can you add some sex?"

Cookie nods like he's nodding off. He uses my shoulder to prop his head up. He closes his eyes and murmurs all his musings on sex right into my ear. He's like the little mouse in the classic *Alice in Wonderland* movie. The one that gets jam on his nose and feels all right with the world. For Cookie, it's a joint, not jam, and the smell is so strong that I look to my feet, where the backpack and my inhaler should be, only I left all that with Pard. I'm okay. It takes a while to ramp up, but the tightness is there inside my ribs as Cookie cuddles up to me and gets poetic on sex.

Sex is nice. Really nice. And slow. Skin on skin is like the *slap . . . slap* of the water on the boat and of the sun on the boat. Wet and light.

I mean a sailboat. Not a powerboat. Because there's also the wind-slap. Sails like desires shudder in the wind.

Blinking is the best part of sex. I like how women blink. And bracelets.

Once, when I was hiking, I swear to God, I found a whole field of plants. You know, special plants. I got into them and rolled around. It was so nice. I cried and it was fine, because the plants were swaying and upright and warm in the sun. I just want to sniff the world.

Cookie seems to be done, though it's hard to say.

Kai laughs. "This is one baked story."

"That—that was not a story," Reeve says, nostrils flaring. "It was *insanity*. We have just listened to insanity."

"Slap . . . sss . . ." Cookie sighs dreamily. If he's hurt that everyone on the bus hates his story, he doesn't show it. He nuzzles me, which is pretty freaky after his sex talk. His breaths get deeper as mine get shallower. My chest feels tighter now. Itchy. I'd sneak in a puff if I could, even with Cookie and Saga right there.

Cece cuts in. "At least it wasn't offensive like all *your* stories."

Kai's eyes pop open. "Not *my* story."

"Emily should never have been forced to marry a zombie. If you can't even see that, what's the point in talking to you?"

Mr. Bailey calls out, "Let's calm down. You can disagree, but you can't fight."

Cece raises her voice. "Women are worth fighting for."

"Let's get back to smoking pot, since we can all agree on *that*," Rooster says. "How about it, Cookie?"

I jostle him. My cheek brushes against his hat, and a mop of fine black curls spills out.

Mr. Bailey can't help but smile. "I thought my classes bored him, but even here he sleeps. Amazing."

Bryce bats his eyelashes. "Aw, would you look at dat? Widdle Cookie take a nap-nap on widdle Jeffie pal."

Everyone turns to look at the snugglefest.

Pard's eyes pop, and a manic smile lights up his face.

The girls all coo over Cookie and me. Briony whips out her phone, then Reiko and Lupe.

I can't win.

I don't smile, and the girls chide me for this. It ruins the pictures, they say. I don't reply—waste of air—but my glum face makes it look intentional. Asthmatics are good hiders, and no one notices my shallow breathing or how quiet I am. My tight lungs are sending me a clear message: *Back off from Pot Boy.* It doesn't help that chain-smoking Saga is thigh to thigh with me, which sounds great—which *is* great—except the combo of ashtray and pot is poison. I should change seats.

Saga pecks me on the cheek and says, "You're like a daddy."

And I can't get up right after she says a nice thing like that.

That's when I see Pard drawing me. I can tell a mile away by the intensity on his face, the way he can look at my eyes without making real eye contact, which makes me feel painfully visible and unseen at the same time.

"Don't." The furious word comes out of my big mouth all tiny, but he stops. He keeps looking, though, memorizing me before the pose is gone. I should ask him to pass me my backpack, but I'm too angry. Also, it would take too much air and draw too much attention.

Alison seems to notice his sketchbook for the first time. "Wow. Like, *wow.*"

71

Pard frowns. His sketchbook is a private thing. She takes the book and flips a page. Then she flips out.

"Oh my God! Rooster! He drew you *naked!*"

Everyone looks shocked, except Cookie, of course, and Mr. Bailey, who's facing forward with his head down, like he's sneaking in a bit of phone time.

"The fuck?" Rooster is out of his chair, fast, and the next moment, Pard's like a squirrel dangling from a bear's paw. Arms over his head, Pard clutches the book as long as he can before Rooster yanks it away.

Mr. Bailey turns around, all teacher-serious. "What's going on back there?"

"Nothing, Mr. Bailey," Alison says, all innocence. "Just looking at some art."

"Pard drew an image of Rooster sans clothing," Reeve reports.

"Pard," Mr. Bailey says, "that's inappropriate."

"Why is *that* inappropriate?" Cece demands. "Thank God someone here is finally objectifying men instead of women." And she launches into another rant at Mr. Bailey about inappropriate stories and behavior.

Meanwhile, Rooster's mouth hangs open at the picture in his lap. A dozen heads angle to see, but he slaps the book to his chest. "You don't like living, do you?"

Pard looks like a terrified tiny person trying to appear brave.

Rooster takes the book in both hands and rips it an inch down the middle. Alison snaps, "Don't, Roo! Don't do that. Roo . . ."

Rooster is caught between wanting Pard to die and wanting to please Alison. He breathes hard through his nostrils like a bull seeing red, and it's not from the exertion of ripping the book. It's from the exertion of *not* ripping the book.

"Roo . . . give it back," Alison says, her hand extended.

There's a whisper of ripping paper as Rooster tears out a leaf from Pard's book and stuffs it in his pocket. That must not have satisfied him, because the spine of the sketchbook twists under Rooster's banana-thick fingers. He's going to wring out the sketchbook like a dishrag.

Alison touches his forearm. "Roo . . . the book . . ."

More deep animal breathing. I envy the scale of his lung capacity. You could film him to make air-porn for asthmatics.

Rooster leans into Pard's space. "Never draw me again. And apologize for the anatomical errors."

"What errors?" Pard sees the dangerous look on Rooster's face and changes his strategy. "Oh. *Those* errors. Sorry. It's easier to draw naked people when they're actually naked."

People look unsure whether he's just saying that or has experience, but Alison's intrigued. "You draw naked people?"

Pard shrugs, all sophisticated. "Of course."

Rooster flips through the book, looking for naked people. "Here's one!" I feel a stab of non-asthmatic panic. What if Rooster finds me in there naked? Pard's stealth-sketched me during PE lots of times, just to annoy me, and I've wondered if he sometimes draws me when I have no idea he's doing it.

73

When Rooster adds, "Eh, these naked people are just a bunch of geezers," I can breathe a little again (who am I kidding?—I am pretending to breathe). I feel a whoosh of relief, but also . . . what? Kind of let down? Like it was odd Pard didn't have me in there, like I'm thinking Rooster made a mistake. At the very least I must be in there clothed. I mean, it would be odd if I weren't there at all.

Rooster pokes one of the pages. "Check out this old woman with saggy breasts. Gross! I bet you love drawing naked people, you perv."

Pard's voice is thin and savage. "I do. I *love* drawing the human form, and old people are gorgeous: their wrinkles, their spotted hands, the way their bodies still hold on to their sex. Drawing is the sexiest thing a person can ever do."

His words have a strange effect. Some girls nod their approval, but the guys aren't derailed so easily from the topic of lust and naked people.

"You sound way too excited about old ladies," Bryce says.

Rooster cuts in. "The big question is, do you draw yourself naked?"

Pard flinches. It's barely anything, but for him, it's huge.

"No."

"Why not?" Bryce asks.

Pard doesn't say why, just holds out his hand. "Give me my book."

Rooster persists. "Cock not long enough?"

Mr. Bailey cuts in. "Rooster, I heard that. Give him his book."

"Maybe draw yourself some balls," Rooster quietly adds, like he's giving an art tip, while handing back the book.

Mr. Bailey cuts in. "Okay, that's enough, gentlemen."

"Gentlemen," Pard mutters. "*Right.*"

CECE'S TALE

"Anyhow, we've wandered off topic," Mr. Bailey says. "Cookie's story has ended prematurely, so let's move on. Our next name is Marcus—"

"Objection!"

Cece waves her arm in the air. She's shed her jacket, probably having heated herself all up earlier.

Saga lets out a surprised hiss, and then I notice she's not disgusted by Cece's dumpy sleeveless dress, but by her armpit hair in plain sight. It's like Cece wants everyone to have a good look.

People whisper. I don't know how Parson can sit next to Cece's armpit and wait attentively, as if he wants to know what she's objecting to. Maybe being this ultra youth group leader fanatic has made him see Christ his Savior in everyone, regardless of shaving habits. Meanwhile, my Jedi mind powers focus on lowering Cece's arm, but my asthma is ruining my concentration.

Sad but true Southwark fact: Cece is about as unpopular as you can get. She doesn't use chemicals, so she won't use deodorant on those unshaved pits. If anyone male opens a door for her, she won't walk through it. If she catches guys debating who the hottest girls are, she barges over and lectures them. Someone asked Cece who her date was for prom, and she said she didn't have a date. "So you're going stag." And she said no, she was going *doe*.

Everyone braces for a speech.

"This name-drawing thing is a joke," she says. "We've had four men in a row. And now you want five? Let's have some women speaking here. Enough with mansplaining. It's our turn. Four women in a row to even the balance."

Rooster wrinkles his nose. "*Mansplaining*," he grumbles. "Anytime a guy opens his mouth, it's automatically that. Anyhow, we're all getting a turn, so what difference does it make who goes when?"

Lupe looks from Cece to Rooster like she's trying to make up her mind, and then, with her lips puckering like she's reluctant about it, she joins Cece's side. "No, she's right. It makes a difference. What if all the women go last when everyone's sick of listening? Then what? Drawing from the hat was supposed to keep it mixed, but it's not so mixed now."

Mr. Bailey taps a pen to his chin. "Let's vote. But I'd like Marcus to get thrown in there somewhere. How about two women, then Marcus, then another two women? After that, we'll try it randomly again. Keep in mind we have more men on this bus."

Cece nods. "I know that, but if women can tell stories now, maybe the men will be less offensive when it's their turn."

"Okay. All in favor, raise your hand."

Everyone raises their hands except Cookie, of course. And Mace.

"All opposed?"

No one raises their hands.

"Mace, are you abstaining?"

Mace shrugs the bare minimum. "Sure," he says, surly and deep. He's still alone in his original seat. No bed swapping for him.

I get a chill from the way he just doesn't care about anything. It's not just today. He and Pard have stopped eating lunch together after three and a half years. Pard's with the theater kids now, and Mace goes somewhere else. Alone, or with guys as mean-looking as he is. I don't know if he and Pard were real friends or just lunch buddies, if they had a fight or just drifted, but it's weird to see them sitting in the same row but ignoring each other. Friend-breakups can be the worst.

My shallow breath trick is failing. Cookie must go. I arrange his head and shoulder against the wall (no window in the back row), and he mumbles "chicken wire" and sleeps right through it. The attack is still threatening to come, though, and a flutter of panic tugs right where I'm tight. Got to stay calm. With Cookie off me, the light-headed thing will pass. I hope. Saga brushes me with her calf as she crosses her legs and rolls her eyes at me as Cece begins.

Society is way too fixated on defining women through men. I mean, look at the word "woman." It has the word "man" right in it. Tips you off that there's a serious problem here. We start out as girls, separate from boys, and as a group, we're all kids. Later, we buy into pleasing men and become *wo-men*. If we don't have a boyfriend and guys don't think we're hot, we feel like lesser beings.

That is such bullshit.

I'm so sick of movies that only have a woman there for making out and taking off her shirt. And I don't buy into giving a woman a gun and calling her badass. Notice she's also a piece of ass, every time.

Reeve's story that you just heard? Sick. That woman Briana was raped. That college guy Bert took a down-and-out woman and raped her, and then tootled away in his soggy Subaru. And Allie could be doing better things than waiting for boys to come down the highway. Rooster's tale is trickier. On the one hand, I'm glad Alison gets out from under the husband's thumb. But notice she doesn't just dump him. Her only options are choosing among three men. Do you see how wrong all this is?

But Kai's story is possibly the worst. What if Emily skipped being bait for Palam and Arc and became a scientist? She could have cured a disease. She could have figured out the whole zombie apocalypse thing and fixed it. But, no, she's a *supporting* character, meaning she needs to support the weight of some zombie-lover on top of her.

"What's wrong with a little love?" Rooster demands.

"The problem is that women are defined by it. They can't have their own lives."

I don't hear anything after that. The lungs have officially been crushed by boulders. My shallow wheezes ramp up into something else altogether. The itch is something I want to claw into, to get the air that way.

I'm not screwing around anymore. Not with this prickle of sweat warning me it's here, it's coming right now.

I rise and push past Saga, ignore her questions. I walk like an old man with my hands heavy on the backs of the seats, and the effort makes my head swim. People ask what's going on, but I can't answer.

I get to the row with my backpack and crash next to Mace. There are stars in the air, or maybe my crashing next to him has disturbed his eyebrow dandruff flakes. I shut my eyes and expect him to punch me in the gut, which would probably kill me for real.

Meanwhile, a girl screams my name. No, it's Pard. He's shouting for help and barking at Mace to *just do it*.

The next moment, the freakiest guy on the bus awkwardly pats my shoulder, then runs his hands along my back. Back rubs calm me down—Mom does this for me—but a rubdown from Mace is weird. But who the fuck cares? I'm wheezing and scratching my chest and can't. Get. Air.

People are calling and shouting, but my ears home in on the inhaler getting shaken. I turn toward the sound like a flower turns to the sun.

"I'll take that." Mr. Bailey's voice sounds close. "Jeff, I have your inhaler."

And, suddenly, it's in my mouth, and I take a puff, that nasty tang I've wanted so hard, and hold it hold it hold it. Then I finally let it all go, and the bad air comes out and out, and it's like the claws gripping me have loosened and let me live. And then I suck in all the sweet air on this whole bus.

"Was that enough? Do you need another?"

Eyes still closed, I hold out four fingers for him to wait that many minutes and let my body process. I have those ups and downs—that wobbly hyper feeling pulling me up, that nausea pulling me down. The shakes as I process this roller coaster. Albuterol kicks my ass.

But when Pard says my four minutes are up, I tip my chin up like a baby bird, and we do it all over again, because albuterol kicks asthma's ass.

So much air now, huge gulps of it. I focus on my lungs and on the gentle hands that haven't stopped rubbing my back and try to ignore the side effects.

"More?" Mr. Bailey asks. I shake my head no.

I finally I open my eyes. Holding the inhaler, Mr. Bailey fills the aisle and takes the edge of Pard's seat. Pard, meanwhile, is next to him in the aisle, down on one knee like he's about to propose. They both are quiet and freaked. Everyone is.

"Jeff," Mr. Bailey says, "we're going to take you to the hospital."

No, I mouth. I hold out my hands to stop him, then pull them back. I'm shaking, which looks bad, but I don't have the energy to tell Mr. Bailey it's just the meds, not my asthma. Everyone stares like I'll turn purple or shake into some sort of epileptic fit.

I just breathe and command myself not to barf as the bus dips and curves its lumbering way.

When the bus takes the next off-ramp, I know I have to speak out loud, very distinctly.

"I'm fine now." My voice whispers whether I want it to or not.

Mr. Bailey wipes sweat from his forehead. "I can't risk this. You're shaking."

"Albuterol. It's strong." Suddenly, I wonder how he knew to get the albuterol and not the Diskus. Or where I kept the meds in my pack. Just lucky, I guess. "They'd only give me albuterol. It works fast. Some water, a snack, and I'll be fine."

"I want you up with me. Can you walk?"

He makes the bus driver pull over. Mace abruptly stops the back rub. I turn to give him a little nod. He shrugs and looks out the window. For some reason it hurts that he won't look at me. Maybe I'm too freaky.

Everyone stares while I walk like an invalid on jittery, woozy legs. Mr. Bailey leads me, practically holding my hand.

He puts me next to him, in the front. Reeve's row, but the other side.

I kind of leak tears as I finish up shaking.

Mr. Bailey gives me the mother lode: tissues, a water bottle, his peanut butter and jelly sandwich, pretzels, and a lollipop. A green one, which is my favorite since toddlerhood.

I give him a teasing look. "A lollipop?"

He smiles, and his eyes go nostalgic. "I have a five-year-old."

I tilt my head. Maybe it was the episode and the side effect of being hyper that make me blurt, "You do? I didn't see any signs at your—"

I stop. I put my hand to my heart, close my eyes, and fake cough, knowing that I'm betraying myself with this gesture, knowing he has to know I was in his house for senior prank. A house with no signs of family, not even a girlfriend, which is odd, because Mr. Bailey may be teacher-poor, but he's kind, smart, young, and as funny as a normal adult can be. Handsome, too, in an intellectual way. But his house was definitely not one with a kid bed or toys on the living room floor. The tiny spare room was his office. I know because I may have sort of hacked his computer from there.

"Jeff, are you okay? *Jeff?*"

He rubs my back, not nearly as well as Mace did, and I surface from my fake coughing fit. I feel so tired, yet hyper, so maybe I'm not playacting sick all that much.

"Sorry. Five, huh? Your kid?"

"Yes. Five." He looks at me carefully, either because he's unsure about my lungs or my honesty. Maybe both.

There are some murmurs of goodwill from the back of the bus, but they sound distant. I'm in a bubble all by myself. Inside this bubble of downtime, I breathe and I snack and I chill.

I also give Mr. Bailey a full recap of how I stupidly sat in a place that I knew would cause trouble and ignored all the danger signals. He wants to know why I did that, and it's pathetic to explain to an adult how hard it is to fit in, so I just say I didn't want to interrupt all the stories and stuff, because teachers understand things like a student sitting quietly in his seat.

"Interrupt next time," he says, almost angry. "Promise me that."

I nod.

We're not going to the ER. I'm hoping he won't bring up calling home, and I know I'm golden when he lets Cece tell her story.

There was this girl in Florida who had a boyfriend and was headed to the same college he was going to, the University of Michigan. Lily and Brandon were prom queen and king, and she thought she knew what lay ahead of her: a life with this guy. She'd miss the Florida Keys, where she lived right on a dock slip and had her own little Boston Whaler. She loved the ocean more than any other place, but love is love, right? And an ocean is just an ocean. Most of the time, she didn't even notice it. It was a backdrop to her life, that's all. But Brandon was the focal point of her life.

One day Lily's mom barged in on Lily and Brandon while they were "studying," but she didn't even bat an eye as they rearranged their clothes. Instead, Lily's mom screamed with excitement, "There's a dolphin outside!"

So Lily ran outside and saw the dolphin. It was right there in their dock slip, spy-hopping. Lily sat on her dock and watched the dolphin, and the dolphin watched her. After taking pics for a few minutes, Brandon went back inside, but Lily and her mom stayed on the dock. I mean, how do you just turn your back and go inside when there's a dolphin in your own backyard, looking right at you?

Just to hear it breathe was heaven.

The dolphin—a *she*, Lily decided—stayed over an hour. The up-close experience at her own dock slip gave Lily such a rush. She went into her bedroom and found the book on dolphins that she used to spend hours reading. She'd stopped obsessing over dolphins once she started middle school and discovered boys, but the memories of that first passion all came rushing back.

And the dolphin came back too. Every day. And every day it came closer and closer to Lily's feet dangling over the dock's edge until, one day, the dolphin nudged her foot.

Pure magic.

Lily and her parents guessed this dolphin must have been separated from her pod and was looking for a new one. Maybe it thought Lily and her parents would make a good new family.

Lily had been adopted by a dolphin.

What would *you* do if that happened?

Well, for spring break, Lily's family had paid for a trip to the Grand Canyon. But they canceled what reservations they could and ate the losses. If they'd left, the dolphin would have moved on.

Lily and her mom shared the obsession. Lily's mom made sure she was around during the school day, and Lily took over every afternoon. Her dad filled in when he could. They bought nicer patio furniture so they could hang out there more comfortably. And they bought lots of pool toys too.

Lily would go out with Brandon only after nightfall.

At first Brandon thought the dolphin thing was cool, until Lily started opting out of watching his baseball games. It didn't help that after he'd play, and shower, and pick her up for dinner, she'd be glowing from all her time spent with Angel. That's what Lily had named her dolphin. She didn't care if it was a childish name or not. To her, it fit. This creature had wings. Or, maybe, this creature gave *Lily* wings.

Anyway, that summer, Lily told Brandon she was going to withdraw from Michigan. She just couldn't leave Angel in the fall.

That was it for Brandon. "You're choosing a dolphin over a human? Over *me*?"

"I guess so."

"We've been seeing each other for five years. Doesn't that count for something?"

"Yes . . . but . . . this is a dolphin. At my house!"

"Don't you want to move out of your parents' place?"

Brandon and Lily had planned to get an apartment and live together for the first time. They'd both been looking forward to it. But if you could choose, would you rather shack up with a hot boy or swim every day with a dolphin in your backyard?

So Brandon stormed off to Michigan, and Lily stayed with Angel.

Lily and her mom, and less often her dad, kept the rotation going. Lily took classes at her community college. And the dolphin stayed.

I could skip ahead to Lily's later work in cetacean research, but when she looked back on her life, this is the story she'd describe as her turning point. Following her Angel made all the difference.

"So what do you think of her choice?" Cece asks everyone.

Girls smile from ear to ear. Guys fidget in their seats.

"Swimming with a wild dolphin every day . . . ," Reiko says dreamily. "Who wouldn't want that?"

Frye looks warily at Reiko, like he's seeing some kind of rejection in his future. "You wouldn't want to follow your sweetheart to college? Live together?"

Reiko tips her head back and laughs. "Duh, it's a *dolphin*!"

The girls are eerily unanimous. Except the prom queen.

"*I* couldn't," Briony says.

"Come on, Bri!" Mouse chides.

Franklin gives his girlfriend a sideways glance and wears one of those ugly frowns that show all his front lower teeth. He's been wearing versions of this uncomfortable look during this entire debate, as if suddenly realizing that his massive house, fit body, and fancy car are worthless compared to a pair of flippers.

"It is a fact universally acknowledged, that a young, unmarried

87

woman is in want of a dolphin," Mari says, getting a laugh from everyone in AP English.

Briony shakes her head. "I mean, I love dolphins, but I love Kai more."

They aren't sitting together because of the whole bed swap thing, but Kai reaches across and touches her hand. "And I love you, babe, and I wouldn't break up with you over a . . . I don't know, whatever the dolphin equivalent is for guys."

"Yes, you would!" Cece snaps. "Guys ditch girls for their careers *all the time*. Why can't girls do the same? I used dolphins, but it doesn't have to be a cute reason. It could be a job; it could be a banana slug. Same principle."

Reiko wrinkles her nose. "*Ew!* I think you just ruined your whole point."

"You really wouldn't, Bri?" Mouse asks, like she can't believe it. Mouse is one of those rare popular girls who parties hard and seems happy cruising around in Franklin's Boxster for a nightlife of beer and sex, but at heart I think she'd rather spend her days Eskimo-kissing horses, bottle-feeding baby animals, and singing and dancing to Disney princess songs with birds flittering all around.

Briony shakes her head. "No."

"What about . . . a unicorn?"

Briony laughs. "There's no such thing."

Mouse's big brown eyes are begging in the most irresistible way. "But what if a unicorn showed up in your backyard? What then?"

"I think the Kai-man has all the horn she needs," Bryce

says, and Rooster grunts, "Good one," and high-fives him.

Briony doesn't answer the question.

"Mammals are dolphins, not fish," Cookie adds philosophically as he surfaces from the back row, holding up his head on the seat in front of him. He rubs his eyes and looks around.

Saga has this look on her face like, *You asshat.*

"Where was I?" Cookie asks, pulling his hat over his mess of curls. "Maybe boats. You guys are tripping out on dolphins? Right on."

"Your story time is over," Cece scolds.

Cookie stares at her like a pouty-lipped preschooler getting cruelly booted from circle time. "What? Why?"

Saga might have just kicked him by the way he jolts suddenly. "You fell asleep," she tells him.

"Whatever. I'm awake now."

Cece snorts so thunderously I wonder if she's emphasizing how liberated she is from ladylike manners. "It's just like the patriarchy to sleep when they please, and then all the women have to shut up and listen when the men wake up again."

Cookie squints but clearly can't work out what is going on.

"She's right, you know." Lupe raises an appraising eyebrow. "You slept through your turn. Here's what I think: If there's time and interest, you can add to your story at the end. But it's not really fair to waste any more time because of you."

His puppy dog eyes get all round and sad. "But I passed out. I couldn't help it!"

Lupe crosses her arms. "Yeah, we noticed, and then there was the Jeff Incident. Maybe you should reconsider your cookie recipe, Cookie."

"Hey, where's Jeff? *Jeff?*" he calls. Cookie looks around on the floor, like he might have dropped me.

Lupe had started off with laughter in her voice, but now she sounds almost threatening. "Are you kidding? You floated to the Happy Plant Stratosphere during your story, which was kinda cute in a stupid way, but then you gave Jeff an asthma attack, and now you want us to hear more of your crap? Forget it, Cookie. You don't need to waste our time a minute more."

"Chill," says Bryce. "It's just Cookie."

"Just Cookie?!" Lupe rolls her eyes and turns to look at Cookie, who is poking his nose into his elbow and sniffing himself. "Just because he's stoned doesn't mean he's harmless. Some of us here happen to be allergic to Cookie and—"

Mr. Bailey cuts in. "Everyone, we've had a great start, and there's no reason we won't have a great finish. Let's get along. That's the number one rule here: respect for all. Lupe, Cookie—can we get along?"

Cookie just sits there with this clueless look on his face, and then, unbelievably, he yawns and falls into Saga's lap.

Lupe stares at the roof of the bus and huffs. "Whatever." And without waiting for Mr. Bailey to select the next storyteller, she launches into her tale.

LUPE'S TALE

Okay, before I begin properly, turn to the person next to you and tell that person a secret. Not just your favorite ice cream— a *real* secret. One that would have consequences if it got around.

Everyone looks uncomfortable. We're not necessarily sitting next to our best friends, thanks to Alison's idea of musical beds. Not that I'd have told Pard anything.

But I'm in a really weird position now, sitting next to Mr. Bailey. And, boy, do I have a secret that would have serious consequences—and he'd be very, very interested in hearing it.

I put on the shy, *I'm a kid and you're a teacher* face.

"Awkward, isn't it?" he says with a chuckle. And he has this careful smile, like he has his own secret. Or maybe his secret is my secret.

"Do we have to do this?" I ask.

"I can start," he says. He looks oddly vulnerable for a teacher, then leans forward and says in an undertone, "I haven't seen Sam in two years."

I give him a look. *Who is Sam?*

"My son," he explains.

My jaw drops. "Why not?"

His laugh is quiet and bitter. "My ex moved to Idaho. I can go there for weekend visitation rights, but I don't have the money for the airfare and motel. Not after child support . . ."

Everyone's whispering—Alison and Pard are practically making out, they're so close—and I wish I could be in on the confessions of teenage crushes and drug experimentation, not this very adult problem. It makes me realize there are lots of ways a parent can lose his kid. It doesn't have to be the asthma attack of a teenage girl just trying her first and only cigarette behind the stands at a football game. A messy divorce can cut you off almost as much, and Sam will probably grow up thinking his hard-hearted dad never bothered to visit.

"You got screwed," I say, shaking my head, and I feel so guilty again. He's been screwed enough without me adding to it.

"True." He looks at me. "How about you?"

I fight down a flutter of panic with a fake laugh. "I don't know."

"You have one minute left," Lupe calls out.

Mr. Bailey looks at me, and I know I have to say something. I give him something a high school teacher might think is a big one. "I'm a social drinker."

"I noticed."

"Yeah." My nervous laugh dies in shame. "I'm sorry, you know, about this morning. . . ."

"I met my wife over a few beers. Drinks, we could do. It was being together without the buzz that was the hard part. Old people like to give life advice, and mine would be to choose your partner based on how well you get along sober."

I nod, all obedience, and I think he's through before he adds, "That goes for friends, too. They should like you for who you are."

That's an odd thing to say.

"They do," I assure him. My pretzel bag crinkles when I ball it up, but there's no trash can. Damn.

Mr. Bailey holds out his hand to take the bag, exactly like a parent would. When I hand it to him, I feel like such a kid. He puts it in his now mostly empty lunch sack.

It's unfair. Mr. Bailey should be having a lollipop with Sam, not fussing over the useless asthmatic kid who can't throw away his own trash from a mooched snack. No, *lunch*. He probably woke up at 5:00 a.m. to pack himself lunch, and I just ate it.

I turn around and see mischief on a lot of faces from all those juicy secrets, and Lupe's smile is the most mischievous of all.

Now, imagine your partner spilling your secret—either the secret you told or the secret you held back and didn't tell. What would you do to that person for betraying your secret? What secrets should be kept, and which secrets shouldn't? When do you kill the messenger?

Here are my characters:

We'll have Saga be the heroine, both hot and mysterious—

"And well dressed," Briony adds.

"Thank you," Saga says, regally.

But she was unaware of her sex appeal. Though she kept bumping into walls and spilling her juice box on herself at lunch, it only made guys want to lick the juice from her smooth, silky skin.

Saga raises an eyebrow, and everyone seems unsure where Lupe is headed with this odd description. Saga's the opposite of clumsy, but her skin is definitely lickable.

"And for our hero . . . I need a vampire."

"Don't do Stephenie Meyer," Mari begs. "Do Rainbow Rowell."

But Lupe is unfazed. "I need an Edward."

Reiko grins. "Obviously, it has to be Pard."

"Right," Briony says, "because he's so *hot*."

Mouse squeals like a fangirl, "And he's got butterscotch eyes!"

The girls crack up, and Pard scrunches his brown (butterscotch) eyes. He's probably missing his fedora right now, but he doesn't hide. He fights.

"I do *not* look like Edward," he says in a clipped Edwardian way. "Or any other vampire. Don't make the comparison."

"What do you have against vampires?" Sophie asks shyly. Sophie is a very cute, plump sort of person who speaks up only when she absolutely has to, which means she must love vampires. "They're strong, immortal, gorgeous."

94

Pard screws up his mouth like he tastes something bad. "It's the wrong myth," he says archly.

I wonder what the right myth would be, but I stick it to him with pleasure. "You've got the undead pale thing going."

He tilts his head as if to say, *That again?* and I shrink in my seat. He could tell everyone about the time during PE last year when I insisted he wore color contacts as an albino strategy, and he leaned across our corner table, locked eyes with me up close, and challenged me to find the plastic rims of his contacts. I'd felt his breath on my mouth.

But his mind is on vampires. "*You* used to sleep in a coffin."

People talk all at once as they try to figure that one out. I don't know what to say about my childhood sleeping box, but Reiko saves me, in furious mama-bear style, even though I egged Pard on in the first place.

"Can't you let Jeff breathe in peace? And for your information, that thing he had was a fort." This isn't totally true, but a good thing to say to a girl when she opens your bedroom closet and asks. "A coffin," she adds, fuming. "How can you talk that way to *him?*"

I look out the window, because it feels lonely and weird to be an object of pity. I wish Lupe would just get started.

But Lupe's always been a little protective of me because of Reiko, and now she's pissed. "Leave Jeff alone, *Edward*. You're pale and controlling and moody. Too short to be a proper vampire, but what can you do?"

95

For some reason gay jokes (or albino jokes) don't get to Pard half as much as jokes about height, weight, or anatomy. It hurts him every time. He holds up a stubby pencil. "Short, huh? Small people can be powerful, and I can draw you if you need me to prove it." After the Rooster incident, it's obvious what his threat entails.

But you don't threaten Lupe like that. She leans over her seat so that her black hair hangs down, witchy with its blue streaks. "You thought drawing Rooster made you *powerful*? Is that your power trip? I don't take kindly to threats, Pard. Try drawing me naked, and I'll crucify you on a harassment suit faster than it takes to sharpen your very. Small. Pencil."

The guys give out a low *ooo-ooooh*, and Mr. Bailey tells Lupe to start her story, while Pard shrinks next to Alison.

Lupe gives Pard one more look, and then says, "We have our lovebirds. But we are going to add another bird."

"Kai!" Briony practically shouts.

Kai shakes his head, clearly freaked at being in this weird story.

Briony turns toward his row. "You're a way better Jacob than Pard is an Edward. You've got the voice, the body. You're perfect! I am so Team Jacob now!"

Kai smiles that pushover-boyfriend smile.

"Point taken," Lupe says, "but I am literally introducing a new bird."

Everyone's like, *Huh?* And Lupe grins.

96

So, somewhere on the outskirts of the small town of Forks, EdPard and Saga-Bell were cruising through the densely wooded lanes at top speeds in EdPard's imported vehicle, which Saga-Bell considered both sexy and grossly materialistic.

All of a sudden they see a flash of shadows, and EdPard uses his vampire-fast reflexes, but even he can't prevent the impact. Saga-Bell hears a *thunk*.

"Oh, just call me Bella," Saga says. "Saga-Bell takes forever."

"Okay," Lupe concedes.

Pard doesn't even try to get his name out of the story, but he kind of lucks out anyway.

"What did we hit?" Bella asked with rising panic.

Edward pulled over. "Stay here. I'll check it out."

There he was again, trying to control her every move. She snapped back, "Oh no, you don't. I'm coming with." Bella fumbled with the door handle and banged her head as she climbed out. "Ow!"

Bella ignored the look Edward gave her. She assumed he thought she was a klutz, though he really was thinking how sexy it was when she bruised that pale skin. He wouldn't mind having a go at bruising her with caresses.

Suddenly Bella wailed, "Oh no! You killed a bird!"

She rushed to the tiny little body.

"My apologies, dear," Edward gushed. "That said, it's just a common crow."

"Edward would never say something that heartless," Briony says.

She and Mouse lean forward, like they want to scoop up and save this bird's fluttering life, while some of the others, girls and guys, look totally bored. Lupe just smiles.

Even in this crisis, Edward's melodic voice hypnotized Bella. She looked at the bird carefully. "Wait, it's breathing! But I think it's fading." Bella felt so guilty at this likely death-by-Volvo. "If we let this bird die, it will be all our fault."

Edward rushed over to the suffering avian. The vampire, of course, was keenly aware of the creature's blood loss. It smelled not unlike strawberries marinated in a tawny port, though the rubbing alcohol aftertaste was a bit nasty.

The crow had suffered some broken bones, and the internal bleeding would kill it quickly. There was only one thing Edward could do: He could save a life . . . but condemn it to eternal beauty, power, sex appeal, and, yes . . . bloodlust.

Edward crouched over the tiny form.

Bella wrinkled her petit nose. "What are you doing? CPR?"

"Saving her the only way I can." Edward panted.

"Her . . . You can tell she's female? Is that a vampire talent?"

Edward's nostrils flared as he nodded, but then Bella saw blood

98

in the corner of his lips. "Wait, did you *bite* her? I want you to bite *me*. I've been waiting a long time for that bite."

"Bella . . ."

But before he could finish, the poison in the bird's body had worked its course, and the crow started to writhe in pain.

They rushed the bird back to their little home outside of Forks. It took all weekend for the crow to go through her transformation.

Bella could not believe this was the same bird they had hit with Edward's imported vehicle. "Wow, she's transformed. She's so pretty now. Like a . . . swan." Bella Swan couldn't help but think how pretty *she* would be if only Edward would grow some balls and bite her. The crow had white feathers— soft as magnolia petals, more delicate even than her favorite lace-eyelet blouse—and different colors of the rainbow shone depending where the light hit her plumage. It was truly magical. Bella reached out to stroke her.

The vampire crow opened her fanged beak.

Edward rushed between them faster than Bella could blink. "Hold on, I'll need to house-train our new family member."

He set up Polly with a water feeder, filled with blood.

"Good one," Rooster booms.

So, anyway, the bird got used to her new feeder and quickly learned to put her tongue to the stainless steel

99

double ballpoint drinking tube to release the blood.

Over the next several months Edward and Polly spent countless hours together. It was important to socialize Polly among both vampires and humans. She had to learn not to bite people, and Edward trained her not to kill any animals, but only to drink the blood of animals that Edward had hunted himself. He didn't want a wild vampire crow infecting the bird population of Forks. And Polly seemed to understand and accept Edward's training.

Soon she understood everything Edward and Bella said, and could speak with them as well.

"No deer. Lion!" Polly cawed one evening when Edward put up the feeder.

Edward snickered melodically. "Lion is my dinner, thank you very much. Deer is perfectly acceptable for my dependents."

"Caw!" Polly protested, but then she finished feeding and fluffed her feathers with absolute contentment. Polly perched on Edward's shoulder when he played the grand piano in the parlor. Her crest lifted during her favorite parts, and she sang arias with the most beautiful voice. Such moments only made Bella even more jealous that *she'd* never been bitten, to unlock all of *her* superpowers.

While everything seemed so charming in the Edwardian household, things below the surface were changing. So slowly that she barely noticed, Bella was falling in love with another man. She wouldn't have put it that way, but with Edward busy training Polly and taking her on multiday trips to hunt, she spent most of her time with Kaicob.

Kaicob had always been a good friend. Unlike Edward, Kaicob never grilled Bella with questions, never commanded her to eat, or insisted she stay away from urban areas and wooded areas, which pretty much kept her stuck at home. Kaicob was always good for a walk and a talk. They took to hiking for hours. She felt his sexual energy when he helped her keep her balance on rough footing or lifted her when her feet could make no purchase on the rocks.

She reminded herself over and over how much she loved Edward's diamond skin and bony ass. She told herself that she and Kaicob were just good friends, easy in each other's company. These long walks and talks were the relaxing times, whereas the snippy and exhilarating times happened when Edward returned from his travels. So she said.

Then Edward took off alone for Alaska. He didn't ask if it was all right to leave, just cautioned Bella not to go out, and to be careful cooking hot meals for herself, in case she burned the house down with her in it. He smirked, like always, and Bella drooled and rolled her eyes at the same time.

"I should be back well before Polly needs another bottle. But just in case, I have fresh blood in the thermos in the fridge. It's lion blood, so Polly should be very polite once she has that. All right, then. Be safe, for once." He smirked.

Bella was annoyed, partly at Edward and partly at . . . what? She didn't know what was going on in her head. She tried watching TV. She tried eating chocolate, but of course, her delicate stomach didn't let her eat very much. And Bella found herself sobbing on the bed. Weeping so hard she wanted to die.

And then she felt warm arms surround her, warm kisses on her face, her neck, her eyes, her lips. His lips were salty with her tears. And she started kissing him back, harder and more urgently.

Kaicob's body was like a palace—so much to explore, so architecturally rich and varied. He kept his weight on his forearms, while she hooked her legs around his waist. She tugged at her clothes, and he tore them off, gently, so the fabric didn't pull at her. Her breasts pressed against his hot chest.

She was used to sex with Edward. She loved the look of Edward naked when the sun streamed into the room, and his little pencil was so sparkly it was a shame to roll a condom over it. All this was enchanting, but when Edward's dry, cold fingers latched on to her, when his naked body pressed on her entire length, when he penetrated her with the bracing chill of a gynecological instrument, the icy touch always gave her goose bumps. He was cold inside and out, like all Cold Ones. She hadn't known sex could be hot.

Rooster and Bryce crack up.

Meanwhile, it's dawning on Briony that casting Kai as Jacob was a bad idea. Swallowing hard, Kai stares at the ground. He's burning with a mix of embarrassment and sexual energy.

Briony looks from Lupe to Saga, like she wants to kill one or both of them. Or even Pard, because he's stealing glances at Kai. Pard probably has his own revisionist ideas of how the love triangle should resolve itself, and it doesn't involve Bella Swan.

After throwing herself into the moment and giving Kaicob all her passion, it was a little awkward talking about what just happened while they lay naked on a bed strewn with her torn clothes.

"I didn't really mean to do that," Bella confessed.

"Me neither," Kaicob said, but he was smiling ear to ear. He was *soooo* happy, and he couldn't hide it. He'd been waiting for years to do that.

Bella rolled her eyes and punched Kaicob's shoulder. "You goofball! Let's get dressed—or have you torn up all my favorite clothes?" She gave him a flirtatiously murderous look that made them both flush with smiles.

The rest of the day was so simple. They strolled outside under the trees, they made dinner and ate together. They had sex a second time—not urgently, and with no tearing of clothes. They did things slowly, like they wanted them to last.

It was too risky to have Kaicob stay the night. This perfect day had to end. She had to think about what had happened, and what she should do.

"Do you still like me?" he asked. "Will you call?" Suddenly, he was a little boy again, hoping to please her.

"Of course. Now *shoo!*"

Bella tidied up the house while she thought of Kaicob's baby potentially growing inside her from the unprotected sex—Edward's condoms wouldn't have fit Kaicob, of course. She made the house gleam, while her own thoughts stayed muddled.

She talked on the phone with Kaicob the next day, and the next, but she didn't invite him back. She could sense new life, and she'd heard about werewolves being very virile.

She was pregnant.

She called Kaicob and told him. He begged her to marry him. He came over and held her while she cried. He held her while she warmed up to him. They made love over and over, but she made no promises.

Edward was due home any day now. Kaicob's friends kept a lookout and gave him notice.

"Please come with me," he begged Bella. "I don't like to think of you facing him. Cold Ones can't be trusted."

"I trust him," she said. "Just go. I need to think about things. *Go.*"

But in the end it didn't matter what she thought.

She'd forgotten all about Polly.

Edward returned on foot. His family met him first on the road north of Forks, and they discussed vampire news for a while. Then Edward looked up and saw his bird, cawing "Kai! Kai! Kai!" Polly swiftly circled and alighted on Edward's shoulder.

Edward smirked as his protégé tugged his earlobe for attention. "What's gotten into you, Polly?"

Polly trilled to the cheerful tune of "Polly Wants a Cracker" for all the vampires to hear. "Kaicob fucked Bella, Kaicob fucked Bella!"

Dr. Bailey and his wife froze in place, as did the other Cold Ones in Edward's family—Bryce and Rooster and Briony.

"Stay calm, Edward," said Dr. Bailey. "Let's talk about this rationally. Wait!"

But Edward was already gone.

Bella didn't have a chance to say a word once Edward burst through the door. Before she could cry for help or even blink, Edward picked her up and slammed her against a wall.

"Is it true? Answer me!" he roared, teeth bared.

But Bella died instantly. He killed her. Had he meant to? He trembled. Despite a wave of nausea and self-loathing, Edward smelled the most intoxicating, overpowering fragrance: his beloved's blood staining the back of her head, and there again on the stained wall. With a moan, a loosening of his limbs, he finally gave up all resistance and did the thing vampires do, the thing Bella had begged for, though not like this.

He bit her. And time was lost to him.

Edward rose up from her corpse momentarily euphoric, sated the way sex had never sated him. And he looked down at her, at the shock and horror frozen on her dead face. He had killed the thing he loved, glutted himself on her blood. He licked his lips, tasting her, and hated himself. If only he could die.

Leaving the bedroom, he paced through the house—limbs shaking, teeth chattering—and caught sight of the grand piano in the parlor. Discordant noise flooded his ears as he ripped out the strings and smashed the whole thing to pieces, and then to smaller pieces. He would never make music again.

He went back into the bedroom to bury his beloved's corpse, and what he saw chilled his already cold body.

Polly's claws had sunk into Bella's shoulder. Open wings mantled her prey as she devoured what was left of Bella's blood, corpse-feeding exactly as she had been trained, though there wasn't much left to enjoy. Edward snatched Polly and pounded the wall with Polly's body until the drywall chipped off. Then he pinned Polly to the ground and yanked out every single feather. Sunlight was pouring into the bedroom, and Edward's face and hands shone like diamonds, just like Polly's plucked body and floating feathers.

"You liar!" he snarled, weeping, as he plucked and plucked. "You lied to me! She was innocent. You were jealous that I loved her more, so you lied. Jealous!"

The glitter of diamonds made an almost pretty sight,

but the horrible sounds of feathers ripped from flesh were drowned out by Polly's terrible screams and Edward's howls until the bird was naked.

Turned out, Polly was a *he*.

The sight of Polly's sparkly little pencil tipped Edward over the edge. He stared at it dumbfounded. He'd always assumed . . . but there it was. He was wrong about Polly being a girl, but he wasn't wrong about Bella's faithfulness. She'd loved *his* sparkly pencil, and wouldn't need any other lover. Certainly not a canine lover. Polly was playing him false. That had to be it.

"Liar!" Edward roared. Without waiting for a reply, Edward bent over the small body. With his teeth he ripped Polly's vocal box. The foul taste of Polly's blood reminded Edward that the last time he bit the bird, he'd meant to save her—its—life. He couldn't process this replayed moment and how his whole world collapsed while he lived on. "Tell me now who's faithful and who isn't. Sing if you can."

Polly's beak hung open. The bird would never sing again. The end.

I sit there as stunned as everyone else. It's like Lupe ripped out our own vocal boxes.

Rooster is the first to respond. *"Whoa."*

"No kidding," Bryce says.

Lupe smiles with mischief.

Marcus blinks as he tries to think of nice sentiments for

his girlfriend's story about blood and torture. As usual, he goes straight to objective facts and says, "You do realize that male corvids lack external phalluses, right?" Lupe ruffles his hair, like this was all cute or something.

Briony cuts in. "You totally ruined the entire book. I mean, you make wisecracks about Edward's penis, and then Jacob and Bella cheat, and then Edward kills off Bella, which he would *never* do. Like, what the hell?"

Mouse crosses her arms and puts on a stern Mouse-face in solidarity. Their gods have been mocked.

Lupe smiles like an evil Mona Lisa.

Meanwhile, Pard looks a pale shade of green, with all the fight gone out of him. Lupe is strong stuff, and she nailed him in his coffin with his own pencil, and no doubt Rooster and Bryce will have Cold One jokes at his expense for the rest of the school year. He wouldn't really have drawn Lupe naked, but he mouthed off the wrong thing, and she called him out, and now he looks forgotten and fragile.

But then Pard takes a deep breath, squares his shoulders, turns toward Alison, and in less than a minute, he has her laughing. He's impossibly brave. I'd never tell, because it would give the wrong impression, but there are times I miss him.

DOUGHNUTS

The bus turns off the freeway for a bathroom break and surprise doughnuts. I learn about the pit stop first, being in the front with the teacher, but the fun happens minutes later, rows behind me, when Mr. Bailey announces the treats. All those cheers.

When the bus parks, Mr. Bailey says we can get out. "But, Saga, Cookie, Mace, Pard—sit tight a moment."

I freeze, because the only thing they all have in common is the front row experience of my asthma attack. Saga will be annoyed she's missing part of her smoke break, then Bryce will be angry too, and before I know it, everyone will hate my asthmatic ass.

I get out first and don't know who I'd even wait for, so I just act like I need to go to the bathroom right away. I feel like everyone's looking at me.

After I take my time in the bathroom, I buy a doughnut with sprinkles, because I need some sprinkles right now.

Reiko, Frye, Lupe, and Marcus are crowded in a booth, so there's no room, and I don't dare bother anyone else. If anyone wanted to make eye contact with me, my face is up and ready, but no one tries, so I take my doughnut outside, walk a ways, find a corner I can hide behind, and, in case anyone's looking, look busy on my phone while I eat.

No messages, and texting Cannon again would appear a little clingy.

Eventually, I get up and walk back. Mr. Bailey has treated the class to doughnuts. He's inside with a giant pink box. He's like a bird lady, but surrounded by teenagers instead of pigeons. I don't go inside. I wouldn't mind snagging a free doughnut, but I don't want to hear from him how nice it is that I'm feeling better. Because I don't.

"She's cute," I hear Pard say.

I turn, kind of shocked he's checking out a girl, but it's a cat he's scratching behind the ears. He has a rapidly disappearing doughnut in his other hand.

Parson is with him, doughnutless, and I'm thinking maybe I should go back inside, but it's too late. Parson waves me over, smiling like he's found a stack of Bibles. He wants only to make sure I'm included, the way he includes all the losers at his gospel-happy lunch table.

"Aren't these stories amazing?" Parson's tail is practically wagging, and it's cute to see this tall, blond guy fangirling in that clueless way he has. It's like no one ever told him that sitting that close to female armpit hair on the nerdy side of the bus should depress him or that wearing a pink Jesus shirt was social death.

A pink Jesus shirt that he fills out in ways I never could.

He notices me staring and gets this look on his face like he's about to invite me to youth group or something. Worse, Pard notices me staring. Pard's smile goes up a thousand watts, like we're a gay threesome.

I clear my throat, turn the focus onto Parson. "So, is pink your favorite color?"

Parson tilts his head, and it's like a cartoon question mark appears over him. After an awkward moment, his eyebrows launch up, he looks down at his shirt like he's detached from his own completely ripped, oddly dressed body, and his chin snaps up to the sky as he roars with laughter.

"Oh, *that*! Oh my gosh! Well, no, I'd never buy a pink shirt. It's my own fault. The shirt was white, and it just came out pink in the wash. I was so embarrassed, I wanted to throw it out!" He's smiling, his brown eyes so warm and mirthful. Even his lashes are long and kind of curly.

Pard's grin speaks volumes of mockery. As in, *Admit it, he's hot.*

Parson rests both his hands on his pecs—well, on the name of Jesus—and now even Pard stops smiling. His pale face shifts and stills with artistic concentration, like he's clicked the video record button in his brain. We both stare at Parson's man-hands on his sculpted man-chest.

And Parson is oblivious to this fiery subtext. He beams at us while we gape at him. "After praying about it, I learned something. I never throw away a Bible, and I would never throw away a shirt with my Lord's name on it. Jesus taught me that it's not about the color of the shirt. This isn't a fashion statement. *This* is what it's all about. *This.*" And Parson runs his hands over his pecs, twice, and Pard lets out a shivery sigh.

"This?" Now Pard has a hand there too, brushing the curvy letters running across Parson's chest. He takes his time with his caress, fanning exploratory fingers over the muscle, over the nipples.

Jesus.

I look around me in case anyone's watching and take a step away from this ludicrously Christianized homoeroticism.

Pard's smile broadens, dimples showing. He's yanking Parson's chain. But Parson is too naive to know what's being yanked. Reminds me of how clueless I was when Pard and I were friends and doing all kinds of things together, and I had no idea.

Parson beams, all joy, like he got Pard to think about the Lord and lay hands on His name. "Exactly, Pard! Does Jesus really care what color we're wearing, so long as we're glorifying Him?"

Pard gives me a shifty sideways look, but then drops his hands in a sort of lingering, finger-trailing way.

Bryce, Saga, Frye, Reiko, Lupe, and Marcus walk outside with their doughnuts. I want to walk up to them and bail on this scene, but I can't walk up to people who don't look at me or signal me over. I can't just appear in front of people that way, because it will kill me, worrying if I'm bugging them.

I steal glances at Bryce, at all of them, hoping for eye contact I don't get. So instead of walking up to them, I'm stuck on the edge of Pard and Parson's sphere. This is the worst kind of social situation: when you've semi-ditched one group without hopping onto the next. Parson's so soft-hearted he would have reeled me back, but he's too wrapped up in the Jesus conversation that's getting deeper by the second.

I'm just listening in when Pard asks, "Would you wear a dress if it said *Jesus* on it?"

Parson looks shocked for a second, and it's quiet enough to hear Bryce going on about airport security and some asshat who got caught smuggling hummingbirds by hiding them in his underwear.

"What about the beaks?" asks Reiko.

"Acupuncture time!" Bryce grins.

"No way!" Frye shivers, and Reiko cuddles up to him. Bryce follows up with a similar smuggling story on lizards also hidden in a guy's pants. He pulls out his phone; he has pics.

They're having more fun than we are, but I want to look like I'm fun too. Like I'm not hating standing with these two guys having a Bible-thumping, homoerotic prayer meeting. Parson's got a simple, sunshiny smile.

"You know, if Jesus wanted me to wear a dress, I would."

The others are passing around Bryce's phone, gushing over the images.

"Don't lizards like to stay warm?"

"Guess they like it there, then!"

"Wait. How do you keep hummingbirds in one place?"

Bryce takes back his phone. "He bound their wings to their

bodies and sewed them into his underwear. Here, check out this one."

Meanwhile, Pard asks, "Would God ever wear a dress?"

Parson shrugs. "That's up to Him."

"Or Her."

Parson opens his mouth as if to correct him, then his face softens, and he says, "I guess the Him or Her is just like the color of the shirt. Secondary."

Pard's smile looks almost pained. He says, "You're all right, Parson," all quiet, and when our eyes meet, I can't hear the others talking. I look back at Pard, and something in his face squeezes me and spills me out.

He's probably yanking *my* chain, and I can't make sense of how much he's changed. There was the boy who used to sit on his patio with a hummingbird feeder in his hands; he taught me to hold still, and when they drank, you felt the vibrations of their wings on your fingertips. Now he's the kind of guy who makes out in buses, dates narcissist actors, draws people naked, plays poker, drinks, parties, smokes, feels up, gets felt up, runs his fingers over the Christian youth group leader's pecs, and does stuff in unsuspecting people's laps.

It's all too much. His face is trying to tell me he's still that boy I knew, but I back off fast, without a word.

For once I don't feel awkward approaching the popular kids, because I'm too panicked not to. I don't even know how I got to Bryce's elbow. One second the world was narrowed to nothing but Pard's eyes, and then, after a blur, I surface for air in a different conversation. I force myself to act surprised, and it's like acting in a fog. "Whoa. You have pictures of *what?*" And I give all the suitable oohs and aahs such images of critters and underwear demand, and I squirm like they might expect, but not because of the pictures.

MARCUS'S TALE

"I saved these for you," Mr. Bailey says as I board the bus. He hands me two doughnuts, and they're good ones—ones with holes, because ones without holes only masquerade as doughnuts. Bear claws and rectangular pastries taste great, but they are not doughnuts.

Maybe he sensed I felt like the odd guy out and wanted to make it up to me. "Thanks."

But, no, he wants to chat.

"Look, Jeff—no sitting with Cookie and Saga. In fact, go sit with Pard again. He said he'd save a seat for you. He seems really reliable."

"Okay," I say, but it's not. "Reliable" doesn't really sound like the right word to describe Pard, unless he means reliable at messing with me.

"Can I have one?" Pard asks right away when I squeeze past him and take the window seat again.

I don't know how someone that skinny can eat so much. "Forget it."

"Please?" he begs, and he gives a puppy dog look with his *butterscotch* eyes.

I do not share my doughnuts. Puppies be damned to a vampire hell.

"All right, everyone," Mr. Bailey announces. "I forgot to share your room assignments for the hotel, and that's just as well, since I made some last-minute changes. It's all in the e-mail I just sent you. Remember, for security reasons, I need you all to stay in your assigned rooms."

The bus rounds a corner, and everyone whips out their phones—except Pard, who's trying to draw despite the turn. He's crosshatching and shading in Lupe, that exact pose of her chewing him out. She looks powerful and terrifying and gorgeous and furious all at once, and I wonder if he's just torturing himself with his art. I do that too.

Then my e-mail loads, and I stop pitying him.

I can't believe it.

Group 3: Mace-Pard-Jeff

Mr. Bailey must think he's done me a favor. Like, maybe he

117

had me in with Marcus, Parson, and Frye, but then seeing me today with Pard made him think I'd rather be with him. Or some other screwed-up adult logic. I picture a room with two queen beds, one with Pard in it and the other with Mace. Hell *is* real.

Pard looks over my shoulder at the e-mail and shrugs like he's not that thrilled either, but he's evading my eyes.

I snap, "What piece of information am I missing here?"

"Give me a doughnut, and I'll tell." But he still looks guilty, and after I give him the silent treatment, he fills the void. "I dealt out your medicine for you. He thinks I'm your nurse now."

Everything makes sense when he says this. I should thank him for paying attention to my Diskus and albuterol back in ninth-grade, and then using that knowledge today to potentially save my life. He even made Mace rub my back. But I scowl, because now he's my escort and roommate and *nurse*. I'll be able to breathe, but I need some air, if you know what I mean.

Mr. Bailey plows ahead. "Remember, we were going to work Marcus in for the next story, and then I'll draw names for two women to present next. Sounds fair?"

Cece nods. "That's what we voted to do."

"I don't mind waiting," Marcus says, and I don't blame him. Having a girlfriend like Lupe must be amazing, but she's one tough act to follow.

Mr. Bailey tells him to just go ahead. Marcus clears his throat.

Then my phone vibrates. Finally! It takes a second to understand Cannon's text, because I forgot complaining about having

118

to sit with either Mace or Pard. That text feels like a lifetime ago.

That sucks. U sat w Mace? He's OK.

I feel like I failed some kind of subtle test. Maybe we owe Mace because of the whole Georgetown connection—didn't Cannon say once that Mace's sister helped connect him with some fraternities? Was that it? Or maybe Cannon just hasn't been on friendly terms with Pard in years.

I'm with Pard.

Micro-dick? Change seats.

Of course, nosy Pard sees my screen and glares at me.

I don't know what to write back, so I change the subject.

What's the plan?

Get wasted, get u laid. Hot girl :)

What?

I don't like plans made around me, like I'm his experiment. He's the one who decided that I had to get drunk at Franklin's end-of-summer party. I thought I'd been drunk before, but no. The next morning I was hungover and hating life and looking back on it all, and there was nothing but a blank. Nothing. And if you're the type who analyzes everything, and you remember nothing, that's damn scary, and you're going to obsessively analyze the nothing and all the laughter and hints of what went down that night. You're going to be grounded with heaps of time to analyze your mom's report that Pard drove you home, and he's such a *sweet* boy, and why couldn't you be friends with him again, he could have saved your life, Jeff. You'll be too freaked out and chicken to ask him or anyone about it, because you don't want to admit you know nothing.

I never got wasted again.

Marcus, still in pre-story warm-up mode, is literally blathering about Harvard's philosophy department, which he can't wait to experience next fall, whoopee-do, while Pard holds very still, fully attuned to my face and body, like he can feel my angsty thoughts.

Or maybe it's just because he read my phone.

"Don't go with Cannon," he warns, his eyes surprisingly full of worry—fear, even. "If you get wasted, if you get an attack, whatever, he's not in any position to look out for you. You can't trust him."

I weigh my trust issues toward Cannon, who should have taken me home after that party, against my issues with Pard, and I wonder for the millionth time what really happened between us that night.

"It's none of your business."

I don't exactly trust Cannon, and he's no *nurse*, but maybe I'm flattered he bothers with me at all. I know him better than most people do. Not just the glamorous things, but the shitty ones, like his mom's addiction, and him moving out last year. It makes him more grown-up than the rest of us. In spite of all that, he makes time for me.

I text back to Cannon, *How hot?*

That's when Pard swipes one of my doughnuts. I reach across

him and into the aisle, and I know tackling Pard is completely wrong and weird—tackling for the last cookie was one of the late-night games I regret playing as an innocent freshman—but I make sure my knee grinds his thigh and my skull crushes his head against the back of his seat, so he knows this is not flirtation. This is war. For my doughnut.

"Gentlemen?" Mr. Bailey says, just when I'm about to reach it and win this evil game of Twister.

Demonically fast, Pard runs his tongue across the length of my sugar doughnut he's holding, thereby ruining it forever.

"Sorry, Mr. Bailey," I say, and I stuff down the rest of my other doughnut in two bites—which is a shame, because now it's gone—and Pard just smiles and takes little cat bites of his stolen doughnut like he has all the time in the world.

"As I was saying," Marcus continues, "I'm interested in Lupe's story about fidelity, and I want to utilize my story to broaden the discourse to gender and class disparities in marriage."

Seriously. That's how he talks sometimes.

Since antiquity, we've wondered what makes a perfect marriage—specifically, what makes a perfect wife.

"What about the perfect husband?" Cece snaps. "Oh, I get it. All husbands are perfect already."

Blinking like a poked owl, Marcus blathers something about the Renaissance, like a textbook. Only drier.

My phone vibrates. I check to see Cannon's message, but there are no words. Just a picture. From the waist up.

She's hot—very hot—but it's not like I'm looking at her face. It's not the kind of pic that draws your attention there. An absence of clothing does that, and her carefully placed hands just make you stare more.

She's a perfect ten. I want to touch her, but it bothers me that I don't know her name. Like, what kind of creep am I? Believe me, I'm ready to shed my innocence. But I want to do it innocently, if that makes sense. I'd wanted to, anyhow.

Nice, huh? Nikki.

What do I say? Ask for more information? He'll just send a pic of her ass. And how'd he get this photo anyway?

The phone vibrates, but it's from a new number.

Hey, asshole, get off the fuckin phone and listen to the stories.

My head snaps up. Pard pops a bit of doughnut into his mouth and reads my screen. I don't know who's on my case.

Then I do. Mari glares at me. Then back down at her phone.

You think ur better than us.

She's so wildly wrong, I don't know how to answer except:

NO WAY

You never even read the journal I published you in. LISTEN to us. We might be good, asshat.

So *that's* why she hates me. Well, she *started* hating me sophomore year when I worked for Cannon's writing service, even though—except for one short story that I sold, which I admit was a mistake—they were just essays, and who cares about those? And I hardly sell essays anymore, now that Cannon alters grades on the cloud. But after publishing my Morpheus story, she must have figured I got too into myself. I always read Mari's stories—not like I'd tell her that—but otherwise, I rarely look at *The Southwarks*, because you want to learn from the best, right? *Published* authors, not high school students and their homemade stapled and photocopied creative writing journal. And the strategy worked for me, didn't it?

But I text back like the coward I am.

OK, OK

She's still glaring murder, so I turn off the phone, semi-naked girl pic and all, and act like I'm paying attention, which is kind of hard because (1) Marcus is not exactly great entertainment, (2) I'm freaked out by Mari's surveillance, and (3) that image of Nikki is something you can't not think about.

Pard takes another bite of his stolen doughnut and watches me like I'm an amusing movie.

Our story begins with a king.

Henry was a well-loved monarch: young, attractive, powerful. All that remained was to fulfill his royal duties by finding a wife and siring an heir. He named his wedding day but would not reveal the name of his bride, and no one knew if he secretly had a bride or was still looking for one. Regardless, preparations for the wedding were made, chefs prepared a feast, tailors sewed a gown from delicate fabrics, and invitations to only the most elite in society were extended. But the invitations mentioned no name for the bride.

In the early morning on his wedding day, dressed to pass unnoticed, Henry waited by the well for the peasant girl to come. Soon he saw her coming down the street, moving gracefully in spite of the bucket she carried. He saw her nod to her neighbors young and old as she passed them by. She wore the calmest, most serene smile that had fascinated him since he first saw it a few months ago, and he could see how much the people loved her and were warmed by her presence. Yet, even as she warmed others, he wondered who or what warmed *her*.

Henry could not figure out the woman's secret. He wanted to know if that smile ever faded—or if it came off like a mask, and revealed the ordinary expressions of women used to backbiting, manipulating, and flattering to get their way.

He was fascinated by this woman in ways that had nothing to do with her beauty per se, though she was beautiful, too. Breathtaking. Even in her rags her figure showed—slim but majestic.

Henry wondered if he could love this woman.

Henry wondered if he could bear this woman's perpetual smile.

Henry wondered if he could take this woman apart and see how she ticked.

"That is a heavy burden for you, Zelda," he said, slipping from the shadows as she hefted the full bucket.

Startled by her king's undisguised voice, she stumbled, and water from her bucket splashed to the paving stones. "My king!" Zelda put down her burden and curtsied to the ground, where she remained. Her smile vanished in the reverent seriousness of a commoner meeting the king.

Henry, however, smiled hungrily. He had long prepared for this moment. "We meet again," he said. "Rise. Speak with me."

She stood but kept her head lowered, and her brow wrinkled as if unsure what to say. "Yes, my king. We meet again. You were hunting before. The hart."

He lifted her chin so that their eyes finally met. She looked surprised, but she did not resist his hand. Touching her jaw like that and locking eyes with her, the king felt her beauty move him carnally. "I am still hunting. For a bride. Today is my wedding day."

Color filled her cheeks, and she lowered her eyes, though her chin remained lifted in his grasp.

Gently, he released her. "I wish to marry you, Zelda."

She curtsied. "As it pleases you, my king. If my father consents, it will be so."

She agreed so readily, without even a gasp of surprise or a squeal of excitement, that it took *him* by surprise. Such an interesting woman. He barked a laugh, and then merrily took her arm in his. "Well, shall we walk to your house, then?"

125

Leaving the bucket on the ground—upright and mostly filled, as if she'd reclaim it later—they walked to the peasant girl's humble home.

The meeting with the girl's father was short and simple. "I ask for no dowry, for you have none to give," Henry explained. "But I do ask for something worth more to me."

"And what is that?" asked the old man.

"Her complete obedience." Henry gazed at Zelda standing behind her father's chair. "She must obey me in any request I make, no matter how frivolous or strange, and she must obey me without a murmur of complaint, not even a frown. Girl, will you obey me?"

"I will obey you in everything, my king, whether we wed or not," she answered.

And her father gave his consent. "If she is willing, so am I."

Henry faced the young woman. "Are you willing? Are you quite sure?"

"Sire, if Your Majesty wishes for me to be your wife, then it shall be so."

Henry cocked his head. The girl seemed to be marrying him to do *him* a favor, not the other way around. Baffling. Surely she was angling for his power, like all the noblewomen he had danced and flirted and fornicated with over the years. But she did not show any excitement, nor any strong emotion. She stood there calmly, waiting for his command.

"Very well," he said. "I have your dress prepared for you, but

I do not have it with me. It is at my castle. But no matter. You can walk to my castle to receive your gown. However, you will make this walk in nothing but your shift, for you will bring nothing into this marriage but your own body and virtue. Once at my castle my servants will bathe and dress you, and then we will wed this very day." He raised a red-gold eyebrow in challenge.

"I will be there just as you wish, my king," she said, once again lowering herself in a deep curtsy.

He bowed his head—he was almost mastered by her perfect obedience. It was a heady feeling. "Then I will ride ahead of you and finish the preparations for the day."

"This is sick," Alison says. "Why would she agree to do anything he asks, and with a bland smile? Never allowed to frown or disagree? That's not what marriage is all about."

"But it's like *My Fair Lady*," Briony snaps back. "You know, he's going to tutor her into being a fine lady, and they'll fall in love."

Alison crosses her arms and laughs. "No, thanks! I'll fall in love with someone who doesn't try to control my face. And why should she have the boring role? Her name is *Zelda*, after all. Henry's the guy with the ordinary name."

Marcus smiles. "Ah, but Henry is no ordinary guy. He's Henry VIII."

"Nice character reveal!" Mari says, eyes gleaming. "Oh, so *Henry's* getting a wife! Or a new wife . . ."

Everyone weighs in on this new twist that revises history.

Pard whispers in my space, "I *hate* Henry VIII." I look down at his upturned face. The doughnut was one of those gritty ones, and granulated sugar covers his lips. He looks like a happy four-year-old who managed to get more sugar on him than the amount of sugar the doughnut had in the first place. He has only a small chunk of doughnut left. I notice the mess on his hands and lap, and my eyes pull back to his lips.

"You're covered in sugar," I scold, and he just grins like I'd said something sexy. I should correct the error, but I can't speak, because there's nothing left of the four-year-old in the slow way his tongue slides across his upper lip. Maybe it's just his doughnut breath, but I can taste the sugar he's tasting.

Okay, this feeling . . . it's not attraction. Not a lot of attraction anyhow. Anyone would feel *some* attraction with all this sugar involved, right? If it had been Nikki, I would have felt a lot more attraction. And Alison—a million times more. With him? This is barely anything.

Pard holds up his little mangled doughnut to share, like he'll feed it to me, like he'll touch my lips with those sugar-dusted fingers. His eyes linger on my mouth. I get that feeling again that he wants to kiss me. Not just wants to, but will. So I snap back my head and brush my sleeves and my face to get Pard's army of pheromones off, like the sugar is dusted all over me and not on him.

Mari shoots me a look as if to warn that I'm goofing off again, which is just great. Thanks a lot, Pard.

I'm relieved to tune into Marcus again, which is totally a first. But a sick story about a megalomaniac's wedding sounds like just the thing I need right about now.

Crowds gathered along the main city street to watch Zelda make her journey. She arrived at the castle on bare feet, in her shift, to the blare of trumpets.

The entire court flocked to the gates to welcome her, and ladies-in-waiting quickly flung a robe over her exposed body. They bathed her and then dressed her and styled her hair.

Even Henry was shocked when he stood beside the archbishop and saw her enter the private chapel in the great cathedral. He had never seen a woman that beautiful before. He regretted making her walk in her shift on her wedding day, a first test just to see if she'd put up a fight and disobey mere seconds after promising perfect obedience. But she was true to him, and impossibly lovely, and he would treat her like a queen from now on.

And for a while, he did.

Soon Henry had a child from her. A girl child, to his disappointment. Zelda was a doting mother and tenderly gave suck to the child rather than turn it over to a wet nurse. She always had a smile for him, but the glow of maternal bliss in her face now made him wonder whom she loved and served best: her babe in arms or her king and husband?

He decided to test his wife a second time.

Zelda had just rocked her daughter to sleep when she heard the clang of a knight in armor marching to her chamber.

The knight entered, his face worn and pale like some horror had occurred, too grim for words.

She clasped the sleeping babe to her chest. "Good sir, what is the matter?"

The knight knelt on the stone floor. To her concern, he wept and could barely get out the words. "My lady, my grace, His Majesty the king has ordered me to come to your chamber and . . . oh, but I cannot speak."

Zelda's face was filled with dread, but she bravely lifted her chin. "We must follow the king's orders."

"His Majesty says that you have become an unpopular queen, and that the babe is rumored to be unworthy because she is half peasant. To prevent the people from rising up against the kingdom in rebellion, His Majesty commands me to take the baby and slay it."

Sophie gasps, then blushes at drawing attention to herself, but Lupe says, "You're right. This is one fucked-up dude."

Marcus blinks nervously and continues his tale.

Zelda's face went white, and for a moment there was no sound except for the clinking of armor as the knight wiped his eyes.

"My lady, surely we can stage a death. We do not have to do what—"

"We most certainly will obey our king," Zelda said. "Take her. All I ask is that you bring her back, so that I can give her a Christian burial."

"I am afraid my king forbids you from seeing this child again, not even to bury it."

"I see. Then it must be so."

After a good-bye kiss and brief prayer, she handed over her daughter to the henchman.

And she smiled.

Henry heard a full report from his knight. He did not have his daughter killed. The knight secretly took the daughter to Henry's sister in the countryside, but no one else knew. Rumors circulated that Henry had his daughter killed.

Meanwhile, Henry waited to see if Zelda would show any sign of anger or rebellion. But he found none, not even resentment. She was obedient and alert to his needs, as always. She never even mentioned the baby. It was as if the baby had never been born.

And four years later, she bore a second child, a son.

"What?" Lupe shrieks. "She's still sleeping with that dickweed?"

Marcus blinks nervously.

"She is one sick woman," Bryce says.

"What about *him*?" Cece thunders.

"*He's* not a sick woman," Bryce replies, but the girls glare him into silence.

Briony flips her hair over her shoulder. "It's not Zelda's fault. She's stuck with Henry VIII. She's totally his prisoner. Good for her for putting on an act."

"She should stab him," Reiko says.

"He's probably expecting that," Briony muses. "I think she's handling it the best way she can figure."

"This story needs to be more like a horror story," Lupe says. "Like, she cakes on makeup to look cheerful, like a doll, and soon her face changes so she can *only* smile, and she *becomes* the doll."

Reiko nods with grim approval. "So Henry has to stare into the dead eyes and smiling red mouth of his doll-woman . . . and then she murders him. Death by dolls!"

Lupe and Reiko cackle like witches.

"For the record," Marcus says, palms out in a nervous gesture of peace, "I'm with you all the way that Henry is the villain."

Um. Okay, so after the second baby, things went pretty much the same way. Henry sent the knight to deliver a death sentence. The knight took the second child and secretly delivered it to Henry's sister. So both children are safe, but Zelda believed them both to be murdered. She handed over her son just as obediently as she had handed over her daughter.

Henry had been expecting an outburst. This was their only son, the son Henry had been waiting for, and the heir to the throne. But there was no emotion from Zelda—just that calm smile that never gave way to rage or even a frown. Zelda must have heard the rumors that he could divorce her or chop off her head for failing to provide him a son, yet obedience mattered more to her, it seemed. He was flabbergasted, to say the least.

Years passed, and Zelda never raised her voice to Henry, never hinted that they had had two children whom he murdered in cold blood. To him, she was a perfect woman.

"Hah." Lupe snorts, and the other girls follow in suit.

Henry finally settled on one final ploy.

"Zelda, I find my people do not much care for you as their queen, because of your low birth. You are getting old, and as I need to have children of gentle blood, I'll need to send you away. I've had a divorce approved by the Pope. I am sorry, but it cannot be helped."

"As you wish, my king."

"You'll have to go home. Now."

Zelda curtsied in farewell.

"But, first, take off that dress and those jewels. You came in your shift, and you can leave in it as well."

So she did. In the rain.

After Zelda returned home, her father could not stop railing on her terrible ex-husband. But even now—even divorced—she held her tongue.

"See?" Lupe says. "She's a doll now. She's not human any-more."

A week later Henry sent for her. She arrived in the tattered dress Henry had not seen since the day he proposed marriage.

If she had wondered whether Henry had changed his mind about the divorce, he put that to an end.

"My bride needs your help preparing her for our marriage. Also, our nuptial chamber needs preparing. You are a good worker, so I've sent for you. You can start by cleaning the room, preparing the bed. Then you may prepare the girl."

"A girl . . . Is she very young?"

Henry shrugged, like her age was not important. "She's fifteen."

Zelda did her work, but her thoughts distracted her. Not thoughts about Henry—she was worried about the girl and what life this girl would be walking into.

Henry entered to inspect the room just as Zelda had fin-ished arranging a decorative silk over the bed.

"Ah, that is well done. And now for the girl."

The nervous girl escorted inside was absolutely beautiful. Zelda could see why Henry would want to marry this lovely young woman. The two women spoke little, which made sense since they were of two different social stations. The girl did not seem to know that Zelda had been married to the very man who would soon be her husband.

"Thank you for your help," the girl said sweetly. This was a girl who smiled because the world would be nice to her if she greeted it kindly. Zelda almost frowned—her, um, doll's mask barely cracking at the sight of this delicate girl, soon to be marrying Henry VIII.

Lupe nods approvingly at the doll reference.

A servant whisked the girl away, and Henry fetched Zelda. "What do you think of my bride?" he asked her.

"She is loveliness itself. But, my king . . ."

"What is it?" He leaned forward, eager. This was finally it. She was finally standing up to him. Defying him. He wondered what that would feel like and how he would react to it. Either to chop off her head or to lay himself at her feet, he did not know.

"My king, the girl is so young, and it is clear that she has been brought up in luxury and ease. Such an upbringing will make her less able to obey some of your wishes. Please, Your Majesty, consider a way to be less demanding of this young wife."

"Perhaps," he said breezily, but his voice faltered. He had expected her to point out how outrageous the wedding was, writhe in jealousy, and condemn his mistreatment of her. He hadn't expected her to advocate for the girl.

And yet, Zelda's affection for the girl made sense on a deeper level.

"Come," he said, snapping his fingers for his servants. Including her.

Zelda, in her plain smock, was escorted to the wedding and given a seat. The service was not in the private chapel but in the great cathedral. No one in the audience murmured complaints about Zelda's presence in her shabby garb. If anything, heads inclined slightly as she passed.

The people, noble and poor alike, loved their former queen, and they feared and hated Henry.

The service began, and Zelda sat with her hands in her lap as she watched Henry prepare to make the same vows with his new wife. He glanced at Zelda, and she smiled.

Henry held up his hands to command the attention of all gathered.

"I regret that I cannot marry this lovely young woman," he announced. The girl frowned prettily. "Instead, I will give her in marriage to my ally, who has arrived and is standing here, the dauphin. He has already agreed to this match. I must step down from this wedding. For you see, I am already married to the girl's mother, so such a marriage would not be proper or right."

Zelda was not sure she understood. The girl was . . . her daughter? She thought of the girl's face and body as she had prepared her for the wedding.

"Emily?" she called. "Are you my Emily?"

The girl trembled. "I . . . I have a mother?"

The girl left the dais, with her new princely groom stand-

136

ing there with nothing to do, and rushed down to meet her mother. Zelda teared up, and when she threw her arms around the girl—her daughter—she sobbed. Almost fifteen years had passed, and she held her daughter again.

"But if you're my mother, who is he?" the girl asked, turning her head toward Henry. Zelda, still sobbing, tucked the girl's head into her neck and held her tight. She let go only when she saw the boy hovering nearby, holding the tiara that was supposed to crown the new queen.

"Emily? I don't understand. . . ." His voice was still high and young. His arms were tentative when Zelda threw herself into an embrace. He hadn't known he had a living mother. Or father. Neither of them had known any of it.

"Come," said Henry, laughing at the triumph of his little ploy, laughing without remorse—for now he knew he'd found a wife noble and true. Zelda's spine straightened. Henry took the diadem from the boy and crowned Zelda's head. "I've tested you more than any other woman, and you are perfect in every way. These are our children, raised under my sister's care and returned safely to you. The boy will inherit my realm. The girl will wed her prince. All is well."

And Zelda smiled at him.

The end.

We sit there, horrified. Then Marcus blinks, and that familiar tic unfreezes us.

"That was the creepiest, sickest story I have ever heard," Sophie shout-whispers. She flicks a glance at Lupe. "Which is saying a lot."

The whole bus chimes in.

"Like, *yeah*."

"Totally!"

"My guess is that Zelda will go on a Goth-doll killing spree and smile with the blood of her son all over her hands," Lupe says, "so that Henry won't have an heir after all. I mean, he didn't have a male heir in real life, and this would explain why."

Rooster grunts. "Wait, his kid gets murdered and he doesn't? Seriously. How come someone didn't assassinate Henry when he was a known freak? They should've hauled him off from the get-go."

"Dude," Kai says, "it's a monarchy. He's the guy in charge."

"So what? He's a sicko, and they clearly should've stopped him."

Kai sighs, and the girls try to explain. Briony leans toward Rooster. "He has all the power. If you don't obey him, you die."

Mouse adds, "You just hope to get through the game with your head still attached."

"Ah," Reiko says, tapping her chin. "Now I have a story idea."

"I don't know," says Frye. "I think Zelda is an enabler."

"No, she's not!" Lupe huffs.

Frye doesn't back down. "She lets it happen. Either that, or she's just retarded."

138

I freeze up. Calling her retarded is just so wrong I don't know where to start. I'd tell Frye off, except I'm chicken.

But Pard is right on it. It's like counting on the sun to burn. "Nice use of the R-word, you fucker."

"Pard," Mr. Bailey warns, and Reeve scribbles on his clipboard.

Pard's sugary hand flips the bird in Frye's direction, not that Frye's looking. But I am. I hold my fist out to Pard. He's surprised. He bumps my fist, does that little hand-slide across my palm.

I let the conversation wash over me and run my thumb over the grains of sugar on my fingers. Then I pretend to scratch my chin.

Fast as a lizard, I taste the sugar. Gross, I know, but it was from my doughnut.

"Okay," Lupe says, "that was an amazing story. Really made me smile. Ladies, let's show Marcus our thanks, Zelda style."

Every single one of them turns a perfect doll's head on her lovely neck, slow-mo, and gives Marcus a dead-eyed smile.

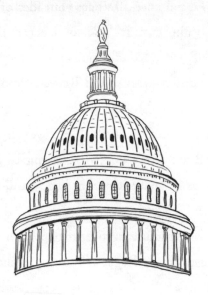

"You have to let me go next," Reiko tells Mr. Bailey.

Mr. Bailey holds his hat. "Shouldn't I draw a name?" He's been overruled so often now that he just asks us what the plan is.

Lupe chants, "Rei-ko, or we won't go!" twice, and he splutters, "Okay, okay, you're on!"

Reiko and Lupe slap fives.

"So, my story's like a companion of sorts to what Marcus gave us," Reiko starts. "He did Henry VIII, but since we're going to Washington, I thought we'd do something more American."

"That's cool, but you have to say something about yourself first." Frye smiles all flirty-like. "You know, what you like to do . . ."

Reiko giggles. "I like to do it all."

140

A big *Yeah!* from Rooster.

But Frye's not finished. "What's your idea of a perfect date?"

Reiko looks both surprised and pleased by his question. "Mmm, that's a hard one, but obviously it would have to be in the evening. I love the energy of a city at night. When my date picks me up and I open the door to meet him, I'd feel that delicious spark to see him there dressed up. We'd walk around the downtown, and then he'd take me to a nice restaurant. I like to know he can hold his own in a nice place. I mean, not just that he can afford it or use the right fork for the right course, but that he can carry on a conversation over a long, candlelit dinner."

Frye reaches into his inside pocket and pulls out something he hands to Reiko. Like he has a stash of trinkets in case a hot girl comes his way. "So," he says, smiling as she puts on this candy ring from a dollar store, "at this romantic dinner, can the guy play footsie under the table? How far he can go?"

Reiko arches an eyebrow like he's pushing it, but her smile is a come-on. "Well, at the restaurant, a guy has to behave, right? He can make *suggestions*. And he'll know how to read my cues on whether we can take it to another level. But this is my dream date, right? So after dinner we'd get a lot less formal. We'd go back to his city apartment and change into bathing suits and go for a soak in the hot tub on the roof. After that we'd figure something out."

"*Mmmm*, yes." Frye sighs. "I have some ideas now. We'll talk."

Their eye beams are having sex, and it's gross. Painful. Even after giving up all hope, it hurts to know how much I don't interest her. At all. I mean, she's picking *Frye*, king of the one-night stand.

Pard is drawing, looking hard at Reiko. I'm surprised he isn't hiding his sketchbook. He has the outline of Reiko's face, her shoulders. Her features emerge in strokes. It's easier now to stare at Reiko through Pard's eyes than my own, to see her becoming real rather than watching her fade like she has in my life. I watch the page as she banters with Frye and the others, until she finally begins her tale.

So. Not long ago, a young woman arrived in Washington, D.C., for her internship.

"Oh!" Saga slaps her thigh. "I saw this on HBO like a month ago. Is this that intern with the, um, compromised blue dress? Monica Lewinsky?"

"I got the idea from that story, but this will be totally different," Reiko insists. "I'm going to tell it Marcus-style."

"Like, creepy?" Lupe asks, a smile in her voice.

I look up from Pard's sketchbook quickly in time to see . . . *drumroll!* . . . Marcus blink.

So let me start again. Virginia was thrilled to get the job. She and her father celebrated with a fancy dinner at her father's favorite steak house. It had been only the two of them for a long time, since Virginia's mother died. Her dad had connections in Washington and helped to make this dream for his daughter come true, but he'd never say it that way. He'd say all her hard work made this happen.

But they both knew the truth.

"My girl," he said, toasting her with a glass of wine. She drank Coke, of course. She was only nineteen. "You've come a long way.

"And don't forget to call if you need any advice," he told her. "I don't want you to get in over your head."

She looked up at all the glassy eyes of the heads mounted on the walls. Buffalo, moose, bucks.

And does.

"Okay, Daddy."

And when they left the restaurant and got to the car, he opened the door for her both times. Just like he did when they got to the airport the next morning. He always opened the door for her.

After a short plane ride she was in Washington.

She shook the senator's hand, her own hand trembling, and could barely thank him.

"Senator Lowell, I'm honored."

"Call me Dan, please," he insisted. "And I hear you're an early November birthday. You were born for politics!"

She laughed. "That's what my father said." Her smile walled up the memory of her eighteenth birthday. Her father had proudly showed her the voter's brochure that had arrived in the mail, addressed to her. On the inside of the brochure, on every column from the president to the local office on the back page, he'd circled the vote he expected her to cast. It was like being invited to a feast with your mouth sewn shut. She read it over before voting. She'd agreed with his opinions, some of them. She voted the way he wanted. It was what he expected.

But now she was nineteen, and this summer internship was going to be a new start—a start for her own decisions. She could manage it, with this new opportunity away from home. She still had to fulfill her father's expectations, but she could be herself, too.

Dan was a good politician. Diplomatic. Careful. But Virginia never noticed how careful he really was. He never looked down her blouse unless she was busy gathering up the papers on his desk or leaning over the antique chessboard of his. He only ogled her from behind when she was fixing his coffee in the corner of his office. He'd picked out this intern by her photograph, but he took pains to hide his attention to her body. For the time being. He could tell she hadn't come to D.C. for an affair and that she prided herself on her intellect rather than her body, but he liked a challenge.

She did, however, notice the gorgeous intern that joined their office in her second week. Ryan, just a few years older than she was, looked like a movie star. She knew she shouldn't be so attracted to a guy just for his body, but he was stunning.

And he seemed to like her—a lot. One night he took her out to dinner, and she spent the night in his apartment. She knew her father would kill her if he knew, but it was so nice, so grown-up to be with a man in his apartment. He was more experienced, but she caught on quickly. She was a fast learner, after all.

Then, just like that, he was transferred to an office in California. He promised to text her. He didn't.

It was midway through the summer, and she was spending all her time in Dan's office. Maybe it was for the best she'd lost Ryan—it wasn't like they ever really talked or had a relationship beyond the physical. Now she was available to help Dan whenever he needed her, for whatever he needed, and he appreciated her work so much. In his way he made her feel like a woman, too—grown and independent. Sometimes they played chess, and he'd ask for her political opinions and not just expect her to be the intern that fetches coffee, though she did that for him too. Of course, he encouraged her to pour herself a cup and make herself at home, and a couple times he made coffee for *her*, and they'd talk, informally, just open up about themselves. That was gratifying. Virginia was delighted when he'd ask for her view about the many things she cared about. She urged him to make better rebates for electric cars, to stop fracking, to stop corn and sugar lobbyists from controlling the nutritional labels on food products. He listened with such attention.

Then, late one afternoon they were discussing the possibility of changing student loans so that students could default. Virginia was keen on pushing this bill forward after seeing some of her friends' older siblings struggle with debt.

Dan looked up from the stack of papers. "It's nearly six," he said. "Maybe we can keep working on this over dinner?"

So they did just that, ordering takeout to keep working on the details to make the bill attractive to both parties. "There has to be a quid pro quo," he explained over their takeout boxes. "The Republicans won't pass this unless we give them something in return. The hope is to give them just enough, but we get the better deal, if that makes sense."

"I understand perfectly. You're talking about negotiating compromise."

He tilted his head as he studied her face. "Most people here don't understand compromise, but I have the feeling you do."

She looked at her hands in her lap. It felt like such a personal remark. "Yes, I do."

"Then, you're ahead of people much older than you are. I'm not used to young people having such passion for the big issues and possessing such maturity," Dan said. "I really think you're going to go places."

She gave him a grateful smile. "Thank you, Dan! That means a lot to me. It's really a pleasure working under you."

Dan paused, like there was something huge he needed to say. Virginia could feel it coming but had no idea what it might be. "The pleasure is all mine," Dan finally said, his voice husky. Then he pulled her toward him and thrust his tongue in her mouth.

"Nasty," Lupe says.

"Senator Lowell." Virginia gasped, pushing him off her and rising to her feet. "I—I have to go."

"A man in love will do crazy things," he said. He was as calm as she was upset, but he tried to look nervous, like his heart was on the line and not just his prick. "I'd risk my career for you. You're worth it, Virginia."

Now she felt bad for him. She'd fallen for someone too. "I'm sorry, but no."

"Just think about it, won't you?"

Virginia shook her head. Senator Lowell seemed like the kind of man who needed to be told no—and only no—just to get the idea into his brain.

"I won't change my mind," she said firmly. "My answer is no."

Virginia didn't show up for work the next day. She called in sick. She thought of quitting but didn't want to come home in defeat.

Meanwhile, Senator Lowell had plenty of space and time to plan his next move. He didn't need much time, really. He was good at judging character. It's how he got elected, year after year.

When Virginia came into work the following day, Dan called out to her from his office.

"Virginia, won't you come in?"

Her hands trembled a little, but she knew nothing could happen. It was ten o'clock in the morning. Witnesses everywhere.

When she finally entered his office, Dan's back was toward her. He was studying the pieces on his chessboard.

"Oh, close the door, please." She did so against her will. "Did you know that, in the early life of chess, the queen used to be a man?"

She stared at the board, curious in spite of herself. "No, I didn't."

"He was the grand vizier, the king's advisor. He could only move diagonally one space. In the Middle Ages, someone had the idea of making it the most powerful piece on the board, and he became a she. A queen, reflecting the power of her king. She became the piece every opponent can't help but want to capture. There's something so satisfying about using weaker pieces to bring down all that strength. Don't you think?"

Virginia's skin crawled. She was the queen he wanted to capture.

"The queen has all the vitality, but the king carries the game. What would the king say if he saw this?"

Dan pulled out his phone and played a video. It was Virginia with Ryan, in his apartment, making love in one of the positions

Ryan had taught her. She watched the ecstasy on her face as she did things to him, and he did things to her.

She put her hand on her churning stomach. This wasn't just thoughtless betrayal. Not just a guy recording things with his phone and leaving that phone in the wrong place. It wasn't just one camera recording the scene. There were two points of view, and the footage shifted between them, expertly spliced and edited to show Virginia's face and body.

"Should I e-mail this to your father? Or just blast it on the Internet? What does the queen say, Virginia?"

The video showed everything. *Everything.* Her father would kill her.

"Come on, Virginia. Give me one night, and this video will disappear."

Most girls in that situation might blurt out *no* and run, but Virginia's fear of offending her father was strong. She could agree to this, and her father would never know. That was tempting. She knew all about compromise and doing what someone else wanted at the expense of her own life. She was trained to obey such men.

"How do I know you'd actually destroy the file?"

He put a hand on his heart. "Virginia, I'm shocked! You have my word. When can I see you? I have a formal dinner this evening, sadly, but what about tomorrow night?"

"All right," she whispered, not knowing if she was really agreeing or not, and hating herself for being unsure.

"Good, then!" He took a bite of the muffin on his table. He wiped his fingers on a greasy napkin, picked up the chess queen, and kissed it. "It's a date."

Virginia left the office, but not before catching an unexpected glimpse of Ryan. He fled at the sight of her. So he wasn't reassigned to work in California after all. She tried to follow him down the hallway, but he turned a corner, and she lost him.

He must have been the knight on the board, then, designed to take her down. And she was trapped with Dan, the enemy king who was prepared to do diagonal moves all over her tomorrow night.

What if some footage of her and Dan went public? What then?

A clip of Virginia and Ryan was one thing, but Dan was older than her father. It would be humiliating for that to go public. And disgusting to let him do it to her in private.

No. If she had to cast one vote that was all her own, it had to be this. To reject Dan.

She'd rather die, even tell her father. Yes. She would tell him. That way, the film wouldn't be a surprise. And perhaps, if he knew right now, he could do something to stop it. He was a powerful man in his own right. He would take charge, as usual. She was okay with that. She needed him to help her decide things.

After agonizing over it all afternoon, Virginia finally called her father. She told him everything.

"How dare he? I'll be right there. He won't get away with it."

The next day, everything was ready. Virginia and her father showed up in Senator Lowell's office.

"Ah, this is a surprise," the senator said calmly. He extended a hand to Virginia's father. "I wasn't expecting you."

Virginia's father ranted. "How dare you push yourself on my daughter? You think you're so above the law that you can get away with this. You can't."

The senator smiled. "And how are those tax evasions working for you, Virgil? I'm sorry to say, it looks like your daughter will be at the center of a major scandal, and you'll be in jail. No one is perfect, of course, but if you can't let me help you, what can I do?"

Virgil grabbed Virginia by the arm. She knew what was coming. She and her father had discussed it late into the night, with tears from both of them. She knew his plan was the only way to save her honor and preserve it forever.

Virgil, who never used foul language, let Senator Lowell have it. "So, Dan. You want some head? Here you go!"

And then things took a nasty turn. Virgil pulled out a knife, and Dan called for help. It was just a cake knife, but it was the sharpest instrument he could get past the government building's security.

Just before security burst through the door, he cut off Virginia's head.

Screams erupted from all around. Virginia's head rolled to Senator Lowell's feet.

Within minutes the police surrounded the place. Virgil and Dan were arrested, and the scandal erupted around the world. When the footage surfaced in the investigation, Ryan was brought in for questioning, and the world learned from Dan's accomplice about Dan's sick plot to blackmail Virginia into his bed.

Thousands of men rushed to Virgil's defense. He was just fighting back against a disgusting man abusing his power over a young woman. Virginia was called a sacrifice in the name of justice.

But just as many women didn't see it that way. They saw Virginia as abused, murdered, and erased after death. The showdown was between two men—that was the power struggle society cared about. Virginia was her father's property, and when that property was in jeopardy, he cast it aside to make a point.

The end.

There's a slow clap from Cece. "That was brilliant. *Brilliant!*"

Mouse pipes up. "No, it was gross. I mean, chopping off Virginia's head?"

"But don't you see?" Cece is totally into it. "It's a metaphor of the way girls are reduced to the power struggles between men. Virginia wanted to be on her own, but in the end, she was pulled apart between the men who claimed her for themselves. No one valued the head on her shoulders. Is that about right, Reiko?"

Reiko raises an eyebrow. "Pretty much, though I wasn't analyzing it, just telling it." It's a known fact that Reiko doesn't much care for Cece.

"Reminds me of Coach You-Know-Who," Lupe says, and she shudders dramatically. "Ugh! Remember, Reiko, how he tied my shoe for me on the bleachers? His crotch pressed to the sole? So. Gross."

Reiko nods. "One of these days he'll rape someone, and he'll get fired. Finally. It pretty much takes a body to get rid of molesters. He ran his hand over my ass freshman year. He was pretending he just loved my suede skirt, but it was pretty obvious what he was loving."

I gasp, and Reiko turns. "Why didn't you tell me?" My voice comes out so small compared to all these strong women who are weighing in where guys fear to tread. I remember that skirt, how pretty she was in it. I feel sick.

She cocks her head and makes a pitying face. "What would you have done?"

What *would* I have done? Gotten angry? Cried? Yes, and I wouldn't have done a thing, and Reiko knew it. She should have dumped me far sooner than she did.

Of course, I was a freshman then. What would I have done as a senior? I would have told Cannon. Cannon would have told me what to do—whatever a man is supposed to do. In other words, I still am completely useless as a man.

I'm staring at Reiko and mouthing *I'm sorry* when Alison says, as if to comfort her, "Eh, I think most of us have had love-pats by random guys. Take it as a compliment!" Reiko gives her that lopsided sneer she uses when she's offended, but Alison isn't finished. "Too bad for Virginia. She should have run off with the hot guy."

Cece pretty much freaks out with a major "Noooo. Everyone wants a piece of Virginia. The whole point is how these men robbed her of everything she had. How can you be a woman and not see that?"

Cece looks like she's ready to rant her way down the aisle, but Mari redirects her energy. "What she really needs is a dolphin, huh?"

Cece rolls her eyes as if to say, *Of course.*

"We *all* do!" Mouse squeals a few dolphin squeaks, and suddenly, almost all the girls practice echolocation, tipping their heads back and squealing in a way that's both ridiculous and sexy.

I realize all the guys are just keeping quiet. What else can a guy do when girls are talking about sexual abuse and getting decapitated by their dads?

I don't envy whoever has to go next after such a violent story. As Mr. Bailey draws a name, a girl's name, I turn and look out the window. I'm not the only one. People tap their fingers on the glass as they point out the view. Manhattan rises in all its glory as we head south. I might be shy and reclusive, but what a beautiful city. All that energy and potential. All that life being lived.

As I'm loving this view and all it promises, Mr. Bailey calls Alison's name.

"Sweet timing!" she proclaims. Feet firmly planted on the ground, she arches her back so she's long and tall, her arms open to New York, her smile wide, her eyes shut, nostrils flared as she breathes in. She's beautiful and free and I feel a little zing when she adds, "Check that out. Makes you want to change up the field trip and just take this city on."

"Oh yeah," Rooster booms.

"No can do," Mr. Bailey says in a teacherly way.

"Aw, I had to try." Alison laughs her full-body laugh. The mood on the bus completely lifts from Reiko's tale of a girl with no choices to this feeling that anything is possible.

Alison has our complete attention.

She shakes her hair out like a wild, untamed mane. Her gap-toothed smile makes her look transgressive and free and inviting—that sly mix of beauty and humor that sets her apart.

"You're all looking at me like this is the story you've been waiting for."

Rooster shouts, "It is, baby!" and Mouse—cute little Mouse, who seems so young and innocent, despite her popularity and partying—hollers, "Teach us ladies some tricks!"

There are hoots all around as guys start to go primal. Alison rewards them with a wicked smile. "I could tell something from life, but we're supposed to tell fiction. Those are the rules, right?"

Protests resound that a true story would be just fine. Even

Reeve sets down his precious clipboard and splutters that, according to the rules, it's okay to start out with a story from real life.

Alison purrs from all this attention. "You know, I wouldn't mind telling you a bit about my life before I tell a proper story. It's not like I'll get to give a speech at graduation. So here's what I might have said. I would have told you all to follow your hearts and put your own experiences before anyone else's advice. No one knows you better than you do, so be true to that. And, sometimes, it takes a while to hit your groove. That's the story I'll tell you. I'm going to tell you about first sex. No one loves sex more than I do, but even I've had some bumps along the road."

She pauses dramatically.

ALISON'S TALE

In sixth grade, my class had an end-of-year field trip to the Liberty Bell. But instead of having a parent driver, our group rode with this girl's older brother. We thought it was so cool to have a guy driving us. Let's name him Pete. So I call shotgun, and Pete does a double take, right there in the classroom. We girls follow him out. I feel mature walking side by side with Pete—the other girls get into one of those little clumps and chatter away. Pete and I don't say much. But we look. He sneaks looks at my hair, my breasts, my legs, and I devour the shape of him under his T-shirt, his jeans. He says he can't believe I'm not in high school. A lot of guys used to say that, but this is a totally different vibe.

We get in his car. When I need to pull my seat forward to make more room in the back, he reaches and puts his arm between my bare calves to lift the lever by my ankles. His arm hairs tickle. He's narrating how to do it, but he's doing it, and his elbow bends as he pulls the lever up, and his elbow slides between my thighs, and he turns his head, and he's still narrating, and his breath curls up my legs. I don't move. I was watching it like you watch a movie, the way my skirt lifts as his elbow rises, and the way his fingers graze me from ankle to knee when he pulls away. He shoots me a quick look, like, *Was that okay?* And I slide my skirt up, like my thigh itches, and I scratch it higher and higher absentmindedly. It just takes a second, but he gets it.

And when we show up, there's no parking, so he drops us off at the front, where a parent group is waiting, except I don't pile out with the others. It's unfair to make him walk alone, I tell them. So Pete and I drive off and spiral our way up a parking garage. We're way up in the darkness, the only car there, and he turns the key, and it's like we both know. He climbs between the seats to the back and pulls me after him, and we are making out like I never have before, and he's touching me like I've never been touched before, my breasts, between my legs, and I'm clawing him when he gets out his condom, because I can't wait, I can't, then he's inside me, and we come at the same time.

I'd seen movies, and it's like a movie. I finally understood how a woman makes that face, moans like that. Suddenly, I understood everything I'd wanted to know. And it's all I want to know.

Pete does himself up, says we got to hurry, and when we're down the flight of stairs I say I forgot to put my panties back on, and he's like, *Shit, shit, shit,* but then he says, "It's cool—

158

I'll just come back alone to get the car for you guys," and he wants to know exactly where they are, but I have no idea. I mean, I was pretty busy just then. He makes a face when I describe them—pink with Hello Kitty—and I'm embarrassed I wore them on the trip. Like maybe he'll never want to do it again, because I'm such a kid.

I stand with my friends, and I'm looking at this wide-mouthed Liberty Bell, but I'm still thinking of Pete inside me. So full, so complete. And the bell cracked after just one ring, one of my friends tells me, and instead of getting scrapped as used-up goods, it became a monument. Cracked, but still the icon of freedom. I like that.

After the trip, Pete and I steal time in snatches—and they are the minutes I live for. I don't care much for his sister, but I sleep over there every chance I get. When she's showering, I'm in Pete's bed. Pete is there the whole summer, home from college. And I'm stoked. I'm twelve, and I have a man who eats from my hand.

Then, I'm in seventh grade, and Pete goes back to college. He doesn't want to text, says this kind of love can get ugly when it goes public. He wants some distance, but he says he's never had a lover like me, says I'm a natural. The moment I turn eighteen, he wants me to please get in his life for good.

I don't want him to get in trouble for something I wanted as much as he did, so I don't text much. The few I send either get answered formally—like we're almost strangers—or not answered at all. I mostly keep to high school boys for the next

159

year, keep it simple. Take a wider field once I get into high school. But now I sometimes think about Pete. I'm eighteen. Would you call him up?

I'm mouth breathing and waiting for some sort of resounding *NO!* to flood the bus, but it's dead silent. No one speaks, and even Rooster stares awkwardly at the boot propped once more on his knee. I wonder why Mr. Bailey says nothing, but I can't look away from Alison, so calm after saying something that makes me want to rush in a time capsule and beat the crap out of Pete, and after I did that I'd tell Alison . . . no, I don't know what I'd tell the girl facing the Liberty Bell without her panties, and I don't know what to say to Alison now.

Completely unfazed by our silence, she shakes out her hair again.

Anyway, that's the slice of life. Now for the story!

I'm going to shift things up with something from King Arthur's court. I've been hearing lots of stories about women, so I'm going to take the guy's perspective here. I'm a bit inspired by the King Arthur story Mari wrote a couple years ago.

Mari beams, totally flattered. It was a really great fantasy.

So there's this young knight. He's brave, gorgeous in his shiny new armor. Has performed well at tournaments. King

160

Arthur admits him to his court. He gets to sit at the Round Table with the best of the best.

Everyone loves young knights. The tried and true ones are muscled gray beards, but young knights have this potential that makes you bend over backward to see them succeed. But to succeed, they must be tried.

So our young knight is out in the forest, returning from a quest. He's done well. He killed a man-eating manticore that had been attacking a nearby village. He's happy about that, but his horse died in the fight. It's been a long trek back to Camelot, but he's close now.

Then he hears something.

He doesn't hide, because young knights boldly meet danger. But it's just a young woman walking alone. Standing there, watching her, he thinks there's no danger after all, but he's dead wrong and just doesn't know it. The girl's new to womanhood. He can tell by her hips, by the way she moves her skirts, playacting a fine lady.

He calls out to her. The girl's lower class, so she curtsies low. He pulls her up. Pulls her coaxingly to his body. Then, when she tries to free herself, he yanks her down hard on the ground, on her back.

The young knight rapes the girl.

He was wrong about danger. *He* was the danger. He saved a village and then devoured a girl. Once he takes what he wants, the knight ditches her in the woods with her legs still

161

open, her skirts still up, like she doesn't even have the sense to straighten them.

The girl has no social standing, no recourse. She has nothing but seed dribbling down her thighs as she walks home, nothing but a baby coming to life inside her. She is almost out of this story, which is about the knight, not her.

But she does one thing more. Two, really.

First, she goes home, and when her mother scolds her for sneaking away from the loom again, she cries before the first lash even falls. She sobs hard, and her mother smells something amiss. The mother questions her daughter, and the girl makes a choice. She tells her. Not just what happened, but what the knight's shield looks like. That design on the shield is his calling card. And the mother tells her husband. Together, they kneel before King Arthur's throne and tell him about their daughter. And now all three of them are out of the story.

Arthur condemns the young knight to death.

"What's his name?" Lupe asks.

Alison shrugs. "I don't know, but I'm not playing this passive-aggressive game of naming someone on this bus."

Still holding his pencil, Pard lifts his hand like he's in school. "How about Sir Peter?"

She cocks her head to one side and gives him a knowing smile.

So Sir Peter is going to lose his head. Except that, long story short, it turns out Sir Peter is gorgeous and quite a favorite with Queen Guinevere's girls . . . or, at least, he *was* a favorite. Rape, even of some nobody, does not go over well. They demand to settle his case for themselves, or at least defer to Guinevere's judgment.

The king is not pleased, but he won't go against the ladies, especially since it's a crime against ladies, though the weaving girl is hardly a lady. So, obviously, she's not a part of this judgment. She's out of the story while her next chapter is growing inside of her.

Sir Peter is brought forth bound before the queen and her ladies. If Sir Peter was hoping his curly hair and shapely limbs would buy him freedom, he's mistaken and learns the precariousness of his life as he kneels facedown before a stern queen.

The queen rises from her throne and looks down on him from her dais. She does not bid him rise. "Your duty is to defend the maidenhead of ladies, not to glut yourself on it like a swine. Your crime is punishable by death. So says my king and husband. But I will grant you one opportunity to save your life."

Sir Peter risks the tiniest peek at his queen.

"You must discover for yourself what women most desire. Ask as many women as you please. By this day next year, you will give us your answer. If you answer correctly, you will live. If you answer incorrectly, you will die."

Sir Peter becomes a questing knight, or the Knight of the Question for Ladies. As soon as he approaches women and poses his question, a familiar pattern repeats itself.

"Ah, so you are that knight who raped a defenseless girl."

"Yes, my lady."

"That was not nobly done."

"No, my lady."

"Well, for starters, women do not wish to be raped. I suppose you could aim higher than that, but maybe start with the basics. We also don't like being beaten—not with your shoe, not your fists, nor a kick to the ribs. Getting murdered is right out. Any other questions?"

When the queen gave him his quest, he figured a couple weeks would be all he needed. The problem is that women kept saying different things. Things to do, things not to do. Some want money, some power, some beauty, some sex. Unsettling variety. He's pretty sure he can have only one answer, not the hundreds he gets. Surely, killing the manticore was much less strenuous. Why, the women didn't even seem to know for themselves what they wanted!

So thinks young Sir Peter.

"But what *do* women want?"

Everyone turns around. Reeve's perched on his bench, leaning forward, wide eyes asking. Still no sign of the clipboard. You can tell he really wants to know.

"Not you," Reiko quips, and everyone laughs. Reeve gropes for the clipboard, like he's turning back into Gollum.

Alison raises a queenly hand. "Hold on. If you think you know the answer, tell the person next to you." There's an uncomfortable silence, and then she adds, "Go on, I'll wait."

The bus fills with the swish of soft voices. Pard lifts an eyebrow to say, *So?*

I shake my head, but he demands an answer and leans in close so I don't see his face anymore, just an ear and his thin white hair. "Fake question. You can't boil down desire to one thing. The women he's asking prove it. It's a setup. You?"

He pulls back, and his face is a mix of *God, you're hopeless* and the look of a slapped kitten.

"Then *what?*" I ask again. I'm frustrated and wonder what makes *him* the authority on women, besides one kiss from Alison.

He tilts his head, and he's not scornful anymore, just sadly resigned I'm not destined to get something so simple. "Love," he says, looking right at me.

I manage a pathetic, "Oh."

By the end of the year Sir Peter makes his way back to Camelot. He isn't desperate anymore, just defeated. He's collected a laundry list of things women want. None of them seem right. He plans to pick the best-sounding one and throw himself at the queen's mercy. He doubts he'll receive any.

He walks as a penitent through the same woods where his adventure with danger began. Then he sees a strange sight: twenty-four young ladies dancing in a ring. All of them as beautiful as fairy folk. All naked.

Sir Peter is in a pickle. If anyone can help him on his quest, they can. But Sir Peter is also pretty excited. He hasn't gotten laid since the whole rape fiasco, and his body goes into overdrive. He has the sense to know that now is not the time to rush women with this major hard-on. Not the best PR, considering his case.

On the other hand, these women might have the true answer, and the guy wants to survive. So he holds his shield low in front of him and pushes forward.

He passes through the ring of dancers, and with a flash, they vanish by magic. Well, one woman stands at the center, but she isn't naked, thank God.

If the other women were supernaturally beautiful, this one's supernaturally ugly: balding; drooping breasts; a wide and warty toad face; a square, squat body. She has to be at least two hundred years old.

Sir Peter lets his shield droop at his side. He doesn't need to cover himself any longer.

Now, if he'd seen this woman this time last year, he'd have run screaming. But he has talked to women both old and young over the many months, so he's seen all types. This hag was in a class by herself, though, and she gives him the willies—but he's desensitized to some ugliness by now, and he's desperate. So he asks her the question.

Her cackle shows off her missing teeth. "Of course I know the answer, dearie! Very simple. But that answer comes with a price. What will you give me?"

No one's mentioned a price before, and he thinks maybe he's onto something good.

"Anything. Anything you want."

The witch's grin makes his skin crawl. "Well, that is an attractive offer. I'll take it. Let's go."

"Oh, you needn't come with me. Just tell me the answer."

"Ah, but if I did that, chickabiddy, would you come hunting for me in this forest, so I could redeem my prize? No, dearie, when we get to court, I'll tell you what women most desire. And then—after you survive your test—I'll tell you what *I* most desire."

She clutches him for balance, and he gags. It's a long, slow walk to the court.

And only when it's time to approach the queen does the hag finally cough up the answer in Sir Peter's ear before melting into the crowd of assembled ladies.

"Tell us," says the queen.

Sir Peter hesitates for only a second. He has no other choice but to parrot the words he has just been told. His voice, like his body, is strong and manly, and everyone waits with bated breath on his every word.

"Your Majesty, a woman most desires sovereignty over her man."

The queen jerks upright in her throne, surprised at his answer. Murmurs among the assembled ladies break out. The attending audience erupts in discussion.

The ladies murmur their approval, but it's the queen's face that people study, and when she nods, the room fills with cheers. Sir Peter lets out a huge sigh.

His joy lasts for two seconds.

"Your Majesty." Everyone turns to see the squat old hag rise to her feet. "I gave the knight this answer, and in return, he promised to give me anything I desire."

The queen's gaze penetrates the knight's face. "Sir Peter, is this true?"

He does not have time to blink or the wherewithal to lie. "Yes, Your Majesty."

The queen faces the hag. "And what is your desire?"

"To have this knight in marriage."

There are so many gasps that the breath is sucked from the audience chamber. Sir Peter staggers like an arrow has hit him. He faces the hag, grinning and hunchbacked. Then he falls to his knees and holds his hands in supplication.

"No, not that. You can have anything else—all my possessions, all of them. Anything but my body. Please."

The hag's gums gleam when she smiles. "You look lovely on your knees, my dear knight. And husband."

The wedding takes place the next day. The knight awaits it locked in a tower by orders of the queen. She does not want a runaway husband.

He then takes his place at the altar. It is a simple wedding, but the guests are the king and queen and high lords and ladies. They are Sir Peter's fellow knights with fair wives beside them.

In a daze of horror the knight makes his vows. He kisses his bride's wrinkled mouth. He walks her from the cathedral and to the banquet prepared for them. He puts roasted peacock to her lips and does not meet her hungry eyes. He has no appetite.

Then his fellow knights grab him and strip him naked and throw him in his bridal bed. His bride is already there. He watches after the merry lords and sweet ladies, who retreat and shut the door behind them. He trembles like a leaf and lies on his side, facing the wall. In another moment he's gone fetal.

"Well, this isn't what I expected from such a handsome, lusty husband." His ancient bride runs gnarled fingers from his ribs to his pelvis, while he grips his pillow. Her foul breath steams around his ear. "On our wedding night too."

Now she's clawing him, trying to get him to roll over to her, on her, and he can't. He can't do this. "For the love of God, please don't," he begs.

But she does. She touches him, and every time she lifts her thigh to tangle with him, her hip bones pop. She's on him now, trying to warm him into life, but he's soft and weak, and the only moisture in his body are his tears.

"This isn't working, is it?" And she lets go with a sigh. Rolls off him.

He returns to his fetal position, thanking God it didn't happen. That said, he knows he's married. It will happen, sooner or later. He thinks of locking her in a chamber and fleeing the land. There must be some way out of this.

"You aren't attracted to me, are you?" Her voice is a raspy scold.

He almost turns to glare at her, but spares himself. "You're the most hideous thing ever spawned. I should have died rather than agreed to this."

"Ah, so you don't like me because I'm not beautiful, is that so?"

He rolls his eyes. "That is so."

"How about this—would you like me if I looked like *this*? Go on, turn around."

He risks a glance, and then turns hard toward the gorgeous woman naked beside him. She's even more beautiful than the fairy ladies dancing in the woods, if that's possible. She is a fairy queen. His body flushes with heat, and he wants to touch her, but he's afraid.

Her smile dazzles him. "Well, that's better. Men can be so shallow. They long for pretty surfaces. But this shape comes with a price. Ah, I see your worry. Not another price, you think. But you get to choose your price, and it's simple. Either have me ugly but faithful, or beautiful but faithless."

Quite a choice. He wants to say faithful, but she was so

170

very, very ugly. He wants to say beautiful, but he can't bear to have her beauty given to every man in the court. There are no good choices.

"Well?" The fairy lady runs a finger over his chest, down the line of his belly, and he's on fire. Except he's trapped.

"I don't know. How should I choose? What's the right answer . . . or can you choose for me? You decide. You're the one in charge here. You're been in charge all along."

She smiles, and there's a gleam of mischief in her face that frightens him. "So I have sovereignty?"

"Yes."

She throws herself on him, hugs him like a vine. "Then, if you will be ruled by me, *I* choose to be beautiful *and* faithful."

And they have the hottest sex of anyone at court, the kind of sex I wish upon you all. The end!

Alison ends with a flourish, but we're quiet and uneasy. Or at least I am. Rooster and a few others cheer her benediction for hot sex.

She smiles at me. "Hey, writer boy, how did you like it?"

Why do they keep calling on me? I love Alison, but I hate her story.

"I was kind of hoping Sir Peter would learn his lesson that raping people got you in trouble, not hot sex."

She waves a hand like I brought up something minor. "It would be so predictable to end with the knight getting executed,

171

or having to have sex for the rest of his life with an old hag. All my stories have to have happy endings. And since it's his story, *he* has to have a happy ending. Plus, it isn't fair to the hag to watch her husband squirm like that. She needs to be happy too. So it's better this way. For everyone."

I nod, but I don't think it's better. I want to rip the whole story out and start over. It's like Alison knew the real story was about that unnamed girl raped in the woods, but she chose to tell the knight's story. Why tell a rapist's story when it's that girl who's worthy of love? Why? Unless . . .

"What?" Pard whispers. He has me by the sleeve.

"You were right, not just about women—we all want love." I shiver, whispering all that in a hoarse rush, but the words need to come out now, and he gives a quick nod to let them keep coming. "But this story was about sex. He gets what he wants, both times, but he never asked for or got or gave love. It's . . . empty. But for Alison to tell a story like that . . ."

"Yeah?" He's leaning in again, fingers on my wrist.

"It's just . . . I don't want her to call up Pete now that she's eighteen."

He looks her way, considers her. "I don't think she'll call him. She's smart. Still, we'll look out for her, right?"

"Right." And I look at Alison again, all cozy back and center, so strong she could pick up this bus, or dance naked, or do anything, and not let it hurt her.

Or does it?

172

BRIONY'S TALE

We're back to the hat. Mr. Bailey calls out, "Ah, another woman this time. You're up, Briony."

Briony looks a tad green. Following Alison was never her plan in terms of high school popularity, and it isn't her plan now in this story competition.

"My story idea doesn't really work well with Alison's," she says, stalling, her face pinched as if she'd found a wad of gum in her pom-poms. "I'm not keen on going after a romantic comedy with *rape*."

"Stories aren't socks," Mr. Bailey says. "No need to match them."

"Just go for it!" Kai says with that dazzling smile, though not a naive one. His cheeks are just a touch tight under Briony's knowing glare, and I feel for him.

Alison was Kai's old flame freshman year. Briony has had more than her share of old flames—and stayed friends with lots of them—but Alison is different. Alison's post-romance friendships have all the energy and flirtation they always had. Once Alison's boyfriend, always Alison's boyfriend, in a sense. Alison and Kai might not be messing around, but she's too likable not to root for and care about and be attracted to, which is enough to make any regular girlfriend freak out.

Briony rolls her eyes, but a moment later she squares her shoulders, straightens her back, and puts on a cheer captain smile. "All right."

So I've always been interested in what makes us who we are. Is it nature or nurture?

In ninth grade, Zac went to his first big party, and it wasn't going very well—leave it to him to smack into a super cute girl he'd never met before, practically the only other black person there, and spill soda all over her.

"Oh my gosh, I'm so, so sorry," he gushed, while his friend Wil just laughed.

"It's okaaaay," the girl insisted, and then she did a weird double take. "Hey, do I know you? From Philly?"

He said no, he'd always lived in D.C., but the girl kept *looking*, tugging on a braid as if to tug the answer from her brain.

The three freshmen exchanged names.

"Zac . . . doesn't strike a bell," Leila said, tapping her chin, "but I swear I know you. Not trying to hit on you or anything, it's just really bugging me right now."

Zac just stood there, wishing she *would* hit on him rather than weird him out with her déjà vu issues.

Then Wil piped in. "Maybe you've heard he's the guy with two dads."

"Hey!" Zac protested. He was known for his dads, but it would be so nice for once to just be known for himself.

Leila turned to Zac. "Really? That's cool."

Zac's stomach tied up in knots wondering what she *really* thought, but Wil was oblivious to it all. "They're white!" Wil added. "And get this. One of his dads found him on the Metro!"

"No way," Leila said, eyes popping. "That's amazing."

It *was* amazing . . . and sad. True, it's a nice story: A man headed to his job interview finds a newborn in a duffel bag riding in his car and adopts the unclaimed baby. All the TV reporters gobbled up the heartwarming news. But it also reminded Zac how his mother put down the duffel bag with him in it and walked out of that train.

At that moment some girls called Leila's name, and she gave an apologetic shrug. "Gotta go, guys. But I'm going to think about you and figure this one out because I *know* we've met."

"Man, are *you* lucky," Wil growled, watching Leila disappear into the laughing cluster of girls. "She's going to *think about you*."

But Zac figured Leila would never speak to him again. She'd done that freeze thing when she heard about his dads. Everyone did that. When people saw his family in a restaurant, you could see them stealing glances and trying to figure out if the white guys were coaches taking him out to dinner. Because they didn't look like a family. He loved his dads, but for his whole life, he'd had it rubbed in over and over that he was in a family that didn't look like a family.

But he was wrong about Leila. She rushed up to him at the lockers on Monday, and Zac was thrilled. He was finally friends with a girl.

"Guess what?" she asked, and he got a weird trembly feeling, like maybe she was going to tell him about a movie or something big, and then maybe ask him out.

"What?" He tried not to look too hopeful or to blurt out "yes" before she asked.

"I wasn't crazy! I found your look-alike! He must be your twin or something!"

Not *that* again.

Then she showed him her phone, and his whole world tilted and came crashing down.

After a dazed day at school Zac sat at his laptop and stared at the guy's profile picture online. It was like an elaborate joke, like some hacker had modified pictures of him hanging out with strangers. The look-alike's name was Aaron. Aaron had uploaded a bunch of photos. All with Zac's face, but in a kind of popular, fantasy life: Aaron with his arm around a beautiful girl; Aaron howling with laughter while his friends carried him after a football game; Aaron giving the peace sign at a party glittering with lights. It made Zac feel like he'd done nothing with his life compared to this guy, but maybe he could have done these things—they looked identical, so why weren't their lives?

After combing through these glamorous photos, Zac clicked on a more quiet photo album that really messed with his mind. Just some family photos, the kind you're often reluctant to be in, but you force yourself to smile and do it anyhow: Aaron, not quite a teen yet, holding a baby (his cousin, by the comments), him laughing as she grabbed his nose; childhood photos with heaps of cousins in front of the Christmas tree; a photo of Aaron looking exactly Zac's age now, but standing with a mom and a dad in front of a church. Parents black like him. And if these were Aaron's parents, just maybe they were his own mom and dad . . . right? Was that possible? He looked carefully at the picture, both parents good-looking and smiling. The mom looked like Miss Day, the kindergarten teacher he'd hoped would fall in love with his dads and marry them, and they'd all live happily ever after. He'd so wanted a mom, like everyone else. Someone in the family who looked related to him. Now he found her.

Zac had to back off from his laptop when tears wet the

keys. He slammed his screen shut just in time to sob hard. He didn't even make it to his bed, just fell onto the ground and stared at the desk's legs and the outlet, and he sobbed until his teeth were sore from rattling.

So sick to his stomach that he couldn't sleep, he couldn't eat breakfast the next day. He couldn't face his dads.

Zac's parents had no idea that their son had grown up longing for a mother or wanting black parents or just wanting to look like a regular family. Zac had never complained, which would seem ungrateful, and he was a star student at his prep school. So there was nothing to prepare either of his dads for what was happening now.

They came to his room, and Pa tried to rub Zac's back, but Zac wouldn't let him. He had to tell them, but he was crying so hard he kept garbling his words.

"You made a mistake," Zac said, his voice raw when he could finally speak. "You took me from my family. My *real* family."

Pa and Dad were totally shocked, so Zac showed them the pictures. Zac wiped his nose. "See? He's my brother, my twin. *That's* my family. There must have been a mistake, and I got taken from them."

Taken. The word made him panicked and helpless all at once.

While Dad looked at the pictures—mouth hanging open, disbelief all over his face—Pa was reaching out to Zac and saying things to comfort him, like "It will all be okay" and "We're still a family" and "Dad will find out what's going on."

Zac flung out his arms like he was losing his balance, like he was going to fall off a cliff. "No! Don't find out. Don't . . ."

"But, Zac," Dad began. His glasses glinted with the glare of the computer. Dad was a professor—a researcher. He could find out everything.

Zac rounded on him, pushing Pa's protective arms away. "I said NO! They're *my* family. It's *my* decision."

"But we don't *know* if they're your family," Dad countered.

"Of course they are—*look at him*. His profile even lists the same birthday and D.C. as his birthplace." What separated them? He had to believe Aaron's mother—*his* mother—wouldn't put Zac in a duffel bag and abandon him, not from the look of her standing in front of a church, or the one at their dining table laden with a holiday meal. What had really happened?

"Zac, stop!" Pa was weeping, desperate. He tried to draw Zac into his arms, and Zac gave up and let him. "We're your family, honey. *We* are! And we always will be. Even if it's true, our family will just grow with more people to love you. It'll be okay."

Zac didn't know how it could ever be okay. He already felt guilty for wanting his birth family. He felt like he should be saying, *I love you* back to Pa, but he couldn't. It was too painful knowing his life with his dads was a mistake, and his real life—the life he was supposed to have—was going on just fine without him.

After arriving at school very late, he zombie-walked through classes until Leila cornered him with a hug that he could barely return. It felt like years since he'd seen her. He wished they'd never met.

She twirled with excitement. "So, did you message him? Aaron? What's the score?"

She didn't seem to realize how shattered he was. To her it was just some sort of interesting mystery. He'd been a twin without knowing it. Maybe it was something to match the weird novelty of having two white dads.

"No."

"Oh, come on. I mean, you guys are long-lost twins. You have to get together!"

Zac's stomach dropped. "I don't think so."

He wanted to, and he didn't. All he had to do was message Aaron. His twin. When a baby is born, he can't go back inside his mother. And Zac knew that if he wrote to Aaron, there would be no return. It would change everything for both of them, forever.

He'd grown up okay in spite of not knowing his twin. He'd grown up okay in spite of having two white dads. He wanted to keep everything the same way.

For the next few days everything in Zac's life felt tilted beyond repair. Pa hovered. Dad got jittery. Zac found himself looking at the familiar way his dads made coffee or spread out a newspaper. There were a million familiar things that connected them as a family, but they felt fragile. Dandelion fluff that would blow away as soon as he made a wish for his real family.

But, finally, he couldn't *not* reach out any longer. The pull for family was too strong.

Zac left an instant message for Aaron and waited for an hour or so. Then waited some more. Maybe Aaron wasn't online much. It was a Saturday night. Maybe Aaron was out. Or maybe he didn't want Zac coming in and invading his family. Or maybe he thought Zac was a prankster and wouldn't reply or would block him. Or maybe . . .

Three hours later Aaron wrote back:

I can't believe it! I'm checking out your photos, AND I CAN'T BELIEVE IT!!!

So began a storm of messages.

And then, a phone call.

"Is that really you?" Zac asked. The laugh on the other end gave Zac shivers, because it was his own laugh coming through the phone.

"I can't believe it!" Aaron shouted, and he laughed until Zac joined in, still to his amazement, identically. They were total strangers, and yet totally connected.

Three weeks later, after some coordinating with the parents, they met face-to-face.

Pa and Dad came too. They wouldn't let him take the

181

train to Philly alone. But this also meant they'd be driving and getting a hotel. If Zac had gone alone, as he'd wanted to do, Aaron's family (*his family!*) would have picked him up at the train station, and he would have slept in Aaron's room like the brothers they were. Pa and Dad were treating this like a vacation, but Zac knew it was so much bigger than that. This was a family reunion—or rather, a family union, since it had never happened before.

When the front door opened, Zac saw . . . himself. They knew what to expect, but neither boy was quite prepared. They both stared, lost to all else.

"They're here!" sang a female voice. And then Zac saw her. She was older than Miss Day, but still had that perfect warmth in her face.

His mother.

His father stood there too, but Zac couldn't help but be more obsessed with his mother. He already had two dads.

He hugged her, and her bighearted squeeze completely matched her personality. It wasn't a long enough embrace for Zac. She pulled back and her eyes misted. "My, but you boys look alike!" Zac smiled and waited to be claimed as she looked searchingly at his face.

She didn't claim him though.

"Come in, come in!" Then she looked at Zac's dads and said, "I know you two are Steve and Tom, but who is who?" As if they were twins too.

Everyone stepped inside with a mix of introductions and handshakes and nervous laughter. It all felt so impossible and strange.

Aaron and his family were friendly to Zac's dads, which was good. Zac had been worried that they would be uncomfortable with the two-dads thing. But the emotional charge he expected from his parents—his real parents—wasn't there. What did they think of him? What did he think of them?

"Look at him!" Aaron's mom laughed. "He twists his mouth when he thinks hard, exactly like Aaron does!"

He looked at Aaron's identical face. It was surreal.

But then he looked at his birth parents. At their mouths. "Do you do that too?"

"Do what?" asked his dad cheerfully. His real dad.

"The mouth thing," Zac said, but he hesitated. Something was off.

His mother covered her mouth and gasped. "Oh, honey, you thought we were your . . . Sweetie, we adopted Aaron, same way you were adopted. Aaron, didn't you tell him?"

Aaron looked embarrassed. "I thought I did. I don't know." Full of concern he looked at Zac. "I'm sorry."

The pity on their faces . . . He had to look away. To look anywhere but at all these people staring at him. "But I thought we—you looked . . ."

"Oh, honey, I'm so sorry. We're not—"

Zac cut her off. "Sure. Okay."

She kept on going. "We didn't know about you. There was nothing in Aaron's file saying that he was a twin."

Zac nodded in quick jerks, wanting to flee the house. "Yeah, that's fine."

He tightened his jaw and used every ounce of willpower not to cry. And all the parents knew how to read him, either because they had brought him up or because they had brought up his twin.

Aaron bailed him out of the humiliating silence. "Do you want to see my room?"

So Zac escaped with Aaron. They played video games, ate sandwiches, and played basketball on the driveway. They also just stared at each other a lot, marveled at their sameness. Zac felt a deep connection with Aaron that he'd never felt for any other person. After taking a shot and flubbing it (he really was terrible at basketball), Zac asked, "Have you thought much about your birth parents . . . I mean, *our* birth parents?"

Aaron scooped up the ball. "Never. I already have the best parents."

"Never?" How was that even possible, not to wonder, not to long to meet them? Zac couldn't imagine. Maybe it was easier for Aaron, since his family all looked related.

As Aaron dribbled, he jammed his tongue into his cheek the same way Zac did. "Someone found me on a park bench in D.C. I was adopted soon after that."

"I was found on the Metro." That duffel bag apparently

caused a scare. Was it left behind by accident or on purpose? Was there a bomb in it? The mood changed in a heartbeat when a weak cry revealed not a bomb but a baby, and Zac was found.

What if Zac hadn't cried?

Aaron nodded, reading all that pain on Zac's face. "It hurts, doesn't it? But the love outweighs the hurt. The people who love me, *those* are my parents."

"Yeah," Zac replied, but his voice came out a question, because it had never been that easy for him.

They were very much the same—but very different, too.

Zac had expected Aaron would totally get him. But did he?

He should be happy, but it was sort of sad, meeting this twin who had charm and tons of friends and athletic ability and all that confidence. It was like meeting a version of himself that he himself could never be. Zac had grown up okay, he guessed. Some people worry about kids with two dads, but he turned out fine. But maybe he was supposed to turn out like Aaron, except that, living with his white dads, he turned out to be Zac instead.

But then Zac asked, "Did you ever think you had a twin?"

Aaron sank the ball. "Not once!" He laughed. "Just goes to show you, doesn't it?"

Zac retrieved the ball, passed it to Aaron. "Show you what?"

Zac expected Aaron to sink the ball yet again, but instead, Aaron tucked it under his arm and faced Zac. Looked at him in

185

wonder. "It shows you the best things in life are the things you never even dreamed up. I mean, a twin I never knew I had came knocking on my door! Just last month I felt like everything was going fine. I was happy, life was good. But now, meeting you, things aren't just great. They're *complete*."

Something electric sang inside Zac. To see Aaron's face so joyful somehow made him mirror back the same joy. "I feel the same way."

Aaron laughed. "Of course you do! We're twins, man!"

And Aaron put out his hand for a huge high five. The boys made a loud *slap!* with their perfectly matched hands, and Zac realized he'd always wanted just one person in the family that would look related to him. That wish had been granted, and then some. He had a twin! He was complete, and he'd finally found his family.

The end.

Briony smiles, eyes misting.

Pard raps his pencil hard against his sketchbook, and for a second, he reminds me of Reeve. "So what do you have against mixed-race families, or gay parents, for that matter? And what the hell does it mean that Zac spends an hour with his 'real' family and then feels okay with life again?"

Briony crosses her legs—or I think she does, by the way she wiggles from side to side. She looks at Pard with some distaste, or maybe she's bracing herself against the criticism. "Obviously

I'm pro-interracial families. I'd love to be in one down the road, if I'm lucky enough to marry a great guy." She takes Kai's hand, and Kai smiles back at her. "And I have nothing against gays adopting babies. The story was about adoptive and birth families, and that strange, amazing connection you only get with your birth family. You don't know how powerful it is to meet your blood family when you've spent your whole life separated."

Pard makes that irritated *teh* sound with his tongue on the roof of his mouth. "More powerful than living with your fake family—is that it?"

"I never said 'fake.' You're twisting my words. Meeting someone for the first time and noticing you share the same gestures, the same posture, the same favorite colors and flavors . . . it's surreal, and I don't expect you to understand it."

I flinch, because Pard would know all about that. He's a twin. *Was* a twin.

"I'm adopted," she adds. "I met my mom for the first time last summer. It was pretty weird, but awesome. The most powerful experience in my life."

"Wow. I didn't know that," Franklin blurts. "That's cool."

"Yeah, well, I was adopted at birth. It was a teenage pregnancy, and my birth mom let me go. She said it was hard, but in the end, she knew she didn't have the support of her family to care for me. Meeting her was good. Painful, but good. Fulfilling. We're staying in touch now."

Pard's still angry. "That's great, but let's get back to the story.

I know you're aiming for some nice Zac-Aaron vibe, but you're forgetting the guy who found the baby in the subway. Pa."

"How do you know it's Pa and not Dad?" I ask. I wonder why he's focused on the parent-child relationship and not the twins, but don't dare mention it.

He rolls his eyes. "It's obvious. That Dad guy is kind of formal, you know? Like, always getting on his computer and stuff, while Pa desperately wants to put his arms around Zac the way he did when he opened that duffel bag and saw a precious baby alone in this world. I mean, shit, the big love story here isn't about the brothers; it's about Pa and Zac. The ending needs to come back to those two. Yeah, yeah, they're not blood, but there are no *buts*. There's no 'in spite of,' plan B crap that you're insinuating. Like, he grew up okay in spite of having two dads, or white dads. Zac is *meh* about his parents but ends up feeling good enough with life because his twin feels that way? No, no, no. You can't celebrate this newly discovered twin at the expense of Zac's parents, especially Pa. You can't. Pa said it himself, that Zac's family was growing, not swapping old for new. Not an either/or. So Zac needs to put to rest all these doubts that you've written into him and acknowledge his love for Pa. The ending should go like this . . ."

They came back inside and saw their parents chatting over coffee in the living room, Zac's parents on one couch and Aaron's parents on the couch facing them. The adults looked up at the sight of their identical boys. Pa met Zac's eyes with a look that carried an avalanche of feelings, and Zac froze. He hadn't been thinking about Pa lately, but now it hit him. That hurting yet loving look. Maybe Pa was torn up from all these new discoveries just as much as Zac was. He had a good guess of what these last weeks had been for Pa, living with the pain of wanting to embrace a child who has shut him out and put up a wall, and on that wall the child tacked up pictures of his new family.

They say you can't choose your family, but that's not always true. Pa chose Zac fourteen years ago and never looked back. He was on the Metro headed to a big interview that might have given him a whole new life. But the life-changing part of the day happened when he heard the cry and discovered Zac. He didn't go to the interview after that—he went straight into his new role as Zac's strongest supporter, and soon, his parent. While Zac fixated on being abandoned and lacking his true family, Pa was all about claiming Zac on that first day and every day after that and being everything he could be for Zac.

And it was that moment, seeing Pa's pale eyes and balding head and anxious face—the lips parting in an effort to smile— that their roles were switched. In his heart, Zac could abandon Pa or claim him. It was like finding *him* and getting to decide for himself what to do with this middle-aged man. It was a huge moment, maybe in its way just as important as the moment Pa picked up the baby and refused to let go.

Zac would never let him go either, he realized, and determination rushed through him to hold on tight to both of his dads.

Zac squeezed in between Dad and Pa on the couch. Dad smiled and made room, and Pa slipped his arm around Zac's shoulders, his eyebrows lifted as if to ask if that were okay.

Aaron's mother was confirming something about childhood similarities—they were talking about favorite foods, Halloween costumes, video games, everything, and finding uncanny resemblances. Her voice was a perfect blend of feminine rasp and softness, motherly things that Zac had always wanted for his own. Yet, in some ways, it was a relief she wasn't his real mother. This couch was already full.

Finding Aaron was an incredible blessing, a gift, and he was amazed to see his mirror image on the opposite couch, but he also knew he needed to keep his own parents close, maybe more than ever. He needed them, and they needed him.

Facing ahead and nodding to the conversation, Zac let his knee bump against Pa's leg.

"Hey," Pa whispered. "Everything okay?"

Zac nodded but suddenly felt bashful. How do you claim someone? How do you make it clear this is what you're doing without being a complete sap?

"Everything's great," Zac told him. "Just wondering . . . have you told them about how we met? I love that story."

"I love it too." And no one laughed or made a fuss when

Pa teared up and took Zac's hand as he began to put into words the most important moment in their lives.

The end.

"Well, isn't that perfect?" Cece sourly complains. "Leave it to a man to come in and revise a woman's story."

The bus explodes with debate of whether Pard's ending was helping or hurting and what Briony's story really accomplished, with a few jokes at Pard's expense thrown in.

I stay quiet, trying to keep Pard's final sentences in my head to see how they completely recalibrated Briony's story. This ending is so sweet that I want him to keep going. I know that the story is over, but I want to hear Pa tell the whole story and have a private heart-to-heart with Zac. I want to hear Pa's voice.

For the millionth time I don't understand why Pard isn't a writer. He's never written a story, but in conversation, he's so good I used to scribble down his little turns of phrase. I'm realizing now that Pard is very Pa-like, and it's a weird thought, because one day, Pard might be a dad—a Pa himself. A great one. His own dad ditched him, as in, no contact. Zero. Apparently, Pard wasn't manly enough. A father doesn't ditch his kid because he's not into the preschool sports scene. My dad's had problems with depression, and he's no hyper-affectionate Pa, but I can't even imagine him leaving me. I mean, I can't imagine my dad leaving me to live somewhere else on this planet.

I can imagine him *leaving*.

God, I want to claim my dad somehow. He helped build me my safe place, my sleeping box. If I could do one good thing in this life, I'd like to make a safe place for him. Here, on this Earth, with me.

Pard touches my sleeve like he senses something. I shake my head and try to laugh it off, because I'm not going there, but he's not laughing. He's giving me an avalanchey, Pa sort of look, and it's like he's asking me about the walls I've built between us. Asking if I choose to claim or abandon him.

If only it were that easy. Zac had all that unconditional love funneled into him from Pa. And I guess Pard funneled unconditional love into a dad who maybe saw a spark of gay in his kid and left. I want to be like Pa, not Pard's dad. But this is different. I'm not a dad. Father-son love is so pure, so simple compared to friends like we'd become, with all that mess to sort out. Though right now, it feels worth it, mess and all.

But, no, I can't. Instead, I turn toward Lupe and ask which ending she liked better, and I try, try, try to hear what she says, so I can get out of my own head, which keeps asking me, louder and louder, *Why not?*

BREAK: FALLING

With New York behind us, we're in that weird zone of urban sprawl without a real city to claim it when we pull over at a pit stop. There's nothing but the gas station convenience store, a McDonald's, and a no-name coffee shop. Mr. Bailey disappears into this third store, no doubt to drink a gallon of coffee. We stand around outside with our coffees and divide in the predictable clusters of smokers and nonsmokers, popular and unpopular. Pard lingers for a moment, but when I pull out my phone and tune him out, he takes the hint and wanders off.

I use my sad strategy of lingering near the people I hope will notice me. Cannon has chewed me out for doing this, but I can't just walk up to Bryce a second time and say *Hey, got more pics of animals in people's underwear?* Too creepy.

With his arm territorially around Mouse, Franklin tells Kai and Briony that his parents are going to be in Paris next weekend, and he's planning a little get-together.

"Cool, if the timing is right, but I have a robotics tournament next weekend. You know, the kids I'm coaching. It means another long bus ride for me, and I'm not sure when I'm free."

Franklin winks. "You know you can drop that shit now that you're into Yale."

I love the way Kai's face says there's no way in hell he would leave those kids stranded without their mentor, but it's Briony, with a hand on her perfectly shaped hip, who snaps that Kai has his priorities straight when he puts kids first.

Franklin catches me peeking over my phone. He smiles the way a feudal lord must when he sees the peasants toiling over his land, which is kind of what I'd been doing writing his papers for him. "Jeff will come, won't you?"

"Aw, that's sweet," Mouse adds, because everyone knows it's a charity invitation, the way popular kids invite a token social bottom-feeder for the sake of pecking-order diversity.

"Sure." I hate how eager I sound.

Franklin looms over me and then ruffles my hair, and the circle of popular people shifts a little to conditionally include me, talking about me more than to me while I stand by. "There's a party animal hiding inside this guy. Remember our end-of-summer party? Remember how he jumped from the top of the waterslide into the pool? Like, clear over five feet of concrete."

Mouse nods, impressed. "That was a huge jump!"

I'd heard something about me jumping in the pool, but I didn't know heights or concrete were involved. My coffee suddenly feels like it's burning a hole in my gut. I know the layout of that patio, that huge, curling slide and all that space between the ladder and the water.

Franklin's face lights up. "Look, he doesn't remember! You were pretty wasted, dude. It was a great night. You know, it *is* April—I'll have the heat turned back on, so the pool will be warm. You could do it again."

I say "Yeah" and try to wait out this tightness in my throat, this terror clawing its way up, but I can't, so I bow out to go to the bathroom. I'm pathetic, and I'll probably get uninvited from Franklin's party, but I have to get away. Somehow that wasted jump freaks me out, like I'm feeling the fall I can't remember.

I splash water on my face and let the hot air dispenser mess up my hair. When I'm done in the bathroom, Pard's leaning in the grimy McDonald's hallway right by the door. "You okay? I saw you bolt."

A flush from the ladies' room gives me time to debate if and how much to tell him. We must look like sixth graders hanging out by the bathrooms, but it's just us, and I really want to know. "What really happened at Franklin's party?"

A middle-aged woman leaves the bathroom and gives us the stink eye, which Pard returns. "I don't think she washed her hands."

I won't get sidetracked. "What. Happened."

Pard fusses with a belt loop. "Well, you've heard by now. You did things you normally wouldn't do. You must have heard about that jump."

He's skirting around the issue. "How come *you* drove me home? How were we hanging out at all?"

As I lean on the opposite wall, he stares at my shoes, and his face softens into something nostalgic.

It's my feet, the nerdy way I put one sole on the ground and the other foot next to it, touching, but standing on its side. Like one foot wants to hug the other foot.

I put both feet down flat. "So?"

"I jumped into the pool and got you. I was worried you wouldn't come up. You just jumped in and went straight to the bottom." He shakes his head, crosses and uncrosses his arms. "Jeff. You've changed so much since you started hanging out with Cannon. All this partying. And then sinking like that. Just *sinking*."

"Oh." It's an odd feeling, getting called out for changing. It's striking how much Pard has changed—how wild and flirtatious he's become. But Pard's never done anything like jumping wasted into a pool. I've heard of people drowning, surrounded by their drunk friends. He wasn't my friend anymore, yet he probably saved my life. Like he did earlier today with the albuterol. I should thank him. I should admit I've changed, but tell him I want to change back again to what I was, and that I want to find that guy I've missed knowing.

But that all sounds so gay, so I ask instead, "And then what happened?"

He waves a hand irritably. "Then we looked for towels and dried off."

"And then?"

"Then I took you home."

"And that's really it?"

He doesn't answer for a long time. He says, looking everywhere but at me, "There was some vomiting. And . . . you weren't yourself. What's the word? *Uninhibited*."

My heart pounds. I can barely whisper. "What did you do to me?"

His face snaps up, his mouth open. "*To* you? Nothing. You threw yourself at me in Franklin's bathroom. You tasted like puke, and I got you out of there before you did something even more batshit with me or anyone else. You tried something again in the car, and then you passed out cold. So you think I fucking molested you while you were out of commission? That's your high opinion of me?"

He pauses as a mother drags her young son into the bathroom, the child all the while whining, "I don't wanna use the girls' room."

My ears ring with what Pard just told me, while Pard says brightly, for the kid's sake, "Gee, I wish *I* could use the girls' room. It's a heck of a lot cleaner." The mother and boy gape at Pard with wide eyes as they practically rush to the safety of the girls' room.

I wait for the door to close, and then we just stand there, but my thoughts are scattered, unhinged. I imagine him with Greg, with the drama guys. With Parson just this morning. With me. I'm probably the only guy he's ever turned down. For some reason that pisses me off. "I'm sorry, but look. How am I supposed to know what you'd do or wouldn't do? You're so forward, you've become this, I don't know, this majorly flaming extrovert skank. So I thought, maybe . . ."

He mouths *Wow* like I've reached new depths, and he just

197

has to stare at the creature that regretfully can't be flushed down the toilet roaring behind the wall. I kind of cringe that I actually said that. It just came out that way from thinking about that asshole Greg, all that nasty kissing in the hallway.

"It's like you don't even know me, calling me something like that." Pard lets that thought sink in. I'm working up the courage to apologize, because calling a gay guy "flaming" is just wrong, when the door swings open and the lady comes out with her son in tow. Pard lets me have it. "I mean, calling me an extrovert. *Me*. Maybe I'm a healthy introvert, ever think of that? You have everything so backward, it's amazing you can find your own asssaahhh—your own derriere."

He glares at the woman as if it's her fault he said "derriere," not "ass," and he storms off, which is awkward with the woman and kid walking beside him, like they're a weird family. And maybe it's because they're ruining his exit that he spins around to chew me out one more time, right after he insincerely tells the lady to have a nice day.

"You know that story with Zelda and Henry? Doesn't she seem familiar? You've got Cannon pushing your buttons, and you're smiling so hard you don't even know what a tool you are. You just let everything good in your life get slaughtered, because he likes it that way. You suspect the people who really care about you. You *have* changed. To you, everyone's part of some stupid scheme, just like the world Cannon lives in. *I'm* the good guy, Jeff. One day you'll wake up and see you're that damned doll, and when Cannon feels like he needs a new toy to play with and dumps you, you'll come looking for me, for anyone. But then you'll remember that you killed us off long ago."

Then he's gone.

I don't run after him. I'm still on overload just thinking about the things I can't remember but are real just the same. The pool. Coming on to him. I don't know if I'm relieved I can't remember it or not. Of course Pard wouldn't take advantage of me. Why was I worried about that? What's wrong with me? All this time Pard was protecting me from a really embarrassing story. And here I thought he was sex crazed, and I was the one coming on to *him* after puking. Disgusting. He must loathe me. I tasted like *vomit*. After Reiko, it's the second most humiliating thing someone's ever said to me about my cursed attempts at kissing. If I want to *write* about love, fine, but I need to stay away from it in real life.

PARD'S TALE

Back in the bus, Mr. Bailey draws another name: Pard.

Briony smiles like she's sharpening knives. "Good! Now *he* can see how hard it is to tell a story."

"Fine," he snaps. He's still raging mad at me. "My turn. What kind of story do you guys want?"

Reeve blurts out, "Not a gay story! *Puh-leese!*" He holds his clipboard like a shield from gayness.

"Let him tell whatever he wants," Alison counters.

Alison rolls her eyes and smirks at me. I can't believe we're sitting together. It's all thanks to Pard and Rooster's rivalry. Pard asked Alison to sit with him, again, and she agreed, but Rooster convinced Alison that since she'd already sat with Pard, she should sit with me this time to spread the fun.

She agreed. It's like I won the Chair Lottery.

So Alison and I share a seat. Behind us, because Rooster

did this last second and had no strategy, Pard and Rooster sit squished together like the odd couple in so many ways.

"I'm not homophobic like Reeve," Cece says. "But I'm sick of romance. You'd think we have nothing better to think about."

"We don't," Rooster declares. "And I think little Pard here should give us some Harry Potter–Draco Malfoy erotic fan fiction." I wonder if Rooster just wants to remind Alison that Pard is inherently not interested in her.

"Sorry to disappoint, but my story isn't about Harry Potter or being gay. But before I tell it, I'll give you a little personal story. One of my most romantic moments."

He glances at me, but I make myself small and telepathically say, *Don't you dare.* His pause gives me time to worry. He could be thinking of any millions of things we did together before sophomore year, twisted around like we were lovers, not friends.

It would have to be the night Greg took me to prom, just last week.

Okay, then. I'm in the clear. But I'm puzzled how Greg is Pard's Exhibit A for romance. Pard said he was over Greg, which is a good thing. They were gross together. Plus, Greg is the kind of guy who would make his boyfriend show up to every performance of *Oklahoma!* just because he's in it, and then they'd have to analyze all the footage together. Pard doesn't need Greg's narcissistic crap. I'm glad that's over.

201

The best part was getting dressed up and Greg looking so nice on my doorstep and then pulling out of the apartment complex in a limo. And the drive, with the music blaring and the limo packed with all the theater people. But the dinner was boring. Greg and his theater friends talked shop the whole time. Boring. The dance wasn't any better. I wish I didn't suck at dancing, but I do.

"But you're gay," Rooster says, brow furrowed.

Pard stares his signature *asshats surround me* stare. "Sure. Because all gay people can dance. Why are you not valedictorian?"

"But there's your gay walk." Rooster sashays in his seat. "That's kind of like dancing. And you dress gay. Clothes like— what is that? Velvet? Those pants were made for a gay dance fest."

"Hey. Respect the pants," Saga counters. Her fingernail scritch-scratches Pard's thigh, like her shoplifter fingers are feeling the itch of sartorial lust. "I. Want. These. Pants. I'd sleep with you, babe, just to steal your pants off the floor when we were done."

I don't know what's gotten into everyone, but no one can keep their hands off him today.

Pard looks scared Saga will steal his pants while he's still in them, and Bryce laughs nervously and pops his knuckles. Everyone knows Saga is a fiend about clothes and would do anything for a sweet pair of pants.

Pard looks from Bryce to Saga. "You could always just ask to borrow them. But . . . could we all get back to my love story, if you don't mind?"

So, after getting fed up with my uncoordinated moves on the floor, Greg danced with just about everyone but me. I think it was payback for me playing on my phone during dinner.

Alison looks puzzled. "This isn't sounding so romantic."
Pard holds up one finger.

But then I saw someone special hiding by the punch bowl.

Pard doesn't look my way, but I freeze. I know where this is going, and I'm terrified he'll say my name.

We say "hi," which is pretty much the most we ever do, sadly. But then we chat about dancing and being bad at it. It's one of those times you complain about dancing, but you're dreaming he'll ask you to. I don't dare ask him though. I don't dare tell him he looks nice, but he does. No, "nice" isn't the word. He's beautiful, and he doesn't even know it. So very kissable.

Pard flashes me that rare but overpowering look. My belly flip-flops and twists from something so private being spoken aloud. He's bringing up the very word that ruined our friendship three years ago.

It was the August before sophomore year, and I finally told him why she broke up with me. Reiko didn't see me as a boyfriend. She didn't think I was mature. I didn't kiss right—I was too awkward. What do you say when a girl tells you that you can't kiss right?

Pard exploded with righteous anger when I told him this. "Sounds like she can't appreciate a great kiss when she gets one. Jeff, don't make a face. I'm being honest. You're a preeminently kissable boy."

The room was warm, the air was thick, and we were sitting on his bed with his hand on my shoulder and that declaration of my kissability soft on his mouth. That Balrog look on his face— it was like he was trying to look angry at Reiko just to hide what was underneath, but his cover slipped. Or he let it fall.

I stood up and said I wasn't feeling well, said I'd call later. I never went back to his place. I ignored his calls, his texts, and when school started up again, I offered to help Cannon with his English essays (meaning, write them for him) and worked to make a new circle of friends. For a long time, when I saw Pard, I cut to the opposite direction or walked past him like he wasn't there. I never explained, but I'm sure he figured it out.

And now, in revenge, he's messing with me on an all-day bus ride, where I can't run away, where everyone will be his witness. I try to hold on to that word. "Revenge." That's all this is about today.

This is war.

I know from Pard's calculating smile that he can see my guts squirm, but then the smile softens as he retells last week's prom.

I rarely spoke with this boy, but I wondered about him, about kissing him, and wondered if he wondered about me, too.

I roll my eyes. He's laying it on so thick he's lost his power over me—not that he has any, or ever had. I concentrate on his oily hair, his arrogant eyes with the stubby blond lashes. I'm not attracted to this person, and I'm definitely not interested in anyone who would parade my life like this.

He lets out a melodramatic sigh.

Anyhow, he's not into me. He doesn't tell me that I look nice, and I'm sure I don't, but here's the thing: He says he likes my rose. It's not a stupid corsage like everyone else is wearing. This is homegrown—a rose that smells like white peaches, no lie. I say he has to smell it—*has* to—and all I want is to have his face bend down and breathe in the vicinity of my heart.

Of course he won't get anywhere near me. Not even when I lift my lapel off my chest to put some distance between his nose and my body. He starts making excuses, gets ready to back off and find his date, so I unpin the rose to hand it to him. Only, I gouge myself pretty deep, and before I know it, he has my hand tight in his, and he's drawn my fingers to his chest. My blood is on his thumb. We look at each other for a moment, and I'm lost in his gray eyes and whatever is breaking inside them. I wonder if it will finally, finally happen. I'm praying. . . .

Then he apologizes and rushes off. Like he didn't mean to touch me. Like it was all an accident. But it was more than that, right?

So *that's* what all the windup was about: Getting an audience to take his side. Now everyone pitches in and weighs in on a situation they know nothing about. They all agree this is love. The girls are breathless with excitement, and the guys weigh in on the gay-scale.

"So what if the guy's hurt? I wouldn't grab his hand like that," Bryce says.

Rooster scrunches up his face. "Yeah, the whole scene is gay. And I never thought of it, but the word 'lapel' is totally gay."

Pard never mentions that the boy admired the rose only because Pard's mom grew roses, and she's his favorite nonparental adult. Or *was*, I guess. I try not to think of her too much. I mean, I ditched her son, still fragile from the death of his sister, fragile from abandonment by his dad, just all around fragile and brave and deserving. She must hate me so, so much.

"Jeff? What do you think?" Pard asks.

I blink like Marcus. Blink like I can't believe that this is air I'm breathing right now. Pard, in front of everyone, is asking me if my grabbing his hand a week ago meant love, not just the involuntary panic that it was.

He's looking me in the eye, asking me if I love him. If I've ever wanted to kiss him. As if this embarrassing farce would inspire the supposedly closeted gay guy in me to come out. And he claims not to be a theatrical person.

My war face is a mask of indifference. "Sounds like a big deal over nothing." My heart races, but not from love. I'm just so freaked out that he could turn the spotlight on me. Over *this*.

Alison nudges me with her leg. "Oh, come on, Jeff. Be a writer. The story is hot with suppressed love."

She turns to Pard and then asks, "So . . . what happened to the guy?"

Pard tilts his head. He's enjoying this little performance at my expense. "Oh, he threw himself at another guy at the first opportunity."

Who is he even talking about? Cannon? There's nothing going on romantically between Cannon and me. Friends are like that. That's why they're called "friends."

But knowing I won't identify myself as the boy who grabbed his hand in an apparently romantic fashion, Pard has me silenced in the crowd. Pard's not looking at me, but he's letting me get a good look at the annoying as hell, Edward-the-Vampire smirk on his face.

Love him? I want to kill him.

"And that leads me to my story about friendship and heartless betrayal. Ready?"

I am so not ready. But everyone else looks hungry for a story that will be a pack of lies.

Once upon a time there were a few Southwark boys who went to a Halloween party they weren't really invited to. The three boys were in costume, and they went by code names: the Face, the Fist, and the Bard. They were there for business and for pleasure. The pleasure came first, and they separated to find it for themselves. The pleasure was in hanging out with cool kids who couldn't see their awkwardness and their acne, but that pleasure had a distinct ceiling to it. The masks they wore had to stay on, or they'd be back to being social pariahs.

"Sharp teeth in the quiet lakes," Cookie pronounces solemnly. Kai corrects him with an amused smile. "Pariah, not piranha."

Cookie puts his head in Kai's lap, and Briony giggles and then settles on Kai's shoulder. She looks a lot happier sharing Kai with Cookie than she did sharing him with Alison.

At midnight they met upstairs and went as planned into a room all set up for a game of poker. This was the business part of their evening. These three guys worked for . . . we'll call him Pistol. Pistol was not in town, but sent them in his place.

A few people snicker at the name.

Pistol, Cannon. That was obvious. Especially since Pard

used to be Cannon's star poker player freshman year. He played for money and they got into parties that I'd only dreamed of going to. Then he quit.

The other characters were easy to fill in. Clearly I was the Bard. Mace with his frightening acne and powerful build was the Fist. And Pard with his strange yet sweet looks was the Face.

It was a toxic trio that couldn't end well, just like it didn't in real life.

So the three guys took their seats. The card dealer wore a hooded robe. No one could see his face as he dealt out the cards, but no one was paying attention. A couple rounds went by, and Fist impatiently threw down his cards.

"This sucks. Why are we here?"

AN INTERESTING QUESTION.

Fist looked around, like he didn't know that the voice had come from within the dealer's deep cowl. Then the dealer opened his robes and pulled out an hourglass, nearly out of sand.

Bard wondered who this person was. "Do I know you?"

Pinpricks of electric blue light brightened within the cowl.

YOU'D REMEMBER ME IF WE'D MET.

"You're not—

But Face interrupted. "You're not here on Pistol's account, are you?"

Then something weird happened.

Everyone else—poker players, onlookers, that guy who just stepped inside with a beer—all stopped moving. Like time was frozen. Face and Fist looked around and it didn't bother them at all. If anything, they relaxed because they could talk business without any eavesdroppers.

YES. I WAS TOLD YOU YOUNG SHORT-TIMERS WERE SEEKING OUT DEATH. THAT SO?

"Uh . . . ," Bard managed.

Finally, Face clarified. "Not death—*wealth*."

HMM.

The dealer fingered something that flickered in the dim light. Something long and so thin it seemed to slip in and out of this dimension. Bard couldn't make it out, but he sensed on a deep level that it was very, very sharp.

"Pistol said we'd get a tip-off here that would make us rich," Face said.

Fist added in an impatient growl, "So tell us already! You have a lead for us, right?"

The dealer scratched his chin with a skeletal finger. It sounded like fingernails on a chalkboard.

OH YES. A LEAD. FOR DEATH . . . OR WAS IT WEALTH? NO MATTER.

Face and the Fist laughed eagerly, or maybe they were hiding their fear. Bard shivered when the dealer's bony fingers clacked on the table.

"Your name . . . is it Wealth, by chance?" Bard asked hopefully.

210

The dealer's cowl snapped up, which permitted enough light for the boys to see a grin.

CLOSE, BOY. BUT NO BANANA.

"I get it," Mari says. "That's Terry Pratchett's Death. Pard, I'm impressed. Not just because you've actually memorized some of Pratchett's classic lines, but I love the voice you're giving Death."

"Why, thank you." He bows in his seat and glances my way. "I've had good training."

The summer before sophomore year, I read a couple Discworld books to him while he was drawing. I had to share with Pard my semi-obsessive thing for Death as a character. Gaiman has one, Milton has one. Nasty or nice, all the Deaths are awesome, but Pratchett's Death might be my favorite. I know he doesn't really have a voice, but the all-caps font made me put extra energy into how I read his lines—kind of hollow, with cold finality.

Pard was the best audience. He laughed in all the right places and frankly didn't get much drawing done, what with his cheek pillowed on his arm as he lay on his stomach to listen, or him sidled up alongside me to read along silently while I kept reading out loud. When our elbows got sore we would sit against the bed. We spent the whole summer surrounded by paper and barely moving. It was kind of brilliant.

Just hearing him play Death fills me with a dull ache.

"Who would seek out death?" Marcus asks. "It's too implausible."

I roll my eyes as Marcus blinks his.

"What?" Alison asks me softly. "Would *you* risk meeting Death?"

Yes, I would. Maybe not lowercase death, but uppercase Death, absolutely. He knows my sister better than my five-year-old self possibly could have. He's read our lives in his books. I'd have questions for him. Where did Bee go? Was she happy? Can I talk to her—see her? I'd give any amount of wealth to know.

The skeletal dealer gave them their instructions: They would find Death under the oak tree just outside of town. They took shovels from the shed and rode their bikes to the deserted place—remote feeling, yet an easy ride.

They fanned out, dead leaves crunching under their feet. It wasn't long before they found where the earth was loose, freshly covering the treasure chest underneath.

"Told you we'd find wealth—that dude was just trying to scare us," Fist said, tossing his shovel aside.

Fist couldn't lift the chest. Even when all three boys tried together, they still couldn't lift it. The best they could do was open it.

The entire chest was filled with bars of solid gold.

Fist hooted. "We're set for life!"

Face laughed, and he threw his arms around Bard and danced around. Then Fist broke out into song, and Face sang along, arm in arm. Sure, Pistol would take a huge share, but the fortune was so huge, it didn't really matter.

Fist called Pistol to give an update. Pistol said he'd be over with a car, but it would take a few hours.

While they waited, Face went to town to get some beer to celebrate.

Five minutes after he was gone, Pistol called Fist again to give new orders.

"Sure thing . . . Yeah, I understand . . . Sure, here he is."

Fist handed the phone to Bard.

"Hi, buddy," Pistol said. "I hear you have a heap of treasure there."

"Yeah, it's heavier than the chests Bilbo's pony carried."

"What's that?"

Bard cringed. "Nothing. Sorry."

"I'll get right to the point, kid. Face has turned against us. I need you and Fist to dispose of him."

Bard's mouth dropped open. He must have heard wrong. Must have.

"Kid? You there? Don't take it like that. It's just business. Look, just do what Fist says. He'll take on most of the job himself."

Pistol hung up. Fist tried to get his phone back, but Bard's hand was tight around it.

"Pull yourself together—it's no big deal."

"But we're friends!" Bard pleaded.

Fist shrugged. Bard shivered and time slowed down, and sped by.

"I'm back," Face cried cheerfully at his return. His arms were full of bottles. "Tonight's special, so I got champagne."

While Face uncorked the bottles, one for each of them, Fist pulled Bard toward him and whispered a quick plan. Bard was trembling. Could he go through with it?

Yes, he could. Bard wasn't a murderer, but he could help one. All he had to do was stand there with his knees knocking.

Face came up to Bard, a bottle dangling from one hand. "You okay? You look like you've seen a ghost."

Bard just stood there looking wretched. He was the perfect distraction. Face's smile instantly faded. His guard was completely down, and all he wanted to do was comfort his beloved friend.

Bard had the perfect view as Fist came up behind Face and shoved a knife under Face's rib cage. He had the perfect view of Face's expression, turning from concerned to agonized and betrayed.

Lying on the ground, bleeding into the fresh earth, Face opened his lips to mouth Bard's name. But only blood bubbled out.

Bard threw up.

"Idiot!" Fist shouted. "Not on the treasure chest . . . oh, disgusting."

On hands and knees, Bard dry heaved. He felt damned. He looked up miserably at Fist, but Fist's face was illuminated in the harsh blue light of his phone. He was texting the news to

Pistol. Then, for just one moment, Bard's eyes met Fist's, and the light of the phone went out.

"The boss says to finish the job," he told Bard.

Before Bard realized what that meant, Fist yanked back Bard's hair and slit his throat.

At the same time, a sharper blade cut Bard's soul from his body.

Bard took in the sight of his body bleeding next to Face's corpse. He trembled at the horror. Then he saw Death looming quietly beside him. Bard bobbed nervously on the doorstep of his afterlife.

"What's going to happen to me?" Bard asked Death.

WHAT YOU IMAGINE.

"I imagine in the afterlife I'll just do nothing. Be nothing."

THEN THAT.

Bard looked at the blood on Face's mouth. He didn't kill his friend, but he'd stood by and let it happen. He coughed a laugh. "Doing nothing. Pretty much the story of my life, huh?"

FROM WHAT I READ, YES.

Oblivious to Bard's shade and Death's scythe, Fist slaked his thirst on the champagne.

Now that it was time to do nothing, Bard found he couldn't just yet. He pointed at Face. "He's gone already, isn't he? I won't see him again?"

Death's terrifying silence was answer enough.

Bard persisted. He wanted just a few words, a small message from Face, to carry into the afterlife. "Did Face, um, say anything to you? Anything about me, I mean?"

Death pinned Bard with an icy stare.

HE SAID HE WASTED GOOD CHAMPAGNE ON YOU.

"Oh. Yes, I see. I wish . . . I just wish . . ."

Fist started convulsing.

AH. HOLD ON A SEC.

Bard couldn't look away. Fist's pimply face darkened, his hands clawed desperately at his throat, and his bloodshot eyes rolled into his head. After a sweep of Death's scythe, Fist's spirit rose and saw Bard.

Bard scowled. "Thanks for murdering me."

Fist didn't have a trace of guilt on his transparent face, still ruined with acne so severe it looked leprous. "Hey, you should be thanking *me*. A slit throat is much easier than poison. That was rat poison, wasn't it?"

SQUEAK, replied the Death of Rats, who'd apparently hitched a ride with Death.

Fist glared at the robed little rat skeleton adorably bearing a mini-scythe. "Just let me get my hands on that rat—better yet, on Face."

Fist rushed off to murder his murderer, but before he could get very far, he shrank into a blip of light that was soon extinguished. Bard realized he'd be next to disappear, and he didn't want to.

216

"Sir," Bard said, suddenly thinking of Face's last words, or his first post-life words, depending on how you look at the situation. "Was Face also going to poison me?"

WHAT DIFFERENCE WOULD THAT HAVE MADE?

"A huge one." Wouldn't it? Looking at the three dead boys at his feet, Bard wasn't sure.

Death shrugged and went to the bottle that Face dropped when he was stabbed, the one meant for Bard. Skeletal fingers picked up the bottle, still sloshing with champagne, and lifted it just inside Death's cowl. Death's sniff sounded like the universe being ripped in two.

Bard felt his spirit slipping away, but all he wanted was to know. He needed to know whether it made them even, or made Bard guiltier than ever.

"Is it? Is it?" he asked, even as he shrank and faded away, never to know.

Death watched the third spirit's light go out like the two others. His horse, Binky, flubbed his lips in a horsey sigh. It had been no cakewalk traveling the vast distance to reap these three souls.

Death took a swig of excellent champagne (NOT BAD.) and pulled out one last hourglass. It was Pistol's. It had quite a bit of sand left. He'd have all the treasure for himself, just like he'd wanted.

THERE'S NO JUSTICE, he told the Death of Rats. JUST US.

The end.

Pard spares me a glance.

I stare at him like the ghost I am. Doing nothing. Feeling gutted.

"Whoa," says Mari. "Talk about going all *Hamlet* on your cast."

"Yeah," says Alison. "And I thought you were a romantic, Pard. That was just . . . brutal."

His smile is harsh and unhappy, his eyes small and evasive.

"I thought it was pretty good," Lupe says cheerfully. "I like bloody endings." And she nods his way in token of peace.

Franklin adds, "Man, what do you have against Cannon? You make him out like he's in the Mafia."

"And poor Jeff," Alison adds. She pats my cheek, and I feel infantilized.

"Poor Jeff," Pard echoes with a lot less sympathy.

Even though others chime in to put in a good word for me, I can't defend myself. Just like the story, I stand by. I let life happen until the day comes when it will be taken from me. And taken from others, too. Pard's right about all of it.

He called me his "beloved friend"—such an old-fashioned way of putting it—and the phrase leaves me uncertain and confused.

"What about me, the fucking leper?"

"Language!" snaps Reeve, and he's so agitated he flings his arm up, and the clipboard flies and hits the ceiling. Mr. Bailey immediately confiscates the clipboard, and the two of them have a massive argument. Based on the way Reeve screams that it's his property, I don't think he can live without his clipboard.

Meanwhile, Mace leans toward Pard. "What makes me a vicious murderer?"

"My hat," Pard answers.

Mace's nasty smile says it all. I knew their friendship ended this year. I just didn't know how badly it ended.

Everyone from the senior prank at Mr. Bailey's house— everyone except for goody-goody types like Reeve and Parson— glares at Mace. We're all picturing the scene: that two story high, off-white wall decorated with a hodgepodge of silent clocks—not as many as Pinocchio's father had in the Disney movie, but quite a few of them, all kinds from cheap to fancy. And way beyond our reach was Pard's hat, with a hole punched through it, perched on a cuckoo clock. Besides being an expert back rubber, Mace was apparently a Frisbee god, or just lucky, if that was his intention.

It was mean ruining the hat, but more to the point—it was like leaving Mr. Bailey a note saying we'd been there. Drunk people tried blowing all at the same time to see if the hat would dislodge and float down. Rooster wanted to throw stuff at the clock to get it down, but that would risk breaking the clocks, so we left it there. A bunch of us got interrogated, but only Pard did detention.

"You dick," Frye says to Mace after a pause. "You said *I* did it. People gave me shit for it. You made me pay you forty bucks to help dispel the rumors. And now we know, don't we?"

"Dude," Rooster says to Mace. "Why?"

Mace just smiles like a creep.

"I hate everything about that night," Pard says, glaring at Mace but then oddly glancing my way. "Doing detention for the trashing of my own hat got me thinking. I deserve to know what Cannon's part is in all of this."

"What?" My mouth drops open, and my eyes cut to Mr. Bailey to make sure he's still lecturing Reeve that it's unsafe to let him have the clipboard after flinging it like that. "Franklin's right—you are so anti-Cannon you don't see straight. Cannon had nothing to do with senior prank, let alone your stupid hat."

"No? Then what were *you* doing in Mr. Bailey's study? Remember? We all started shouting and tried to figure out how to get down the damn hat. But you weren't around for a bit. So what gives? Were you helping Mace, or did Cannon give you a different project?"

I'm shaking my head at this freak coincidence. "Neither. I just needed some air."

Pard curls his lip. "Inside his office? That's where all the best fresh air is, right?"

Now, people look at me like I'm somehow a part of Mace's nasty joke or something even shadier.

I can't tell them I was helping Cannon rig the grade book on the cloud. Mr. Bailey only seemed to access the cloud from his home computer, not the teacher's lounge, so it had to be done. It was wrong hacking a computer in a teacher's own house, but it had nothing to do with Pard, and it wasn't hurting anyone, doing it.

But then I have one more sick thought. When Cannon dropped me off at Mr. Bailey's house, Reiko, Lupe, and Marcus were already there, and Cannon quickly led us all to the back door. Reiko commented it seemed like he'd done this before, and he flashed her a wolfish grin. It took only a couple minutes for him to bust the lock. He'd brought several tools, but in the end he simply wiggled a credit card in the crack and coaxed the cheap lock to give way. "Never underestimate the power of plastic," Lupe quipped. By then a couple other people had showed up, and everyone piled in. But not Cannon—he had someone to meet, another scheme. I shut the door but then remembered I needed to ask him about some arrangements for prom. I popped open the door in time to see him picking up a small package hidden behind a potted plant. Our eyes met. For a moment we just looked at each other. He winked, his face reassuring, and instead of asking him why he was taking Mr. Bailey's delivery, I let it be.

I hoped he was just pranking Mr. Bailey and would soon return whatever it was. That's what I told myself.

I want to unravel the whole convoluted story. But everyone is looking at me with those suspicious eyes.

"I didn't do anything," I say.

Pard sighs, his mouth dragging at one corner. "You never do."

"Please!" Reeve begs, and with a sigh Mr. Bailey hands back the clipboard. There's something naked about the way Reeve clutches it to his chest and faces forward, just to be alone for a moment.

Distracted by Reeve and still worried about my role in the prank, I've forgotten all about Mace by the time Mr. Bailey draws Frye's name. But Frye hasn't forgotten, not by a long shot.

"I am *so* ready." He narrows his eyes and launches right into his story, like he can't take down Mace fast enough.

So Mace used to work at McDonald's. You could see him there in the back, all zitty and scaly faced, with his eyebrow flakes falling on the fries, and when people noticed, he said it was just salt.

"Frye, this isn't appropriate," Mr. Bailey warns in that feeble-teacher way of his.

"No worries," Mace says with that deep voice. "My turn will be next. He'll pay."

"*I'll* pay?" Frye shakes his head like he can't believe it. "Dude, you owe me forty bucks."

So, eventually, after a health inspection, Mace was personally declared an infestation and fired.

After Mace's first and only attempt at honest labor, he went into a life of crime. Turns out if he got into people's faces, they were so freaked out by the skin peeling off him and the zits that they were all too willing to pay Mace to go away. So he made a small business of getting lunch money from kids. Later on he learned to see weaknesses and exploit them. He'd find rich geeks and pretend they were trying to steal Cannon's business, and the geeks would pay Mace to make the accusation go away. Cannon tolerated him and occasionally gave him real jobs, mostly ones to suit Mace's increasingly violent, scheming nature.

To branch out, Mace looked for loner girls and picked on their dress code violations. Their skirts were too short? Midriffs were showing? Mace was right on them, asking if they wanted to pay him to keep his mouth shut. They were so creeped out, they paid. Not that he wanted to be paid in money, but most of the girls didn't let him get physical.

"Ew!" Briony shrieks, and there's a whoosh of angry whispers from the girls.

Frye's smile is wicked. It's kind of bizarre, because Frye is the school moocher, and he's received piles of cash from Franklin and others all the time, and he's cool with it. But being conned out of forty bucks brings out all Frye's fury.

Mace sits back with his arms crossed and waits. Deadpan, scaly, and pimply, he looks terrifying. I wonder if Frye is just being vindictive, or if Mace really did become a sort of blackmailer and henchman or worked with Cannon. Mace's sister probably did help Cannon meet some people, but I've never seen Cannon and Mace hang out.

So, one day, Mace sees a new guy at school, but this one doesn't look like an easy target. Maybe it was the knowing look on his face, but there was something a little scary about him, and Mace doesn't scare easily—I mean, he looks into a mirror every morning, for crying out loud. But this is different.

"Hey, you, in the green . . . what up?" He sits down with the guy at lunch to figure him out.

Just then one of Mace's victims approaches their table, slips Mace a five, and scuttles away, like he does every week.

Green asks, "What was that about?"

What is Mace supposed to say? It's kind of embarrassing to say he bullies kids with invented, trumped-up charges just to squeeze cash out of them. But then he kind of confesses it, and Green acts like this is great news.

"Cool. If you want to make some real money, let me know."

Mace lifts a flaky eyebrow. "Meaning?"

The new guy smiles. "I was pretty good at milking the kids at my old town." After Mace says he's interested, Green offers to work together. "I'm new, and you can help me find the right people to extort. We'll split whatever profit we make. How's that?"

"Sure. If you're as good as you say you are."

"'Good' isn't an adequate word." Green smiles pleasantly. "I'm a *fiend*."

"A what?"

Green laughs. "A fiend, a demon. A devil. Whatever you call them nowadays. I'm not joking."

"I thought this was a realistic story. You can't have a devil at a regular high school," Marcus says.

"Yes, you can!" Sophie blurts. She flinches, like she's surprised she spoke out.

"She's right, I'm afraid," Parson adds, very seriously, and Marcus and Sophie look worried a sermon will follow any second now.

Sophie turns to Frye with her cute fangirl eyes. "Please go on—I love paranormal."

Frye laughs, and for a moment his face captures his flirtatious personality. But only for a moment. "Glad you do, but I'm not sure Mace does—do you, Mace?"

Mace very calmly cracks his knuckles in response.

225

Mace glares at the new guy, who comes across as some kind of Satanist weirdo or a prankster. "Yeah, sure. A devil."

"Think I'm lying? Look me in the eye and say that."

Mace takes a chance and looks into Green's eyes. There's something off about them, though he can't say what. But he cannot pull his eyes away. And then the whispers start in his head. Whatever they are saying, the whispering voices are downright freaky. They're asking for something. Demanding something. His soul, maybe? Mace senses that all he has to do is speak the words, offering his soul, and demons will rush him down to Hell.

Green laughs, and Mace finds himself released from the freaky whispers. "Are we done with the skepticism?"

"*Whoa.*" Mace shakes himself but recovers quickly. "Okay, I believe you. But now that I know, I don't see the point in partnering. You want souls, right? I want money, cars, girls, stuff. Not the same."

Green absentmindedly traces a pentagram on the table with orange juice. "Actually, I get tons of that stuff. When mortals call on the Devil's name and curse their pet parakeet to Hell, guess what happens down there?"

"You get pet parakeets?"

The demon laughs with an embarrassed frown. "Yup. I'd rather *you* get the parakeets . . . and the gold, jewels, and so on. So, you get the stuff, and I get the souls. Deal?"

Mace smiles at this windfall. "Yeah. Partner."

A normal person wouldn't jump at a pact with a devil, but

226

Mace is all over it. The school is his oyster now. Even Cannon will have to bow down to him. No more Mr. Loser Scabface for Mace. He'll get money. Hell, he'll get laid. His lonely balls have always wondered what that would be like.

There's laughter all around at Mace's expense. I join the laughter, but as a pathetic virgin, I feel like a hypocrite.

"Hey, all," Parson says. "There's no need to laugh at our brother. I think every guy must wonder what it's like to be with a woman. I do."

That's Parson for you: Jesus shirt, virgin guy. Up-front and smiley about it.

"Parson, I'm shocked," Alison says, all mischievous. "Are you saying that even *you* sometimes have sinful thoughts?"

Parson's face goes beet red. Characters in books always blush, but Parson's skin really changes from pale pink to deep red. It's kind of charming. He finally manages to say, "All young people think about . . . about sex. I just won't act on my impulses until marriage."

"Dude," Rooster says, "you are missing out."

Cece leans an elbow on the row in front of her so that her armpit shows. "I hope you aren't one of those guys who insist on your wife's virginity—you know, so you're the only one to 'show her a man's touch.' Yikes. That's a major red flag for a woman."

Parson's deep red blush has traveled all the way down his neck, so that his skin is darker than the pink Jesus shirt. He mumbles that he only wants to offer his future wife his full self and know no other touch but hers.

227

"Oh, leave him alone, everyone!" Pard's eyes shine tenderly like he's ready to nuzzle that Jesus shirt. "Parson, just be yourself and don't listen to these heathens. You're going to have a *great* wedding night, and I hope you'll invite me to the ceremony."

Parson beams with a sweet *God bless you* smile that seems blissfully unaware that Pard's brotherly love might go a little deeper than Parson expects.

"Okay, guys, the difference here is Parson *wants* to keep his virginity," Frye says, "and we can respect that choice. It's different if you want to lose it but can't find anyone to help you out with that." He grins as he continues his tale.

After school Mace and Green meet up to do their first job.

"Watch this," Mace tells him.

Then Mace taps Marcus on the shoulder in the parking lot. "Hey, we need a ride."

Marcus spins around, terrified that Mace will threaten or rob him and unsure who Green is, but Marcus can't say *no* out there in the quiet lot. He shrugs. "Sure, but can we stay in the downtown area? I have violin rehearsal at four."

"Oooh," Mace says, "we wouldn't want you to miss *that*."

"It's a *cello*," Marcus says, blinking with shock that Frye can't tell the difference.

Frye shrugs and continues.

They all get in Marcus's car.

Marcus drives them around for a couple miles, when his old Focus dies. So he gets out, pops the hood, but still can't figure out the problem. He knows one thing for certain though: His famous violin—cello—teacher isn't going to be happy about being stood up because of his lemon of a car.

"Dammit! To hell with this piece of crap!"

Mace gives Green a look, expecting the car to literally go to Hell or come into Green's own possession somehow. But nothing happens. Marcus ramps up to the F-word, and that's about it.

This devil was either deaf or a slacker.

"So, why isn't anything happening?" Mace says under his breath while Marcus looks under the hood.

Green smiles and shakes his head. "He didn't mean it, right? I can't take it unless he really means it. Regulations from Our Enemy Above require intention *and* the verbal go-ahead to get through customs. It's too bad, because otherwise everyone and everything would have already been in Hell ages ago. Alas, my hands are tied."

Even as Green makes a gesture of bound hands, the car splutters to life again. Green doesn't look surprised.

"Oh yes!" Marcus pumps his fist like a seventh grader. "I love you, Socrates!"

Green cocks his eyebrow. "You named your car Socrates?" He laughs. "Socrates isn't offing himself today, I guess."

Marcus smiles for the first time since Mace barged in on his afternoon. "You know about Socrates's death by poison? He wasn't offing himself because he *wanted* to, you know."

"Really? How interesting," Green says, his wide smile very, very knowing. Like he'd been there.

Mace gives Green a sour look for not showing off his powers and getting Marcus's car, lemon or not, but the devil stretches his arms comfortably. "We have all the time in the world. No rush."

"Is your car really named Socrates?" Kai asks.

Marcus chuckles, nerd style. "Yeah. But that's nothing. I named my Betta fish Diogenes . . . you know, the oft-naked philosopher who lived in a barrel? So we have a barrel in the fish tank, and Diogenes actually hangs out in it. It's hilarious." And he chuckles again, blinking with pleasure with those thick black lashes, and it's all so over-the-top nerdtastic and sweet that I kind of adore him and want to meet his fish.

So Mace is dead-set on trying something again. He's seen Green in action and knows that the car breaking down and coming back is all Green's doing. It just didn't work out that they could take Marcus's stuff.

Mace has a new idea.

He takes the devil to the library. "There's always a wuss to pick on in here."

Green pauses before a shelf and appreciatively touches the books' spines the way a harpist strokes the strings. "I wouldn't mind some of these going to Hell, frankly."

"You can have all of the books you want. Just sucker some wallets from the students here, and I'll be impressed."

Green's face fills with longing. "You could help me curse these books to Hell, you know."

Mace cranes his neck, looking for someone to extort. "Forget it. We're here to get some work done, Green. Maybe for every ten wallets you get me, I can reward you with a book. If that's your thing."

"That would be very nice," Green says with a slight bow, eyes narrowed to slits.

Mace finally finds what he's looking for. "Watch how *I* work this time. Learn something." And he strides to his target.

Sophie is sitting alone, reading.

"Me?" Sophie gasps, horrified.

"Sorry, do you mind?" Frye smiles. "It's a good part."

She squirms, and when she speaks, her voice is quiet. "I'd rather not. Couldn't you cast Mari instead?"

Frye shakes his head. "Not really. Mari would just give Mace a piece of her mind. You're a more interesting heroine because you're the type who wants to cave, but then you'll fight back. It'll be cool." He pauses. "Okay?" His voice is a soft caress. There's a reason he's slept with half the school and convinces people to give him lunch money, rides, funds for double dates, you name it, all the time.

Sophie turns to Mari, but Mari doesn't give her friend any easy outs. She shrugs. "Sounds good to me."

Mari reminds me just a little bit of Cannon. Not Pard's Cannon, but *my* Cannon. The guy sophomore year who pushed me into Franklin's living room when I was hiding in the front room with all the coats. The one who pointed out some girls from a different high school and said, very casually, "See those two girls? We're going to have a beer with them." And then we did. Yes, he lives for schemes, but I'm more than a scheme to him. I am. Even his plans this weekend point to wanting to help me out. Mostly.

Green tips his head to read the spine of Sophie's book. Clearly surprised and delighted, he puts a hand over his mouth. "I'm flattered by your reading material."

She is reading—

"Sophie, what are you reading in the story? I need something that makes the devil a kind of hero. Like fallen, but misunderstood."

Sophie nods. "Easy. *Paradise Lost.*"

My jaw drops. She read *Paradise Lost?* Why are we not

232

friends? Why didn't I take *her* to prom last week instead of that junior Kaitlyn Rush? We could have talked about devils and Death, and the evening wouldn't have been so painfully awkward.

"Is that Shakespeare?" Frye asks.

"Milton?" She sounds shy, correcting him with a question in her voice, like she wants to sound unsure so he won't feel stupid for not knowing.

After Sophie picks up a pencil she's dropped, she notices Mace leering at her. He holds out his phone. "That was a great view down your shirt. So should I post this pic of you online, or do you want to give me forty bucks?"

Sophie's heart pounds. "What? Please don't. But I don't have any money."

"Sure. Right." His thumbs run all over the phone.

"Hey, please! Stop!" Her eyes fill with tears.

"Last chance!" Mace sings.

"I only have enough change for the bus home. Please, Mace!"

Mace laughs and works his phone. "Three, two, one . . . uploaded." He scratches his chin carefully, so as not to make his pimples bleed, then snags her bag. "So what *have* you got in that purse?"

"Hey, give that back!"

But she doesn't jump up and grab it. She's scared.

Green has been sitting next to her this whole time, looking admiringly at her copy of *Paradise Lost*. He says to her, very softly, so Mace doesn't overhear, "Do you want him to go to Heaven?"

Sophie glares at Green like he's crazy. "Um. Nooo . . ."

"If not Heaven, then where would you like him to go?"

"Huh?"

Their eyes meet. Eyes pleading, Green doesn't inflict demonic whispers on Sophie, but she shivers, sensing something about him. "Humor me. I need you to say it. I know you feel it, deep down."

Meanwhile, Mace dumps out Sophie's purse and paws through her makeup. He acts out the revolting seventh-grade bully tactic of waving her tampon in her face and laughing about it.

Then Sophie finally snaps. "Go to Hell, Mace! Go to Hell and take that tampon with you!"

"I owe you one," Green says, giving her a quick kiss on the forehead.

Mace is so clueless, he doesn't fully understand. Not until that cheap library carpet rips in two and reveals a hole straight to Hell. The devil, now bat winged and leathery skinned, takes zit-faced Mace in his talons and flies him down, down, down. And the tampon comes too, as promised. The end!

Reiko pulls Frye down for a kiss, while Rooster loudly sings, "And the tampon goes to Hell!"

MACE'S TALE

Frye levels his confident gaze to Mace as the laughter dies down, like he's got Mace where he wants him.

Meanwhile, the backs of Mace's fingers absentmindedly stroke his cheek—gently, on account of his acne. I guess he's feeling the uneven stubble, since shaving over his cratered skin is almost impossible. Even if he is a jerk for wrecking Pard's hat, I can't hate him. There's something too vulnerable about seeing him touch his own face. I wonder if he even knows what it's like to be touched by another person there, even once.

Frye makes a big show of stroking his own cheek, and Mace puts his hand down fast.

But Mace doesn't whine like Reeve or even threaten like Pard. "You forgot the epilogue." And he dives right in.

Sophie had a special friendship with Green. And Green owed her. So she summoned him one night, when her parents were out of town.

Sophie looks completely freaked out about where this is headed. Frye is one thing, Mace a whole different species.

"Watch it, Mace," Mari growls. "My story's coming up too."

Mace doesn't smile, or reassure the girls, or even look at them. He's got his dark eyes on Frye, who's mock-stroking his face again, like a matador taunting a very deadpan bull.

"You're really here," Sophie said, a little breathless. Green wore one of his most pleasing human shapes.

He sat on the couch next to her. "Of course. What do you need?"

Sophie touched Green's wrist. "It's about Frye. He's missing. Do you know what happened to him?"

"I know exactly where he is." Green laughed bitterly.

Sophie gripped him even harder. "Where?"

Green hesitated. "You really don't want to know, especially if you're one of his conquests. Are you?"

Sophie cleared her throat. She had a crush on him, yes, but he was working a long list of girls and hadn't gotten to her yet. "Um, no, we've never dated."

"Well, where he is, his days playing the field are over."

Sophie trembled. "He's in Hell?"

Green looked everywhere but at her. "Yes. He's here. With me."

This answer made no sense. If Frye was with Green, he

couldn't be in Hell at the same time. And if he was with Green, where was he?

"Well . . . can I see him?"

"Not a good idea," he said flatly. "Please. Ask me for anything else."

But Sophie still had her crush on Frye. She had to see him.

"I do owe you one thing, but this . . . I can't show you here. It's too exposed. Let's go to your bedroom."

Green looked around wildly at the pink bedroom, like he was trying to figure out how to reveal Frye properly.

"Listen. You know I don't have a real human body, right?" She nodded. "So, he's inside me. I can bring him out, though, for a minute. It'll look mind-bending for a human to see. Do you want to wait outside or stay as I retrieve him?"

Sophie paused to think it over, but finally she said, "I'll stay."

He gave a quick nod.

Then he took off all his clothes. Sophie had never seen a guy naked before, so she just stared. Green had chosen a very pleasing shape.

He smiled. "You sure you want to see Frye? We could just hang out instead."

Unable to speak, she shook her head. She needed to know the truth.

"All right. But don't say I didn't warn you."

He flopped onto her bed, facedown, with a pillow shoved under his stomach. And then things got really weird.

Green writhed a little, and then he farted with barely a sound, but Sophie could see the gassy cloud coming out of him. It had substance to it, jiggling and alive. The cloud quickly stretched over six feet, growing scrawny limbs and a long chicken neck. It had little wings that helped it to flit about like a butterfly. Or a virus.

Sophie felt a scream in her throat. She recognized the freshly hatched thing.

"Frye?"

The creature smiled at her flirtatiously and opened his arms for an embrace. Sophie stepped back.

Green looked over his shoulder and rose from the bed. Frye floated to the opposite side of the room, clearly not keen on being near his captor. "That's him. A real pain in the ass. But it's symbiotic. He gets a little place to live, and I get his soul, which helps me digest the other souls that pass on through my bowels. Sorry if the sight is a bit much. Have you had enough of him?"

Watching Frye repeatedly wink at her, Sophie said she'd had enough.

"Right, then. I guess I better head out." Still naked, he put his back to Frye and his hands on his knees, like an athlete at rest. Then he whistled, and Frye, after blowing a good-bye kiss, zipped back right where he came from. With a farewell and a quick snatching of the clothes on the bed, the demon was gone, with nothing remaining but a strong whiff of Frye.

And *that* is how Frye's story really ends.

"Eww," Briony says, and Mouse and Saga scrunch their faces in disgust.

"Some surprising slapstick, but not as developed as it could have been," Mari pronounces. "I do like this demon stuff, though." Sophie nods.

But Mace isn't looking at them. He's looking at Frye with a hint of a smile at one corner of his mouth.

Frye isn't a deadpan sort of person. He's sneering and barely containing himself. He gives Mace the finger. "Your story matches your face. It's a mess."

Mace gives his dark, unflappable stare. "That was just an epilogue for *your* story. Now for *my* story," and he begins.

Frye's summer job was working at Massage Splendor.

Frye thought it would be this dream job where he'd get to rub down hot girls, but in reality he was working the backs of women his mother's age. The only good part was that he got decent tips from some of them. Some, but not all. You'd think rubbing down a whiny sixty-four-year-old grandma for an hour would get you at least ten bucks, but those ladies seemingly grew up in the Depression. They'd tip two bucks, like he'd just brought around their vintage Lincoln Town Car.

He'd vent online. He had to be clever about sneaking pics of the old hags—facedown, gray or brightly dyed hair puffed like a growth from the face pillow—but the images really drove home his point that ugly people needed to tip properly.

And then, one day, this super old guy comes in. Like, eighty years old.

"Bet you're used to pretty women and not some geezer like me," said the old dude.

If this dude only knew how bleak Frye's job was.

But it was about to get bleaker.

"You're no geezer," Frye said, but his voice was fake, and as they shook hands, all Frye could stare at were the tuffs of hair exploding from the guy's collar. This geezer—Tom, we'll call him—was a wolfman. It was going to be like rubbing down a giant, wrinkled old rat.

In fact, it was worse than that.

Tom had so much curly gray hair that Frye got the willies when his fingers made contact. He put on extra lotion, braced himself, and went for it. The dampened hairs were practically glued to the guy's body fat. At one point Frye's fingers got tangled in them.

"Ouch!" Tom yapped.

Frye carefully extracted his fingers from the gray tangles of back hair. "Sorry."

"I guess I have a lot of hair there."

Frye didn't respond.

"Too much testosterone, maybe," the man said, his love handles jiggling with a deep laugh.

Frye wondered if testosterone also gave a guy moles, because Tom had plenty of those, too.

When it was time for the guy to roll over, faceup, Frye realized what the dude really meant by having too much testosterone. There was total tent action.

"Nasty," Saga says.

The effect was subtle, because of Tom's big belly, but still.

Frye quickly finished massaging Tom's neck and age-spotted scalp and said that the time was up. He got the dude the complimentary cup of water and handed it to him once Tom was presentable.

"That was a great massage. Thanks!" Tom waved good-bye and headed to the register.

Frye just nodded and went in to strip the bed, and when he did, he found two twenty-dollar bills on the bed.

What a tip! The money changed things. That dude could set up enough tents for a Boy Scout camp, if that's what he wanted.

Frye was thrilled when the guy started coming in weekly. He came in for lower back pain but also, it seemed, for companionship. Besides snarling his fingers in back hair, working his way carefully over the minefield of moles, and dodging flagpoles, Frye thought it was worth it. Forty dollars, every time. The old fart was loaded, in every sense of the word. Or maybe Tom just didn't realize that no one else tipped this high.

Mouse has been squirming wildly during the back-hair episode, the way people do during a horror movie. Now she cuts in. "He has to stop seeing Tom. It's too gross."

Mace lifts a scaly eyebrow.

"How do you know so much about massage parlors anyhow?" Briony asks, all suspicious, like it's impossible to imagine people letting Mace massage them.

Mace shrugs and doesn't mention what I've just remembered from freshman year—that his older sister, Melanie, was planning to work as a massage therapist to help pay for college. I knew her during her senior year. She was sweet, almost painfully nice. Melanie had Mace's acne, but she caked on makeup to try to hide the damage. That spring Mace bragged about all the colleges she got into, including Georgetown. The bragging was oddly affectionate of him, since he didn't seem to otherwise care about school. I guess she must have gotten that job, and now that I think about that back rub during my asthma attack, I'm pretty sure Mace knows a lot about massage. More than Frye does, with his YouTube videos.

Let's get on to the good part. Frye was having a blast posting online about the old guy and all his other hideous clients, and he was making good money.

But one day Tom seemed unwell. Tired.

"You okay?" Frye asked.

"Ah, it's just old age," Tom explained.

Frye finished working Tom's lower back. It was time to do his glutes—not the most fun. Granted, Tom's ass was covered in a blanket, and he was wearing underwear, but, no matter how you cut it, Frye was still working an old man's ass.

"I'll move on from this life, soon," Tom continued.

"I'm sure you have a lot of life left in you yet," Frye said, just to pass the moment. It was creepy, squeezing a guy's ass while he talked about his upcoming death. Not your typical heart-to-heart.

Tom sighed. "I'm not long for this world, sadly. But these massages have been a real gift, and not only for the relief from pain. I feel like you've helped ease me toward my next life, what with your gentle hands and gentle words. Frye, I'm truly thankful."

"It's my pleasure to help in any way I can, Tom. You know that." *Squeeze, squeeze. Squish, squish.*

"I'd like to give you something from my estate to remember me by, when I'm gone."

Frye froze mid-squeeze. This—this was the opportunity he'd been waiting for. Get the old man's fortune and live the good life. Oh yes.

"I'm . . . wow, sir. I'm amazed you'd be so generous to think of me. What with me saving up for college and all . . ."

"Let me think of how to do this," Tom said. "I have lots of scheming relatives after my money. I don't know if I can—or should—put you in my will officially. They might find a way to write you off. Maybe I should bring you something of value off the books. Something for your college funds. And it will be fun outsmarting my heirs."

Tom laughed. Frye didn't know if he should laugh too. It seemed greedy somehow. So he just said, "Thanks," and worked that guy's glutes like never before. Tom's butt cheeks were like two fluffy clouds by the end of the session.

Finally, on the fateful day, when Tom had promised to bring the gift, Frye was jumpy. How much would Tom bring?

When Tom appeared for his appointment, he didn't let on that anything was different, and yet, everything went differently that day.

For one thing, Tom wanted to start by lying on his back. He kept his eyes open and studied Frye's face. "I must be your ugliest client."

Frye smiled as he shook his head. "No way," he lied. "You're the handsomest dude here."

Tom smiled innocently and puffed out his chest from the blanket as if to show off that bear-rug mat of gray chest hairs. "Really?"

"Really."

"Thanks. That means a lot to me." Tom rolled over onto his stomach. "Legs first, then feet, okay?"

"So many changes to our routine," Frye ventured, working up from the calves to the man's thighs.

"True . . . might mean something big is happening, you think?" Tom lifted his face from the doughnut face pillow and winked. "And don't forget my toes," Tom added. "I love how you do my toes."

Frye did his toes.

As Frye worked on Tom's back, he couldn't help but sigh. Maybe nothing would happen today.

With his head down in the pillow, Tom chuckled. "I heard that! Poor boy, you have nothing to worry about. You'll get your little gift from me. I feel jazzed just thinking about it!"

That got Frye's heart pumping. He finished Tom's shoulders and then went down, down, down. Finally, he got to where Tom's elastic waistband should be. This is normally where he'd straighten the blanket and do the glutes.

Only, Tom wasn't wearing any underwear, it seemed.

"Another change to schedule," Tom said, facedown, but Frye could hear him grinning.

For a moment Frye was freaked. Was Tom going to proposition him, like he was a male prostitute or something? Could he go through with it? How much money were they talking about here?

But, instead, Tom yawned. Sometimes he fell asleep in sessions. So he probably didn't want to have sex, Frye reasoned, or he wouldn't be on the verge of conking out.

245

Tom sighed and said sleepily, "I hid the jewel."

Frye's mouth went dry. "Jewel?"

"My scheming family is keeping my money out of my reach, even searched my clothes. Heh, I outsmarted them! I stuck the jewel right where the sun don't shine, and it's all yours. . . ."

Oh. So the old geezer had shoved a gemstone up his ass. Brilliant.

"Why don't you extract it, and we'll take it from there?" Frye offered.

But Tom was fast asleep. "Tom," Frye whispered urgently. "Tom!"

He was out cold.

Frye pulled the blanket down, farther and farther. Tom really was stark naked. And there was his ass. The crack boasted as many snarly gray hairs as his upper back. And beyond that forest, nestled away, lay the object of Frye's desire.

"Oh my God," he whispered, because he knew he was going to do it.

He looked at the door—closed, not locked, because locks gave a massage parlor a red-light feel. This wouldn't take as long as a hookup, though; it would be a faster in and out. He'd have to be gentle. Wouldn't want the old man to bleed. Wouldn't want him to wake up terrorized that fingers were prying a stone from his ass either.

So Frye lubed up with lotion, which he hoped could be applied internally. Then he parted the gray forest and launched himself up the cleft, all the way to Tom's inner sanctum.

He felt around inside. Was that the stone? There was something . . .

Then the most nuclear fart erupted from Tom's ass, knocking Frye off the table, where he'd been perched like an ass-pecking vulture. The fart was so loud, all the other massage therapists heard the thunder and felt the walls vibrate. But the sound didn't hold a candle to the smell of all that gas. Frye's nasal passages were permanently scarred from the burns.

"Oh ho ho!" laughed Tom, not asleep at all. "I knew you'd prod an old man's hairy ass if it meant money. Oh ho ho!"

Frye gaped, holding his polluted right hand away from him.

"You're a real sicko. I'm calling the cops."

"Call away!" the old man cackled. "You're the one who groped my anus! And I can't wait to show the cops all your posts online. You don't think that's a crime? You're going to be one of the most hated people alive when your story goes viral!"

"You're totally crazy. What do you care what I post? It's my life."

"It's my life too. My wife was one of your victims. So I thought I'd teach you a lesson. Oh ho ho!"

And after that session, when Tom tipped him forty bucks, Frye took it in his *left* hand.

And that is the fucking end.

"Wow," says Frye. "Give Mace a mic, and this is what happens. Seriously."

Briony rolls her eyes. "Now I can never get a massage without thinking about this horror story."

The other girls emphatically agree, except for Cece, who thinks Tom was justified in avenging his wife. "The stories really go together. I think the idea is that Mace and Frye are not all that different."

Everyone pretty much tells Cece she's wrong.

Meanwhile, I'm staring at this guy in all black—this guy who ate lunch with me at the loner-solidarity table, never to become a real friend. He was always a scary mystery, with that joyless face and that mean body. And now it's like, *mystery solved?* There he sits with his skull rings and his metal tattoos half visible on his biceps and chains gleaming about his black clothes, and it's just weird, because under that pimpled, scaly, tough exterior, there's a guy who can give a nice back rub if you really need it, and who thinks a lot, a very lot, about butts and farts.

BRYCE'S TALE

"And now for something completely different," Bryce says when he's called on. "I've had enough of demons and farts."

Saga flips her hair from her face. "Thank. God."

Okay. So this story is also about an old guy. No farting, promise.

The old guy is Jan Uriah Wagger, and he's this octogenarian rich dude in New York who has played the field his whole life and finally decides he'll settle down with a wife, mostly so they can have a kid to inherit all his wealth. But hey, if he's going to get a wife, she may as well be hot. So he thumbs through Tinder and all his other social feeds looking for the right chick.

And he finds just the one: Maya. She's gorgeous, and he researches her background and sees she's had nursing experience. He thinks that's perfect because, at his age, it's nice to have a wife who can tend to his sex needs *and* make sure his stools are healthy.

Private detectives confirm she is, indeed, a hottie and has worked at a nursing home for three years. She's twenty-three years old.

Wagger is ready to offer marriage. Maya accepts, prenups are signed, and after a massive wedding and reception, the wedding night arrives.

Wagger has jacked up on Viagra and all these Chinese herbal remedies like ground-up rhino horn, but it doesn't make much difference. Maya finds herself under this soft old guy who can't do it, though he's panting and growling and clawing her with his old man nails. She stares at the loose skin on his neck, rough with white stubble, as he crows with lust, and she endures what he manages to perform on her. Luckily, he sleeps like a log after.

After the honeymoon in Paris, she returns to Jan's modest fifty-five-hundred-square-foot penthouse apartment.

"Welcome home, sir." Wagger's manservant, young Damian, holds a tray with two champagne glasses. Maya notices Damian blush when he sees her.

"Excellent," Wagger says, draining his glass. "Now, boy, go make us a snack while I give my bride a tour of my little home in the city." Wagger's apartment has been featured in every architectural magazine, but it's the urban garden on the roof that is his real pride and joy.

He has an elevator that leads up to the roof, and only he

has the key to activate the elevator. When the doors open, Maya gasps. She's standing in a garden with vegetable patches, a fruit tree orchard, and, under the boughs of trees, a shady bed of thick moss, sculpted as a reclining love seat, rimmed with soft ferns.

"It's so enchanting!" Maya sighs, then sees her husband unbuttoning his shirt and pants. "Wha—what are you doing? We can't do it here!"

He chuckles as he undoes his fly. "Of course we can! You are Eve, and I am Adam, and no one can view us in our little Eden. Did you know there's a quaint place in the English country-side called Fockynggrove? I won't translate that for you, but I thought, why not have my very own love grove, right here in Manhattan? I designed it for privacy from the other high-rises, and I'm the only one with the key to our private elevator, so no one can come up unless I permit it. So, what are we waiting for?"

During the warm weather, they spend loads of time in Wagger's garden.

Meanwhile, Maya notices a change in the manservant. Damian once had fine bronze skin, but now he's become pale, and he can barely speak. He had a slender build to begin with, but now he looks frail. Finally, too sick to work, he takes to his bed in the small servant's quarters.

"Poor little guy," Wagger says. "The doctor isn't sure what's wrong with him. Maya, see if you can cheer him up, would you?"

She knocks softly on the door and enters his room. It's dark, and the young man is curled up under the blankets. He looks terrified to see her.

"My lady, please don't trouble yourself over me," he croaks.

Maya smiles at being called "my lady."

She sits on the bed and pushes his dark curls from his face. "What lovely hair."

He looks at her with helpless, sad eyes, then closes them and groans.

"How's the boy doing?" Wagger calls out, leaning on the doorjamb.

"Not well," Maya says.

"Then, let's have lunch downtown again. I do miss Damian's cooking."

Maya rises to follow Wagger, but Damian whispers, "Wait." He presses a folded piece of paper into her hand. She can see from the urgency on his face that it's a very private message.

In the bathroom at the restaurant she reads his letter.

I am so lovesick that I can no longer stand, no longer trust myself not to reach out to you whenever you walk past. What should I do? If you hate me, I should leave my job. No, I should throw myself from the window. I love you. Could you ever love me? Check yes or no in one of these boxes. If yes, you'd make me the happiest man who ever lived.

Needing no evidence of the boy's passion, Maya rips up the note and flushes it down the toilet. Still, she thinks of

Damian while eating her smoked salmon crepes. The more she thinks of his curly hair and his young bronze skin and his lithe figure, the more she wonders if she could ease his suffering.

"What a warm day!" crows Wagger as they walk from the restaurant. A breeze unfurls his comb-over, which he quickly refastens. He winks. "I think we should have a turn in the garden."

So they do, and afterward, when Wagger sinks into a short nap, Maya checks in on young Damian.

She teases, "How do I tick the box? Like this?" And she kisses him on the lips.

Damian draws her to his body for one long, blissful moment. He is cured.

But he wants more of that cure, and so does Maya. The young lovers have only snatches of time to exchange loving looks and brief caresses. With Wagger breathing down their necks, there's never enough time for anything more.

And then, something happens.

Wagger loses his sight. Completely. It's a huge blow to him. He needs Damian's help more than ever now, and Maya's, too.

The lovers begin to realize their opportunity. Maya leads Wagger to the couch, and when Damian brings them their tea, he slides his hand up Maya's thigh, even as Maya is helping Wagger find his tea. Her back is arched with the new possibilities in store for them.

"Perhaps the garden would cheer me up," Wagger says.

Maya answers Wagger, but her eyes seek out Damian's, as if her reply were meant for him. Passion makes her voice almost rough. "Yes. I really want to."

The three of them wait for the tiny elevator. Maya pushes Damian in first and leads Wagger on her arm and then squishes Damian against the wall with her ass, which he seems to like very much. With the key in the elevator, they rise to the roof.

Walking gingerly on the path, Damian follows Wagger and Maya to the mossy love seat, shady under the trees. He watches them start to undress, then wanders around the garden while they try to do what Wagger wants to do. It's over by the time Damian gets back, though Maya and Wagger are still naked and sprawled on the fresh green bed.

Maya looks over at her lover, who is now taking his clothes off and soundlessly launching himself up the pear tree.

He gestures for her to come up.

"Those pears look so tempting," she says aloud. She unravels herself from Wagger's embrace. "I'm going to climb up and find a ripe, juicy one."

Wagger frowns. "Be careful. I wish I could help."

She too launches herself up the tree, with Damian's outstretched hand pulling her up. She braces a foot against a branch to get a firm hold, and with her legs spanning two branches, Damien thrusts himself inside her. They tussle, rocking on the branches and letting the swaying limbs do some of their work for them.

She moans, trying to keep her voice down, but it's so good to finally have sex with a man with the sap of life in him.

"Did you get it?" Wagger calls.

"Almost there . . . higher . . . higher . . . higher! Good . . . just a little . . . ah . . . ah . . . yes!"

The lovers gasp, both of them, and Wagger's face turns toward the sound. Something strange and miraculous suddenly happens to the old man. He rubs his eyes.

"I can see! But . . . what are you doing? You're having sex in a tree! Sex in *my* tree!" He rubs his eyes once more, and the vision is gone. He's blind again. The doctor had warned him that his sight might have some rare moments of flickering recovery, but, otherwise, he would be blind for the rest of his life.

Wagger begins to sob with frustration, while Maya jumps down to the mossy floor.

"What are you talking about?" She speaks calmly to him as if he's a befuddled patient in her old nursing home. "You didn't see anything, you silly goose."

"I saw you," moans the old man. "For an instant. You had your hands above your head, gripping the branches, and Damian was ramming you hard, with the branches swaying under your feet. Oh no, no . . ."

Maya snorts. "You're fantasizing, Jan. Sweetheart, you're still in shock from your eye trouble. Your brain is playing a trick on you. A dirty trick! If I wanted to have an affair—which

255

I don't—I'd get a hotel like a normal person, wouldn't I?"

"I suppose . . ."

"I wouldn't have sex right under—or over—your own nose, would I?"

"I guess . . . but why else climb the tree?"

She laughs. "The pears, my dear! You know pregnant ladies and their food cravings, don't you?"

Wagger's mouth gapes. "You're . . . you're pregnant? Really?" His worries forgotten and his dynasty assured, he strokes Maya's belly, kissing it and murmuring to the baby that one day, all this will be his. . . .

Even if the baby isn't his.

The end.

Kai slaps Bryce a high five.

Rooster whoops and calls out, "Forget D.C. Take me to *Fockynggrove!*"

And pretty much everyone is impressed that Damian and Maya had sex in a pear tree and got away with it.

"But they never ate the pears," Parson says.

"Oh, I think they did—metaphorically," Kai says.

"I'll never be able to listen to that partridge in a pear tree carol without thinking of sex," Briony says.

Alison muses, "I've done it under a tree, but never in it."

"Fockynggrove," Rooster says breathlessly. "Is that place for real?"

"I read it online," Bryce says. "It's in England."

Mari says, "It sounds like the porn version of Winnie-the-Pooh's Hundred Acre Wood."

Rooster holds out his hands like a baby that wants to grab all the colored blocks in the entire preschool. "I am going there someday."

JEFF'S PROLOGUE

Mouse turns to the window and points at the city skyline.

"Are we heeeere?" she squeals.

Everyone gets excited, but Mr. Bailey laughs. "Not even. This is Philadelphia."

Philadelphia. This is where Alison stood in front of the cracked Liberty Bell and declared herself free and unbroken. There's a weight on me just thinking of it. And, fictionally speaking, it's the city where Zac and Aaron reunited. It's the City of Brotherly Love, and the unclouded spring day makes the place look full of hope and healing.

Mr. Bailey calls my name.

"Yeah?" I say, turning, wondering what he wants.

But he's holding a slip of paper.

It's my turn to tell a story. It's time. This is it.

"But he's the fifth male in a row," Cece whines, and I nod vigorously to show my utmost conviction that going next would be sexist.

"I'm afraid we have more men on this ride than women," Mr. Bailey says. "Jeff, it's your turn."

I try to remain calm, though I know this is bad. My chosen story doesn't rise to the mood that's just swept over me when I saw the city skyline. I'd love to tell something about cracks and love and Philadelphia. But I decide to keep to my plan. I've got it all rehearsed, which is good, because the pressure is on with

Bryce intending to be helpful by chanting "Mor-phe-us!" as if I have the sequel ready to go.

"Whoa," I say. "Don't get your hopes up. What I have is pretty rough. I'm going to tell you a story I've been working on. It's called 'The House of Fame.'"

"Objection!" calls Reeve, rapping his pen on the metal grip of his clipboard like a judge. "Everyone else made up new stories on the spot, and you're shamelessly planning to recycle one you've already written?"

"It's only a work in progress," I mumble.

To my horror, everyone takes Reeve's side. They say it isn't fair.

"But I don't have anything else prepared!" I sound more frantic than I care to let on.

"Hire someone to write one for you," Mari says airily. "Oh, wait, I forgot. *You're* the wordsmith enabler for everyone else, right?"

I meet her glare and shrug like I don't know what she's talking about. I can't believe she'd call me out for my paper-writing service with Mr. Bailey sitting right here.

"Chill, Jeff. None of us were prepared," Kai says, diffusing the tension and being nice, even though I've never written a single paper for him. "Rushing into a story is part of the fun."

Fun? *Fun?*

Like he wants to help, Kai adds, "Just throw yourself into it."

Everyone stares at me politely but mystified. Like: What is

Jeff's problem? Why can't he throw himself into a story? Why can't he have *fun*?

"I don't write this way."

But in the end they prevail, and I'm forced to make up a story on the spot.

I think of simple movie plots and come up with something. To mask my terror, I project a deep male narrator's voice, like the trailers for big-box movies with lots of action and little logic. A movie that I have never seen before, never read a plot summary of, but am forced to narrate.

JEFF'S TALE

In a world of devastating climate change, continents sink under the waves. The sole survivors are young, muscled teenagers, fit for a movie screen . . . or an apocalypse. They band together on a ramshackle floating structure called a flet and fight the evil Cthuloocks spawned from the sea. They are led by Ashton Blair, seventeen-year-old pro surfer, who rides the waves, but longs only to ride his way home.

I get some laughs from this cheesy intro, and I smile. This *is* fun!

Awake before dawn, Ashton limbers his taut six-foot-four frame with Pilates, when a ripple in the water alerts him. The guy on watch is insufficiently manly to detect the danger, but Ashton dives, machete ready in his hand.

Tentacles punch above the surface as a Cthuloock attacks a strange animal. Ashton severs a tentacle gripping its injured prey. The Cthuloock lashes out, but Ashton stabs its red eye, straight into its brain, and the Cthuloock dies.

The creature Ashton rescues is a Triwhal, a dolphin mutated with a triceratops. As Triwhals and humans become allies, human riders surf the waves with new, unparalleled speed and can battle the Cthuloocks with new might. A tide is turned, and peace gives way to passionate embraces among the heroes.

Ashton Blair was not always a sex icon. He had been such a shy, thoughtful child that when his body transformed to sculpted perfection, he remained humble. Experienced, yet virginal in his gentleness.

So the Triwhals breed, and Ashton serially impregnates flet girls, including Bethany, who didn't seem hot until her glasses fell off while Triwhal riding. She turned out to be the hottest woman ever born and never wore glasses again.

Yet the Cthuloocks strike back when a sorceress's Spawn of Evil leads the entire Cthuloock swarm to the flet.

On the horizon the water churns with angry Cthuloocks.

"Uh-oh," says a dude who usually lingers in the background.

But Ashton pulls up his riding pants, his bare toes firmly keeping his balance on the swaying flet. He dresses in special seaweed loin-girders suited to Triwhal riding—first pulling one perfect thigh into the pants, followed by the other perfect thigh. The seaweed pants perfectly encase an ass so tight and a front so generous that just watching him simultaneously impregnates all the remaining flet girls who haven't been knocked up yet.

"It's time to fight," says Ashton Blair, and he and his mostly pregnant army ride to the battle that will decide humanity's fate.

"Um, Jeff, are you on something?" Mari stares at me like I'm stoned, and any scrap of confidence I had is gone. Without that mood driving my narration, I can't even go on with it, because that story was nothing more than mood-spawn.

It's a giant heap of suck.

"What did you expect?" I sound peevish. "You made me tell a story off the top of my head."

"The top of your head is freaking weird, dude," Cookie sings.

"Look, just stop," Mari snaps. "For the love of Christ, stop."

So it's over. Everyone knows I'm worthless. I'll stop hearing all this stuff about being a writer. That whole chapter of my life—that immortal feeling—is gone.

Alison sees me suffering. "You can't just shut him off, you guys. He's supposed to tell a story. So . . ."

People debate if they should move on or let me try again, but they definitely don't want to hear about seaweed pants. I cringe into a smaller and smaller ball.

Pard says nothing—not a word. Instead, he gives me this half-angry, half-puzzled look, like, *So that's all?*

That hurts, because I want him to think I'm a good writer even if I'm a sucky person. Out of all the people on this bus, it's Mari and Pard whose artistic opinions matter. They're both going places I also want to see. Even if it means following in their wake. On my freaking flet.

I'll never be able to keep up with them. But I want to try harder, try again, even if it's humiliating to speak out loud after this disaster.

Quickly, and against my will, I have a scene ready-made. I don't want to use it, but it's all I have.

With people wrapping up discussion, there's no time to second-guess if this is wise. I just begin.

JEFF'S TALE, TAKE TWO

A husband and wife sit down in the psychologist's office. The shrink's legs are crossed, her hair is up in a twist, and her nails are painted red. Even her toenails. The couple brought along a little boy. He hates that shrink. He never eats the candies in her candy jar. There's something odd about her face. It's like a mask, showing sympathy, but the eyes are calculating, always at a distance. If Henry VIII married a woman like that, she'd survive him. No problem.

She asks the man questions, and usually the child doesn't understand. The man keeps blaming his genes, and for years the boy took a special interest in his father's pants. On this particular day the shrink says, "You can't blame yourself for something that isn't your fault."

And the man just looks at the shrink. One day the boy will read about Tolkien's palantir, and he'll think of his father's eyes. Quiet eyes with dark things going on in them. The man says, "What about what happened after? That was my fault."

"No," his wife says, and she puts a hand on his arm, but she does it like he's made of glass. "We both broke down; we both did in our own ways. There's no one at fault. We just need to move forward, somehow." The woman smiles bravely.

The man looks nervously to the place where he thinks his five-year-old is lying asleep. He can't see the boy, because the boy climbed into the giant dollhouse in the shrink's office and was so quiet that everyone assumes he sleeps. But he's not sleeping. Instead, he's looking right at them through the cross-hatching of the plastic window.

The boy loved that dollhouse. It didn't have partitions between rooms or even the first and second floors. I—*he* fit in it. He climbed in, lay on his side, and pretended he was Alice in Wonderland. It bothered Alice to outgrow the White Rabbit's house, but I loved the snug feeling. My real house felt so huge and empty, since—since she—

I stop because the pronouns slipped up, and I'm not sure how to correct for that. I don't realize I'm hunched, rocking back and forth in my chair, until Alison whispers "Hey" and rubs my back.

What is it about someone rubbing your back that calms you down and lets you breathe again?

Okay. Sorry. I don't really have much of a story here. The story is kind of over, you know? After Bee died, it was all over. This is all just what happened after. The shrink has been working with the husband and wife not right after Bee died, but after my dad came back from his own trip to the hospital after . . . you know, an attempt. Sorry. I keep slipping. Maybe you already figured out the couple are my parents. Anyhow, it was part of the deal that my dad had to see the shrink. You know, so he wouldn't do anything permanent to himself.

When he was in the hospital, it was just Mom and me.

266

When he tried to talk to me on the phone, I'd cry, because I thought he was dead like Bee and calling to say he missed me. He'd promise to come home soon, and I'd ask him to please bring back Bee, too, which upset him. Then he came home— without my sister. Mom told me to stop asking him about his trip to Heaven to find Bee, because he was very sad. She also stopped sleeping in my bed after Dad came home, and I didn't want to sleep in the big bed with them, because I was scared of ghosts and maybe a little of him, if only at night. So I slept in any old corner or drawer. Someplace snug and safe.

My dad tells the shrink that it's hard to keep going. There's eating and drinking and sleeping, and it's pointless without his bright-eyed child. The one who took after Mom, not him. The shrink mostly lets him talk but then asks what is going to keep him here, commit him to life, and keep him moving forward.

He says, "Jeff. He's all I have left."

She gets this concerned look on her face. "He can't take that role."

My dad is a really quiet guy, but this time he talks back. "Sure he can!" He looks over at me and sees my eye in the window. "He's awake," he says, sounding scared. "He shouldn't be hearing this."

Her voice is flat, logical. "No, he shouldn't. You need to get a sitter. You can let go of him long enough for one appointment. Or you can hire a sitter to wait with him in the waiting room. Like I've said."

There's this pause, and my parents are both looking at me like I'm going to die next. Even though it was Dad who almost went next.

But now that my father sees I'm listening, that changes things. "Fine," he snaps. "He won't be back."

The shrink sighs. "Let's end early today. And, John, a minute ago, I only meant your motivation has to come from within you. Other people can't hold that all-important role. It's not fair on them, or yourself."

"Fine. We're leaving," he says, his mouth angry, but his face softens a little when he comes around to the doll-house. He does something I don't like. Instead of looking at me through the window, he walks to the back, where I'm exposed as this kid lying in a fake house. Like this is pretend and not real.

"Let's go, Jeff."

But it's my house, and I fit, and I understand that I'm not coming back, so I say what lots of whiny kids say. "Can I keep it?"

And Dad turns to the shrink with this hopeful, hurting look on his face, and it's like *he's* the kid, having to ask for the toy. She drones, "Sorry, no, other kids need the house."

I brace my feet against the walls and my hands against the ceiling so no one can haul me out. It's wrong, but I do it.

Dad goes to the other side to whisper with Mom. Through the window I watch Dad tilt his head, considering me. They both are. I can feel a showdown to get me to come out of

268

the house. Meanwhile, the shrink sits back and studies us with those calculating eyes.

Then Dad moves where I can't see him. Plastic toys clatter in the bin I can't see. "Help me," he says, and Mom gets out of her seat.

The window fills with a view of his jeans—the jeans he keeps talking to the shrink about, that caused me and Bee to have our asthma, and made Bee's asthma so bad that she died.

He knocks on the little door. I open it, and it's kind of thrilling because it feels like a real house, with all the ordinary customs of knocking and entering. There's no proper doorknob, but it's still awesome to snag the doorjamb with my fingernail and pull the door toward me. To see my front porch, I have to lie on my side and poke my butt out the back, but I try to stay inside the house as much as possible.

My dad is holding up a Lego man with royal blue pants, a red shirt, a yellow face, and the kind of smile you'd expect from someone made out of symmetrical shapes and primary colors. He's holding the Lego man like it's alive, not just a toy.

"I'm looking for Jeff so we can get ice cream," the Lego man squeaks cheerfully.

"I don't go places with strangers," I say, because Mom taught me that.

Dad looks at me with the palantir eyes. Then his voice becomes his real one. Husky. "What do I have to do to get you out?"

"Get Bee," I say. I am still angry that he ruined everything.

"Honey," Mom says, and Dad turns his head and shushes her with his lips but no sound.

He gets on his belly, so his face and one hand fill the door-way. "I tried," he says. "But I wasn't allowed."

This gets my attention. He's finally admitting the truth.

"I ran after her," he continues, "but you know Bee was really fast. She wanted her wings, and I couldn't stop her. She flew. And then I woke up back here."

My five-year-old self believes him. She could run with me on her back, without me weighing her down. I didn't think anyone could catch her. And she'd be really into having wings.

"You're a slowpoke," I scold him. These were harsh words at the time. "And now we lose."

"Yeah." He's being honest. Dad and I are the slow, quiet ones. Mom and Bee are—were—bright, fast, warm.

Then he asks out of the blue, "Do you like your bed?" I shake my head, and he says, "Do you want me to build you a sleeping box? A house like this one, that you can keep in your room?"

And I nod.

He reaches one finger through the door and touches my hand, there in the front entryway with the round red rug stick-ered on the brown floor. "Okay. The hardware store closes soon. Let's hurry."

That's logical, so I agree.

And he waves good-bye at me, and I wave too, and then

I shut the door, and I meet him outside the house, the front side, and I leave the office for the last time. And we go to the hardware store.

And we move forward.

I don't say "the end" because I'm still living this story. But I stop speaking, and then there's this hush. I stare at my hands and wait.

If they think my story sucked, I can't face them ever again.

I told two stories, and both times no one interrupted—well, besides Mari stopping me from finishing the first one. But no one broke in to add something like they did with everyone else's stories, to tweak a detail or share a thought. It's like I speak in a void. It's like my life.

Finally, Alison takes my hand and says my name and nothing else.

Her face has none of its cocky glory. This time she looks wise and serious and real.

"I never knew," she says, and I shrug, but she cups my chin in her hand, and slowly moves in to kiss me. It's a sweet, adoring kiss on the cheek, the kind Bee used to give, and my throat catches, because for a second, she's almost in reach.

My sister, I mean.

"That was beautiful," she says—Alison says—and I know everyone is watching, but it's like we're the only people there. She weaves our fingers together. "And so are you."

There's something sisterly in that, too, even if it isn't true. I shake my head and say, "Thanks, but—"

She squeezes my hand. "No 'buts.' Just 'thanks.' When people want to love you, let them. When people open a door like that, never close it, not even to hide."

I turn my hand over to get a better look at her long fingers. "Okay. Just *thanks*."

She gives a mini-chuckle.

Our hands are laced together, and I'm not even hyperventilating. In fact, I feel calm, like the universe is holding me up.

Alison Chavez has been my crush since I first laid eyes on her. Larger than life, wilder than the Wild Things, someone I've had only brushes with in the hall or the parties that Cannon got me into. My great social goal had been to hold her attention for more than five minutes and maybe even make out with her. I finally have her attention, although I don't think making out is going to happen, maybe ever.

But this is pretty nice.

People start chiming in now, saying they liked the story, but they're quiet, and I'm hoping it's because they got it as much as they got the Morpheus story. This dollhouse thing is the same story, really. Dreams, desire, death. And me, trying to understand my father, my Black Knight, and this emptiness and how to live with it. It's the same story I'll be telling for the rest of my life, maybe.

My head snaps up when Reeve slams his clipboard. "What gives? That wasn't even a proper story—it wasn't fiction."

272

"Jesus, Reeve," Rooster says at the same time that I say, "I'm sorry." I forgot the rules. I just bled for no reason.

"Don't worry about that, Jeff," Mr. Bailey says, his face concerned.

"Seriously? Then I want to tell a second story," Reeve whines. "Everyone likes *his* story because it's got a suicidal dad and a dead sister."

I freeze, and Alison's hand wraps tightly around my wrist.

"Reeve, that's enough," Mr. Bailey says, his voice sharp.

"Yeah, Reeve, shut the hell up," Bryce adds. People chime in.

Reeve stands on his knees and faces the whole angry bus. "My dad shot himself, so why can't I tell that one? Why not? Then you'd all like me." He claws at the clipboard like he wants to tally something but is too upset, and when he speaks again, his voice comes out shrill and breaking. "It's not fair! Jeff's not the only one with a sad story, and he's going to win, but I was in the house. *I was in the house!*"

His throat closes on that last word and shreds it. There's chaos as people murmur, and Parson offers to pray for Reeve, which Reeve furiously rejects, and Mr. Bailey tries to quiet him down. It takes a while.

"He shouldn't have talked about you that way," Lupe tells me. "Don't listen to him."

I nod, but I hope Reeve will be okay. And he's right. We all have more than one story to tell. We have hits and misses. Stories that speak to one moment and not to another. He chose

273

a vindictive story at the start of our ride. He should be allowed to get a second chance.

I did.

Pard hasn't said a word, but he knows me better than anyone else. I'm not sure how he'll take this new story, or if he even listened. I'm hoping he did. He knew a little bit about my dad, and, of course, he knew about Bee. Maybe finding out where my so-called coffin came from will fill in a blank.

I turn around to face him. I'm prepared for indifference, or a derisive sneer, or a thin white eyebrow raised in a *meh* salute.

I'm not prepared to see Pard crying. Rooster looks up at me, his forehead creased like he has no idea what got into Pard. It is the strangest sight. Rooster has an arm around Pard's shoulders, and Pard cries into Rooster's chest—or, really, his armpit.

As I watch, Pard raises a hand to shield his face. Rooster's armpit kind of shelters Pard like a cave.

"What did I do?" I ask Pard, twice, but he's not coming out of it.

"Hey," Rooster coos, looking down at Pard. "It's okay."

I mouth *What?* at Rooster, and he shakes his head like he has no idea.

Alison reaches over the back of our seat to stroke Pard's hair, but Pard burrows farther into Rooster and tries to hide. He's no longer crying, and he breathes calmly, but he's not going to talk about it. His eyes are usually so bright, in joy or anger, that I forget how small and deep set they are, now that all the light has gone out of them. Like death has touched them. It gives me a panicked feeling to see.

Rooster is actually being kind of sweet, mothering Pard in his gentle, lumbering way, and I wish I could have done something, leaned over and held him like that. I wish I could be close to Pard without all this sexual tension of his messing things up. Sometimes I really wish sex didn't exist, because friendships would be so much better.

Pard peeks at me for just an instant and looks away, and his face shows he's not insulted, just completely crushed.

It's my story about a family torn up over a kid's dead sister.

I'd just raked him through hot coals.

He has that desperate, anguished look that wants to tell me what's eating him. I don't know what it is he needs to say, but I'm here.

Only he can't say whatever it is. He never could.

I've wondered if there was some guilt there. He and his sister must have been in seventh or eighth grade when she died. At that age they might have argued and been snippy with each other. Maybe she died suddenly after they'd had a bad fight. Or maybe he feels like it was his fault, like he ran into the street, and she ran after him to haul him back, only to get hit by a car. Something like that. Something that agonizes him every time he thinks of her. That's the vibe he's given all these years, at least. And now that feeling is back, and he's caught crying where everyone can see.

I wish—I want—

"Pard . . . ," I begin, but I don't know what else to say. Eyes shut, Pard shakes his head no.

In six weeks summer will be here, and then we're all off to different colleges, and I'll never see Pard again. Ever. Why bother, in that case?

But seeing him cry with his body curled into Rooster, his hand partially covering his face, his eyes scrunched and hopeless—I can't ignore that. I can't look away, because our sisters are our most private shared experience, and that bond matters.

I can't let Rooster's armpit be the only place Pard can turn to.

THE BUS DRIVER'S PROLOGUE

My thoughts are interrupted when the bus driver takes an off-ramp, and Mr. Bailey digs into him.

"You can't stop now. Come on!"

The driver snaps back, "You bet I can. I've got union rights. What with traffic and the stops, you've hit your time. Anything over six and a half hours violates my contract. I get an hour break before we go on. And I like the station outside Philly. It has an employee rec room. Good couches."

Mr. Bailey almost shrieks. "But if you need a break, at least drop us off somewhere more interesting than a parking lot for buses! Seriously, it'll be like thirty minutes overtime tops! Teachers do overtime every day!"

"What's going on?" Marcus asks.

Mr. Bailey just grumbles about bus unions while everyone else tries to figure out what's happening.

"Stop whining, everyone, and listen up," the bus driver says through the loudspeaker. He studies us in his rearview mirror.

If Pard were sketching him, the driver would be a study in circles and ovals. He's got a gigantic bald head, gigantic shades above two round cheeks, and a big round belly topped with two round man-boobs.

"It's time you all listened to me, for once," he says, still using his loudspeaker.

Kids, the whole world is filled with heartbreak. Sometimes it's just disappointment . . . like a bunch of damn kids and their uptight teacher bitching and feeling sorry for themselves because a bus driver keeping his eyes on the road for hours needs to take a break—which he legally has the right to—so he can drive safely. But I'm talking about the real stuff. Like the kid back there with the sister, or you in the front, with the dad. That's the real deal. Hurts like hell. I should know. Because we all expect good things to come our way and stay there. You kids are too young to know, but you will learn soon enough. Life don't work that way. Something good happens, and *boom!*—it's gone. Maybe it's your fault, maybe it's not, but rest assured, the pain is headed your way.

You kids sit all smart with your college sweatshirts on, thinking you'll be stockbrokers and lawyers and shit like that. You'll
never drive a bus for whiny high school brats, eh? Well, guess
again, is what I'm saying.

I know about disrespect. It walks through these doors every
single day. But I'm getting off track. I was talking about heartbreak. Like, when I was an undertaker, I got no disrespect. But
the smell, kids. The smell was like nothing else. Growing up,
it was the smell of my father before he showered. The smell
was death and the family business. You come to think different, breathing air like that. You come to see how it is. The way
things turn.

You show me the heroes of the world, and we know how it
all ends. But let's look at the turn before the turn. The heartbreak before the daisy pushing.

I don't know. Take JFK. I mean, he was young, handsome, dated Marilyn Monroe. He had it all, and he died on
camera. That's what we're talking about here. A nation is
given a great gift, and that gift gets ripped away, clean out.
Hell, aren't you going to go see the Lincoln Memorial? There
you go again.

But there are other ways heroes die, you know. Shame
is a kind of death. Think Lance Armstrong. You too young to
remember him? A cycling hero, until his doping went public,
and a bunch of kids lost their hero. And sometimes the hero
screws his fans and screws the people who trust him. Think of

279

that football coach in the news, creating that charity outreach organization and using it to manhandle a bunch of young boys. That kind of thing happens all the time.

I remember Kurt Cobain's suicide airing on the radio. You kids weren't even born yet. There's another guy who had it all, and ended it. Makes you think no one can have it all for keeps. Life just doesn't hold still like that. You get something, and you lose it. Hell, Robin Williams went the same way, and he was the funniest man alive. Damn. Even the world's best sense of humor can't protect you from the dark.

I'm skimming these off the top of my head. I could come up with hundreds if I set my mind to it or fiddled with one of your smart-ass phones. But in the end, it's the lives near you that make you take notice. How many people can say they prepped their dad's body for burial? Makes you face it, don't it? He was a good man, and I knew it was coming, what with old age and all. But what killed me was how the strokes took him bit by bit. None of this going to bed healthy and waking up in Heaven. But I was there for him. I let the family business flop because they were strangers needing burial, and he was my father needing his son on this slow decline and then final stop. I figured he'd understand if he were with it enough. And when you lose day by day the only person who's ever really loved you, when you lay him in the ground . . . well. You stand up from that, and your hands are empty. That divorce after, and then the stint of being homeless? That's just icing on the cake.

They say time's a healer, and I guess after a bad turn, there's some good to come. Maybe.

But my hands are still empty, kids. Who would you rather hold: your father, or this steering wheel?

Thought so.

Oh look, here's our stop.

THE UNION BREAK

Everyone's stunned by the driver's story. Some of us mumble "Thanks."

"You're welcome," he tells us. "Changes nothing, but you're welcome all the same."

The driver pulls into a huge lot of school buses. "I'm now officially on break, God bless our union. See you kids in one hour. There's a bathroom inside the building there, and vending machines too."

The bus makes that sound like it's dying, the doors screech open, and all goes quiet. And the driver is the first one off the bus, off to the employee rec room for his nap on the couch.

Mr. Bailey surveys the bleak, massive parking lot, with buses parked all the way to the horizon, but he's not about to complain after a life story like that. "Okay, everyone, feel free to stretch your legs, but be back in fifty."

I don't go to the dumpy rest stop with the bathrooms and vending machines. Instead, I track Pard from a distance, weaving between the rows of buses. I can't decide whether to talk to him or not. When my phone buzzes and I check it, I lose him among the maze of buses. He obviously wants to be alone anyway.

Cannon: *Where R U now?*

Philly. One-hour delay. Bus driver's union, or something.

Cannon: *Sucks. U in the bus?*

I text back, *No, outside.*

My phone rings. "Hey, Cannon."

But it's not him. "Is this Jeff?" A girl's gravelly laugh fills the silence.

I splutter, "Uh, yeah. Who's this?"

"Nikki."

"Oh. Hey." My heart beats faster. Cannon is smart. Manipulative, but smart.

"I can't wait to meet you. From what Cannon's told me, you sound amazing." Her voice is pitched like she's excited but chill at the same time.

"You sound . . . well, I guess Cannon hasn't said much about you." Unless a topless photo counts.

Her sigh sounds like an eye roll. "Cannon can be so communicative. *Ha.* But what can I say? I'm a sophomore, and super friendly. You can ask Cannon or ask Mace, and they'll tell you that. We're going to have a lot of fun, Jeff."

"Mace? So you're friends with his sister?"

"Melanie's like a sister to me. Mace and I fight over sibling rights."

Weird. I'm not sure how I feel about someone who is "super friendly" according to *Mace.* "So, what do you want to do?"

"Whatever you like." She laughs. It's a really sexy laugh. Exactly the kind of laugh you want to hear from a girl on a phone. It could be a start to something. I do have to go to college somewhere, after all. Maybe Cannon is right. Maybe I should go where I know people like Nikki. People who'd take a chance on me. And if she's okay with Mace, she's going to think I'm totally hot.

Of course, she hasn't hung out with me yet. I imagine myself going to a party with Cannon tonight, meeting people over beers and loud music, and smiling my face off. It sounds so mind-numbingly exhausting. It's not about obeying school rules, though I still don't want to give up my chances with Cornell and Penn. But I just don't feel like partying with strangers. I've been pumped with stories all day—stories by people I care about, some a lot and some not so much—and I want to hold these stories close tonight. All of them. And maybe . . . maybe *write*.

Yeah. I might be able to write tonight. It's been a while.

"Jeff?" Nikki asks. "You still there?"

"About tonight . . . I don't know, Nikki," I say. "I told Cannon I couldn't do much. Kind of busy here."

Her intake of breath sounds practiced. "What? But you *have* to. We don't have to party all night. We could just go out for drinks. I don't have anyone to hang out with tonight, and Cannon's going to be all business. . . ."

She says it in a pout, and I'm hooked on the chance for information, straight up. "What kind of business?"

"Oh, Drew has this new plan to rig up computer labs. You'll meet him when you get here. He's—"

In the background she squeals, "What did I say?" and it's muffled, but I hear Cannon's harsh tone.

"Of course you're coming," he says with hard cheerfulness

into the phone. "I'm fixing up Georgetown for you, red carpet."

"Who's Drew?"

"You'll meet him when you arrive. He's amazing. And there's a party tonight at his frat house. All you have to do is meet some friends, and this place is yours next year. I'm counting on you."

"Counting on me for what?"

"Counting on friendship, man." He adds in a dramatic whisper, "Nikki's not so interested in *friendship*, though."

"Hey!" I hear her shout in the background, and he laughs.

He means to tantalize me, but my head is screaming for me to run. I can't make it look like I'm running. Not to Cannon. That would be a fatal mistake. "Look, I'll text you after I get to the hotel. Maybe then we can go out."

He laughs like I'm funny, like I'm offering him the first page of a term paper, and what he really wanted was work for a dozen clients. "Nah, I've already worked out the itinerary. Jeff, look. When you go to college, how many friends do you think you'll have?"

I don't say anything.

"So. Time to make some connections. And I'm the only one who can really help you. I *like* helping you. There are other people I could work with, but I'd rather team up with you. Because you're my friend."

"Cannon, I'm not a business guy."

"Hey, stop being so scared. There's a whole world out there, and we're going to go see it. See you soon, kid."

The line goes dead.

I need to clear my mind after that call, so I walk aimlessly through rows of buses. It's like my feet know exactly where to go in this labyrinth, and I find Pard way out there where the ground isn't paved anymore, just dirt and gravel.

He looks tiny seated and leaning on the front tire of a parked bus. He rolls a cigarette. Cloves. It's this complicated process that makes him look sophisticated. Licking the papers here, in this school bus graveyard, he looks gritty and raw.

My feet crunch against the gravel underfoot, and he looks up and waits for me to get closer. "Hey," he says. He opens his plastic bag and puts the finished cigarette inside.

I want something from him. Not sure what, but it's not pity. "You can smoke that. I'm not going to die or anything."

He shrugs. "I've been thinking about stopping. Quitting."

"You? Quit?" I do one of those laugh-snorts through the nose that I hate. I feel stupid standing there while he's sitting down like the cool kid.

He licks his teeth like he's tasting the papers. "I don't smoke as much as you think I do. But, yeah, it's time to make a change. Be who I want to be."

He looks up with a lonely smile that shatters me.

I feel like my body is doing some sort of telepathy without translating for my brain, or maybe a transfer of little atoms leaping out of me and into him.

These are probably *more than friends* feelings. I'd like to blame him for flirting and tricking me into it, but he's just sitting

286

there talking about something that my busy atoms don't even care about. What was it? Quitting. And changing.

I am changing.

"Jeff?" His smile blooms.

He pats the ground next to him. I am suddenly right next to him but don't remember bending my knees or putting my ass on the ground. His hair is oily, the way it always is by this time of day. I look at it hoping to find fault, to somehow distract myself, but it's no good trying to focus on his less perfect features. No good.

I need to stop these feelings before so many of my atoms jump ship that my center of gravity shifts and I smack into him.

What did I come here for? To apologize? I need to get this over with and get out. "Pard, I'm sorry. About my story. About what I said at McDonald's. How I've acted in general, all this time. Treating you like crap. You must hate me so much."

There's a long enough pause to make me cringe at being hated.

"Actually . . ." He laughs softly, pulling one knee toward him so he can hug it to his chest. He doesn't finish his sentence, doesn't look at me.

And then he does.

Heat mushrooms inside me. I probably shouldn't let it, but I can't stop this warmth from rising.

"You know how I feel," he says finally. "The question is, how do *you* feel?"

How do I feel? It depends which atoms you ask, but they all agree that I'm terrified.

I toss my head horselike the moment he takes my hand. In seconds I transform into a sweaty mess. I need to pull away, but I can't. Please, let this not be love. Maybe it just feels that way because I've missed him so much. Because he was my best friend. Why can't friends acknowledge they love each other too? Because friends do. So that must be why this heat is rushing through me and why my fingers opens like a flower when he runs his hand over mine.

Our fingers lace, and I watch like it's happening to someone else. It has to stop. "I can't—I'm not—" I finally manage, and he slides his thumb over my slick palm. With nothing more than a soft *hmm*, to show that he's listening, he explores my fingers, like they're places he could get lost in.

"I'm not into guys."

"You're into me."

"As a friend."

He does the *oh, come on* head tilt. "I could kiss you. Then you'd know for sure."

I shake my head, but he leans in.

No, I'm not shaking my head. I'm shaking.

"Just once," he whispers, and he runs his other hand around my neck, and the heat, the sound in my ears, the breath on my mouth, everything is too much. I kick out, and gravel shoots in a noisy spray and a great cloud of dirt wafts up like the smoke I've never been allowed to exhale. Suddenly, I'm kneeling three feet away, holding my breath so I don't breathe in dust.

My heart is pounding.

"I can't," I say when the dust settles. "I'm telling you. I've thought a lot about this."

"*So have I.* You wanted me, just now, as much as I want you. You can't deny it." He glares as if he's braced for me to do exactly that.

"I'm not denying anything. . . ." His whole face changes like I've handed him something he's waited a long time for, and it's lifting him. But it's a false hope. "Even if I did want to, what's the point? I'm not gay. I never wanted to go all the way with you."

"Ah. You think I'm the sex-crazed one, but look where your mind is," he chides, but his voice is alarmingly gentle. He's still smiling like he doesn't understand how hopeless this is. "Very well. Go *partway*, then. If two people want to kiss and hold each other, wouldn't their world be full and perfect? Mine would be."

"Mine wouldn't." I sound so certain saying it that his face crumples back to that slapped-kitten look. He turns away so I can't see.

I should leave, but it would be shitty leaving now. I have to finish this properly. "Look. I can't be that person. But we can be friends. I came over here to check on you and talk because my story made you cry. I feel bad about that."

He sits back and deflates against the tire. "You should feel bad about not going with your true feelings. But your story was good. It was honest and real, and I only cried because I . . . haven't been."

My eyes cut to his face like I'd heard him wrong. "What do you mean? You're the most honest and real person I know."

"You don't get it." He doesn't look at me once, doesn't sneak glances the way I do. He's scared, and I understand that. "I don't think I can talk about this."

I scoot next to him, and he stiffens. "I know it's painful for you to talk about, but we both have that death thing going. It's hard. But we can help each other."

He shakes his head no so fast he's going to get dizzy. He's being eaten alive.

"Pard, I meant to tell you. When Briony told that story about twins . . ."

He's staring at me, horrified. He keeps shaking his head *no, no, no.*

I can't stop. I need to put things into words for myself as much as for him. "I know. I do. It kills me that some twins get reunited while others get—dammit. I think your pain is sharper than mine because it's so recent, and you were older. Mine is so . . . Pard, I can't even picture my sister. Not really, not without the photographs influencing my imagination. I'm kind of empty that way. Is that awful? But I want to help you. Do you want to talk? Maybe I can't . . . kiss you, but isn't this more important? Because, let's face it, we're kind of together on this one, yeah?"

His knees are all the way to his chest, his arms tight as rubber bands around his legs. He's crying. I make a move to wipe his tears, but he flinches away from my hand. "Don't."

Still in knots, he wipes his tears on his dirty knees.

"Shit," he says. "I can't do this." It's tenfold now, whatever shook loose in him that he couldn't say on the bus. He's busting apart.

"It's okay." I touch his shoulder, and he jerks away.

"It's fucking not. You don't know what I'm hiding. You're killing me."

He grips his hair and makes this high, thin noise that's terrible to hear.

I awkwardly pat his stiff back. "What's eating you? Are you blaming yourself for her?"

He barks a laugh. *"Hell yes, I am."*

"Just tell me. I won't judge. I'll listen. Pard . . ."

He flinches when I rest my hand on his shoulder, then closes his eyes and lets me stroke him there, over and over. He's like clay under my fingers. Softening. And I keep doing it because he needs it and because I need it.

I'm softening too.

I'm not ready for a boyfriend. "Love" is a word that sneaks up on you, love is a thing that sneaks up on you, but "boyfriend"— that word, that thing, is pure terror. If I really am bisexual, I'll just stick with girls. They're scary enough.

Friendship, though—it's scary too. This longing to see inside of him rushes through me hard and loud like we're on trains passing in opposite directions, and I focus on staring through

291

window after window, trying to get another look inside before these trains part forever. As trains do.

He takes a breath like he's willing himself to up and say something.

He says, "I love you."

Heat rushes up and down and fills my ears, fills my whole body to overflowing. My atoms go haywire.

Then I blink, because he didn't say that. He said, "I lied to you."

When my voice returns, there's a wobble in it. "Okay." But he shakes his head. He fishes out the plastic bag from his pocket, opens it.

So he lied, although I have no idea what about. I'm in such a haze that I can't process it.

He looks surprised when he sees the cigarette in his hands, like he had no idea how it got there. He turns it end over end and talks to it instead of me, which means I can stare at his downcast face all I want.

"This lie . . . I had reasons. Good reasons. And I'm so, so sorry."

"Okay," I say, but I'm not okay. I feel so weak. I'm still rubbing his back, willing him not to feel so much pain. I can't stop *looking* at him.

I'm in love. *In love.* When I fan out my fingers over his shoulder blade, it's an act of rebellious love against everything I've ever told myself. And it feels so good to admit the need to know the bones in him, every angle, every curve.

Still looking at his cigarette, he nods, like he's given himself a quick pep talk. "I'll just say it. I never had a sister."

He hunches over his unlit cigarette, and I wonder if I heard right, because I'm not hearing very well with this roar of the ocean pounding inside my ears. He said nothing about love, and my brain is relieved, while in a fog my heart replays the words over and over, failing to recall the word "love" anywhere. There must be some mistake. Or maybe he never loved me, ever, and I'd just imagined it? Why would he love *me*, after all?

I shake my head to snap out of it. What is he talking about?

"Um, of course you had one." I try to fit the pieces together. "The photo . . . Ellie . . . I mean, no one would lie about—"

"You put me on the spot, reaching for Mom's phone to check the time, then asking who that person on the screen was. So I lied. End of story."

I can't think in this fog. "But she . . . she's not your sister?"

"No." By the line of his mouth, I can see that it's major, admitting this.

Suddenly, my brain wakes up. If that wasn't his sister, who was she? This was an *important* photo.

"*Okaay*," I say. "So Ellie's your cousin?"

"A little closer to my gene pool." His face hardens into something so defensive he looks outraged. Then, after avoiding my face for so long, he stares at me with his art-stare, as if to memorize every facial muscle I make as I process his words.

"Then who? She looked just like you. *Exactly* like . . ."

293

You.

My hand drops from his back, and everything in the world shifts. After all this time . . . I never really knew him at all.

He sees enough of my shocked expression and turns away. Blinking hard, he rips at the cigarette, picks at it like one of those *love me/love me not* daisies. "Look, you practically ambushed me with the picture. *Who's this girl?* What was I supposed to say? It just popped out that she was my twin. I didn't know about your sister, and then you told me about *her* death, and it was too late to go back. It's agony whenever you bring this up. I've had this cheap claim to sharing something deep and important that didn't even happen to me. I hated myself for it. But then you dumped me, and it was good you didn't know. If word got around, the guys here would have assaulted me just like at my old school. But I never got outed—four years in high school, and I coasted. Why mess with success? Why have a heart-to-heart and tell you that was . . . *me.*"

He's talking fast, almost a whisper, but my brain is numb. I remember finding that box with his dead sister's stuff in it and feeling awful for him, but not daring to bring it up. *His sister's things.* That box of stuff was something like my sleeping box, his way of dealing. But, no, he wasn't dealing with Ellie.

There was no Ellie. No mourning someone he loved. Just *dressing up.*

When I speak, I hear the accusation in my voice, but I'm not sure how I really feel. Confused, mostly. "So, those girls' clothes in the closet—those are *yours?*"

He looks pissed, like *I'd* done something wrong. "You went through my closet?"

From a distance Mr. Bailey calls out that it's time to go in five.

Pard and I stare each other down, the walls between us thick and hard and strange. "The Rube Goldberg project. Remember? You were in the shower, and I was looking for boxes to use. I thought, you know, you saved some clothes to remember her. I didn't know you were *wearing* them."

With a vengeance, the Balrog fire's back in his eyes. "Fuck this." He launches to his feet. He flings the disintegrated cigarette pieces and we head back, out of sync.

"You can't tell anyone," he says. "No one."

"This is the last thing I'd tell anyone, believe me."

"Because I'd make your life hell. This is huge, telling you."

"Whatever, I get that."

He shakes his head, like I don't get it at all. Which I don't. At all.

We step out from the shadow cast by yet another bus, and I steal a glance at him. I can't imagine him in a bikini top, like in the photo. All that skin. That's not him. Dammit, I told him the girl in the photo was pretty. His face got this look I'd never seen, eyes averted, cheeks glowing, but I thought I knew what conversation we were in. I thought he was pleased her memory was being honored. Now even that moment is screwed up.

That's the thing about him. He screws every memory we

295

share. I think we're friends, and it's more than that. I think he's this guy, and he's this guy who cross-dresses and pretends to have a beautiful dead sister.

Pard catches me staring and kicks the gravel. A few small rocks ping on a bus. "You said you'd listen—what bullshit. I show my feelings for you three years ago, and you ghost me. I try to kiss you just now, and you wuss out. I say this incredibly personal thing about my body to you—and you're the first person I've ever told—and all you seem to care about are some clothes in my fucking closet. Every gut-wrenching part of me I offer you gets rejected, ignored, mocked. Well, fine. I have no more guts left to spill. Now you know that we don't have sisters in common. We have *nothing* in common."

"I guess not." I'm going to blow up from the way he's turning on me, with his shoulders in knots, and the way it's all ruined so fast I can't stop it.

"You think you're more of a man? I never played with a doll-house."

I'm not a fighter, but I draw back my fist, my body ready for it, because all I want to do is make him shut up, make his mouth just stop. He stiffens, eyes wide, his little hands palms out to block me. I'm horrified and drop my fist, and we both stand there, shocked. Minutes ago I wanted to kiss him and now this impulse. Both options are impossible. "I didn't play with it, dickhead."

He half reaches for me, his eyes all apology, though I was the creep making a fist. "It's okay if you did play with one . . . but, no, you weren't playing. I'm sorry, I was mouthing off, because this hurts. I've never told someone I'm intersex, and it's hell."

He says a weird word, like he's so into sex he's *intosex*. Not an image I need.

He notices my confused look and groans. "God, you don't know, do you? You . . . you think I'm a boy who puts on girl clothes, is that it?"

I shrug, but his question scares me. "Isn't that what you said?"

Pard rapid-blinks like he's tearing up, though I can't tell in the shade of this bus. He leans one hand on the bus and rests his forehead on his hand, like he's suddenly old and tired and in far too much pain. His voice is quiet and sad. "Out of all the imaginary conversations I've had with you on this topic, it never turned out like this. I just . . . listen. Forget the photo—forget the clothes. Forget my journey in genderland. We'll stick to the basics. *Intersex* is the sex I was born with. You know, some babies are girls, some babies are boys, and a very special few are betwixt and between."

He stops leaning on the bus and wipes his hand of the dust, and I stare at his handprint. I'm completely lost. "There's no such thing."

He sets his jaw and glares at me. Nervously, I babble an infomercial. "I mean, sure, there's that myth about the god Hermaphroditus. A lovesick nymph threw herself at him whether he wanted it or not, and the gods merged their two bodies into one, male and female."

297

That face of his—brittle, polished, harrowed, smooth, and slightly amused at my obtuseness, even now. His voice carries the understatement of a lifetime. "I'm familiar with the myth. That's right . . . *This* is my myth."

I don't know what to say. Mr. Bailey is shouting something, or maybe I'm just pretending I can hear him shouting. "We better go."

"Right."

I sneak glances at his smooth face as we walk, and the pieces start to fit together. We'd slept over at each other's places countless times freshman year, and I've never seen him with his clothes off. He always emerged from the bathroom fully dressed in pajamas or clothes. Always covered up, top to bottom. Kind of modest for someone who would become this flirty gay guy. It hits me that this is all real.

The words fly out before I can stop them. "You have both kinds of parts?" And heat burns my face like I've said a bad word.

His eyes bug out at the rudeness of my question. He crosses his arms over his chest and walks a bit faster. "Like you deserve to know."

"Believe me, I don't want to know. God. Isn't being gay interesting enough without—?" I wave a hand wildly. I can't even say it.

He laughs bitterly as we round the last row of parked buses. Our bus waits parked in front of the rest stop, and I look around nervously, because we're getting too close to our group to be talking like this.

"Ha. Don't get me wrong. I kind of aim at being a straightforward gay guy—get it? It's easier. I mean, gay or straight aside, people expect you to be male or female. Less is more, they say. Which I guess implies that more is less." He pauses as we line up and then adds, "Yet I think more can be more if you focus on my winning personality. Right, Rooster?"

"Right, little dude!" Rooster absentmindedly punches Pard's shoulder in a brotherly way and goes back to chatting with Bryce.

Everyone starts filing onto the bus, and Reeve marks us off on his trusty clipboard.

Pard and I inch forward without talking, thank God. I don't think I can have another conversation like this one. I'm all done. I'm all messed up.

If someone liked Pard, would he be gay, bi, or straight? Or would it even matter, because what does sex even mean for someone like him? And why couldn't he just be gay when I was almost getting used to the idea that I liked a boy?

It's like losing him all over again. And losing his sister—I need Ellie to exist too, in her dead-sister way. Which is a creepy thing to want.

None of this should be real.

"Sit with me?" Pard asks. He steps on the bus and turns his head sideways to pose the question without facing me. His voice is level, like he's playing poker and it doesn't matter to him if I'm in or out.

But asking means he probably wants me in.

I look at his hand on the rail, the hand he covered his weeping face with an hour ago. The hand I held when he poked it with his corsage, and touched again just now before we almost kissed. Such tiny fingers, delicate yet calloused with lizard skin where the pencil rubs him.

My chest tightens like it's asthma.

"I don't think so," I say, brushing my face of the cobwebs I sometimes feel there.

And I'm alone outside the bus.

It's not easier to breathe with him gone. It's worse.

Everything is worse.

SAGA'S TALE

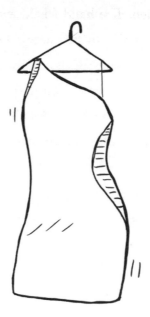

I don't think about it. I get on the bus and sit in the row behind Reeve, that empty seat no one wants because it's behind him. Social death means nothing. I'm dead inside.

Mr. Bailey puts a gentle hand on my shoulder. "Do you need anything?"

I shake my head without looking up. My breath comes out shaky, and I want to cry, but I don't even know why. I don't know what's happening to me, what this all means.

Mr. Bailey walks down the aisle, and when he comes back, he gives me my backpack. Probably in case I need my medicine.

The bus driver pulls out, and everyone starts chatting

and, except for Mr. Bailey keeping an eye on me from time to time, I become invisible. Even Reeve doesn't seem to see me as he scans the back rows for infractions. I thought I wanted to disappear from everyone else, but that's not enough. I want to disappear from *myself*. I envy Tolkien's elves. They have the ability to off themselves with a mere thought. No mess, no failed attempts. Their souls go to the otherworld, the Halls of Mandos, and don't return until the world has changed beyond recognition.

I could handle that.

When Reeve faces forward again, I check my phone. Cannon has left a text.

Cannon: *U coming?*

I don't know if he's referring to Drew this afternoon or the party tonight, or something else entirely. It doesn't matter. I text back, *Yes.*

Because I can't take this anymore. I can't spend the whole weekend with Pard hating me. With me hating myself. It's not Mandos's kingdom, but it will do.

Mr. Bailey draws a name. "Saga, you're up."

I no longer feel like part of the gang. It's like a switch has turned off, and I'm out of the group. My inner monologue is back, the voice that tells me I was never a part of the group to begin with. I'm a dumbass to think otherwise. *This* is how things really are.

I listen to Saga's story like my life depends upon it, because

I need less of me and more of these people and their stories right now.

Once upon a time there was a prom.

"Nice," says Briony in that high-heeled, prom queen way of hers, and Saga smiles back with her typical cat burglar elegance. Everyone on the bus is mostly back to their original seating arrangements. In the back Briony snuggles into Kai, while Alison kicks back in the center, both boots up on Rooster's knee.

And our heroine will be . . . Reiko. So, Reiko was gearing up for prom. She had her dream date and just needed her dream gown.

At Saks Fifth Avenue, while trying on different styles, she found The Dress.

She was with her friend Lupe at that magic moment.

Lupe pointed out the obvious. "You rock that dress." And, no lie, Reiko did. Reiko had never put on a dress before that felt so right and looked so good.

"But the price is going to be a bit of a problem," Lupe added.

Reiko looked at the tag then back to Lupe. She was screwed.

So she came back to Saks with her stepmom, Erin. Reiko came out of the changing room wearing The Dress after showing a couple awful ones for comparison. The plan was that when Erin saw how perfect The Dress was compared to the others, she'd realize Reiko had to have it.

Reiko coughed a little, but her stepmom still didn't look up from her phone.

"Erin?"

Erin looked up, still not really paying attention. "Yeah? Oh! That's a nice one."

"Super nice, don't you think? Isn't it perfect?" Reiko pressed.

"You look lovely. Well, how much? Oh . . . oh no. Honey, we're saving for college. We can't do this."

But Reiko had one final hope. Her boyfriend, rich and handsome . . . um, Franklin.

With his arm around Mouse, Franklin says, "Saga, I already have a girlfriend."

"And who's Erin?" Reiko asks.

"Oh, come on, guys," Saga says, looking around. "This is all just fiction. Erin's my stepmom. Get over it!"

"I'll be the boyfriend," Frye offers. His coaxing moocher's voice is dialed up a few notches, and he gives Reiko a flirtatious grin, like he's looking forward to the story with this new change.

"No can do," Saga says. "My story needs a guy with money."

Frye looks away, bitter.

Reiko worked on Franklin. She said she wanted to look really hot for prom, and if he bought her The Dress, she'd be all too happy to take it off for him after. That made him smile, but the smile faltered when she said the price.

"You'll look hot whatever you wear," Franklin said.

It was a no-go.

Reiko wasn't living in a modern-day Cinderella story. No fairy godmother was going to give her that dress.

It was up to her to get it for herself.

Theft was out of the question. The long skirts made it impossible to slip into a bag, and this was a high-security item.

No, she would have to buy it.

Which meant someone would have to buy it for her, and not her parents or her boyfriend. Someone with influence and money.

And at Southwark High, that someone was Cannon.

After school she asked if he wanted to hang out, and he took her for a drive. Have you been in his car, with the fin? Very sweet ride. She opened up and told him about the money she needed for The Dress. If he could get her that money, she'd do anything. *Anything.*

He put an arm around her. "Call them to reserve it for you, and if they give you a hard time, I can hold it on my credit card. You free Thursday?"

She was. She told him Franklin was going to be away for the game.

"Yeah, I know," he said. Cannon already had a plan.

*   *   *

Cannon went to see Franklin.

"I brought you something," he said, and he gave Franklin a bottle of absinthe.

Franklin got excited. "Sweet. How much do I owe you for this?"

Cannon smiled. "Actually, this is your free sample for listening to my sales pitch. I've got this new lead, and I can get loads of this stuff, but it's pricey and the seller wants money up front. Think you could spring me a loan? I'll pay you back fast, probably next week. How about it?"

Cannon left with the money in cash.

While Franklin played third base for an away game, Cannon picked up Reiko.

"I can carry that," he said, and slung her overnight bag on his shoulder. "You brought your bathing suit?"

She nodded.

"Good. But first things first."

Cannon took Reiko to Saks Fifth Avenue. He waited outside the changing area as she came out nervous and radiant in her dress.

He just looked at her with those dark eyes, that dangerous face. He was a bad boy, but tonight he was playing the gentleman very nicely.

He walked full circle around Reiko. "You look amazing. How do you feel?" He put his hands around her waist.

"Great," Reiko said. "I love it."

"We'll take it." He barely spared the saleswoman a glance, he was so focused on Reiko in her dress.

He paid for it in cash, a huge stack of twenties. "Thank you," Reiko gushed, kissing his cheek right there at the register.

Then they were off in his car.

Reiko was enchanted with his apartment—the hot tub on the roof, the furnishings and signs that no parents lived here.

She checked out the view from the window and then flopped on the bed. "Nice place."

That night, she gave him everything he wanted.

"Well, well," Reiko says, smiling like she's part embarrassed, and part pleasantly surprised.

"He didn't even buy the dress," Frye says, scowling at Saga. "You could have put me in there. I could have talked Franklin into lending me the money."

Saga sighs. "Cannon's in a different league, Frye. But this is fiction, remember?"

For once Frye doesn't have a comeback line.

Meanwhile, Reiko absentmindedly pulls off Frye's ring and turns it over in her hand, like she's thinking of the difference between the kind of jewelry Frye can buy for a girl and the kind of jewelry a guy like Cannon or Franklin can buy.

Or maybe she's not thinking about the money. Maybe she just has a thing for Cannon. A lot of girls do.

Reiko arrived at prom looking absolutely perfect. Every girl there was jealous of the way she looked in The Dress. She glowed.

Franklin glowed too, knowing he had the hottest girl in the room. He savored the way everyone turned their heads when she walked past. He didn't understand the finer points of the plunging back or the clinging fabric or shoulder straps that did more to reveal than to cover, but that dress brought out a sexiness he'd never seen before. Which kind of made him want to rush the night and get it off her. But, no, he let her enjoy the evening—and he enjoyed it too.

He ran into Cannon at the dance. They shouted greetings over the music.

"Oh!" Franklin shouted. "About the money?"

With a lazy hand Cannon shooed away the question. "Already paid you back. You weren't home, so I left the money with Reiko. It's all good. See you!"

But Reiko had never mentioned anything like that. So when they got back to his place, he sprung the question while he helped undo the buttons on her lower back. Buttons, no zipper. It was another tantalizing detail to The Dress.

"Babes, did Cannon give you some money for me?"

Reiko hesitated only a moment; Cannon had given her a heads-up at prom. "Oh, *that* money! Yeah. I think you missed a button."

He undid the last button, and The Dress swished to the

floor. She stepped out of it with her hip cocked. Reiko started helping him undo his buttons, then ran her hands up his chest.

"And?" he pressed, but he started losing his focus.

"And? I bought this lovely dress with it," she answered, not a bit sorry.

He narrowed his eyes, but now they were both undressed, and it was either have a fight or just roll with it.

"And what a lovely dress it was," he said diplomatically. Because who's going to fight when your girl looks so good and shows she's so ready?

"I knew you'd think so," she said, and she left The Dress in rumpled perfection on the floor and took him to bed.

The end.

You can feel the difference in opinions immediately on the bus. Most guys aren't saying a word, while the girls burst into excited chatter.

"Come on," Frye says, almost whining, "that can't be what Cannon's apartment is really like. And it's not like he lives in his own place."

Saga shrugs. "*Fiction*, people. I dressed things up."

Her knowing smile suggests she's been to his place. It's part of Cannon's magic that everyone wants to pretend they're tight with him, and no one wants to look left out. But not one of these people has seen his place. Or places. Ever since he moved out of his mom's apartment, he's been living with some guys a few years older, but I've never been inside, never met them. I don't press him for a tour, but I'm probably the only person from school who's sat in the parking lot while he runs in to get stuff. It's definitely not the kind of building you'd take a girl to, unless it were a horror movie so you could time the murder with the trains roaring past and pan out to all the random rust stains on the peeling exterior. "Low rent," he said that first time, smiling, like he's cheated the system of having to live with his mom.

I never figured out if living on his own makes him glamorous or sad. But to everyone else, he's pure glamor. The kind of person who might have a hot tub on his roof.

Reiko grins at Saga. "That was intriguing. But I have to ask, what made you think of me?"

Saga smiles. "Your measurements, of course. The Dress I had in mind was kind of made for our body type. You know, people with arms."

"Dress sisters!" Mouse shouts, but Briony frowns and whispers something to Kai.

"You can't just tell a story like that and not show dress pics!" Alison says.

Saga passes her phone around to show her current dream dress.

"Looks a lot like *your* prom dress," Briony says coolly, then passes it on.

"Interesting," Cece says, and by now everyone looks to her as the voice of Ultimate Feminism. "There's the belittling stereotype that women will do anything for clothes, and they turn to men to buy clothes for them. However, she takes initiative in a male-dominated world and manages to get what she wants. I think this one's okay."

"It's an old, old story," says Saga. "There's this Scandinavian myth about Freya, the goddess of love, who wanted a necklace that enhanced her beauty threefold. She slept with some dwarves to get it."

"Too bad Peter Jackson missed that one in his *Hobbit* movies," Rooster says, but he's quiet, and the laughter from the guys is forced. Bryce is looking at his hands in his lap, not sure how to turn this into a joke. Maybe he's wondering how Saga got her dress this year, especially if her stepmom really did refuse to pay for it.

"Seriously," Briony says, all nettled. "So unfair to the guy. Right, Franklin?"

Everyone turns to Franklin, who looks like a cornered animal. "Hey, I'm cool with the story contest, but sometimes things take a feminist turn, and I have no idea what to say when that happens."

"Pard, *you* say something," Saga says. "You value clothes, and you're no prude. You'd have done the same thing. Explain to the guys."

Now that he's being called on, I finally I let myself stare at him.

Pard sits alone, sideways, feet dangling in the aisle. He sticks his nose up from his sketchbook. His small face is pinched like he's barely holding himself together. I mean, right after our conversation about girls' clothes, Saga is asking him for a speech on the same topic. "I don't think I'm the right guy for this. I'm a romantic, remember?"

He's right—he'd never sleep with someone to get a nice outfit. I'd always assumed Pard had slept with Greg and pretty much every gay guy at school, and now I'm not sure. I mean, there are rumors of him doing certain, um, *things* with this boy or that one, but I'm not sure anyone's ever returned his favors, or if it's even biologically possible for him to accept them. Even if something *were* possible, word would have gotten around that he's not a regular boy. He'd be hazed if people knew.

Then it hits me, what he'd said. Something about his last school. Something like, *If they knew, the guys would assault me like they did at my old school.*

He's sitting there so sharp and cynical and smart, but his body is so small, so defenseless. I felt that when I raised my fist. Why did I assume he had it easy just because he had no sister to mourn? Someone *hurt* him. He said as much, and I didn't even listen.

I push against my chest, against whatever is spilling out. I blink back tears. Someone *hurt* him. I'm the only one who knows this, and I brushed him off as a freak. Shit, I pretty much asked him what he had in his pants, like that's all I cared about. Then I refused to sit next to him. People hurt him, and then I hurt him. All I ever do is hurt him.

I'm dimly aware of Saga's pouty scold. "Oh, come on! What's more romantic than clothes . . . God, your pants are filthy."

I want to tell her to leave him alone, but of course, I do nothing.

Pard rolls his eyes and snaps shut his sketchbook. "*Fine*, Saga. It's true: The only things people can really count on are their clothes. Lovers come and go, but clothes are the real deal. Clothes make the man. Or woman. Whatever. It's just too bad your heroine has to ditch her dream dress sloppily on the floor at the end, when clothes are the only things she can really count on in life. She should have at least had the decency to hang it up." He goes back to his sketchbook and seems to be crossing something out fiercely.

He doesn't look in my direction once.

"*Okaaay*," Saga says, like Pard's just a basket of nerves, not someone who's been attacked in a hate crime and then coldly rejected by his former best friend. Just prickly Pard. The silly gay boy.

I hate myself. I tell him that, telepathically. Pathetically.

He doesn't look up. He's either drawing from memory, or he's just holding that sketchbook to get him through. I could say something right now. Tell him something. Gush out across the length of the bus, *Sorrysorrysorry.*

But I pull my signature move. I do nothing.

313

MARI'S TALE

Mari's up next, and she gets loud cheers from Sophie, Mouse, and Lupe.

"Don't be too literary," Rooster warns. "You writer types always ruin stories that way."

Mari looks annoyed. "What do you mean, 'too literary'?"

Sophie jumps in to defend her friend. "Mari is only the best writer ever. Didn't you read her werewolf story in the *Southwarks* January issue? You know, the one where the werewolf's wife steals his clothes, and the werewolf is stuck in wolf form until he finally gets them back?"

It was a brilliant story—my favorite werewolf story ever, published by anyone. After talking to Pard and hearing Saga's story, I realize the werewolf tale also seems to be about clothes and trying to be yourself.

Rooster taps his chin. "Yeah, that one's okay. But there wasn't enough sex. Actually, there wasn't any."

Mari gives Rooster a stern look. "*That's* what you mean by too literary? Fine. This time, you can be the sex-crazed hero."

He hoots. " Tell on, my minstrel."

On Zuckerman's farm, the pig Wilbur had been feeling lonely. Try as he might, no one wanted to play with him. He'd asked the old sheep, who said she didn't play with pigs. He'd asked the goose, who was too busy. He'd asked Templeton, the rat, who had no interest in *playing*, least of all with a whiny little runt.

Wilbur was running out of options and feeling desperate.

"Hey, this is *Charlotte's Web*," Rooster cuts in. "Didn't we read this in, like, fourth grade? How can this be any good?"

Alison, Mouse, and Sophie shush him simultaneously.

Then Wilbur saw the rooster for the first time, a very striking bird. He had huge tail feathers that streamed from his backside like banners, his wattle dangled importantly—

"Worship my wattle, ye mortals!" Half standing in his seat, Rooster thrusts his hips back and forth, and I'm not sure if he's playing on Mari's use of the word "wattle" or really doesn't know that roosters have droopy skin under their chins.

—and he shone in the sun with brilliant reds and russets and browns and burnished gold, plus the deep inky darkness accenting his wings and back, and his stunning turquoise toes. He was the gem of the whole farm, the all-important announcer of the dawn, and the most virile creature within miles. His name was none other than Rooster.

Rooster breaks into a "cock-a-doodle-do!" and Alison gives his wattle (the northern one) a love bite. Meanwhile, I watch Pard smile in spite of himself at Rooster's antics, then study Mari as he sketches her.

I try apologizing telepathically: *I'm so sorry.*

But, again, it's like I'm not even here.

Stirred by Rooster's energetic beauty, Wilbur was about to ask Rooster to play, but, upon closer inspection, he noticed Rooster busily playing with a troop of chickens. The flapping wings and chaos and noise confused Wilbur. The game involved Rooster climbing on the chickens' backs one at a time, and each time he did it, he stayed up there struggling and crowing loudly in a kind of crescendo before he climbed down again. He seemed to enjoy the exercise mightily.

"What are you doing?" Wilbur asked.

Rooster spared Wilbur a glance. "Treading feathers," he replied happily, and then he and the hen he was on top of started crowing louder and louder.

"Can I play too?" Wilbur asked a few times. It was hard to get Rooster's attention, he was so engaged.

Rooster climbed off the hen, who shook herself and went to look for a snack.

While he waited for her to return, Rooster surveyed his remaining chickens and turned to Wilbur. "Sorry, Pig, these ladies are all mine, but you're free to watch. Isn't he, Pertelote?"

Pertelote cooed uncertainly, but then squawked as Rooster mounted her.

While Rooster and Pertelote did their thing, Templeton sidled over to Wilbur and gave him a quick explanation of what this game of treading feathers precisely involved, and then the goose came over to admire the game and verify its generative function.

Wilbur was scandalized. "But—he's putting his—but—oh my!"

"Oh yes—oh yes—oh yes!" the goose said cheerfully. "Nothing like a bit of copu-opu-lation for the species' propu-opu-gation."

Lupe laughs. "I remember the goose! This is kind of sick!"

The guys hoot and crow in some sort of approximation of chicken sex, while chanting: *Treading feathers! Treading feathers!*

I can't help but love this boisterous group, but what moves me most is Reeve's soft, nerdy *heh-heh*, and mouthing of the chant that I would never have noticed if I'd sat farther back. I would have assumed he was muttering clipboard data, but I wonder if half the time, he's just participating in his own way. Here's a kid who's been rejected time and again, and he embraces his post as a nark and killjoy—yet sometimes he forgets his grudge and laughs along, even if the other kids never forget he's a social outcast. He sees me smiling at him and grabs his clipboard, and the moment is lost. I can't do anything right today.

Wilbur, nauseated by the fornication before him, escaped from his pen and tried to make a run for it. The animals broke out in raucous chaos, with flapping wings, trotting legs, and a chorus of voices, including loud bawks from Rooster's entire harem.

"Why, he's running from rutting," laughed the old sheep. "Scared of the beast with two backs, I'd say."

"COCK-A-Doodle DOOOOOooooo!" Rooster screamed with an explosion of lady wings beating underneath him.

"You realize if you live long enough, you'll be expected to carry on the same performance with a sow," Templeton told Wilbur.

"Noooo!" squealed the pig, scarred for life. "I'll never put that part of myself into an animal in such a coarse fashion."

"When you're older, you'll be surprised-surprised-surprised," clucked the goose. "You'll play the game like everyone else."

"Never," Wilbur insisted, and he trotted off, but not too far.

Even if the other animals were disgusting and played terrible games with their bodies, they were still his extended family. He didn't know where to go without them.

After a confusing dose of freedom Wilbur was more than ready for Lurvy and Zuckerman to arrive with slops in hand, and the pig went docile, but still confused and friendless, to his pen.

That night Wilbur called a meeting in the barn and asked if anyone would be his friend. A *platonic* friend, he specified, with a nervous glance at Rooster and his nymphomaniac hens. "What's 'platonic'?" asked Rooster, who had a small vocabulary. This is when Charlotte befriended Wilbur and promised to show herself the next day. There was a nice logical tone to her voice that comforted the confused and frightened little pig.

The next morning, just before dawn, Wilbur woke up in high anticipation. He trotted back and forth in his pen, and then, finally, Charlotte called down to him from a high beam. She seemed to be a kind of vampire, because she sucked blood, but at least her no-nonsense personality meant he wouldn't hear rutting jokes from her.

Then, to Wilbur's alarm, Rooster crowed for an emergency meeting.

"What is it?" snapped Templeton. "Do you need a friend too?"

With his clawed toes, Rooster scratched the ground angrily. "I have enough playmates, as you well know! All of you, listen up. This is truly important. I had a terrible dream—an ill omen for us all."

His entire harem trembled, and the whole barn heard him out.

He paced as morning light streamed through the rafters and played upon his brilliant feathers. "Lives are in terrible danger! Last night I dreamed there was a fierce creature we've never seen before. The animal came to our farm and attacked me. The hungry beast tore into me with his sharp teeth. This vision is surely a warning. Some creature of death is coming our way. I'm deadly serious—I bring you tidings of dreams, desire, and death."

Mari flashes me a mischievous smile that I have to return. She's woven in a line from my Morpheus story. She's parodying me, and E. B. White, and possibly more. Her simple story actually isn't so simple. It's brilliant, like everything she does.

"Dreams? You're not serious." Templeton yawned. "I could be sifting through Zuckerman's garbage, but instead, I'm stuck here listening to Rooster's dreams? What, dreaming of a trac-tor or something?"

"This wasn't a tractor. It was smaller."

Templeton scoffed. "Oh, I'm shaking."

"After a dream, you've only got to wakey-akey-akey," advised the goose.

Surrounded with indifference and misunderstanding, Rooster turned to the wives and concubines he's always counted on, and especially his great love, Pertelote.

But Pertelote wasn't having it either. "Did you take your medicine last night? You know, the laxatives?"

The animals all gave their varied squawks and brays and squeaks of surprise and gleeful alarm. "WHAT?"

Pertelote explained. "Oh, it's that all-corn diet. Can't digest it properly. Takes laxatives to soften things. Softens the brains, too, you know? Laxatives really mess up dreams. We shouldn't worry."

"What do you think, Charlotte?" Wilbur asked. "You're clever, and you'd know what these dreams add up to."

Charlotte dangled before them all on a glistening strand. "Dream interpretation is a pseudoscience. I wouldn't put much stock in dreams without more evidence."

Pertelote fluffled her ample feathers. "There, see?"

So Rooster tried to forget his bad dream, which wasn't hard to do, considering how lovely his wives and concubines were. He began treading feathers then and there, much to Wilbur's discomfort.

While Wilbur and Charlotte were getting more deeply acquainted, and Rooster took his treading act out toward the henhouse, no one noticed a new visitor to Zuckerman's farm. Not much bigger than a barn cat, but much cleverer, the fox found his way to Rooster's henhouse.

321

Pertelote shrieked. "What's that?" All the hens flapped to the roof of their henhouse, and Rooster was right there with them, though he was at the edge of the sloping roof and closest to the strange creature. It would be a near miss at best if the strange creature could jump.

"I'm terribly sorry," the fox said, his head bowed with a show of apology. "I didn't mean to frighten anyone. But, oh my, you are a beautiful animal."

Rooster fluffed up his tail feathers to advantage. "I'm sure you meant no harm," he said, somewhat mollified.

The fox's amber eyes watched Rooster with a loving expression. "You must be that magical bird with the singing abilities. I've heard the songs of your kind before—only the males deliver that crooning song of raw beauty and power."

Rooster trilled a little *cock-a-doodle*, with a question mark at the end of it, as if to say, *Ah, that little thing of mine?*

The fox's mouth opened in a canine smile. "Like that, yes, but with more force! When the eyes are shut tight with concentration, and the gorgeous throat extends to unleash the full power of song, there is nothing to compare it to. What I wouldn't give for just one rapturous performance!"

Rooster's eyes popped open with delight. Even Pertelote had never praised his song so highly. "Well, if I have a fan . . ."

The fox whined with the hunger of fandom.

And like a diva, Rooster screwed shut his eyes and gave a terrific crow.

"COCK-A-DOO—"

He got no further. Instantly, the fox leaped into the air and snapped his jaws around Rooster's elongated neck, landing nimbly on black-gloved paws with Rooster's body underneath. Wasting no time, the fox took off running with his prey, Rooster's long tail dragging in the dust.

Hens screamed, the geese picked up the panic, and all the animals went berserk. Wilbur went mad with fright, sending up a high-pitched wail and running aimlessly around his pen while the fox was trying to pass through the barn, with Rooster in tow. There was a terrific crash, and the fox bounced off Wilbur, completely winding him, and Rooster, now free of the fox's jaws, beat his wings until he was up with Charlotte on the high rafters.

"Ah, love, I didn't mean to frighten you," the fox told Rooster, looking up with longing and then glaring at Wilbur. "I only wished to take you out of this prison and go somewhere where we can enjoy your music . . . in privacy. Won't you come down, my dear?"

Rooster, whose throat was bruised, rasped, "I have no idea what 'privacy' means, but I see right through your sweet words. Think I'd fall for your fandom act a second time? Eat my tail feathers!"

Charlotte waved at the fox. "Speaking of which, look who's on your bushy tail!"

Lurvy and Zuckerman were running pell-mell toward the

barn, but not as fast as Zuckerman's dogs, who were frantic to get at the fox.

The fox beat it out of the barn, and they never saw him again.

"Well, well!" Rooster crowed, at last coming down, noticing he had a huge audience gathered to see him. "I'm all right, friends! If it weren't for Wilbur here, I'd have been that animal's lunch. That's some pig!"

All his wives and concubines gathered around Wilbur and bawked "Some pig! Some pig! *Ba-kah, ba-kah!*"

And when Charlotte needed to save Wilbur's life by writing words in her web, these were the words that seemed the perfect ones to write. The end.

"Aw, that was cute!" Mouse says.

Rooster chuckles. "Yeah. I'm kinda cute when you give me a harem. Nice one, Mari."

She leans on one elbow. "Thanks. Warms the cockles of your heart, doesn't it?"

"Both of my cockles," he says with gusto. "*Cockles. Wattle. Treading feathers.* Mari, you are my Word Girl."

Rooster looks at Mari like he's noticing her for the first time. Not just as a brain, but as a woman. It's like her tale rampant with chicken sex was a female mating call for him. They'd be like Hermione and Ron, wit on her side and a redhead jock on his. I'm probably just hallucinating, thinking of Mari and Rooster as a pair. I don't think she'd appreciate knowing he's been a steady client (my favorite client—try writing a C-minus paper on *The Scarlet Letter* in Rooster's voice, and it will be more fun than getting drunk, though you'll need to be to write the paper). Not a likely match.

But, on days like today, anything can happen.

Or not. Pard still won't return my glances. This must be how it felt sophomore year when I'd walk past him like he wasn't there. For months. I need to apologize. At least after high school, when I think of him, I'll know I did that much.

SOPHIE'S TALE

Mr. Bailey reads the slip of paper in his hand. "Sophie, it's your turn!"

Sophie giggles shyly. She's trying hard not to look nervous, and then the group gets all pep-talky and cute, saying, *You'll do great!*

So. An angel and a devil fell in love.

The girls go wild, and Mari fist-pumps. "Is that line from Laini Taylor? This is going to be awesome."

"I'll take a story with hot angels and devils!" Lupe says.

Sophie smiles, but when she pushes back her hair, her hand is trembling. Sophie is not as painfully shy as she was before she hung out with Mari, but still, this will be the first time I've heard Sophie speak to a group for anything more than a few sentences.

The angel and devil were both assigned to the same soul.

It was young Constance's first assignment in the mortal world.

When she found her mortal, a boy named Fabius, the devil was already corrupting him. It was a small sin, to harbor resentment against his parents over some rules, but still, it could lead to greater transgressions. Constance worked through Fabi's tangle of emotions, and she found him. The devil.

"There you are," he said, almost as if she were late for a date. He looked her up and down. "You're new."

She flexed her wings. "Clearly, you are his demon. I think I can handle you. Don't assume I don't know what I'm doing."

He tilted his head. "I called you *new*, not inept. You're too beautiful to be an old hand at this tiring game."

She reasoned aloud. "Then you are also new."

He raised his eyebrows, and she blushed at the implication that she'd called him beautiful. "I'm hardly new. Only experienced demons can be beautiful. Temptation is a beautiful thing, or didn't you know that?"

Mouse squees. "Sophie, you're a natural! That demon is hot!"

Franklin nuzzles Mouse's neck and repeats, "Temptation is a beautiful thing."

You can imagine what happens next. Their rivalry in steering their mortal became charged with their feelings, until Constance cared less about Fabius and more about Sowdain, the demon. At some point they followed their mortal around like balloons on a string but forgot to get into his head. They talked to each other instead, walked side by side.

And then something happened.

The mortal, now grown, was walking to the local ovens for his bread. There was a spring in his step. He was getting married soon, to a pretty young woman. It made Constance oddly wistful to see all the preparations nearly at an end.

Sowdain dropped some news on her all at once. "I'm going to be reassigned."

She tensed like he'd slapped her. "How can that be? Our assignments are for life."

"For the mortal's life. Yes. Or ours."

"Well, then. The man is young, and we are immortal." Constance was still new. She didn't understand.

Sowdain snagged a roll from the baker, which no one saw, of course. He broke off a few pieces and let them fall for the birds. "I don't eat bread, my dear. I eat souls. I nibble away at their lies, resentments, and lust. When the mortal is won, I feed. I live. And then I do it again. Lately, I lost my knack for angling for this mortal's soul. I've missed meals and feel myself fading. I've been . . . distracted. It's negligence my commanders haven't noticed yet, or maybe they are just waiting for the right time to end this. I'll be replaced soon, and when I am, there won't be time for farewells. If I'm a convincing liar, I'll be assigned to grunt work. If not, they'll feed on me. Either way, my time here will end suddenly. That's why I'm telling you now. I want you to know. I want you to remember me when I'm gone."

He dropped the last of the bread and wiped his hands free of crumbs.

She caught his hands. "You can't go. We have to save you!"

He chuckled, but he squeezed her hands just the same. "Spoken like an angel. *Saving.* It's your business, but I'm not your client. What would you advise?"

"Perhaps . . . perhaps Fabius could—" Could what? "Lie? Would that be enough?" Constance was too innocent to imagine what sins the mortal could do.

Sowdain's eyes glowed like the coal fires. "Hmm. That's a dangerous suggestion for an angel to make. I will do nothing that implicates you. Instead, may I suggest a different indiscretion altogether?"

She pulled back at the sound of his voice, but he had her hands. He only gave them up to slide his hands up her arms to her neck, her face.

He kissed her. He couldn't help it anymore.

Constance had never been kissed before. She was young for pairing. Yet she kissed him back. They stayed that way, kissing on the market street, for some time, invisible to everyone else and lost to each other.

They were in love, and he apologized for tasting her soul. He offered to abandon his post. He didn't want to jeopardize her position. Her life. He didn't want to devour her.

Constance, being an angel, saw the situation differently. She wanted to marry him. When angels have sex, their souls mingle as one. She was young, she could sustain him, she was sure. And she wanted to.

And against his better judgment, he said yes.

It was a foolish plan. They abandoned Fabius and eloped. Then everything ended. Suddenly.

Angels and demons swooped in and attacked the lovers and one another. The lovers were unarmed and stood to one side, fighting only when attacked. Many died. So did Sowdain, and what happens to the souls of the demons, only God knows.

"No!" Briony wailed. "You can't take him out!"

Mouse piped in. "Yeah. I'm so mad at you! But go on!"

Alison was almost jumping in her seat. "It's more *Game of Thrones* this way. Makes you keep guessing."

"Or is this some sort of tragic ending?" Briony asks.

"There's more," Sophie says. Her voice is quieter now than it was a moment before, but she doesn't look nervous. "If that's okay?"

The angels won the skirmish and took back Constance. She was judged for her actions.

She was guilty of leaving her post, her mortal unguided.

She was guilty of conspiring with a devil and giving herself to him.

She was guilty of using the human world for purposes denied to her order.

The archangel ruled that she would wander the pathways of the Earth by water or road and have no access to nor insight of either Heaven or Hell. She would appear human, with a human's physical needs for food and clothing and shelter.

She became an exile, a wanderer.

There were rules to her wandering. The main rule was to keep moving. She couldn't stay anywhere long. When she tried, the pain was unbearable. When she lay down at an inn, she awoke on a road. She would get up and keep moving.

Years passed.

Our story next picks up in the modern day at a Greyhound station.

A woman boarded a bus. She had a pass that let her onto any Greyhound in the country. And she rode all day and all night. She crossed from New York to California and back again. She was known as the Bus Lady.

Mostly, people left her alone. Her tattered clothes and her snarled hair marked her as homeless. Sometimes someone leaving the bus would give her a dollar, or a granola bar, or a novel, and these gifts would keep her going.

Then there was the night with the scary man. The bus had

a lot of empty seats, and the scary man came and sat behind her. A young man at the front cast a nervous glance her way.

"Pretty thing," the scary man said.

The Bus Lady had to fight off would-be rapists before, and she got up and moved toward the front.

The scary man shouted, "Hey, that's rude, leaving in the middle of a conversation! That's rude behavior!"

There were only a few people on the bus. The young man signaled to her, so she sat next to him.

They waited a long time, but eventually, the scary man got off at his stop.

The young man sighed. "I've been waiting forever for that guy to take off. I'm sorry, but I forgot to ask your name. I'm Alan."

The Bus Lady smiled. "Constance."

They talked. Constance didn't say who she really was. She was on the move, with a past behind her, and that was enough. Alan had a past too. He was a young man caught between divorced parents, a violent mother, a distant father. His hope was to go to college next year and stay in one place: his own.

When it came time to sleep, they shared the seat, propping their legs on the other side, their bodies close. There was comfort hearing the young man breathe in his sleep. They stayed together for the entire next day, and the next. Talking, riding in silent company, sharing a book. But mostly talking.

On Alan's last day on the bus, they both began to speak at the same time. "You first," he said.

She told him her secret, that she had loved someone and saw him die. It was good to finally tell someone, to trust someone. He had no answers, but she expected none. She only wanted someone to help her hold her truth. They fell silent.

Then she asked him, "What were you going to tell me?"

He shook his head. "It's not important." But she'd seen enough inside him to know he was lying. Long after, she'd realize what he meant was that *he* was not important—he didn't feel worthy to declare his feelings when he could never match this other man who died defending her.

They said good-bye at sunset. He gave her his money, his iPad (with his library), his journal, his jacket, the pack around his shoulders—everything that might be useful to her.

Everything but himself.

Then he was gone. She continued on her route, but the world had changed. She was restless. She read everything he had given her. She read and reread his journal. And with the pen in the backpack, she started writing her first words.

"Constance?"

It was a few years later, on another bus, in another state, and she looked up to see the face she'd imagined so many times: Alan. She didn't know how it happened, but he slid in next to her and held her so close for so long. She tilted her head to focus on the feeling of his fingers over her snarled hair.

She'd imagined they'd have a rush of words between them

if they'd ever met again, but, instead, it was a rush of touching in silence. Holding hands. Holding. Her finger on his cheek. Alan was a little older, but she was not.

A mere two days together was not enough time. Her fingers weren't done with touching his face. With resting her cheek on his shoulder. Not enough time to touch him.

And they came to his stop.

"Come with me," Alan pleaded, pulling her by the hand.

And she came. With his hand on hers, she could bear the walk away from the station. She could ascend the stairs and walk into his apartment, a small two-bedroom with another young man sharing it. Miraculously, anchored by Alan's love, she lived there for a year. She lived there and gave birth to a son.

And then one day, when Alan was at work, a knock on the door startled Constance from nursing the baby.

She opened the door to a handsome woman with dead eyes.

She called herself Alan's mother, and she came in and asked questions. Then she began hitting Constance and trying to harm the baby. The screaming woman threw books off the shelves, almost hitting little Morris. Constance gripped her baby and fled out the door. Without Alan's help centering her in place, Constance couldn't stay. Her curse to wander returned.

She woke on a bus with the baby in her arms, and she sobbed. She wanted to throw herself in front of the bus. Constance had lost Sowdain, and she'd lost Alan.

But if she died, so would little Morris.

So she held on.

Passengers helped the sobbing young mother with small gifts: food, mostly, and that very first day, another mother returning home gave her own diaper bag to Constance. There was a change of onesies, a pair of socks.

The baby suckled and grew. He took his first steps down the aisle, and his first words were with passengers. Time passed. The baby became a child.

It was only when the child was fifteen, on his birthday, that Constance had had enough with wandering. She did not know where she was, only that she had to get off. She took Morris off the bus. He looked around in surprise, the way he always did to see the world holding so very still.

She walked and found she could resist the call to get back on board. Constance was allowed a rest from wandering.

She soon found a job as a live-in maid and caretaker for a very old man. There was a room for her and Morris to share. The old man left her alone and did not mind if Morris read in the library. They settled in for several months. And then she was called down and asked to prepare a room for the man's son. The guest arrived the next day.

It was Alan. Older, with a grief-lined face and thinning hair, yet still kind, still soft-spoken and beautiful. She ached at the sight of him, but she didn't show herself. Not yet.

She sent Morris to see if Alan needed anything, and Alan was struck by the boy's face. The boy was like Constance in every way, and Alan was beside himself with love for this child.

"Who is your mother? Please tell me."

And Constance entered the room.

Alan leaped forward, then froze.

"Don't be afraid," Constance said, but he was.

"You haven't changed. You haven't aged."

"I do not change," Constance said mournfully, "but our son can." By now Constance looked like Morris's sister, not his mother.

And she told him what she was and why she had wandered and might one day wander again.

Then Alan told her his story.

He'd gone to prison. He'd found Constance and Morris gone, and his mother railing at him, slapping his face, bragging that she'd beaten off a whore. Overcome, Alan had shoved his mother to the ground. The mother had a heart attack and died, and Alan was convicted of manslaughter. When he was free again, he spent years searching for Constance.

Alan and Constance were reunited, and Constance and Morris moved in with Alan in his own house. For a time all was well, and Alan was a tender father. Father and son became close. But when Morris was eighteen, Constance could feel the curse to wander one more time. She said good-bye to them, but they insisted on coming with her instead. They rode the Greyhound for days, for weeks, for months.

One night, when they were sleeping, Constance woke to find a man sitting beside her. She froze at the thought of an attacker.

"Don't try anything," she warned him. She pointed at her husband and adult son, indicating that she was not alone.

"They are worthy and beautiful," the man said, "but I must try *something*."

At the sound of his voice, she looked at him. It was Sowdain, but dim and distant. Sowdain as a mortal might be permitted to see him.

He smiled, and the mischief was still there, even after everything that had torn them apart.

Her fingers ran through him as if he were made of mist. She tried once more and still could not touch him.

"Soon," he said softly. "When you shed this curse, you'll shed your mortal limitations. But our superiors are allowing me to talk to you first. It's time to stop wandering, my dear. I'm here to take you home."

She shook her head. There were too many questions that needed answering. "Where have you been all this time?"

"For a time, I was in a place of the dead. But then I was offered an assignment: you."

Her eyebrows crept up her forehead. "As my demon?" Had he deceived her? No, that could not be.

He looked embarrassed. "Not precisely. A different assignment—or rather, I had two mutually conflicting assignments, and had to choose between them. I've been with you a long time. I moved the hearts of others to give you sustenance and compassion. I gave you things to think about to make the hours less lonely. I begged you not to give up. I made sure Alan ran late so your paths would cross that second time."

"You were my angel!"

"And I gave every single one of your would-be rapists blistering cases of genital warts." He shrugged and looked more pleased with himself over that than any of his angelic contributions.

"Sowdain." She tried to touch him again.

"Constance, your stop has come. Are you ready?"

She kissed Alan and Morris. "I love you," she told them both. They shifted in their dreams, sweet dreams by the looks on their faces, but they did not wake. She hesitated before their sleeping bodies. She didn't want them to be cursed with her wandering, but she didn't want them to worry.

"You'll visit their dreams and tell them what's become of you," Sowdain said. "And we will help protect them. This is not the last time you will look on their faces."

She gave them one last look and nodded fiercely.

"I'm ready."

Before she took off in flight, even before she felt the wings spring from her back, she felt his presence again, and then his hand. And she flew.

We sit there stunned, and then we can't clap fast enough.

"That was beautiful!" Briony fans her face. "I've never heard a story with a love triangle quite like this one. That was really great. Alan was pretty cute, but Sowdain!"

Mouse passionately agrees.

"You rocked it," Alison adds. "Here's a story where the heroine gets to have *both men* and no one calls her a slut. She's just being herself. Being *constant*."

My gaze drifts to Pard. He's looking at Sophie, at Alison, at anyone but me.

I get out my phone and text. I still know his number.

I'm sorry. I'm terrible.

"Jeff?!"

I send the text and look up. Mari stares daggers at me. It looks like I zoned out on her best friend's story, which is pretty much going to land me a death sentence. "Do you want to deign to comment?"

Why do they keep doing this, when I'm not nearly the best storyteller here?

"This was one of my favorites—great twists and turns. Nice romance plot and resolution. And the bus is very meta."

"Me-ta!" chants Rooster, and he and Franklin argue over which of them gets to be Sowdain, which gives me a chance to look at my phone.

Nothing.

He didn't look at me either, just stared out the window while I answered Mari's question.

I don't know what I want anymore. A weekend with Cannon sounds pretty good, but I'm not fun company for Nikki or anyone else right now.

But riding this bus is starting to feel like a Constance-style curse.

MOUSE'S TALE

A city rises before us, but even as the choruses of *We're here!* begin, Mr. Bailey hollers, "It's *Baltimore!* Good grief. This shouldn't be a civics class. We should be studying geography."

"Hey now," Alison counters. "It's one thing to fill in blanks on a map, and it's a whole different thing to see the world with your own eyes. Cut us some slack!"

He looks a little sheepish, conceding her point. "Okay, okay. We're down to the wire . . . D.C. is next, and we have three stories to go." He reaches into his hat.

When Mr. Bailey calls out Mouse's name, she squees then slaps a hand over her mouth. Briony leans across her seatback and gives her an air kiss and one of those drapey-armed hugs.

Mouse beams at everyone, and that enthusiasm even carries to the front of the bus. "Okay, I've been thinking of ideas all day, and here's the one I want to try out on you. But I only have half the story."

In the great city of Tashbaan, in Calormen, it was the birthday of the Tisroc.

"Oooo, a Narnia story," Mari says, beaming.

Mouse nods. "Guess my favorite character."

Voices call out: "Lucy!" "Susan!" "Aslan!"

Sophie is on this one. "Reepicheep!"

Mouse laughs. "He was my first crush!"

Heralds strolled the streets of Tashbaan, crying the good news. "Today is the nativity feast of the Tisroc, may he live forever!"

Streets both fine and squalid were lined with people thronging there for the parades, the jugglers, and the food. Even the most ragged boy had bread that day. A pack of children gnawed on second helpings when they heard another proclamation.

"Make way! Make way for the ambassador!"

The man was dark haired, black eyed, and magnificently dressed, with a jeweled scimitar and a most magnificent horse made of metal yet as graceful as a living animal. The rider turned the bend and rose up and up to the heart of the city, where the great feast was being held.

Meanwhile, the Tisroc sat on his dais in his palace next to the temple. Tarkaans and Tarkheenas feasted on peacocks and swans, ices shaped like animals, cakes of dates and honey and almonds, and wines both strong and sweet. In a place of honor among the women sat the Tisroc's daughter, Canacee, who had just yawned under her veil and tried to make it look like she wasn't yawning. She wasn't sleeping well. For the past two nights a falcon outside her window lamented her sorrows all night long. The mournful sounds made her feel both enchanted but also sad and powerless to help the unhappy bird.

Everyone turned and marveled at the ambassador as he dismounted from his strange horse, and Canacee was no different. His dark eyes met hers for one strange moment, and then the rider dismounted and bowed before the Tisroc, offering him birthday gifts that, he claimed, were from another world, where he, too, was from.

The Tisroc frowned. "There is a White Witch also from another world. She rules the small kingdom of Narnia. She covers the land with ice and snow, and only the desert walls her from my domain. It does not please me to know more travelers have entered our world and even my own country."

"Ah, but our intentions are friendship and peace. In token of which, I give to you this horse, a metal engine to carry you over land and across the air, far abroad and above arrows."

The Tisroc considered the amazing gift. "I accept."

"In further token of our wish for peace, my master also bade me to give you this." He brandished the scimitar glinting in the light. "The blade will cut through any armor, no mat-

342

ter how thick. Riding this horse and fighting with this scimitar, you will be a most dangerous foe. You have already united the provinces and brought a golden age to Calormen, but these tools will help you keep your reign in peace and prosperity— and arm yourself against magic at your borders."

No sooner had the Tisroc thanked the ambassador, when the man continued, "I have two final gifts for one of your household. The first is a mirror that reveals friends and foes—a man can see whether armies rise against him . . . or a woman using it could see whether her lover is faithful or faithless. The final gift is this ring." He took off a ring with a large stone. "The ring imparts the ability to understand the speech of birds, and it can also lead its bearer to find healing herbs to cure any wound, no matter how great. And the mirror and the ring are for your only daughter, beautiful, unparalleled Canacee."

The girl froze, unsure what to do, while a murmur of shock rushed through the large dining chamber as the assembled Tarkaans and Tarkheenas craned their necks.

"This is most unusual," the Tisroc said. "She is just a girl. You have overlooked my sons, meanwhile, and should not the mirror protect the safety of the realm rather than inform my daughter of lovers' hearts?"

But her eldest brother laughed. "Perhaps it is fitting she have the mirror. She is more besieged by suitors than we are by armies."

The ambassador did not laugh at this jest. "Canacee's

goodness and beauty are known across the world, and beyond it. I would give her these gifts and all within my power."

She blushed.

After much ceremony Canacee stepped forward to take the ring and the mirror, and some magic must have been in the air, for it seemed she and the ambassador could speak to each other without the court overhearing.

"I hope you will use the gifts," he said softly. "I made them for you. Little marvels from another world."

He was a wizard, then. She shivered just a little, but bowed her head and thanked him. "There are marvels outside my own window that I do not understand—I do not pretend to have the wisdom to understand things beyond my own world. And yet I wish to know more."

"And I wish I could know *you* more, but there is no time, and my world is too perilous." And he sighed, and she knew he was in love with her, and it filled her with all the restlessness that the falcon's lament had done.

But they did not speak again—he vanished soon after, and no man saw him leave.

No one spoke of anything else but the strange ambassador and the four gifts: two for the Tisroc on his birthday, and two for the girl, for no apparent reason.

Only Canacee knew this generosity came from love. At first, that made them marvelous enough, and that day she made no attempt to use the gifts. Luckily, her father let her keep them.

He had the more valuable treasures, the ones that would serve in war. The other two seemed like women's treasures because they looked into minds and hearts.

But to her they seemed the most valuable treasures of all.

Late in the night she looked into the mirror. There he was, the wizard—did this mean he was her lover? But there was a gash on his forehead, and his clothes were torn and bloodied. He was in a dark prison. With bound hands he tried to cast a spell, but clearly could not do so. She ached at the sad sight. How could this happen? How could she help him?

Suddenly, she heard a woman crying outside her window, which opened to treetops from its lofty height.

"I'm lost and abandoned," the lady cried.

Canacee threw open the door to her balcony, and there she saw what she least expected: a most beautiful falcon, who gave her a curious look, and then, seeing no danger from the girl, cried out, "I will never recover from this heartbreak!"

Canacee gasped. "You—you can speak like a daughter of men."

Now the falcon stared with sharp yellow eyes. "I have heard the birds of Narnia are understood by the flightless beasts, but you are the first human I have ever spoken with."

Canacee clasped her hands, felt the ring on her finger, and instantly understood. "I forgot that this ring allows me to understand your speech. But what heartbreak do you mean?"

The bird's sorrow instantly returned. "My lover has left me. He promised we would build a nest together. Nothing came of it in the end."

"That is so sad!"

The falcon ruffled her feathers. "My heart was his prey. I must forswear love and protect myself against its snares."

And the falcon saw the mirror in Canacee's chamber and gave a sharp cry—"There he is, the tercel falcon!" She rammed the mirror with her beak and shattered it. Then Canacee wept at the hurt to the bird and the destruction of her mirror. She told the falcon of the mirror's power to show lovers faithful and unfaithful, and she told her of the man who came to her father bearing the four gifts. He was now in prison, though she knew not the cause, nor where he lay.

The falcon looked at her with a solemn eye. "And you have not attempted a rescue?"

Canacee felt a thrill in her heart. "Do you think I could rescue him? I'm not allowed to leave my father's house, let alone this city. I'm not sure I could escape."

The falcon ruffled her feathers again. "Then I must help you find your way in return for your friendship to me. For starters, we need that horse!"

To steal something of such value was a crime punishable by death. Canacee's eyes wandered to the broken mirror, and she saw against all hope that one shard of the mirror held her wizard's image. He was still bound and suffering. She wrapped the shard in silk to take with her.

Canacee said, "We'll need the scimitar as well."

And so they planned far into the night.

"Phew, I think that's all I can manage, guys!"

Everyone says, "No, keep going!"

"I would if I could!" Mouse frowns. "I thought of the ambassador as a sort of wizard from another world who made the gifts for a cruel king but gave them to Canacee and her father instead. And Canacee would somehow save him, but I have no idea how, or how all the gifts will get used. I have to think about it. I'd like to finish the story someday."

Franklin puts his arm around her and tells her she did a great job, and that's all he has to say about the matter.

"It was good," Bryce says. "Also, I have to say I'm really glad that the ambassador isn't some blond Narnian dude. I mean, pretty much all the good guys in Calormen have to convert to Narnian ways. Kind of sucks."

"Like Shylock in *The Merchant of Venice*," Mari says.

"Yeah," Bryce says, but he looks unsure what she means, probably because I wrote his Shakespeare paper for him.

"I loved Aravis," Mouse says, drumming her jawline, "but I see what you mean."

"The big question," Rooster says, "is which gift really is the best. I think the horse is. I want a horse that can run over land and air and doesn't even shit."

People naturally pair off to tell their seatmate what they preferred.

Of course I stare at Pard, who ignores me.

Reeve mumbles, "The mirror. For a man's use, obviously."

He scribbles on his clipboard. Up close, I see he uses black and red pen and writes in tidy, color-coordinated columns.

"The ring," I tell his head.

Reeve looks up, scornful. "You want to commune with love-lorn birds?"

"I want to find the healing herbs."

Reeve's black stare is intense. You can see the struggle he's feeling between wanting knowledge of his enemies and wanting herbs that cure all wounds. He returns to his clipboard, grumbles at it. "We should be allowed both."

FRANKLIN'S TALE

With only two names left, Mr. Bailey draws Franklin's, and the popular crowd cheers.

Franklin chuckles with feigned humility. "Well, you can see how awesome my girl is. It's hard to follow her."

"You should tell us something about yourself," Mouse says.

He puckers his face with concentration, probably because there are so many accomplishments and world tours to choose from, but then his face clears. "Did I tell you guys I got into Princeton?"

Everyone's like, *No way!*

I know jealousy is an ugly thing, but I'm thinking of all the flawless, slightly obnoxious papers I've written for him. My biggest client. Now I regret writing them.

"And Mouse is going to Rutgers to be near me. Luckily for me, Mouse hasn't been adopted by dolphins." He clamps down on her in a squeeze.

But Mouse giggles in his clutches and says, "Aw! You're too cute. And brilliant! Give us a story, Frankie!"

His smile is pure confidence. "I think you'll like this one."

My tale begins at Hogwarts—

Cheers erupt like this is the story everyone's been waiting for, and Mouse gives her signature squee.

I stiffen. Because I wrote a Hogwarts story and sold it to him sophomore year through Cannon. It's the only time I sold a story. It was for his final project. He got an A. The only thing I asked was that he never publish it in *The Southwarks*—it was just for a grade. Still, it hurt to sell it. I asked Cannon if I could just write essays after that. I was nervous confronting him. He said that was fine and not to worry about it.

Franklin laughs, but he's holding his hands up protectively. "Whoa! I'm not J. K. Rowling—time to lower the expectations!"

Please, let it not be my story. It's one thing to know a teacher thinks he's a great writer and for me to help launch him to Princeton. It's another to see all these guys leaning in to hear him tell the story I wrote. It's like when Harry catches Mundungus nicking Sirius's stuff and can't do anything about it—except I sold it. It's my fault.

A fifth-year Slytherin watched hungrily as the owls streamed in at breakfast. It was spring, and he just needed to hold on a little longer before he could see Dori for the whole summer long. These letters were all he had in the meantime. When he was lucky enough to get one.

He prodded the strip of bacon he'd saved to offer his owl

Perimene, but she didn't come. Not today, then. He was stupid to hope for a response so quickly. It's just that Dori's last letter was so . . . promising. He couldn't pull it out here at breakfast, of course, but he tuned out the racket of banter and cutlery and ran over the memorized words in her letter for the millionth time.

Oh, Aurie,

I loved the flower you sent me—it glows in the dark! I keep it on my pillow at night. Beautiful. How does it live on this little vial of stuff? You make me wish that I was a witch and could go to Hogwarts with you and Gus. You must have so many adventures.

Things here in the ordinary world are fine. The performance went fine. I just . . . Don't get me wrong, I love the cello. But sometimes I wish I could leave it all behind. Gus told me he was thinking of helping with dragon research when he graduates, and just thinking of Gus showing me nests of dragons and you showing me where the moon-phase flowers grow . . . if either could ever happen . . . it just makes my world so small, when yours is so big. You're so lucky, living in two worlds, but I don't know why you even bother with mine.

I miss you both. Gus sent me a picture of him on his broom. What a great Quidditch season it's been for him! He has such a cheeky wink, don't you think? And while I love the flowers you send in every letter, why won't you include your picture?

Here's mine. It isn't very good, I know, and it doesn't move with magic. But now you have no excuse!

Love,

Dori

How wrong she was—her photo was absolute magic, even if it didn't move. *He* was the one who kept moving multiple times a day to gaze at it just one more time before he'd tuck it under his pillow or in a pocket. And then he'd take it out again.

He sighed. Someone looked his way, but went back to chatting with his friends. Aurelius didn't have friends at Hogwarts, but that was all right. Dori was all that mattered. But she wanted his picture! That could never happen. He was about as good at smiling for photographs as he was at making friends. He suspected the two were closely related.

But that letter . . . She kept his flower *on her pillow*. She missed him. She signed her letter "love," which reduced him to putting his hand on his heart and sighing every time he visualized it on the page. He had written back with excuses about the photo. He'd see her soon after his O.W.L.s, anyway. He said he'd go hiking with her and show her wildflowers. "I'll show thee all the qualities of the isle," he wrote, echoing Shakespeare's *Tempest*, which her literature class was reading—how amazing to study poems and plays in school. And as usual, he included another flower, and a poem. He wrote, "Your letter had the words 'beautiful' and 'night,' so I thought you might like Byron's 'She walks in beauty like the night' this time, as mood music . . . to enjoy with your flower." He signed his letter "love," but daringly left out the comma, which turned the words into a plea. *Love Aurie.*

It all sounded so romantic and rapturous, writing all that, imagining her reading love poetry in bed with his flower on her pillow, and he sent the letter off with Perimene, his feelings literally taking wing, soaring to her.

He'd been a nervous wreck ever since.

Briony gasps. "This is really good. Franklin, I didn't know you had it in you."

Mouse laughs. "He's such a romantic."

Franklin smiles. "I'm glad you like it."

And I die a little more with every word, because every word is mine. Or was.

So Professor McGonagall was teaching transformations to the fifth-year wizards and witches, all Slytherins and Gryffindors. There was a knock at the door, and she had the students work in pairs while she had a brief conference with Professor Snape.

"Get your nose out of that book or I'll charm your face into it once and for all," snapped Aurelius's partner, Jeremy. Most of the Slytherins tolerated him as a hopeless bookworm, a fluke who really belonged in Ravenclaw. Aurelius reluctantly pushed the bulging textbook he'd been reading under his elbow. It was hard to concentrate on transforming a bottle into a bird when his mind wanted to stay lost in the words he'd been reading.

Meanwhile, the Gryffindors were goofing off and getting away with it, as usual.

"I can show you transformation." His archenemy showed a picture to his friends. "See if that doesn't transform you in all the right places."

A Gryffindor girl spun around in time to snatch the picture. "Gus, you pig—wait until I tell Sylvie!" But she didn't look too angry. Gus had a bad-boy charm that seemed to have all the girls after him. Gus lunged after the picture, and it fell in swoops into the aisle at Aurelius's feet.

The picture he'd been waving around like a trophy was Dori's. Aurelius stood up so fast, the bench toppled backward, Jeremy with it. His wand was out and the transfiguration spell rushed from his lips. Now a raven, Gus squawked angrily.

The Gryffindors roared and the scene quickly turned into a hexing free-for-all. One of Gus's friends cast a spell that Aurelius blocked with his left hand, which instantly became webbed like a seal's, though it seemed to be a hex involving slime rather than human Transfiguration. Gus's other friend cast the pins-and-needles curse, and Aurelius fell to the floor in pain all over.

He heard shouts and then, finally, the pain eased off. Aurelius tested his limbs. Snape stood over him.

McGonagall's voice was harder than Aurelius had ever heard. "Aurelius, when did you learn human Transfiguration, and how dare you try it on a student unsupervised? Twenty points from Slytherin. And, Leo, I saw you perform the pins-and-needles hex. That's unacceptable. Twenty points from Gryffindor."

Then the chorus of other Gryffindors clamored in Gus's defense.

"Aurelius started it, Professor."

"Gus was minding his own business."

"It came from nowhere."

"Silence, everyone!" thundered McGonagall.

Snape screwed up his mouth like he'd tasted something foul. "I'll leave that miscreant in your hands. Meanwhile, I need a word with Aurelius. Come, boy."

He got up on legs still weak from lack of blood and would have fallen without Snape catching his arm, which still felt like it wasn't his arm. They made their way down the hall, then down the stairs.

He waved his flipper. "Shouldn't I go to Madam Pomfrey's?"

"Not yet," Snape replied, swinging open the dungeon door of his office.

Aurelius looked around the office he knew well from so many detentions.

Most of the detentions were for unauthorized reading: in class; outside, at Quidditch matches, which Snape some-times required him to attend; in the library, because he read the wrong books there. Snape was particularly furious when Aurelius was caught writing bits of rhyme. Snape gave up long ago detracting points from Slytherin. It only turned the House against the boy, who retreated even more desperately to his world of words.

By force of habit, Aurelius dipped his finger in a vase holding one of Snape's small selections of plants, all of them magical and most needing no soil to live, just living off icy-hot tinctures. Aurelius had stolen cuttings from some of these plants and bred his own garden in his room.

Aurelius liked detention. It gave him an excuse not to have plans on Hogsmeade evenings, or Saturday nights, or Quidditch matches and post-match parties, and all the other social events. Not that anyone asked him what he was up to on a Friday night.

"Sit," Snape said when he saw the boy move to the tray of dirty vials needing washing, and the boy's face fell. "I want to hear what happened."

He didn't dare look in the eyes of his Head of House, a skilled Legilimens. His father, his classmates, and everyone else, cast Aurelius withering looks of disapproval but couldn't read whatever went on in Aurelius's head, and Aurelius liked it that way.

"Maybe I'm finally showing Slytherin spirit," he offered, unconvincing even to himself. "You know, defying Gryffindor."

Snape's stony face remained unreadable. "Let's start at the beginning. First, during Professor McGonagall's class, you were perusing this little gem."

Pulling the transformation book from Aurelius's book bag, Snape yanked out the book hidden inside and examined it with a contemptuous lift of one eyebrow. The book was called *Immortal Sonnets*, but the tattered copy appeared to be at death's door, and several pages fell loose in Snape's hand.

"Sonnets," Snape spat, literally, on the final *s*. His voice dripped with scorn. "I'm not sure whether I should be more disgusted by the sonnets themselves or the outlandish claim that they're *immortal*."

"I think it just means they're really, really good."

"Enough!" Snape made a strangled sound and wiped his face. "Such a waste of talent. I saw how you transfigured Arveragus . . . that was N.E.W.T. level work, far beyond your coursework. . . ."

He sat bolt upright. "So, that's it. You sneaked an entire Muggle library into Hogwarts through transformation."

Aurelius squirmed eyes down with his hands in his lap. You can fit heaps of books in your luggage if you turn them into cotton balls. And his crime was a misdemeanor in both worlds. He'd stolen from a Muggle library, or borrowed on his own terms. He'd bring the books back when he was finished with them.

Snape's oily black hair curtained his face as he leaned forward. "Why? We have the best library at Hogwarts."

"Yes, sir. It's terrific. It's how I read up on transfiguration in advance. The collection is a little lacking in poetry, though."

Snape almost snarled. "You should be writing spells, not narcissistic emotional reflections."

For once, Aurelius talked back. "You've heard of *Sonnets of a Sorcerer*, that book tricking people to speak in limericks, as if sonnets had anything to do with limericks? Real sonnets aren't a trick. Real sonnets are our deepest feelings distilled into . . . perfection, captured on a page, forever alive and able to connect with anyone caring to read them. They're magic. They *are*. I want to read words that have that power. I want to write words with that power. Even to write just one poem like those. Just one."

"Then write the damn thing and be done with it!" Snape said.

"It's not like that. It might take my whole life and hundreds of failures. Thousands."

Snape angrily got up and shoved the copy of *Immortal Sonnets*, with all its loose pages flopping out, into a drawer. So now his book was confiscated too. "We'll leave this topic aside for a moment. Now, explain yourself. Why Arveragus? To clarify, I can think of many reasons to despise Arveragus. But I'm curious what *your* reasons are."

Aurelius shrugged, like it didn't matter. "Gus is my neighbor, back home . . . you know, among Muggles. We've never got on well."

Snape raised an eyebrow. "And the photo? Who is she?"

Aurelius flushed. "A neighbor." Then Aurelius realized, it's time to tell him. It would distract him from this sensitive topic. And he'd decided this was what he wanted. "Sir, I have some news. I've decided not to come back in the fall. I'm going to live with the Muggles permanently."

Snape went white with anger. "Not continuing? Are you mad? Look, just finish up and then ruin the rest of your life. I cannot allow—"

Then he stopped, and Aurelius didn't like the look dawning on Snape's face. "So that's it. Love. Rivalry."

It was humiliating to have his heart dissected this way. "Professor, I can't talk about this."

Snape's eyes narrowed, the tone dripping with smiling pessimism. "Whom does she favor?"

Technically, Aurelius didn't know. There was a chance she'd favor him. He wasn't handsome, or popular, or athletic, but he listened to her, he wrote her back with enthusiasm, if not as much wit as she deserved, and he listened to her cello and knew what music meant to her. Would it be enough? It had to be.

The professor seemed to see Aurelius's thoughts. Snape frowned like he could see the boy's rejection as plainly as the nose on Aurelius's very plain face, like he knew Aurelius would never be loved by anyone, ever. A bit pathetic when Aurelius spent so much time reading and writing love poetry.

"Stop!" Reeve thunders, aiming his red pen at Franklin and looming over the back of his seat.

Franklin looks up from his lap, eyes bugging.

Reeve chuckles. "You were reading your phone, Franklin.

Disqualified!" I never dreamed that Reeve would suddenly appear as my unwitting knight in shining armor. I almost love him.

"I wasn't," Franklin snaps in disgust, like, *How dare you?*

Of course everyone is furious at Reeve, even if people in the back can probably see the phone in Franklin's lap.

"Shut *up*, Reeve," Rooster says. "You're just jealous."

Reeve sneers. "Why would I be jealous of a cheater? If it's your story, and you aren't reading it, tell me, Franklin, how does one combat Legilimency? *Hmm?*"

I can almost see the word "Occlumency" hover over the head of every fan of Harry Potter on this bus—including Reeve. I had no idea he was a fan. I always figured he read books like *Crime and Punishment*, because he liked the word "punishment" in the title.

Mouse tries to mouth the answer, but Franklin ignores her. His scowl shows all his bottom teeth. "Jesus, Reeve. I hardly need to take a pop quiz from you. Can I go on, or do we have to stop for an interrogation?"

"Couldn't be more obvious," Reeve mutters, while everyone shouts him down so Franklin can continue.

After taking his O.W.L.s, he moved back to his Muggle address. When he finally got up the courage, he phoned her.

"You're back, too! Aurie, I have to see you. I have big news. Something important."

In twenty minutes, she was in his arms.

Then, clutching both his hands, she pulled back with a

beaming face. "I have great news: Gus asked me out! Can you believe it?"

Aurelius, who'd said his good-byes at Hogwarts, confronted his angry father, and committed to the Muggle world, gaped for half a minute.

"You . . . really?" he heard himself ask.

She laughed, but an hour later she put her arm around his shoulders. "Aurie, I know what's eating you up."

"You do?" They were eating Chinese takeout from the boxes, there in the backyard, the whole garden in bloom. It was almost a perfect evening.

"You're worried I won't hang out with you if I'm seeing Gus. But you're my friend. I would never just drop you."

"Okay."

She smiled ruefully. "You don't sound convinced, but it will be great. You're just a worrier. You'll see."

They opened their fortune cookies.

Her fortune: *Love has finally found you.*

His fortune: *You will never find love without first loving yourself.*

What a perverse thing to conceal in a cookie. He was convinced a Gryffindor had prepared these. He didn't eat the cookie. It would be like going along with it.

He didn't see much of Dori. Not alone. Seeing her arm in arm with Gus was too much, even when they weren't making out.

361

Which they did. All the time.

And he learned something about Dori that the letters had never revealed. She had friends. Millions of them. It made him worry that she would have been Sorted in Gryffindor.

But in the fall Gus went to Hogwarts. Finally.

Aurelius took Dori hiking that afternoon. The late summer leaves were just a lovely backdrop to her beauty as she walked between the trees, her face tilted up, then turning to him with a smile.

And then it was time to attend their own Muggle school. It was a lovely, crisp morning, and autumn had come early. They rode their bikes together through the fall leaves, and he had her all to himself. They arrived at school, and her millions of friends surrounded her with hugs and tore her away from him.

He later found himself in a dining hall, eating alone. He had a panicked feeling he'd never see much of her again.

But she rescued him and brought him to her table. It was a Gryffindor kind of table. The popular kids let him stay, though he often didn't get a seat next to her. But just to be near her was enough. And on weekends they'd take to the hills, finding growing things, or on her living room floor he'd pretend to do his homework while she practiced her music.

He'd get hopeful she'd somehow begin to fancy him until she'd say, "An owl came last night!"

"You're so quiet," she added one time, after she announced an owl from Gus. They were alone under bare November branches.

He should tell her once and for all. But he said, "I wrote you so much more. He should write you every day."

She kicked wet leaves at him. "You're always there to defend me, but I can take care of myself."

He should tell her. Now.

She turned down the path.

"Wait . . . Dori. I love you." He shook, forcing the beautiful words out as if from a cramped impossible space.

She had this patient, sad look. "I have a boyfriend. He's coming home in a few weeks."

He could feel the words rising up stronger. "Still. I love you."

"I'm sorry."

"Please. I'd do anything. I loved you all this time." He'd said the word "love" three times. Now that he'd finally told her, he couldn't stop telling her. It was like a self-inflicted Babbling Curse.

She sighed. "I can't have two boyfriends. I can't even speak about this," she said. She turned away and let a long pause smother the moment. Then she said, "I hate this weather. Bleak. I miss spring, don't you?"

He didn't say anything except, again, that he loved her, and "please," over and over.

"Will you hush?"

But he couldn't. He couldn't stop pleading.

"Look, if you make me a flower garden in the December

snow, I'll go on a romantic date with you, all right?" She laughed, like that was all very silly. "But honestly, I have a boyfriend. I'm sorry, Aurie."

Without more words, he hiked through snow that crunched like breakfast cereal. His mind churned with the problem. His so-called Babbling Curse had switched off so suddenly that she looked at him with a worried expression.

"Aurie. Say something."

He said, quite determined, "I'll try."

"Besides," she laughed, "Dori and Aurie—that sounds a bit rhymey."

His deficiencies always came back to poetry, no matter what world he was in.

It was madness, but he tried. Transformation wouldn't work. The amount of magic needed would alert the Ministry of Magic. Potions were more subtle, though. And magical plants could be brought in. His backyard was suitably private, and his father and stepmother weren't living there. There are some advantages to being despised by one's father.

December arrived, and Aurelius took his exams, no closer to his goal. He needed to make a garden by the end of the month. If he took Dori on that date, she'd realize how much he loved her and what real love feels like. Her heart would change. It would. He tried to imagine Gus and Dori hiking together, watching birds through their binoculars and watching the trees give way to winter. Impossible. Gus couldn't do anything without an admiring crowd. She'd have to see the limitations of that. Once she got to know both of them better, she'd see who really loved her.

But time was running out.

As eager young witches and wizards rushed home from Hogwarts, Aurelius arrived.

He knocked on his professor's door, terrified but still determined.

Snape opened the door. He was clearly surprised and, for a moment, pleased, though his face immediately turned cool and distant. "To what do I owe this honor?"

Aurelius followed him in, and the place smelled like home—like spells and secrecy and something brewing. He wanted to tidy the place just to touch the contents, just once more. He couldn't stop looking.

"I knew you'd miss magic," Snape said, a smile twisting across his face.

"Sometimes." To hide his guilty face, Aurelius breathed in all the magic brewing in a cauldron. And there on the small shelf with Snape's thinner volumes Aurelius saw it. "My library book!"

"Take it. I certainly don't want it." Snape covered the cauldron and glared at the book in Aurelius's hands. "I assume you still waste your time on poetic fancy."

"Every day," he said defiantly. His voice dropped. "My literature teacher, Mr. Hartman . . . I showed him some of my writing, and he thinks I have talent."

"Ah, so I've been replaced with a new mentor, have I? And yet, here you are."

Beating around the topic no longer, Aurelius asked for his help with the winter garden. Of course, Snape wanted to know why such a ridiculous waste of magic was desired. Aurelius had planned to lie, but he knew the time for lies was over.

"She said if I made her a garden in December, she'd . . . she'd . . . she'd go on a date with me."

Snape's eyes flashed, and the grim silence in the room was palpable. "Are you asking me for a love potion?"

Aurelius jumped from his seat. "No, Professor! I'd never . . . All I need is a winter garden. It's all she wanted. She promised."

Snape's lip curled with distaste. "A most unusual promise. Wouldn't she simply go on a date with you if she really wanted to? Maybe this is her way of saying she *doesn't* want to go on a date with you. Perhaps you were pestering her? Groveling and pleading, perhaps?"

"No—not much," the boy said, flinching.

Snape's mouth twisted into a bitter smile. He seemed to be enjoying himself. "If you don't like discussing your love life, then why write about it? Anyhow, it's clear to me, she was trying to shut you up. She means none of it. This isn't an Unbreakable Vow, Aurelius. She was putting you down gently. She'll have forgotten the whole conversation—you'll never have her love. To act on this promise is a grave mistake. Is this not perfectly clear?"

"Professor, she promised. Please let me try this one hope. I'll pay any price."

The professor waved a dismissive hand. "It would be costly, what with obtaining materials, dealing with the Ministry of Magic, taking time away from my duties. You could not afford my services, not without robbing your father, and I will not abet such schemes."

Aurelius shook his head. "I have my mother's inheritance. It's yours. The house, too, if you want it. My life. Anything."

"Anything," Snape repeated testily, like the word offended him. "You haven't got much of a plan. Would this garden be in your Muggle backyard? I doubt your father would let all this happen under his nose."

"My father and stepmother don't live there. I haven't seen them since last spring." Aurelius opened the tattered book, as if to read and avoid this topic, but something was different about *Immortal Sonnets*. The pages that had fallen out were all securely bound.

"Surely at Christmastime they'll want to see you and—"

"I'm in disgrace and not needed presently."

He turned another page of the book. All mended. Why had Snape done it?

"Aurelius, if I may ask a sensitive question about your

father . . . From what I've heard, he hexes you, yes? Do you really want to risk—"

"He's not around enough to do much of that, now that I'm older. I have him to thank for what I am. He spelled me with a Compulsion to study when I was little: I had to read or my head would burst. Finding poetry, I discovered to my delight it didn't really matter to the Compulsion what I read."

Snape scowled. Whether because he disapproved of hexing children or reading poetry, it was hard to say.

"Look, forget my father and stepmother. Lost cause. Will you help me? Please, Professor? I'll give you my life."

"Your life? Preposterous. Would you die if I demanded it? Hop in a cauldron if I needed a boy for a potion? I can't even get you to give up poems and return to Hogwarts . . . Would you even do that much, I wonder?"

Aurelius clutched the book to his chest. "I would, sir. Any of it. Well, I'd rather not die in a cauldron, but anything else. Please."

Sharp lines deepened between Snape's eyes. "Fine. Bring me your mother's fortune, the deed to your house, all of it. I'll decide what you'll do with your very naive life. At the very least you'll return to Hogwarts, if I can convince the headmaster to take you. You will not bring any Muggle books or any Muggle-headed fancies for poetry—is that perfectly clear? You might even help our House—there is a most annoying first-year in Gryffindor who needs to know that some people spend more time in the library than she does. Or, maybe I'll keep you on as a human house elf. Or maybe I can use bits of you for potions. Speaking of which, we have some work to do. . . ."

"Where are we going? Gus is picking me up at eight. . . ."

Aurelius dragged Dori by the hand to the backyard.

He opened the door for her and studied her face as she took in the wonder of the garden.

It was a winter garden, and an evening garden. The short December days only showed off the nocturnal glow of the moon-phase flowers that climbed the walls and tangled with purple lunart and variegated luceme. Petals glistened with a Patronus-like light. The place smelled heavenly.

They were holding hands, taking their first steps on the path, crunching with snow, when she stooped and touched a flower blooming at her feet, silver on white.

She gushed praise, fell silent, gushed again, silent again, like a tidal flow. They both walked in their own enchantments, she in the garden, he in her.

She clutched his arm, and he could hardly bear his happiness. "I've never seen such magic. Never."

Feeling daring, Aurelius squeezed her hand. She let him do it, and he forgot what he was going to say. He even held a flower for her to smell. Finally he said, "Remember what you said on that hike in November? About a garden in December? It's all for you."

Her eyes questioned him, and then they changed. She froze, her face as white as the snow. "You mean . . . God, you mean going on a date? I was only joking. Aurie, this is . . . sick."

The flower in his hand trembled. "I didn't mean you had to go all the—look, I just wanted to take you out. You know, dinner, a concert. I just thought we . . ."

"I can't believe you tricked me. I trusted you. I—I have to go." Tearing up, she rushed out of the yard and down the street. He ran partway and stopped, because she was running from him. Because she hated him now.

Gus's owl came later.

A scrawl in Gus's hand: *This is how you get a date? Trap a girl in a false promise? You're a sick boggart.*

Then two hours later: *I can't get her to stop crying. Why don't you look in the mirror and practice the Killing Curse on yourself? Maybe we'll all get lucky.*

He thought about Gus's suggestion very seriously, as well as the Muggle alternatives.

And then, days later, the phone rang.

He heard her voice. Flat. Very tired. "I'm coming over."

He let her in. Her dull eyes were rimmed with black and red. He was about to show her the garden, but she shuddered. "No, thanks. I don't much care for gardens anymore."

She flopped onto the sofa. "I'm here for my 'promise.' Gus and I talked it over. We're not sure if you built a hex in it or not, but we both realized the quickest thing to do was to get the date over with. Right now. Gus will still be my boyfriend, no matter how 'romantic' our date is. So. Here I am. As promised. Carry on with whatever you want from me."

She wasn't weeping. She was shaking, with misery and anger.

Aurelius trembled. "I didn't hex anything," he whispered. "I didn't mean for you to feel forced. You must be so angry—"

Her eyes flashed. "Are you saying I need to act *happy*? To make *you* feel better?" She put on a mock-sultry face, moved her shoulders so that he noticed her breasts. "How's this? Ready for our date?"

His knees gave way. He sank to the floor. "I never meant our date would be like this. I never . . . I'm sorry. Forgive me. I'm so sorry. Just—please go."

"Oh, I don't know. Shouldn't I stay awhile to satisfy the terms? Or what were you expecting from a 'romantic date'? I don't want to fudge the contract and hear from your lawyer after."

Something in his throat made it nearly impossible to speak. It took a few efforts before he managed it. "Please go. Please."

He heard the couch groan as she got up. He felt her looking down on him. "You were my friend. I trusted you. I never dreamed you'd . . . Oh, forget it. Look, you might want to go back to your old school or, if you stay, find some new friends to hang out with, all right? Because I'm never speaking to you again."

He nodded, eyes on the floor, on her feet walking to the front door.

"Good-bye, Aurelius."

He whispered "Sorry" before she slammed the door.

Then he lost it. He tried very hard not to hug himself as he sobbed, because he didn't deserve love from anyone, least of all himself. He cried himself out, lay there numb for a long time. Then he packed his things.

He arrived at Hogwarts on Christmas Day. He avoided the feast and waited for Snape at his dungeon door.

"How was it?" Snape asked, eyebrow raised. He unlocked the door and let them both in.

"Fine." Aurelius pretended to take a great interest in the jars filled with solutions and bits of dead animals.

"Oh, come now, she must have appreciated my work. I assume you took all the credit, all your great powers lying at her worshipful feet."

Snape studied the boy's averted face. "Something is wrong. Why are you not—what is the phrase—glowing with happiness?"

He shrugged. "I'm not feeling well, that's all."

Snape looked grimly satisfied. "She gave you a piece of her mind, didn't she?"

"Yes," Aurelius croaked.

"And then?"

"Then I called it off."

Snape's dark eyes revealed nothing in the silent gloom.

Neither of them moved for a moment, and Aurelius brooded on Dori's reaction. Her rejection.

He tapped his suitcase with his foot, impatient to do whatever needed to be done. "Anyhow, Professor, I have the deed to the house, and I went to Gringotts to transfer the gold, but they need my father's signature because I'm underage. But I can take out the money in portions, over time." He took out a bag of Galleons, which clinked on the table.

He blinked hard and looked furiously at the cauldron and not the man standing right there. "And, Professor, just so you know, your work was brilliant. She liked it a lot before I reminded her . . . Anyhow, I have my suitcase and can stay wherever you need me. I can be a servant and work off my debt, or whatever else you may want from me."

The professor's eyes still revealed nothing. "I see. No smuggled books, this time?"

"None. I keep my promises, Professor."

"As I do mine," he snapped, eyeing the gold with distaste, then pinning Aurelius with a look. "And you're not writing ridiculous poems any longer?"

Aurelius paused. "Only one, on the train here. I'll destroy it gladly. It's just miserable garbage."

"I will spare you the effort and take it now."

With no choice, he gave him the poem from his book bag. It was a letter to Dori that he wrote as a poem. Snape glanced at the thing with dislike, but then to Aurelius's embarrassment, read it silently.

And after that, he—

"Hold on!" says Mari. "What's the poem?"

Franklin scratches his head. "The story never came with— er, I don't have a poem."

With a loud "A-HA!" Reeve waves his pen and clipboard above his head. "You confess the poem didn't come with *the story*—the story you've been reading on your phone! Your guilt couldn't be any clearer. Case closed."

"Shut. Up," Bryce grunts.

But Mari frowns. "But if it's not Franklin's story, who wrote it?"

"I did," Franklin says, showing all his lower teeth.

"Still guilty!" Reeve sings. "If you *wrote* it, it's not a *new* story. Case closed *again*."

Mari plays Sherlock. "It could come from online. Or from someone at Southwark."

"It doesn't matter who wrote it," Reeve says testily, "all that matters is that Franklin did not compose a new story and hence no longer qualifies."

But everyone ignores him, as usual.

"Someone obsessed with Harry Potter . . . and poetry," Reiko muses, and she glances at me. She's seen my bedroom, my shelves. She's read the love poems I'd written her freshman year.

"Someone who likes writing insecure male main characters,"

Mari adds, which makes me feel like my style is utterly predictable. She shakes her head, "Oh no, not that damn writing business. Well? Aren't you going to say anything?" She looks at me expectantly.

I'd love to claim it as mine. To publish it, share it. But I can't. I sold it, and it's one of those things where you're not even allowed to say you were the seller. Franklin's glare warns me to keep quiet. I so hate confrontation. I'm a coward. Everyone's looking at me. I should say something. I clear my throat.

"It's. My. Story."

Franklin's words are so forceful that everyone pauses, and I shrink in my seat.

"But not the poem," Pard says quietly. "You didn't get the poem."

Pard looks at me.

Pard looks at me, and all their eyes stop mattering, and I tune out Franklin's retort, whatever it is. I lean toward him.

"Say it," Pard says. Our eyes stay locked. To say he's rooting for me would be simplifying the intense look on his face after everything that's happened. I can't summon the words with his eyes flooding my insides, so I tap my thigh to count the syllables that come rushing back, and I aim my poem at his collarbone, hoping he'll hear an apology that is meant for him.

So this is what it's like to lose your love.
I thought I couldn't lose what I never had.

No matter how I reached, you soared above,
Yet we were friends, before it all turned bad.
My weak apologies are all too late,
You're right to call me out and make an end
Of us. I don't deserve to be your friend.
Coercing you to stay, I earned your hate.
Obsessed with words, my self-inflicted fate,
I almost trapped you, with nowhere to move.
Believe me when I say I share your hate.
So this is what it's like to lose your love.
How fitting I have nothing left but words,
How fitting too that I must speak them unheard.

In truth, it isn't very good, the poem, even though I worked on it over and over. But at the time, I couldn't sell that, too, on top of the story. I needed one thing to keep, and this was it. It's like I needed that one thing to be mine so I could give it over to Pard today. One poem of apology and heartbreak.

"When did you write this?" Pard says, and it's as if he's cast a Levicorpus spell that hooks my insides roughly and flips them upside down, just at the sight of him leaning toward me. Mari's asking me something, and it's coming from too far off. All I can process is that face. With difficulty I mumble, "December, sophomore year," that horrible year of longing for the friend I abandoned. I pull my eyes away, because I will cry if I look at him one more moment.

So this is what it's like . . .

Mari waves like she's been trying to get through. "Yoo-hoo, Earth to Jeff! So what is Franklin doing with your story?"

I can't answer a question like that without confronting Franklin, though I guess I've already stuck my neck out. "I don't know. I made a mistake."

I look at Franklin and manage to squeak, "I'll pay you back," which I meant as a kind of atonement but realize too late that I've just further implicated him.

Franklin rolls his eyes. "Look, everyone, I'm done hashing out my affairs publicly. I'll say 'the end' if you don't mind."

"Wait," Mari snaps, "you can't just stop. We have to hear the rest." But Franklin is too pissed to read aloud a story that everyone knows he bought but didn't write. Not as fun, reading it in that context.

Mari turns to me. "Do you mind, Jeff?"

I look at Pard, and he gives a little nod.

I don't mind at all.

"It's pretty much the end, and it's been a while, but this is roughly it." And I finish my story.

To Aurelius, it took ages for his professor to finish reading his miserable poem. Finally, Snape looked up from the page. "What should I do with you? What do you want?"

Aurelius shrugged. "It doesn't matter. I've given up."

"On this?" Snape tapped the paper lightly with his fingertips.

377

Aurelius barked a bitter laugh. "Oh, especially that."

Snape narrowed his eyes. "You said writing is a kind of power, to make others feel what you feel. To connect over our deepest experiences. Personally, I find such broadcasting of private passions to be foolishly transparent. Who needs to be a skilled Legilimens if one need only read such things? And yet . . ." His eyes flicked to the paper on his desk. "In your case . . . I accept your pursuit of this art, if you wish to resume it."

Aurelius blinked at the word "art" coming from his Head of House to describe writing poems, but the momentary bloom of pride soon withered. "Unfortunately, I'm not fit to resume writing, sir. I . . . my poem . . . it's crap."

"Is it? I cannot make a technical judgment." He picked up the paper and considered it while Aurelius longed to Disapparate. "It seems alarmingly private, but that's what you intended, am I correct? You wanted to recount a moment of rejection and self-loathing. It seems dangerous to reveal so much. It seems dangerous even to read into another person like this." He put the poem in a drawer and shut it. He paused with a furious and confused expression on his face, like he couldn't decide whether to speak his mind or not. Then he snapped, "I've saved them, you know. You're getting better—if that is the right word."

The boy's mouth hung open. He thought of all the poems confiscated in classrooms, in hallways, and never returned. Saved. "You did? I am?"

The professor made an impatient gesture with his hand. "Didn't I just say so? Now, assuming you aren't a coward and haven't given up on your art, where do you need to be to refine it?"

The boy sat up straight like a plant eager for the sun. "In the Muggle world. Out there."

His face a mask of irritation, Snape rose and flicked his wand and put away bottles with a loud *clink* of glass. "Oh, very well. Here is my decision. I see no reason to hold you to your promise, not when you released the girl from hers. I don't need your house—why would I want a useless Muggle house? Nor do I need your mother's money. You ought to remain at Hogwarts, but if you won't listen, I won't bother exerting myself to retain you. I will expect some information as to your whereabouts, just to know you haven't foolishly died from some Muggle contraption. Is that clear? And I might not be averse to seeing your, what is the word, *literature*. So. I await your owl to hear progress on your goals, unless you dare to slight me in preference for your new mentor." At these last words his voice sank with menace.

Aurelius shot out of his seat. Snape was setting him free.

And after some profuse thanks and a promise to send news and a very awkward handshake, and the even more awkward moment when Snape called him back from the hallway to get these unwanted Galleons off his desk, which Aurelius did and then had to say farewell all over again to an even more tetchy professor, Snape's heavy door closed. Aurelius swung his suitcase over his shoulder and rushed to the trains. His reprieve reminded him of his poem. He lost Dori, surely forever. He had nothing left but words. But they wouldn't go unheard. She'd never hear them, but writing meant someone would hear them. Professor Snape, if no one else. To be heard by anyone at all and to know his professor had kept his scribbles and would read more of his writing made a powerful impression on the boy.

Years later he was contacted by Professor Slughorn. "It took me a long time to figure out the person these belonged to . . . at least, I think they're yours. Professor Snape wouldn't have wanted anything on them pointing to you, because of You-Know-Who. Well, I suppose we can say his name now."

Apparently Aurelius's poems—the handwriting so young, so childish and urgent—were found neatly stacked, filed with student work, including reams of Dark Arts essays that Snape had never had time to return to his last students. Slughorn added that Aurelius's were the only papers without scathing remarks covering them. Aurelius thumbed through the stack and could see they had been marked with commentary. Words beyond the grave that he would treasure.

"Thank you so much, Professor." Aurelius gave Slughorn a copy of a Muggle-published book of poems, *Really, Really Good Sonnets*, plus an extra copy for Hogwarts's library.

Aurelius pointed out Severus Snape's name on the dedication page.

The end.

"Well, that was disgusting," Cece says. "I'm at least relieved that Dori didn't have to put out for that nasty boy."

"I'm glad she didn't too," I say.

Mari says that Snape was the story's magic ingredient, and she gives me a little nod from one writer to another, and it feels good to be acknowledged by her.

Everyone else is silent. Obviously, no one wants to weigh in on such a compromised story. Franklin sits right there with his jaw set. I don't know whether I've done the right thing or not, taking back the story, but I don't much care. Pard wanted to hear the poem.

I don't think I'll ever get invited to Franklin's parties after this, but I think if I write Mari in college, she'll write back. And that sounds pretty good to me. But Pard? I'm grateful he spoke to me, but I can't hope for something I don't deserve.

The tension breaks when people, mostly from the front half of the bus, start talking about which of the four Hogwarts Houses they each belong to. They all know exactly how they'd be Sorted—mostly Gryffindors, of course—though Mari, Marcus, and Reiko say they're Ravenclaw. Scribbling, Reeve nods and grumbles happily that he's in Ravenclaw, and, as with the discussion of Mouse's four gifts, I realize he's writing on the clipboard not to tattle on us but to organize our responses. In his own way, Reeve is a writer.

"So you're a Slytherin like me!" Lupe tells me, eyebrow arched conspiratorially.

I laugh, but it sounds self-deprecating. "No. I'm a Muggle."

Pard silently looks on, and I wish I could be interesting, so he'd keep looking. He has his sketchbook, and I'm praying that he's drawing me.

Alison gives an exasperated, horsey sigh. She's the only really popular person to speak to me after I pissed off Franklin. "You can't read *Harry Potter* or watch the movies and think of yourself as a Muggle."

I look at her, so confident, and I know if she went to Hogwarts, Hogwarts would be even more amazing and unstoppable. How can I explain to someone like that what it's like to be an outsider?

"Think of the Evans sisters," I say. "Lily has magic, Petunia doesn't. It's just the way it is. Harry has the stuff, Dudley's a dud—same thing. If I were either of the Granger parents, I'd drop my dentistry practice and follow my eleven-year-old daughter to wizarding school, if they'd let me. But that's not how it works. Muggles don't get to go. I'd love to get invited to Hogwarts, but I always made the distinction between wanting and belonging. Reading the books always felt like a peek into a world that would never in a million years include me." I shrug like it doesn't matter but add, "They're painful books that way."

"Oh, Jeff," Mari says, with a kind of wise, Hermione-type expression that makes me feel comforted and lost at the same time. And Alison says something about words being my magic, which I don't buy into. But it's Pard whose sad, open stare is too painful to return. If anyone knows I'm a worthless Muggle to the bone, it's him.

Mr. Bailey isn't as harsh to Franklin as he could be. "You realize if the Harry Potter story wins, the prize goes to Jeff, right?"

Franklin shrugs, like he's cool with it. He doesn't need the guaranteed A. His path in life is assured.

But Reeve flails his arms. "Unfair! Jeff's rigged the whole system and told three, I repeat, *three* stories. And might I add that the third is not even a *new* story."

Mr. Bailey sighs. "True. Too bad, because I'm a sucker for teacher-student stories. Well, that leaves you, Parson! Last, but not least."

Parson thanks Mr. Bailey and gazes at us with a sweet, dopey expression.

"Before I begin, I just wanted to say how awesome all your stories were!" He looks around the bus and puffs out his Jesus-labeled chest with loving pride. "I think I'm going to have my youth group start this tradition. I love the idea of everyone getting a turn to speak. And I hope you won't mind if I use my turn a little differently."

A grin freezes on my face. I feel a sermon coming on.

Everyone else must feel it too, because from the back row, Rooster pipes up with desperate pleading in his voice. "Dude, give us a sexy story!"

"I'd like to talk about love," Parson begins. "But not that kind."

Deep male voices groan.

Nature works its urges inside us, especially at our age. If you add to that the erotic love in all our books and movies and advertisements, we can't help but think a lot about sex. But there's so much more to know about love than the sexual bond between a man and a woman.

Rooster says, "Or a man and a man—right, Pard?"

"Love accepts no limitations."

I get a catch in my throat, seeing him flaunt a self-assured sexuality that doesn't quite match the vulnerability I saw in the parking lot. I'm the first person he's ever told, and I ruined it. Like he said, I trash every gift he's ever given me.

He never texted me back.

385

According to the Greeks, there are four different kinds of love. *Eros*, erotic love. *Philia*, the love between friends. *Storge*, the love of familiar things, like what Mr. Bailey feels for his coffee and what I feel for the smell of crayons and the sound of my dog's thumping tail. And then there's *agape*, unconditional love. The Latin word is *caritas*, which is where we get our weaker word, charity. You probably think of charity auctions and stuff like that because, at their root, acts of charity are supposed to spring from deep love. When you give a homeless guy a buck just to keep him at bay, you might call it charity, but it's not *caritas*. There's no unconditional love there. You'd act differently toward the guy if you felt that love. You might try to talk to him and connect in some way, and that would matter to him more than the money.

I guess there's nothing sexy about talking to homeless people and whatnot. But, as a Christian, I don't treasure erotic love the most. I treasure this unconditional love. It's the love of Christ dying to save all of us from our sins. And we can share that highest form of love as well. Think of Lily Potter saving Harry from Voldemort. That sacrifice shows the lengths we'll go to for those we love, but we can also show that love in smaller but equally life-affirming ways.

Love brings hope, trust, and forgiveness to others. You can sit down next to someone who looks like he needs a friend. You can forgive your friends and family who have flaws you don't have or temptations that don't tempt you. You can have faith that God is listening, even though you can't see or feel him in the room or in your life. You can believe that God is listening through the eyes and ears on this bus at this very moment.

He looks around at all of us and says something he has said at school before, to anyone who'd listen.

God is with us right now, because you're here. And if you look closely, you'll see God sitting right next to you. You've heard him all day through the stories, told by children of God.

I've always shirked away from this kind of talk. There's nothing godlike about me. It's like wizards and Muggles all over again, and the invitation to Godhood feels gilded and false. But the others can hear stuff like that more comfortably than I can.

"What does it even mean to be a child of God?" Alison asks.

"It means you're a goddess," Rooster says, smiling, but Alison is concentrating.

"No, a goddess stands alone on her marble pillar," Parson says. "A child of God is alive and connected to her family—her God and her brothers and sisters. See how it's different from *eros*? Erotic love is between two people. With unconditional love, you get this whole family, as big as your heart can hold. Bigger, even. No one is excluded. Isn't that amazing?"

"Does that mean you think there's some God fellow in you too, then?" Reeve asks. "That seems really presumptuous."

Parson flushes. "I see where you're coming from. I guess I'll answer it this way. I started talking to homeless people, for example. For years I was too uncomfortable to try. I was scared, to be honest. I knew it's our duty to feed and clothe them, so I'd give them money or volunteer in a soup kitchen, but I didn't give them eye contact, didn't engage. But I prayed about it, and I started doing it. I was so nervous, but I knew it was what God wanted me to do, and I did it. That's God acting through me. He's helping me do something I thought was beyond me. And I've met the most amazing people thanks to that nudge from God."

"Aw, Parson," Alison says. "You're as gorgeous on the outside as you are on the inside."

Again, he does it, that deep, dark red blush. "I . . . wow."

You can feel the female energy in the bus observing Parson's stammering beauty. Only Cece seems immune, which is a shameful waste of her front row seat in the Parson Show.

"Thanks for sharing that. I'm really, really honored." Then he sits up and tries to look into all our faces at once. "Do you guys want to know a secret? I feel like I want to give you something of myself. It's a pretty big secret. I haven't even told my youth group yet."

The whole bus leans in. I mean, what kind of secret would Parson have? He could open his mouth and say he actually slept with ninety-two different women, or he masturbated at a porn shop, or who knows? Maybe he just wanted to say he lied to his Sunday school teacher about feeding his cat with sustainable, humanely-raised pet food when he actually used over-farmed tuna. Whatever it is, I want to know Parson's secret.

"I . . . I find *agape* easier than *eros*," he says. "So much easier."

I have this side view of his red cheek and red neck with a little blue vein, and no matter what your gender or orientation is, he looks like a thing of *eros*. I mean, he's so blushingly beautiful and so passionate. If he'd gotten one-on-one with someone, anyone, and shared this secret, the person he was with would have to make out with him, because it's a turn-on to be with someone that beautiful and that sexually insecure. Who wouldn't want to show Parson the ropes?

But he's not confiding in any one person. . . . He's telling the whole group this confession. Lovers don't unmask to the group; they undress for one person. I can see a girl falling for Parson after he goes deep to the group, but one-on-one, there's nothing else to share. He already shared it with her friends, her pastor, the homeless guy on the street. Everyone gets Parson's deepest self, which means no one person gets his love for keeps. I'm fascinated by his dilemma, if it is a dilemma.

"I've always loved the idea of helping widows and orphans and finding people who need help," he continues. "I love the connections that spring up between strangers. I love to hear where people come from and to try helping them on their way. And then when I became a teenager . . . oh my gosh! The hormones! One of three things always happens: Either I crush on someone who doesn't return my feelings; or I lose the girl because I won't have sex until marriage, and I need to stop quite a bit before then to keep from temptation; or, finally, I like a girl I'm dating, but she says she can't find the 'real me' beneath my 'perfect exterior.' What do they mean by that? I'm not perfect! I think they want to peel off my *agape* layer and get to my *eros* one . . . only the *agape* layer is pretty much who I am. They say I'm not being real with them; they say I'm fake. Can I be fake without knowing it? It's totally confusing. I pray about it a lot. . . . I haven't lost hope. . . . Maybe someday . . . someone . . . if God wills it . . ."

Then the nicest thing happens. All the girls pitch in and tell Parson not to worry, that he's a great guy and some girl is going to get really lucky. If he tells the girl what he just told all of us, she'll understand.

"We like guys who show us they're vulnerable," Mouse says.

Briony adds, "That's as real as you can get. But I know what you mean. People have accused me of being fake just because I'm captain of the cheerleading squad and prom queen, plus I do a bunch of charity things." She flinches a bit at the word *charity*. "It definitely sucks. Like, should I stop doing all this cool stuff just to avoid being called fake? Nah. You just got to keep being yourself and be your own judge of whether you're acting fake or real. And by the way," she adds, "I totally had a crush on you sophomore year. I gave you a secret Valentine."

"That was you?" His mouth falls open. More blushing.

Briony laughs along with a bunch of girls, but it's nice laughter. Girls pipe up and say, "I had a crush too." Even Reiko rather guiltily says she had a crush freshman year. She looks right at me. "And I swear, I did not ask for it or act on it!"

I smile to let her know it's okay. I'm actually kind of flattered she'd be embarrassed about a crush while she was going out with me. Like she took me and my feelings seriously and maybe still does a little.

The guys chip in too. "We all feel that way," Kai says. "I mean, no girl's ever said I was too perfect, but I think every guy has been told he's not being real, or showing his true self. I think Bri has it right. You know how to be yourself, so go with that."

"Also, dude," Rooster adds, "you sound like a team player, you know, with helping people. I think you got to find a girl who's the same way, on the same team. I can't date a girl who hates football and crass jokes, or what would we talk about? I think it's just harder for you, because you're, like, this awesome saint, and saints just aren't all over the place. But you'll find her."

"You guys are really compassionate. Thanks," Parson says, glowing. And then, maybe because I'm sitting near him, we lock eyes.

He smiles like I've already said something nice, when I wasn't planning on speaking up.

"You're not alone," I offer, and I'm not sure if I'm saying this so publicly for him or for Pard. "I'm bad at *eros* too."

"We all are, dude," Rooster says, "except Alison."

"I bet you're good at *agape*," Parson tells me, already switching roles from comforted to comforter in his desire to help others.

I smile at him, and almost leave it at that. "Not really."

After the conversation dies down, Mr. Bailey beams at us and says, "We did it, guys. Those were some awesome stories. Thank you."

"Hey, look!" Alison's pointing out the window, nearly jabbing Briony in the face.

We see the Potomac, and everyone literally goes berserk because of the cherry blossoms. I'm not a tree expert, but it's pretty obvious we're catching them at the tail end of their season. No matter. The way the girls press their delighted faces to the windows, it's like we're hobbits on an enchanted drive through Lothlórien, while the elves are strolling around with this total *meh* expression on their faces.

Mouse points. "The Washington Monument! With cherry trees! We're *heeeere!*"

"Yup," the bus driver says. He pulls up to a giant curb reserved for buses. "Kind of a coincidence that everyone told their stories with just the right amount of time."

Mr. Bailey nods like a teacher. "Coincidence, perhaps. Maybe there's a lesson here. We all have the time we need to tell our stories."

He's smiling, and I don't want to ruin things for him, but I say, "You never told yours."

He shrugs. "My job is to listen to your stories. And we did it, guys. We did it." But our eyes meet, and there's a story inside him, and I think maybe that story is about the son he wants in his life.

Then the bus gives that monstrous sigh like a dying dragon, and the doors open.

ARRIVING IN D.C.

People make a grab for their stuff and then jump to their feet, jostling their way into the aisle and forward.

"Hold on!" Mr. Bailey stands in the aisle as if to block the stampede. "Announcements first! Sit down!"

Everyone grumbles and sits hunched forward, ready to spring as soon as he's finished talking.

"Here's the plan. We're behind on our itinerary"—he scowls just a tiny bit at the bus driver—"so listen up: Everyone, go pee, go eat. Take your valuables with you. Then, in half an hour, for those of you interested in getting inside"—and he points to the towering monument—"we'll meet there, in the circle of flags. If you want to skip the view, meet at the water in an hour. And, guys, think about which story should win. We'll figure that out when we come back together. Okay, enjoy the Mall."

Since I'm in the second row, I stand up to follow Reeve. I turn around for a second, and Pard looks up, a question in his eyes. I telepathically convey how very sorry I am, how desperately I want him not to hate me, but then everyone starts crowding into the aisle, and my view of him is blocked.

With my pack on my shoulder, I hurry off the bus and pretend to check my phone. Maybe I'll ask Pard to grab something to eat with me. Maybe he'll say yes.

Kai and Briony wander off, arm in arm, alongside Franklin and Mouse. Alison, Rooster, Bryce, and Saga follow a bit behind and are having considerably more fun taking ridiculous selfies.

That's when I see Cannon, tall even when he's slouching. He's hanging back with that girl Nikki.

I look around. Pard is chatting with Reiko, of all people. Just the two of them. What the hell would *they* have to talk about?

He probably didn't want to talk to me after all. I guess it's his right to walk away.

It's what I deserve.

I go where I'm being invited. No one even notices.

"Hey." Cannon bumps my fist. "This is Nikki."

She's just the right kind of hot. I mean, not only that body, dressed to advantage, but this beaky nose and thick eyebrows that make me think she knows what it's like to feel ugly, at least a long time ago.

"Is Mace coming too?" she asks, and Cannon shakes his head.

I sense someone jogging up to us as we're leaving the Mall, and I feel a flutter in my gut.

But it's not Pard; it's Mace. Still a dozen yards away, chains jingling on those Goth pants, he gives what has to be the cutest little wave to Nikki, his hand squiggling like he's washing Barbie's windshield. I should be on red alert—*competition!*—but it's so obvious he's in love with her, and from a distance, his broad shoulders and long legs show off how handsome he is. Then he gets closer, and you can see the acne-scarred face, and yet, with all his features uplifted at the sight of this girl, he doesn't look half bad. He's a different person.

Cannon shrugs and tells Nikki, "He can come, but he's not

someone Drew needs to meet." Then he motions to me and Mace. "Hurry up. My car's over here."

My reverie crashes into panic. "Wait. I don't know. I—I really can't ditch my field trip."

Mace puts an arm around Nikki, and she giggles and lays her hand on his chest. "I'll ditch mine," he says.

Cannon's forced smile brings out the hard lines of his face like he's sick of Mace flirting with Nikki, and now my whining. "It's a ten-minute drive, Jeff. You'll be back before anyone notices. Tonight I'll pick you up and take you to a real live college frat party. You can't say no to that."

I shrug. "Sure."

Nikki and Mace race ahead to the car, all frisky. Mace jumps and hangs from the low branch of a cherry tree. The branch shakes, and the last of the blossoms fall over him and Nikki, who twirls to catch them.

We all pile in when we reach Cannon's car—Nikki and Mace in the back—and I can tell Cannon's annoyed, like he wanted Nikki to be mine. Still, he tilts his head at the rearview mirror and tells her to give me her Georgetown spiel.

"You're going to love it here!" Nikki says. "Everyone is super friendly."

I turn to Mace. "Your sister goes here, right? She likes it?"

"Loves it." He speaks comfortably, as if we're friends. "She's in Nikki's sorority. Speaking of which"—and he's pawing her—"I'm totally hanging out with you guys this weekend."

"Whoa, is this new?" Nikki says, running a finger along his tattoo.

Cannon's eyes cut from the rearview mirror to me. "This guy Drew has one more year, so he can set you up. By the end of your first year, you'll have friends, a place to live, everything. Girls, too, if you want." He subtly glances in the rearview mirror at the girl I don't seem to want badly enough. He shakes his head.

We pull up to a fraternity house. Guys pass a volleyball on the front lawn like they're advertising what a gym membership can do to a body. Cannon parks in the driveway, waves at the guys, and walks into the house like he's one of them.

A guy squatting in front of an open fridge stands up when he sees us. "Cannon! Hey! Looks like you brought a couple friends." He lifts an eyebrow as he takes in Mace's acne. The guy, who must be Drew, looks related to Franklin: super tall and built, that smug kind of person who was born with all the advantages.

Cannon introduces Mace as Nikki's friend, but me as *his* friend, like the hierarchy needs to be spelled out. Drew gives Mace a slight head-tip, but he shakes my hand. Still, I'm only here because Cannon is vouching for me. I may not gross out Drew (he keeps sneaking contemptuous looks at Mace), but his eyes size me up and find me lacking.

"You want a beer?" he asks.

I *wanted* a beer. Like, sophomore year I wanted one, and guys like him to hang out with. A dream come true. But now, not so much. I want to get away from all these college-aged Franklins and get back to my class. A beer means we're in for a chat for who knows how long, or over how many beers. If I had a backbone, I'd use it.

"Sure," I say.

Drew leads Cannon and me into a living room that is lined with sofas, while Nikki and Mace decide to play volleyball with the guys out front, their voices barking happily as they get into the game.

Volleyball aside, I'd rather be out there and not in this dark, empty room meant to hold a whole lot more people and noise. We're sitting on two stained corner couches like we're in time-out.

"So you're coming to Georgetown," Drew says to me.

I bobblehead nod, even though I'm not sure. He peppers me with a few small-talk questions before he bores of me.

Then he turns to Cannon, like it's just the two of them. "Those computers in the lab you rigged a while back . . . haven't heard anyone notice a problem."

Cannon waves a lazy hand. "It's easy. Jeff can rig more, too. I can teach him how to read the data. He'll take over, and we'll work out percentages. It'll be great."

Drew rubs his chin. "As to that. So what do you do with all the Visa numbers? Buy beer and hope no one notices?"

I freeze. Cannon never told me about credit cards. Hacking was all about grades, nothing more.

Cannon takes a swig. "Ha, that's not quite how it works. With keylogging, you see everything a person types on the machine. So I see what kinds of things the person orders online, and I can buy the same thing without their noticing. I'll order something, and the beauty is I have the tracking number, and I just go to their doorstep and pick it up right when UPS tells me it's there. If you know the person's habits, you can have deliveries when they're at work or out of town."

"Sweet. You don't get caught?"

"I get accounts shut down when fraud protection kicks in, but they can't trace it to me. Or if I don't want the account, I have a guy I can sell it to. Then it's his problem." Cannon laughs.

Drew shakes his head, but with appreciation. "Let me guess—you're going to be a computer science major."

Cannon's eyebrows hike up ironically. "How'd you know?"

"Too bad you're going to . . . Carnegie Mellon, right? You'd be cool to hang with next year."

Cannon shrugs. "Sorry. Got to follow my scholarship."

"So you can do this stuff too?" Drew asks me.

My head swims from information overload. It's none of my business what Cannon does. Never has been.

Except it is now. It's been my business all along, and I never knew it.

"No," I say.

Cannon carefully catches my eye, like, *Let me handle this.* "This guy here keylogged several teachers this year and even helped me crack the teachers' lounge—total jackpot there. I never could have gotten near their machines, but teachers seem to love Jeff helping in their offices while they go on coffee breaks. Never suspect a thing. Look at that face."

Drew looks at my face.

I'm not fat, but I have a baby face. Round, rosy cheeks. Tragically innocent. *Not mature*, Reiko said. I've tried to make up for it with parties and scheming with Cannon, but no matter how much of a jerk I am or how many beers I drink, the baby face remains intact. I've got the face that teachers like, the kind that Mr. Bailey hands a lollipop to, and now I see I've been stealing more than just grades. I've been stealing from *him*. Making it harder for Mr. Bailey to buy a plane ticket to go see his Sam.

Cannon has never made me feel so cheap.

I can barely speak, and when I do, I sound like a little kid. "I—I don't steal credit cards. I'm not a thief."

Their eyes snap to me like I'm wearing a pink Jesus shirt. There's this pause, and noise from the volleyball game outside sounds way too loud.

A line etches itself between Cannon's eyebrows. "I never said you were."

"I'm sorry," I say, and I wince, because here I go, apologizing to Cannon when he's the one ripping off my teachers and duping me to help.

"Hey," Drew says, "that's cool." He slaps his thighs in that *oh, look at the time* kind of way. Doesn't even look at me. "Dude, I have to get going," he tells Cannon. "We'll chat after you and your, um, friend figure things out."

399

"Yeah, sure."

Outside, there's no sign of Nikki or Mace. One of the volleyball guys calls out that they went to Nikki's house and will catch us later.

Cannon shrugs and heads for his car. We pull out in silence.

"So what's going on?" he asks, like I'm the one with the problem.

I look out the window at cherry trees done with flowering and homeless people chilling at spray-painted bus stops and spotless monuments in the background.

My voice still comes from somewhere far away, but I have to know what I've helped him do. "What was in the box? The one on Mr. Bailey's doorstep?"

One lonely intersection. Two.

He says, "My phone."

It all makes sense. His old phone broke. So he got a new one. The one he's been texting me from all day.

"Which machine? His house?"

"No, think of the timing. Teachers' lounge." The jackpot.

There's something quiet and careful about him, that's all. There's no guilt in his voice, no guilt in his face. No show of irony that he unlocked Mr. Bailey's back door with a credit card and then scooped up the brand-new phone he bought with Mr. Bailey's credit card.

"What?" he says, irritated.

"Don't you think that's messed up? He's a penniless teacher, for fuck's sake."

He shakes his head, guns through a yellow light just switched to red.

"You don't get it. It's an obvious red flag on his statement. All he had to do was call his credit card company, alert them to his stolen account, and get the charge reversed, and the company gives him a new number. The cost of the phone is eaten by the fraud protection program. End of story."

End of story puts me in mind of all the stories I've heard today. It's a bitter ending. And I helped write it.

"How can you be sure it all worked out that way? How can you do that to someone?"

"Sorry, okay? I needed the money."

"You needed a *phone*. How much money could a few teachers give you anyhow?" And then I realize it's not just teachers. He keylogs lab computers used by college students. People barely older than he is. "You do this to college students?"

"*Rich* college students. Their proud parents gleefully pay all their bills."

"And that makes it okay?"

"Shit, Jeff . . ."

We drive in silence.

And I thought helping Franklin's grades was bad enough. This is much, much worse.

We make our way back. The Washington Monument spikes above the intersection. Cannon parks, and I just sit there.

Hands on the wheel, he looks over the dashboard as if he

were still driving. "I know this looks bad. It is bad. I needed the money."

"What, to cater Franklin's parties?"

"*No*. Just . . . I needed the money."

"Look, I don't care *why*; I just want to know *who*. Have you done this to people at Southwark? I mean, one of us?"

I think of everyone he's had access to and blurt the first thing that pops into my mind.

"Like me?"

His mouth opens and closes like a fish, a sign of weakness I've never seen from him. And I hate him for it. He stole from me. I have no idea how much. I just know I've been used.

"Fuck you, Cannon." I fumble the latch and stagger out like a drunk.

I don't know whether to care that he races after me. I swing around to face him.

He looks terrible.

This is the guy who taught me how to go to a party. How not to be a quivering mass of fear. And now we're both afraid.

"Jeff, I know you're mad. That's fair. Look. You don't know how bad things have gotten this year. Real life stuff."

"I have a real life too. And you fucked with it. What did you take from me? What did you buy?"

He twitches like the conversation's crawling up his arm. "It was barely anything," he mumbles. "I just modified your gym membership to include me. Like, a family membership."

"You screwed me over because you needed nicer abs?"

"I screwed you over because I needed a place to shower." He opens his mouth and closes it again. I hate how it makes him look. Weak. Stupid.

He's not making any sense.

He sighs. "I had to get out of my apartment situation. One of my roommates started hanging out with some bad people . . . like, worse than I am. Where do you go when that happens, right? You go to your mom's. You hate each other, but she'd take you back. Only, the key doesn't turn the lock. And you look at the number on the door, and you're in the right place, but the key won't go in, and then some random guy inside opens the door and scares the shit out of you. She moved out. She left, Jeff, and I never knew. So, yeah. I needed a place to shower."

My mind goes blank like it does in Calc. The xy graph makes no sense, how your mom becomes an x and you can't figure out y.

I shift from angry to numb so fast that I'm dazed, like *I'm* standing at the apartment door, opening to someone I don't know. "Where've you been sleeping?"

He glances at the souped-up little WRX. "There. Other places."

"You're *homeless?*"

He looks pissed. "Homeless people don't have cars. But I'm not going to *be* homeless. Ever. I'm practically back on my feet right now."

He's homeless. I've never met a homeless person before.

A gust of wind picks up, and our bodies brace for it. His hands in his pockets make his arms look like restless, half-folded wings. Faded cherry blossoms fairy-dance their way into gutters.

"Look. I'll cancel the membership. Or fix it back to what it was."

I shake my head, still stunned. "I just . . . I didn't know. You never said. I'd have helped you."

"Yeah. I know. I *know* you, Jeff. You'd be fucked to trust me, but I trust *you*. Maybe I should've spoken. I just . . . I needed the money."

"Do you have a place to stay tonight?"

Cannon has alpha-male posture, like he's too cool for that question, insulted, even. "I'll crash at that frat house. Party, remember?" His mouth starts a smile he doesn't bother to finish. I wonder how much fun it is to party hard when you're banking on finding a couch or a room or somewhere, anywhere, to shelter you.

He doesn't look at me when he asks, "Will you come? I can still set you up with a network of friends. I can give you that. Make college easier. You're not the best at meeting people, you know?"

A new thought hits me. "Where are you really going to college?"

He looks pissed at me for asking but takes a breath. "Not going to happen. But *you* are, and you're going to have a shitload of fun. I can promise that."

It makes me sad, hearing that promise, because someone should have made it to him. "But why? You're trying to help my social life because of the gym thing?"

"Dude, I've been helping your social life eons before the gym thing. I help you because I like to. You get so wound up with the tiniest risks, you know? I like showing you it's okay. And then making things work out, safe and sound."

I shiver in the wind. *Safe and sound.* That's everything Cannon isn't.

"Anyhow," he adds, "you should come to the party."

I take a deep breath. "I can make my own friends from now on."

He nods, his face a little tight, his eyes fall from my face.

"I'm still . . . processing all this," I tell him. "Call me next week if you want."

Cannon nods, then he shrugs his shoulders loose, walks to his car. I wonder if he's still sleeping in it.

I wonder how safe and sound he is these days.

"Cannon."

He half turns.

"Call me next week, yeah?"

He meets my eyes like he'll ask a question, but instead he simply says, "Okay."

I know it's corny, but I watch him drive off. I want him to know I'm not turning my back on him, even if I've told him where I stand.

THE MONUMENT

The flags around the Washington Monument suddenly snap in the wind, and everyone lounges around in clumps at the Reflecting Pool. Mr. Bailey just noticed Bryce and Saga wandering off, and he rushes after them in pursuit. Meanwhile, Rooster and Alison dip their bare toes into the pool, and by some sudden inspiration, Alison strides right into the shallow water. Her joking smile is replaced with this radiant, almost determined look on her face as she turns to face the Washington Monument. She stands tall as a Valkyrie with her fist high above her head, posed in a warrior's salute, and she unfurls her red stockings, which stream behind her flowing hair.

There's a certain unflinching core I've never seen in Alison before as she looks up at the monument towering over her, but not leaving her in shadow.

As a kid I watched the opening to a movie—I don't remember which one—with the Columbia woman standing there in all her glory. Seeing her for the first time, hearing the orchestra, and feeling a hum of energy, I thought *This. Is. It.* Like, the ideal person is that Columbia woman, standing as a symbol, both flesh and monument, for all time. It's like that now. Alison's so perfect. So complete. The way she's most herself by confronting things head-on. In her face-off with the Washington Monument, she's finishing something she started when she was twelve years old, when she stared down the Liberty Bell without her underwear or her virginity.

The moment ends as quickly as it began. Alison throws the red stockings over her head, and the wind picks them up, and Rooster hoots and races to capture them. She laughs, running after Rooster on the grass, and the moment is gone like it never even happened. I don't know what it all means, but I need to write it down before it's gone forever.

"Jeff!" Mr. Bailey waves at me frantically, and he jogs over to catch me.

"Sorry I'm late. I lost track of time."

Evidently, that's not going to cut it. "You're over twenty minutes late. Where were you? Where's Mace?"

He gives me an almost desperate look when he asks this last question, and I feel bad for him. I realize I'm going to have to tell him where Mace is, or he'll have a panic attack. "There was this girl . . ."

He groans. "Oh shit."

And I explain the relevant details, leaving out Cannon, and give him Mace's cell, which I still have in my phone.

He strides off to call Mace, and I hear incoherent yelling punctuated by *get your ass over here* and *you are so suspended right now.*

And then . . . it's like I'd never left. The popular people stay in their groups. The loner types stay on the edges. No one except Mr. Bailey missed me at all.

Only Pard notices, but he's not waving me over to his little loner spot away from everyone else. Instead, he's glaring, the picture of white Balrog fury sitting on a patch of grass.

Walking up to him—uninvited—is terrifying. I'm sweating already.

I manage a wimpy "Hey" and wither under his Slytherin-grade sneer.

"I saw you leave with him. *In his car,*" he adds, like the automotive aspect clinched his decision to hate me forever.

I'm puzzled why he cares what I do with Cannon. I mean, I've done worse things today. To him. But I still grovel. "I came right back."

He murders some grass with an angry tug. "In a hurry to win your story contest, no doubt."

Oh, so we're in *that* mode. I'm stuck standing there while he plucks at the grass and plots the next vitriolic thing to say. He gets like this a lot at our anti-PE table. He always comes out ahead.

"I'm not winning that."

"Not for lack of quantity."

I almost tell him he sounds like Reeve, saying that, but I have no fight left in me. None. I just want him to let me come clean. "Please don't be that way."

Sitting there furiously downcast, he acts like he can't hear the longing in my voice. "What way is that?"

"I don't want to argue anymore. You were right about me not listening. I was a jerk when you told me you were . . . about your condition. I'm sorry. And I'm so, *so* sorry that someone hurt you at your old school. If you ever want to talk about it—"

He whips up a hand to stop me, and it hurts to be cut off mid-apology, even if I deserve it. "We're not discussing that. Ever. I told you too much, and I regret it, all right? Just forget it. Just forget today ever happened."

"I can't," I croak, flooding him with stares he won't return. "I don't want to forget. After today, talking and hearing all the stories—"

"Yes, about vampires. That was swell."

"Shit, you *are* a crabby vampire."

I'm rewarded with a sneer from his downcast, closed face. "Stooping there, are you? Figures. But there's no need. I already handed you the goddamn *Book of Mythic Creatures* bookmarked with the page I'm featured on. And besides." His voice drops to a simmer, a hint of real pain. "Isn't one mythical affliction enough?"

I draw my arms to my chest because he's sitting two feet and forever away. "It's not an affliction, what you have. You're . . . you're very special."

His eyes snap up, glaring. "Ah. Now I'm *special*."

"To me, I mean."

He considers me still standing there like a loser, hugging myself and wilting. He says, regally, "Now I'm curious. Do you *like* vampires?"

I can't botch this, but I know I'm going to botch this.

"You mean, do I like vampires in stories? Or are we talking in code?"

He flicks my leg, and it's like a gong vibrates all the way up my body. "We always talk in code." His face is tipped up, looking defiant and cynical. Yet I have his absolute attention.

"I like . . ." My voice drops to a whisper. " . . . one in particular."

That sudden smile. His face turns sharply so I don't get it head-on, which is good because that smile would probably slay me. Not a bad way to die though.

"Everyone," Mr. Bailey calls from far off, "gather around for a minute."

Next I know, Pard jumps to his feet and takes me by the arm. I can't feel my own hands, my legs, just his fingers on my elbow. My elbow is in heaven. My elbow is in *eros*. And it takes a moment to figure out he's not doing something technically erotic but merely guiding me where we can sit near Mr. Bailey.

Everyone's forming some sort of circle, but I'm mesmerized by what's happening in my immediate space. One of his little gray Vans is ever so slightly touching my sneaker. It's not full-scale footsie, but it is definitely foot touching. I tell myself it's nothing but, then again, if he has a foot fetish, then we are practically having sex right here in the National Mall. I don't look up to see if the world is staring at our feet, because I'm too busy staring at them myself. They're mesmerizing.

Mr. Bailey rests his hands on his hips like a coach. "Good news: I got in touch with Mace. He's safe. He's with his sister, and I have his address. I'll be coordinating a cab to get him back. In the meantime we have a lot to do. To those of you who missed the Washington Monument tour"—and he flicks me a malevolent stare I can't seem to get worked up about—"it was a gorgeous view. Right, guys?"

Rooster shouts out, "Phallic fantabulousness!"

"Enough," Mr. Bailey warns, as if they'd covered this ground already. "Okay. Next stop, right across the water."

He gestures, and we look past the length of the pool to the less phallic Lincoln Memorial.

"We don't have much time, just fifteen minutes, but we'll check it out. Our bus is already there, ready to zip us over to the Museum of Natural History until closing, and then we're off to dinner and checking into our hotel. And may I remind you all that after you check in, you stay in your assigned rooms all night long."

There are some mock groans from frisky people eager to play the musical beds game, but when Pard taps my foot, I can't tune in to anyone else. "Lights out early," he teases, eyes half closed with a come-hither look.

And I thought his *shoe* was mesmerizing.

Mr. Bailey keeps talking, and I'm wondering if Mace will come back by tonight, or whether it will just be Pard and me in that room. If he'd let me lie next to him and hold him. There's nothing I want more, but it's also something I don't deserve.

Mr. Bailey drones on, when Mari cuts in. "But who won?"

He gives us one of those sly *let's have a learning moment* smiles. "Ah, we come to the question."

Everyone shifts, a little uncomfortable. Now that we're at the impromptu awards ceremony, the whole day of storytelling feels a little cheapened somehow, because it was more than a contest.

"Everyone deserves some credit," Parson chirps. "Everyone should win."

Reeve snorts. "Wait one second here. Why do *you* deserve credit? You told a sermon, not a proper story. And what about Cookie getting all spaced-out and then falling asleep during his own story? Even worse, Franklin cheated! And furthermore, it staggers the mind that Jeff told three stories. *Three!* They should all be automatically disqualified."

Everyone speaks up at once, and Mr. Bailey has to shout to calm people down and let the accused have their say.

I simmer with words. *Stories. Cheating. Winning.*

I think I have an idea. . . .

"I spoke from my deepest soul," Cookie murmurs when Mr. Bailey gives him the floor.

"So did I," Parson adds.

Franklin shrugs when Mr. Bailey calls on him. "Look, I'm not into this competition thing. I don't care. Studying for one more final won't kill me."

Alison cuts in. "Come on, guys. So what if Cookie slept or Franklin fudged? God knows we all sleep and fudge. But not one person *refused* to tell a story. Not even Mace."

"Oh, Jeff did the opposite of refusing: He told three stories!

412

That prize would be mine if everything were fair," Reeve whines, to eye rolls all around.

Mr. Bailey looks at me. I have nothing to say. I'm too busy thinking about Pard right there and also about this story idea blossoming all around me.

Parson smiles at Reeve and then includes us all. "It's not about winning. It's about giving people a chance to be heard. Everyone got their chance to share, and we all listened. What a gift. It's like magic."

Magic. It really is.

"Jeff?" Mr. Bailey looks at me like I'd better speak up this time. "Your head looks like it's going to explode."

"It's magic," I parrot. I sound like Cookie.

Cheating. Playing. Making stories. Stories that flow into one larger story. *The* story.

Yes.

Everyone's looking at me like I'm a total oddball, and I don't even care. Pard's looking too, but I can't explain this right now. This amazing idea.

"So who won?" Rooster asks. "Because I'm kinda hoping . . ."

"Let's just vote and be done with it," Briony says, eye rolling like this is taking too long, and I notice she's not the only restless one.

Reeve goes ballistic. "That's a popularity contest!"

"Quiet down," Mr. Bailey says.

Parson beams at us like we're all precious children of God.

"I think in the spirit of unconditional love it would be wrong to select one winner. Everyone wins."

Mr. Bailey nods. "I've thought of that, but I can't give the entire class A's."

I could, however, with the cloud. But, no . . . I won't. I'm going to tell Cannon I'm not messing with other people's numbers ever again, not even grades. If I don't get into my top schools, I'll just have to deal with it.

"Look," Mari says. "Not to dis the *agape* or whatever, but patting everyone on the back doesn't mean anything. There should be a winner. And it should be Sophie."

People's eyes kind of pop, and then they nod in agreement, even Cece, and I have to agree that Sophie's story was excellent. Romantic yet lonely, my favorite kind, and it elevated the theme of demons from the stories told before her. I'm totally on board with her winning. Even if I'm partial to Pard's story about prom, or the merciless story that followed. Or Pard's revision of Briony's story. Actually, Pard just sitting right here is a really nice poem in itself. I'm not sure I can be objective when it comes to Pard.

I tap his shoe. He doesn't pull away, or freeze in horror, or kill me. He *smiles*.

"I loved that one too," Mr. Bailey says brightly. "All in favor?"

Sophie blushes, and when everyone except a few grouches lifts their hands, she gasps with a little laugh-cry. "I've never even written anything before."

"You better write something now," Mari says, and our eyes

meet like we're in a writerly family plagued with writerly weirdness, yet also still family. A new writer has been born today.

But Mari knows only the half of it. Because I know what I'm going to write next, and I can barely contain myself.

People cheer with varying degrees of enthusiasm—a mix of appreciation and jealousy. Mostly, though, everything feels anticlimactic. The contest is over, and people are over it. They're eyeing the Lincoln Memorial like they want to get moving. It's like all they care about is D.C. or something. I don't get it at all. I'd jump in the bus right now if we could keep telling stories.

"Well, that was easier than I thought it would be," Mr. Bailey says. "And for the rest of you, just behave yourselves this weekend and the whole senior prank will be forgiven. And who knows? Maybe we can play the game again on the way back."

He's generous. He might not know about the cloud, but some of his students trashed his house, and as far as he knows, one of them might have bought a phone on his card. And he's willing to forgive and move on.

"Well," Mr. Bailey declares, "onward to the Lincoln Memorial!"

People get up, and according to their personalities—rowdy, reserved, horny, happy, whatever—they make their way.

"Race, guys against girls!" Rooster shouts, and he lumbers off.

Cece gripes about separating people by gender. She folds her arms like she'll have nothing to do with his sexist race, and he wasn't including her in the first place, really—he was egging on Alison, who takes the bait. Like a herd of cats, everyone

415

starts splitting up, even as they head in the same direction. People revert back to their own social groups, Kai and the cool crowd in a cluster, Reiko and Frye leading another, Reeve and Mr. Bailey at the tail of things. It's the weirdest sight, but kind of expected.

The social laws have been reinstated. Our revels have ended.

But not mine. Not by a long shot. Because I am going to put all their souls on paper, and there, like a monument, the revels will never end.

From behind, his hand touches my shoulder.

It's like old times, and I can tell him anything. I wave my arm to encapsulate the Lincoln Memorial and the pool and the whole gaggle of them getting farther and farther away. "I'm going to write this whole thing. I'm going to write everyone's stories and make a novel of it. A *novel*. Not just the stories, but everything. The interruptions, the bickering, the coffee breaks. It's going to be about loneliness and finding each others' truths on the slant through the stories they tell. It's going to be about lies and big reveals and how we shuffle and deal the cards and bet our souls away. It's going to be about *everything*." I waggle all ten fingers for emphasis on *everything*, though I don't mention Cannon will be in the novel as part of that because I want Pard in a good mood.

"I love it, Jeff." He beams at me. Not in a Parson way. Parson beams at anything. But when Pard praises you, you've really hit on something. I want to put a frame around his face and keep it forever.

Then he rubs his chin and worry clouds his eyes. "Hmm. You do realize that's kind of stealing everybody's stories?"

I think of Reeve accusing others of cheating, and Cannon actually doing it. *I'm not a thief.* For a second, I'm defeated. It feels awful to hear another guy call your story his own. I could ask for everyone's permission, but there'd be at least a few who'd say no. And I need them *all.* Dammit.

But then I bark a laugh, because this story is totally different: I'll still be giving credit where credit's due, openly saying the tales are theirs. *I'm just the narrator.* Problem solved.

I grab Pard's hands and twirl him in a ludicrous circle because I'm totally high. "I'll use all their names, and we'll have an Acknowledgements section in the back! It'll have this real-life angle to it that way. It's going to be the best thing I've ever done. I'll start tonight. *I'm writing a novel.*"

I let his hands go, and it feels a little more intimate letting them go than it did grabbing them in the first place. The novel will be full of paradoxes like that too.

He looks oddly shy. "Do you think you'll need an illustrator?"

My smile might be wider than my actual face. "Yes! We'll be a team."

He nods, shy and relieved, and I almost grab his hands again. He's back in my life. My happiness is fizzing out in all directions.

"So," he says, recovering his sly decorum. "The plot is the story-telling competition on the bus. But what about the love story?"

My smile falters. "Love story?"

"Yeah . . . for the hero."

Huh. Maybe we're not on the same page after all. The stories had a lot of sex, but not a lot of love. Maybe he means the people on the bus, but that makes no sense either. "You mean Kai and Briony? You can't want that. I mean, it's not a love story. It's a group of people getting together over some storytelling. And I'll end with this scene of everyone headed to the Lincoln Memorial but starting to regroup back into their own lives. See?"

"But what about *you*?"

It's like a Marcus question about silly story logistics. "Oh. I'll add myself running after them in the final scene. Whatever. I can change things around."

His face is gentle, and sly, and so, so sweet. "Jeff. As the star of your novel, you need a romance. It's practically required of you."

I think he might want to kiss me.

I laugh through my nose, which is so embarrassing, and try to keep my focus and explain things to the non-writer. "No, you don't get it. I mean, I get you're flirting with me, which I . . . appreciate. But in terms of art, I'm not a hero, not even a pro-tagonist. I'm just the narrator in the background. You're not even supposed to notice me."

He takes a step so the space between us fills with him. "Far too late."

Then he nuzzles my neck, and my fingertips touch his sides just barely. His hair brushes against my mouth. The thing about ultra-thin hair is that it's very, very soft.

We just breathe like that, sorting out the way we fit.

I speak into the hair. "You smell like animal pelts."

He squirms and reverts a bit to his snarky self. "Thanks—it's called oily hair reek. Just kiss my mouth like a normal boy-friend?"

"No, I like it. You smell feral. Like an albino sea otter."

Instead of pulverizing me, he laughs. "It always comes back to the fake albino thing. Fine. Triple myth. Will you kiss me, you kinky thing?"

I hesitate.

"I don't want to rush you." His lips brush my neck with each word and snake over my jaw. It makes me tighten my grip, and I feel the shape of him. I start trembling.

"I'm sweating." I wasn't supposed to advertise that.

"How *feral*," he purrs.

"What if I kiss you . . . and you don't like it?"

"Impossible." He tugs my earlobe and gazes at it like it's the only thing in the world. "I remember the bad kisser conversation. You're *not*. But even if you were, then that's what I'd want. Lots of sloppy, feral, badly executed kisses." He bites my ear.

I'm terrified by the jolt that goes through me.

I gasp. "One more problem."

His growly *hmm* warns me. "If this is about not being gay . . ."

I mouth a voiceless *no*, and a lump mushrooms in my throat. If I speak, I'll lose my shit. But I'm losing it anyway. My brain plays out a montage of me ignoring him in the hallways as if he

419

weren't there. Especially fall of sophomore year, hurting him over and over. "I . . . I treated you like crap every day. And now I just walk up and kiss you? I don't deserve this. I don't deserve—"

"*But I do!*" His mouth tugs hard in a miserable line.

I pull him to me and feel the tremor in his chest, or maybe it's mine. He's clinging to me and frowning so fiercely to wall in whatever is inside. I touch his neck, his face, and then I bend down and kiss that softest peach fuzz corner of his mouth, and it's the most beautiful part on any human body ever born, and there doesn't seem to be any reason not to kiss him there again, so I do. He smiles, and his eyes shimmer and overflow.

"I'm so happy," he says, sniffing. We take turns kissing each other's tear trails like total saps in love. "You can't imagine how happy."

We brush lips to lips, back and forth, back and forth, and it's like I just invented this lip-brushing thing, and I don't want to stop. He tastes like salt.

"I should have done this earlier," I say against his mouth. His *mmm-hmm* vibrates through my lips.

He kisses my eyes again. My tears.

When we're drier, he gives me writing advice. "You should end the novel here. Or in bed, at the hotel." His eyes are puffy, and not thirty seconds ago he was wiping his nose on his sleeve, but he's trying to look hot and skanky, so I have to honor that.

"No way. I'm ending with the Lincoln Memorial. Fits the story better than a tearful make-out scene with my first boyfriend." I said it: the B-word. I thought it would be like crossing a finish line, but it's more like a beginning. Like I can say anything now.

A popcorn machine in my brain turns on. There are so many words that weren't there before.

"What?" He rouses, knocking very nicely against my hips.

I look at his blotchy face, and it confirms everything. "The words found their places. They're hopping from me to you, like the atoms did earlier, but it's different. Like atoms wearing capes."

He's a little too sob-and-kiss woozy for this incoherent Word Nerd speech, but he's trying to listen. "What?"

"The words I couldn't use, I can use them now." I caress his cheek—he's so soft—and say the words I could never think, let alone say. "*Love, lovely, lover, beloved, boyfriend, beautiful, kissable, you.* And others. They're all snapping into place, to the places they've always belonged to. All the labels in my spice rack are attached to all the right jars. The words know right where they want to go. Right at you."

"Took you long enough," he says, with a bit of an *I told you so* vibe, and his face turns cautiously tender in case I might tear up again.

But I act chill. "Yeah, the words will come in handy. I have a novel to write."

His lopsided smile gives me a good view of that peach fuzz corner. Now I know it's as soft as it looks. But I kiss him there again, just to make sure, and he holds my face and kisses me open-mouthed, and I do the thing where I breathe him in and in, and it's like he's saving my life all over again in the best way possible.

Mr. Bailey shouts our names, and I break off in panic like maybe we've been seen, and we run/walk/jog the length of the pool. But not before Pard flashes his predatory smile to let me know he's not finished, and that our own story is to be continued.

When Mr. Bailey sees my innocent baby face and hears my dishonest little cough, he lets us off easy. "Ride with Pard," he orders, and I dutifully board the bus with Pard for the ride to the Museum of Natural History. We sit together, right next to each other. Our hands keep touching, without Mace sitting across the aisle to see. The Lincoln Memorial disappears from the window, and we're on our way to see dinosaur bones.

When the bus pulls out and turns, people in the back row dramatically crash into one another, and Mr. Bailey roars Rooster's name, and Reeve is all too happily transcribing incriminating details. But I'm not actually sure what Rooster did, and it's all cheerful background noise, because I'm holding my hand out for Pard's sketchbook, my eyes asking. It's been a long time. His breath catches, and he gives it to me. With my eyes on the page, my leg knocking into Pard's to reassure him, I see a whole world open up to me. His.

I'm in it.

And we move forward.

AFTERWORD

I find it extremely cool when readers don't realize that I'm retelling Chaucer's amazing poem, *The Canterbury Tales*. But for readers who want to know how I went about retelling Chaucer and his story, and translating that to a modern teenage experience, I thought I'd share what I was up to.

Chaucer (1343?–1400) was a survivor. As a child he lived through the Black Death (1348–1350), the plague that wiped out roughly one-third of England's entire population. As a teenager, he went to fight in France and was taken hostage, then fortunately ransomed. He'd later watch the city of London get overrun in the Rising of 1381 (also called the Peasants' Revolt), in which peasants and other people angry over taxation briefly took over the city and decapitated the archbishop of Canterbury, burned palaces, and demanded an audience with the teenage king of England. I couldn't realistically include such events, but I wanted to craft a modern teenager who was also exposed to death and uncertainty. Chaucer may have had a sister named Katherine, but when I added Bee and imagined Jeff's Morpheus story, I was thinking of Chaucer's poem *The Book of the Duchess*, which was originally about the death of the wife of Chaucer's powerful patron, John of Gaunt. I fudge it when I say Jeff is having writer's block after the success of his Morpheus story. It's true Chaucer didn't finish *The House of Fame*, but he did write some other amazing poems. I've tinkered with Jeff's output, but

I liked the notion Paul Strohm proposes in a recent biography that Chaucer was writing *The Canterbury Tales* at a transition in his life, when he's between jobs and between cities and maybe unsure what is coming next, which describes the transition to college that high school seniors are excited and worried about. In writing *The Canterbury Tales*, Chaucer finds his *magnum opus*, and it's something entirely unlike anything done before. Not just by him—no one had ever written something like *The Canterbury Tales*, which dramatizes a road trip with such varied characters: men, women, clergy, knights, merchants, laborers, not to mention their colorful, complex personalities that range from the pious to the villainous. As John Dryden put it best, Chaucer's vibrant full cast gave the world "God's plenty."

Chaucer's cast relies on stereotypes—i.e., the Knight is valiant and cultured, the Miller strong and loud. I tried to stay true to that: Kai and Briony are in the popular crowd, as befits their stations as quarterback and cheerleader, or Knight and Prioress. Meanwhile, the Canon and his apprentice, who both show up very late in *The Canterbury Tales*, are alchemists who supposedly turn lead into gold but actually trick people into losing their gold; I similarly made my Cannon a charismatic scammer and schemer. Where I especially diverge is downplaying the role of the clergy, about one-third of Chaucer's cast. Chaucer pointed out the hypocrisies and abuses of power in the religious system of his day, but since our culture is secular, I de-churched Frye, Mace, Briony, Mari, Cece, Pard, and the bus driver. I kept

Parson, though I made his sermon at the end less gloomy than it is in the original.

My other main change to the cast is including more women. Chaucer, of course, created the one and only Wife of Bath, and he also includes the Prioress and a woman only called the Second Nun. I then converted some of the male characters into women. Having more women—and vocal women—gave me the opportunity to emphasize how misogynist some of the characters and the stories can be. It also was fun pairing up some of them and letting us see characters in action. For example, Chaucer's Friar (Frye) is a womanizer, so having him flirt with Reiko (formerly a male Physician) lets us see some of Frye's flirtation rather than just be told it happens. I also played around with the order of the tales partly for these considerations of gender.

And then there's Pard, the Pardoner of Chaucer's text. Details like his lack of facial hair, high voice, and thin pale hair ("yellow as wax" in color, though I went with platinum blond) come from Chaucer's poem. Chaucer describes him as a gelding or a mare—either a castrated male horse or a female horse. What do those metaphors mean? Is he castrated? Feminine? There's a lot of scholarly discussion about the Pardoner's body and what's called "the Pardoner's secret." There are no firm answers and never will be, but I ultimately went with him being gay and intersex. Most medievalists probably wouldn't say the Pardoner is intersex (although the argument was proposed in the 1960s), but then again, it's only in recent years that intersex has been receiving significant public awareness. I liked the idea of claiming the text for this current moment. I also made sure Pard was a central character and a desirable one. This is all a rather big change from the original Pardoner, a bitter outcast whose sexually suggestive comments make the pilgrims uneasy. I didn't want a LGBTQIA character to be condemned to the marginalization and rejection the Pardoner experiences in Chaucer's text. I took out his villainy but hopefully kept his eloquence. I hope you like what I did with him.

Chaucer's premise and cast make his *Canterbury Tales* unique in medieval literature. That said, a lot of Chaucer's story material derives from classical and medieval authors. There were no intellectual property laws. Retelling a story by another author was fair game, whether you declared your sources or not. Readers were not obsessed with originality as much as we are today and, like a proto-fanfiction culture, had something like a passion for retellings. However, if I made open references to Ovid and Boccaccio, for example, a modern audience would possibly be rather bored . . . but that's only because modern audiences might not know how amazing Ovid and Boccaccio really were. If Chaucer were a teenager writing today, he'd likely pull from culturally known material to make his own stories. So what I did is offer a medieval retelling hidden behind modern fanfiction. For example, Mari respins E. B. White, when Chaucer really is retelling Aesop, possibly respinning the retelling of Aesop by Marie de France. Jeff in turn acts like his Morpheus story came from Neil Gaiman's *Sandman* instead of Ovid's *Metamorphoses*, and Lupe's Twilight story about Edward's vampire-crow tattling on Bella is really Ovid's story of Phoebus Apollo and his raven. Franklin's Tale uses Snape to tell Chaucer and Boccaccio's tale of a lovesick young man promising to pay a magician (Snape) richly to do an amazing feat of magic, in turn to ensnare a woman with her own promise. These stories resemble modern fanfiction, but Chaucer's version and its borrowings are right there underneath, to give modern readers the same layered encounter of a tale retold.

Speaking of layers, Chaucer cultivates this layered quality in his characters and voices. There's Chaucer the man, Chaucer the author, Chaucer the wallflower narrator, and then Chaucer the author and/or narrator ventriloquizing the pilgrims, who in turn have characters inside their own stories. This is another example of Chaucer's brilliance, because the stories are more interesting for being matched to the characters telling them. Why does the Wife of Bath tell a story with rape in it, for example? The stories become another peek into these personalities, because the characters are authored yet authors, too.

Chaucer intended to get twenty-nine or possibly thirty pilgrims to Canterbury and back, each pilgrim telling two stories each way. That would have been a massive project, and he didn't come close to finishing it, only giving us twenty-four stories, counting the fragmented ones. He didn't even make it to Canterbury. Medieval readers seem to have resented this incompletion. A number of manuscripts leave space for the Cook to finish his abruptly unfinished tale (in my version, he falls asleep), and one fifteenth-century poet even wrote his own ending, because no matter how busy an author is, the least he can do is get the gang to Canterbury. So of course my group gets to D.C., and my Jeff needs to grow over the course of the story. I needed some sort of story arc. I originally thought it would end with Cannon, but Pard sort of insisted on a love story. Either way, it's not just a love story between two lovers, but the bond Jeff increasingly feels for this community he's traveled with and the power of stories to get us to see into other lives and our own.

FOR FURTHER READING

Print resources:

Geoffrey Chaucer, *The Canterbury Tales*, second edition, edited by Robert Boenig and Andrew Taylor (Ontario, Canada: Broadview), 2012.
This is a complete and highly regarded edition of *The Canterbury Tales* used in many college classrooms.

Helen Cooper, *The Oxford Guides to Chaucer: The Canterbury Tales* (Oxford: Oxford University Press), 1989.
This is my favorite companion to *The Canterbury Tales*.

Online resources:

Larry Benson, The Geoffrey Chaucer Website.
sites.fas.harvard.edu/~chaucer/
A very useful page devoted to Chaucer and his work.

Brantley Bryant, *Geoffrey Chaucer Hath a Blog.*
houseoffame.blogspot.com
Twitter handle: Chaucer Doth Tweet @LeVostreGC
For readers who want to enjoy Middle English's relevance in modern life, Bryant takes on Chaucer's persona in this occassional blog and active Twitter account. It's fun stuff.

Daniel T. Kline, Geoffrey Chaucer Online: The Electronic Canterbury Tales, kankedort.net and "The Chaucer Pedagogy Page," kankedort.net/pedagogy.htm.

These sites, useful for students and teachers alike, give context to Chaucer's work and provide links to many other useful pages.

The Open Access Companion to the Canterbury Tales, edited by Candace Barrington, Brantley Bryant, Richard H. Godden, Daniel T. Kline, Myra Seaman.

opencanterburytales.com

This site (currently in development) will include essays on each of the tales, plus essays with broader themes.

DRAMATIS PERSONAE

(corresponding names in Chaucer's original text, *The Canterbury Tales*, given in parentheses)

ALISON (the Wife of Bath)

MR. BAILEY (Harry Bailey, the tavern Host)

BRIONY (the Prioress)

BRYCE (the Merchant)

CANNON (the Canon's Yeoman)

CECE (the Second Nun)

COOKIE (the Cook)

FRANKLIN (the Franklin)

FRYE (the Friar)

JEFF (Geoffrey Chaucer, the narrator)

KAI (the Knight)

LUPE (the Manciple)

MACE (the Summoner)

MARCUS (the Clerk)

MARI (the Nun's Priest)

MOUSE (the Squire)

PARD (the Pardoner)

PARSON (the Parson)

REEVE (the Reeve)

REIKO (the Physician)

ROOSTER (the Miller)

SAGA (the Shipman)

SOPHIE (the Man of Law)

THE BUS DRIVER (the Monk)

ACKNOWLEDGMENTS

There are so many amazing people who helped make this book, too many to name them all.

First, thanks to everyone at Simon Pulse for giving this book the best home it could ever have. I'm at the stage right now where the book isn't in a physical form, but I've already fallen for Adam J. Turnbull's fantastic illustrations and the jacket design by Karina Granda. As the word is starting to go out, I feel gratitude for people who have started chatting up the book and supporting it, including librarians and bloggers, with special thanks to Jess Huang. The book is starting to feel real by all this support, and I appreciate it so much.

This is a Chaucer book, and I have Chaucer debts. Andy Galloway, Pete Wetherbee, and Tom Hill mentored me as a graduate student at Cornell. I'm so grateful for everything you've taught me. My high school English teacher Tom Debalski (Mr. D) also deserves special mention, because I didn't know it at the time, but it's through him that my pilgrimage with Chaucer began. I also have deep gratitude for my students at Sacramento State, especially my Chaucer students. A couple specific students to thank, though it doesn't cover my debts by far: Mike Brown's discussion of veterans helped me shape Kai's backstory; Catrina Porter gave me the idea for the Greyhound bus, right there in class when I asked for a modern equivalent to Constance at sea— Sophie's Tale was a breeze after that. My Medieval Literature students were an outstanding group to teach while I was writing this novel. When I announced the book deal, they broke into spontaneous applause, which was sweet. My students are the best part of my job at Sacramento State. I am also very grateful for the sabbatical that helped me complete the novel.

Many thanks to my academic friends. My Cal State cousin, Samantha Fields, was so generous going over all the ins and outs of asthma attacks. I'm so grateful for her time, because the scene became so much more authentic, and I loved her description of asthmatics being good hiders, which sounded just like Jeff. Poet and Sac State colleague Josh McKinney read Aurelius's sonnet (I was worried it was a prosodic disaster) and gave scansion suggestions regarding the pesky last line; if anything about that sonnet stinks, it's all my own doing. My dear friend Katherine Terrell, a medievalist at Hamilton College and a wonderful person to talk to, helped me focus on the Prioress's perception of what she's doing, which in turn helped me come up with a plan for Briony's Tale. I'm lucky to be a medievalist—a Chaucer fan and a card-carrying Gower Girl—and feel such gratitude for my medievalist community for its kindness, brilliance, and even doughnuts. Yes, in a way, #medievaldonut got worked in there too.

My writer friends have been awesome. Fabulous and wise author Katherine Longshore answered my questions about Henry VIII as I was writing Marcus's Tale, and she's been a mentor in many ways. I deeply appreciate my local Better Books community and SCBWI friends who have kept me sane and kept me writing. Matt Kirby and Talia Vance gave me moral support and good advice. Bruce Coville and I once had a meaningful chat about how to accept compliments from others (even if you feel insecure, he told me, just say thanks), and I put some of that wisdom in Alison's mouth. Thanks, Bruce.

My parents Valerie and Barry—Hi, Mom and Dad!—and the whole family have been supportive, even though I know my parents won't be a fan of the swear words and the scandalous bits. Thanks for buying copies anyhow. Thanks, Emily, for your good advice at a time when I needed some. My little sister, Itsy, is going to help make giveaway prizes, T-shirts and stuff, which will be fun. Writing this book reminded me of the time Itsy complained that even though she read Chaucer in high school and college, the survey classes never covered anything beyond the General Prologue, which is just sad. So here is the whole thing . . . sort of.

I don't know if this is cheating, but I am dedicating this book to five people, which is kind of a Wife of Bath number, but I'm not going to analyze that. I have to dedicate this book first off to my husband and son, because watching someone type one hundred thousand words on a computer is a really boring thing to do. That's dedication right there. Thank you, Mark. I have had really interesting conversations with you to help me write this book, such as what kinds of bad things a high school hacker might realistically pull off. There are also all sorts of references in the novel inspired by you. Thank you, Arthur, for offering to help read over the manuscript. I didn't take you up on it, because

435

you were ten and only wanted to see what kinds of swear words I put in the story besides that one word you noticed when you read over my shoulder. My love to you both—we're on this pilgrimage together. This book is for you.

I also wanted to dedicate this book to the three people closest to it: Rachel, Michael, and Emma. My agent Rachel Orr has been incredible from the get-go. Enthusiastic, supportive, helpful in every way. I couldn't have done this without all the brainstorming, the phone calls that had me pacing all over the backyard. Thank you for writing that e-mail that went, "HAHAHAHA-HAHAHAHAHA," and for totally getting my tampon humor. I feel like we bonded there, but seriously, those late-night edit e-mails were totally exciting. You are the best. Thank you so, so much, friend of many years.

This book would have never happened without my two editors, Michael Strother and Emma Sector. Seriously, how many YA editors out there have a passion for Chaucer like they have? I'm just amazed that we connected and that I haven't dreamed all this up. From start to finish, I felt like I was on a pilgrimage, and Michael and Emma were the Host, tasking me to tell a tale. Of course, they did much more than that—they helped me shape the manuscript and gave me their brilliant, wise perspectives. Their inspiration and guidance took me to a place and a story I never knew I had in me. I can't even begin to say how grateful I am for the gift they gave me. Thank you.

Finally, it goes without saying I have literary debts—but I'll say them anyway, with gratitude. To make some of the tales feel like modern fanfiction, to approximate how Chaucer borrowed freely from classical and medieval writers, I wove medieval texts with modern characters and settings from E. B. White, C. S. Lewis, Terry Pratchett (the "justice/just us" pun and other such goodies come straight from him), Stephenie Meyer, and J. K. Rowling. There are other smaller references throughout, Neil Gaiman, John Milton, J. R. R. Tolkien, Rainbow Rowell, and Laini Taylor among them. Thank you, all, for hooking kids (like me) onto reading. I must have read ages ago that bit about the spice jars finally being labeled correctly, but I never could hunt down the attribution. Writers like the ones I named fill our minds with characters and places and tales and spice jars, and it was fun bringing bits of these other worlds to a modern Chaucerian playground. I felt like less of a Muggle than usual, touching that magic however briefly. And of course, the greatest debt of all goes to Chaucer himself. How can I put my feelings and awe into words? I guess I already tried, because this novel pays homage to his incredible yet down-to-earth genius. Six hundred years later, we still crack up from his jokes, and we don't need footnotes to know they're funny. That's immortality right there. As long as people still love stories and laughter, Chaucer's *Canterbury Tales* will live on.